LOOKING DOWN ON
MRS THATCHER

LOOKING DOWN ON MRS THATCHER

Edward Pearce

HAMISH HAMILTON · LONDON

HAMISH HAMILTON LTD

Penguin Books Ltd, 27 Wrights Lane, London W8 5TZ (Publishing & Editorial)
and Harmondsworth, Middlesex, England (Distribution & Warehouse)
Viking Penguin Inc., 40 West 23rd Street, New York, New York 10010, U.S.A.
Penguin Books Australia Ltd, Ringwood, Victoria, Australia
Penguin Books Canada Limited, 2801 John Street, Markham, Ontario, Canada L3R 1B4
Penguin Books (N.Z.) Ltd, 182–190 Wairau Road, Auckland 10, New Zealand

First published in Great Britain 1987 by
Hamish Hamilton Ltd

British Library Cataloguing-in-Publication Data:

Pearce, Edward
Looking Down on Mrs Thatcher
1. Great Britain *Parliament House of Commons*—Anecdotes, facetiae,
satire etc.
I. Title
328.41′072′0207   JN550
ISBN 0–241–12337–2

Typeset in 11/12 pt Sabon by Butler & Tanner Ltd
Printed and Bound in Great Britain by
Butler & Tanner Ltd, Frome, Somerset

For Cecily Pearce

INTRODUCTION

I have been writing sketches for eight years, since Mrs Thatcher became Prime Minister in fact. The sketch is an amphibious thing caught between humour and serious observation of politics. There is a great temptation to think of it as political criticism. But time spent in the gallery of the Commons is also the best way of observing the character and personality of politicians. Accordingly, the sketcher finds himself functioning as portraitist and genre painter as well as being tempted to join the great folk doing landscapes.

Some of the time he is not heavily committed to political opinions. The jokes and the light and shade are what matters.

But one can't always keep that up. Impressions of right and wrong intrude. The characters depicted come also to be judged. Accordingly readers may note the latter part of this anthology darkening as events like Westland, the Wright case and finally Zircon came to dominate politics. Mrs Thatcher, admired for certain strengths, has finally been seen by me towards the end as someone acting tyranically, sending police into the *New Statesman* and the BBC. You either mind that sort of thing or not.

I concluded after years of light entertainment and the sending up of backbenchers with a serious view. Readers are not asked to agree with these late conclusions. This selection, which also includes a number of longer pieces written for *Encounter*, is a combination of running record of events, satire on the comicality of politics and occasional lapses into seriousness. But it is meant to give pleasure and is not conceived out of hostility to politics. One former colleague on another paper took his farewell with a splenetic piece telling politicians how much he hated them. All in all I rather like them, as good milch cows before dairy quotas came in, and as endearing domestic pets. The House of

Commons, with all its faults, is a humane place where one would sooner be than not. British politics is ruder and noisier than say the German or Scandinavian varieties and it lacks the exercise of simple power which is available to US legislators. The Commons is divided into executors, infantry and aspirants (infantrymen putting in daily for a commission). It bounces legislation about, but legislation is certain of enactment. On the other hand while it has no power to remove those in office, competence is permanently in the wind tunnel being tested. Talent is picked out, adequacy ticks over, failure is noted and written down.

Any sketchwriter feels some affinity with a theatre critic or a man watching gallops in the early mornings. We try to notice the Goulds and Rifkinds as well as the folding corpses of question time. In the old Victorian way one seeks to mingle amusement with instruction as well as keeping oneself briefed by listening over a long period.

I spoke of a serious view developing. The Government's wish to misuse police powers against the *New Statesman* and the BBC in Scotland in January/February of this year struck me as deeply shocking, not part of the funny bone of politics. I said so in plain terms as the last clutch of sketches makes clear. It was perhaps not reasonable to expect to criticise Mrs Thatcher in a Conservative newspaper. Even so it was also unnerving to return from a short foreign visit to find oneself dismissed from the sketch for "inappropriate" criticism of the police trawl through BBC Scotland. Naturally the *Daily Telegraph* and I will now go our separate ways. Whether there will be other sketches on another paper I do not yet know. Seriousness has done me no very great good lately; accordingly readers are reminded that most of these contributions are not serious at all, they hope to amuse. Despite its bleak conclusion, I hope that this book will give pleasure and produce some smiles. Gravity is altogether too dangerous.

*At the Labour Party Conference in Brighton in 1979 the
rising strength of the Party's Left wing, later to prove so
electorally disastrous, manifested itself.*

Brighton has its associations in the minds of different people –
the Prince Regent, the race gangs, the Labour party. Nice sort
of place, highly questionable kind of clientele.

At this conference one is put very much in mind of the seedy
criminality of Brighton in the '30s, the race gang element which
inspired Graham Greene's *Brighton Rock*.

In that novel, the victim on the run from the underworld is
being stalked through Brighton's streets by a murderous youth
called Pinkie. With James Callaghan as the victim, this will be
Pinkie's conference.

In the housing debate, standard non-operative revolutionary
prose flows from the rostrum – "Bloodsuckers on the backs of
the workers", "Christ threw them out of the temple", "callous,
indifferent and self-interested", "community, compassion and
the brotherhood of man", and naturally "this reactionary Tory
Government".

Indeed, your correspondent had to draw such nourishment
as he could from the oratorical convenience foods of the Left.

Whatever else it may be, Labour has become the repetitive
party. This is exemplified by a delegate from Worcester who
began excitably, "Comrades, Comrade Chairman, Comrades!"
There was a lot of that.

Actually, Comrade Chairman Mr Frank Allaun, in that sleek
South Lancashire accent of his, implied in his address that some

3

people were only ticket-of-leave comrades – the former Prime Minister perhaps.

Mr Allaun, for a skilled Left-wing operator, gave a good impression of a fairly inept chairman. He summoned speakers variously as: "The comrade with the red pamphlet at the back there", or "The stout gentleman in front with his hand up." For delicately combining the uninformative with the insulting, Mr Allaun did well enough.

When it came to debating the General Election all that was missing was the delicacy.

Mr Tom Litterick, formerly MP for Selly Oak, who sounds like rancour and resentment made flesh and sent to a conference, attacked Mr Callaghan personally.

There has been, he said, waving a bunch of papers, hundreds of hours of sub-committee work put into the preparation of the last election document (and a right receipt for the horrors that would have been), then suddenly "Up comes Jim", at which Mr Litterick threw his package dramatically to the floor amid applause.

From other delegates we learned that the May election had not been a defeat for Socialism (yes, you guessed it, Socialism had never been tried!).

But the real attack on Mr Callaghan came not from some lurking delinquent but from the party's machine-minder. Mr Ron Hayward, with a voice like curdled Cotswold cream, effectively denounced his leader in a week that turns on conference or Parliamentary authority, by saying: "We lost it by ignoring conference resolutions."

As for so-called Trotskyists or Marxists, he didn't call them that; he called them activists. Well, he would, wouldn't he, the old fool!

In a crisp and clever speech Mr Dennis Howell, Under-Secretary for rainmaking and weather changing in the last Government, listed some real reasons for defeat. The party had 80 agents for 630 seats. It had no full-time agents in Glasgow, Newcastle, Leeds, Birmingham, Coventry and Hull. Thirty more agents were essential.

When it came to Mr Eric Heffer to reply he took an oddly capitalistic, cost-estimating, and generally Tory reactionary attitude.

4

"Thirty extra agents would be wonderful," he said, like Mr Heseltine contemplating a new town hall, but it would cost money – £200,000 by 1980. Therefore he begged conference to remit the resolution.

Daily Telegraph October 2, 1979

All proposals for negotations with the Irish factions were haunted by the memory of Mr Whitelaw's attempt to do such business in the early seventies, first at Darlington, then at Sunningdale.

Mrs Thatcher was in sharp and truculent form. Her finger-in-the-eye style of argument continued when she came to our friends in the European Community.

The budget contribution was intolerable but "the battle must take place in Dublin".

For a moment one thought that to the list of Strongbow, Cromwell, King William and other sound chaps, we were going to add the name Thatcher. She was, alas, only referring to the next inconclusive Euro-bumble of EEC Prime Ministers.

Actually somebody will *have* to be sent to Northern Ireland fairly soon, given the doubts which exist about the existence of the Northern Ireland Secretary, Mr Atkins.

It seems that we are back on the all-stations-to-Darlington theory of Ulster political reform – conference vaguely defined, opened to any more or less respectable party, including, perhaps especially including, those like the Northern Ireland Alliance party which spreads golden light on all sides, but don't actually get elected.

In such hazy circumstances Mr Atkins should be happy. He is a nice man, without the bare-knuckle egotism of some politicians, but possessed of such a graceful debility that neither side could be quite sure which of them he was letting down.

He produced the Peter Sellers-like pronouncement that "there has to be such an advancement that we advance and don't go backwards". For such a man to have to handle the knobbly, uncomfortable Ulstermen is hard.

Mr James Molyneaux, the leader of the Official Ulster Union-ists, made it clear at once that his party, the largest, would not be wasting time by going to the conference.

Presumably various secondary and voteless parties will meet the mainly Catholic SDLP at, say, Sunderland and then Gleneagles to no effect whatever, and the immense satisfaction of President Carter.

Not being able to say this out loud, Mr Atkins rolled with the punch between those who accused him of restoring the Protestant Ascendancy and those who suggested unkindly that determination to govern would be welcome in the Secretary of State.

Daily Telegraph, October 26, 1979

MORE JOBS LOST: MPs WILL MISS RHODESIA

Ae fond kiss and then we sever
Ae farewell: and then forever.

Burns's words sum up the spirit in which Labour Africanists took leave of their favourite subject in the committee stage of the Southern Rhodesia Bill yesterday.

Going on about Southern Rhodesia has been a form of employment for Members for a long time now, and with Lord Carrington, if not squaring the circle on this issue, apparently making a fair old parallelogram out of it, many backbenchers evidently felt rather like handloom weavers deprived of their livelihood.

Never again would they be able to talk about Britain standing impeached before the bar of world opinion; there would be no more opportunities to drone on about the legitimate aspirations of the African people under White minority rule.

Some of them last night were broken men. Too old for retraining in some other highly skilled branch of legislative tedium, they are, as their colleagues would put it, on the scrap heap!

However one would pay good money never again to listen to a speech by Mr Sam Silkin (Lab., Dulwich) on this subject. Mr Silkin speaks, as it were, in slow motion. Has the climate of African affairs afflicted him with some indigenous disease, like sleeping sickness?

He didn't want to suggest that everything the Patriotic Front stood for was right and everything Bishop Muzorewa represented necessarily wrong. Presumably the Bishop has some saving grace and the boys with the Czech rifles a few little shortfallings.

The former Attorney-General is the Meadowbank Thistle of debate. But he was not much worse than a number of old Africa hands on both sides who took part in the Rhodesia ceremony.

Mr Frank Hooley (Lab., Sheffield Heeley) conjured up the Commonwealth and something called the Lusaka Spirit.

Mr Hooley would like to see a Commonwealth force keeping the peace. Why he had such faith in that gathering of our far-flung enemies, like Tanzania and Australia, who can say.

Your correspondent had actually fled for a consoling cup of tea when the name of David Winnick (Lab., Walsall N.) flashed onto the annunciator screen, and, knowing high quality nonsense when he sees it, he hurried back into the Chamber.

Mr Winnick is a sort of Labour schoolmaster to end all Labour schoolmasters, bespectacled, somewhat afflicted with an agitated index finger, never at all nasty, but in a fixed state of mild and perpetual recrimination of the sort which occasionally provokes domestic tragedy.

He also specialises in little moralityburgers about "our shameful role". We are not let down. Mr Winnick who, like other Labour Members, dislikes the quick passage of the Bill and the possibility of a fallback settlement with Bishop Muzorewa, said that "Britain would be placed in the dock" if that happened.

We were already in trouble with world opinion because of Northern Ireland, and there was a risk that to defend Muzorewa we would be drawn into a sort of mini-Vietnam. Mr Winnick hoped that we had learned the lesson of Vietnam. (Indeed yes – not to lose!)

There then followed a strangely relevant speech. Mr Stephen Hastings (C. Mid Beds.) remarked that the House had been talking about nice legal points to do with a balanced constitution for all the world as if it had been drawing up rules for Harlow New Town.

The Opposition's amendments called for more time for negotiations. That would allow the Patriotic Front to make their own arrangements. In the last ten days, said Mr Hastings very quietly, terrorists – guerrillas – whatever had been coming in

7

great numbers across the Zambesi. Those captured had been asked (nicely or otherwise) why?

They had instructions, it seemed, to get into the villages and start intimidating. Naturally that would need time, as naturally negotiations would provide it. Just occasionally this platonic House gets a notion of the full nastiness of the world it likes to talk about.

Daily Telegraph, November 13, 1979

Immigration and the rules governing it was a topic of conversation in 1979. There seems no good reason why it should not preoccupy us for ever.

As every schoolboy knows (or as he used to before recent improvements in education) Professor Pavlov proved something rather interesting by the judicious manipulation of dogs, a bell and plates of dog-biscuits.

Yesterday was dog-biscuit day in the House of Commons as Mr William Whitelaw, the Home Secretary, served up a plateful of immigration rules. (One can almost see the wording: "Immibix – your backbencher will love them.")

Mr Whitelaw, oyster-eyed and benevolent, made his statement to assorted cries of "shame", "scandal", "racist", "resign", "National Front" on the one hand and "Yer-yer-yer-yer-year" on the other.

What all this grade two outrage concerned was an attempt by the Home Secretary to tighten up the rules so that Indian fiancés may not use marriage as a route round the regulations and into Britain.

As the Indian fiancé has replaced the deceased wife's sister as an object of fervid contention the salivation was mildly stupendous.

Mr David Winnick (Lab., Walsall N.) – sorry about this – rose and in a foam-flecked and piping passion demanded that "as this whole racist document is clearly the work of the Prime Minister she should be present".

Then, after more noises of the kind which one associates with the better class of county meet, Mr Merlyn Rees, in a towering pique, gave a rather poor impression of being shocked.

8

As an old control-tightener himself (and by implication – or is it imprecation? – racist, fascist and sexist), he had first of all pre-emptively to dissociate himself from his own actions in 1969.

As Junior Minister in charge of savage and callous harassment of immigrants, he had expressed fears about the numbers coming and had acted accordingly.

"I was wrong, Mr Speaker, I was wrong," he said. He then proceeded, by way of what was supposed to be a question, to advance a vast club-sandwich of a protest which actually went on longer (or seemed to) than the Minister's statement.

Skilfully, he tried to set the Home Secretary at odds with what might be called the non-New Commonwealth element, Mr Ronald Bell, Mr George Gardiner and Mr Enoch Powell.

No such caution came from Miss Joan Lestor (Lab., Eton and Slough) who sometimes gives the impression that in the interest of better race relations she might throw herself under the Queen's horse at the Derby.

She quivered with agony at the let-out clause which favours English girls born when daddy was, say, Third Secretary in La Paz.

"This attempt to buy off women who happen to be white in no way mitigates what the Minister is doing to our Asian sisters." Drearily and oppressively the regiment of the good paraded up and down with the ancient vocabulary of the race relations drill yard.

When Mr Sid Bidwell (Lab., Southall) added to his reasoned criticism the remark, "I know the Home Secretary is a very humane Tory," he got himself almost shouted down.

In all this Mr Whitelaw, who has fluffed and fumbled in his day, was oddly impressive, keeping up the civilities without letting down the defences.

Are the Tories undergoing a sea change? Not long ago you only had to level a moral argument at them and they hid behind the furniture. An ethical superiority complex and what might militarily be called bawlweight were Labour's very real deterrent. They are looking obsolescent.

Daily Telegraph, November 15, 1979

The point will be raised with your correspondent's employers

9

that if danger money and unsocial hours are in order something will have to be done about its Press Gallery equivalent!

A tedium bonus one was thinking of calling it. Really! What is to be said about a motion which brings forward in succession Mr Albert Costain (C., Folkestone), Mr Ioan Evans (Lab., Aberdare), Mr Robert Cryer (Lab., Keighley) and Mr David Crouch (C., Canterbury), each and every one of them verbal morphine?

In that company Mr Geoffrey Rippon, normally about as exciting as a plastic bag, glittered with relative felicity.

The debate was one of those Private Member's motions which occur fairly infrequently (perhaps in a humanitarian spirit), and it concerned "Parliamentary Control of the Executive Bodies".

In other words, it was a private little grief session that most of the power in this wicked world is exercised by the EEC Commission, an apostolic succession of Permanent Under Secretaries, Mrs Margaret Thatcher, the Regional Electricity Boards, Sir Michael Edwardes and the French agricultural lobby, but not, alas, by the House of Commons.

The complaints are largely true but for so far as one can see the powers lost are so many pooh sticks – under the bridge and floating downstream.

The response of the House took the form of what a trade union leader once called a "complete ignoral". It was clearly a perfect day for writing letters, sitting on committee or taking the family to the zoo.

Such was their sense of concern that when the fatally fluent (and permanently out of order) Mr Cryer was denouncing the European Parliament as an "empty talking shop," six back-benchers outnumbered three front benchers.

The debate had got off to a grim start with Mr Albert Costain, who moved it. One does not want to be unkind about Mr Costain who is a pleasant and kindly man who looks like a legislative Teddy Bear.

His style of address, however, reminds one of nothing so much as a concrete-mixer working off an under-charged engine; and it is not often that anybody manages to quote (with column numbers) Hansard for 1869.

With Mr Cryer, we suffered, in fact, from some over-tolerant refereeing by the Deputy Speaker, who only started showing cards when Mr Cryer lumbered into the closed-shop issue with the glinting assurance that he was "prepared to discuss it at any time and at any length".

He was anxious to cite the Labour Party as a model for democratic accountability and kept coming back to a curious phrase about "a bubbling of ideas" or later "a bubbling of concern".

The idea of Transport House or, indeed, the Brighton Conference Centre as natural springs from which thermal ideas come effervescing upwards will startle anyone familiar with the dun-coloured desolation of the one or the rat-pit atmosphere of the other.

Just as he was beginning to sound half-sensible, calling for posts in public bodies to be elective (good afternoon, my name is Henry Birtwhistle, I am your Liberal candidate for the Water Board), less patronage, fewer nominees, all good neo-Conservative American stuff, he meandered into British Leyland and the wrongs of Robinson. (What this had to do with the debate Allah may know in his wisdom.)

The firing of Derek Robinson had been a breach of democratic accountability. Mr Robinson had only been seeking to express a contrary view. The shop floor.... (Hang on a minute. Hadn't there been a ballot – secret votes, democratic process and all?)

Like Mrs Thatcher, Mr Cryer deals with gaffes by velocity. He surged on, his own thermal spring of concern. "It was a hasty ballot. There had been no unanimity of view . . . human aspiration . . . the dead hand of conformity. . . ."

It was all rather sad really. Parliament is not very influential. Government keeps it occupied, rather like the young men in Mr Whitelaw's detention centres – though the process here is one of long laborious languor; civil servants treat it as a remedial class incapable of taking in serious answers; membership is a limbo between real life and office.

Yet the debate deploring this state of affairs tended rather to confirm official wisdom. As someone said of King James II's court in exile, "when you hear them you see why they are here".

Daily Telegraph, December 11, 1979

11

This is the first anthologised account of someone sub-sequently to move much higher ... and keep talking.

"Adjectival Ketchup", a term coined by the great Tom Wolfe, perfectly describes almost any speech by the Labour spokesman on Education, Mr Neil Kinnock.

Four-Synonym-Kinnock has the advantage of a sort of eloquence which leaves the steady plodding indignation of most of his colleagues quite outclassed.

Yesterday he was giving a polychrome performance on the Government's decision to charge foreign students the full costs of their fees, an issue to which one looks forward to seeing the Labour Party giving maximum publicity at the next election.

For apparently the Government hasn't got a friend. Against it are ranged the principals of polytechnics, the educational trades unions and the students' unions, the High Commissioners and Ambassadors, and every quango and professional body having, like Miss Prism, something remotely to do with education.

The policy is, of course, also blind, arbitrary, wasteful, heartless, brainless, insular, cynical, careless, dramatic and not surprisingly – incoherent.

It seems that the presence of overseas students in large numbers in this country is a peculiar glory of our way of life. It creates trade and increases cultural ties, it brings in "scores of millions of foreign exchange", and it keeps large numbers of cuddlesome Iranian students hard at their researches to the delight of a genial and admiring British public.

"The students," said Mr Kinnock, "look to us for educational sucker". At least that was what it sounded like.

With heartless compassion he flowed on. It is doubtful if the upping of fees to overseas students has a precedent for iniquity in the doings of the Spanish Holy Office, the *Oprichnina* of Ivan the Terrible or the opinions of Roy Jenkins.

And, as Neil's mam would have told him back in Tredegar, you can put too many eggs in a pudding.

The Secretary for Education, Mr Carlisle, is almost as slate-grey English as his opponent is tropical Welsh, and, to be xenophobic, it was a great day for the English!

The Minister worked his way through the facts. True a higher

12

differential fee had been introduced for foreign students ... by Labour. Even so the numbers had risen from 31,000 to 86,000 in 13 years; 25 per cent of those students came from countries richer than Britain.

Would we now be favouring richer students, as his opponent had put it? Just how many poor students had we ever had? Would the numbers collapse under the new stiff fees?

On the contrary, consumer resistance among those in the market for that valuable commodity, the British third year degree, seemed according to advance early bookings to be very modest.

Oh yes, Labour and its dedication to foreign students – hadn't they proposed a quota system back in 1976 in the hope of getting the numbers down to 66,000 by 1981?

At this stage something seemed to fall apart in Dame Judith Hart, who began to dance around the Dispatch Box and generally make Mr Kinnock look drab and repressed.

Her voice rising to a shriek, she demanded to have it known that Labour had produced a secret document in 1978 which would have been quite different.

Mr Carlisle, as sweet as silk on a retainer, regretted that the election result had denied us detailed knowledge of the plan's contents, something which reduced Dame Judith to frantic and embarrassing cries of "Sit down".

It only remained to quote the last Secretary for Education, Mr Mulley – "We cannot accept the continuing rapid growth in the number of overseas students" – and the last shovelful of earth had been thrown on the Opposition case.

But then, Labour is always being betrayed, not least by its past, which so often turns out to have been really rather sensible.

Daily Telegraph, June 6, 1980

Very occasionally I am tempted into parody, here of Kipling, and by a happy afternoon's procedural delay. Mr Norman St John Stevas at this time was Leader of the House, Mr George Thomas, Speaker of the Commons.

Would you like to hear, oh Best-beloved, how the Order got his Point? Long ago and far away in a bi-cameral legislature near

13

Westminster Bridge all the animals of the Jungle were angry.

The Stevas-Gazelle sauntered around in a clearing and the opposition beasts hung from the trees, wiggled through the grass and generally threw coconuts at him. For the Stevas-Gazelle has charge of a very special Bill called the Housing Bill, and he has to make it law before the animals and birds of the Jungle fly away to Barbados and Gstaad, Forte dei Marmi and Wolverhampton South-East. And the beasts were not pleased with the Bill. They wanted to have the Bill amended, if not cut up into little pieces. So the beasts and the birds decided to waste time so that the Bill should not be enacted, O Best-beloved.

Now just as the snake has venom hidden in his tongue, so the Cryer-creature has great ducts of tedium with which he is able to go on and on and on without pausing. He does not pause for breath, O Best-beloved, or for thought, or for consideration of the environment. And what is true of the Cryer-creature is true of the Skinneroo, the Arthur Lewisotomus and the Lesser Michael English.

The Stevas-Gazelle announced to the Jungle that as well as the Housing Bill they would have to deal with all manner of extra business in a very short time to make up for their naughtiness in losing Tuesday by a procedural manoeuvre. And then at a certain hour they would have to vote on the Housing Bill. Now when it comes to voting there are more great huntsmen and sepoys and native bearers than there are beasts. So the beasts cried "Outrage" and "Intolerable for our dignity and proper conduct" and "Outrage on the procedures of this House" and other foolish customary things.

And the Wise Little Elephant George Thomas, to whom the huntsmen and the beasts all listen, or should do if they are good, said, "Order, order; we can't stop someone speaking just by shouting. That's not the way of this House." Which is a very dubious proposition, O Best-beloved.

The Stevas-Gazelle announced that he had sent the bearer Jopling and the Great Crested Michael Cocks away to a remote stream in the Jungle known as the Usual Channels to make civilised agreement, or, as some animals call it, a fix: and could we please get on with business now?

At which the beasts all rose in their places waving Order Papers, or clutching the lapels of their waistcoats and crying,

14

"Point of Order, Mr Speaker, Point of Order." The Arthur Lewisotomus, who is a very stout and dignified beast, demanded that the Little Elephant suspend him for refusing to sit down in the Little Elephant's presence. And the Little Elephant who knows better than to make a martyr out of an exhibitionist suspended the House instead for ten minutes. But it did no good. For when they returned not only were there more Points of Order and 13 Standing Order No. 9 applications waiting for them: but the Great Foot, who browses beneath the Oratory Tree and who knows where all the secret streams of delay and obfuscation can be found, demanded another suspension.

When the Great Foot said very solemnly and politely, "I fully understand the desire of the House to proceed," the huntsmen were very sad about their Housing Bill. So the Stevas-Gazelle agreed to another suspension and went away to the Usual Channels. When the Stevas-Gazelle returned he brought an in-between sort of beast called a Compromise. The Compromise said, "Beasts of the Jungle, please stop raising Points of Order and in return we will change the Housing Bill just a bit. Which will also please the sahibs in the Great House in Simla."

And beast and huntsman went away thinking that theirs was the most tolerant, sensible Jungle anywhere in the world.

Daily Telegraph, August 7, 1980

The contrast is almost unbearable. After Blackpool the Conservative conference comes like a rattle of matinée tea trays after cockfighting.

After a week of constitutional self-evisceration we watched the Conservatives seraphically debating the quiet calamity of transport like eirenic ducklings on a millpond.

The best copy the Conservatives have is usually Mr Michael Heseltine. The Secretary for the Environment is an eruptive performer who, once a year at conference, so reliably that you could set your watch by him, performs like a roman candle!

The people who organise this conference (and when Conservatives have been organised they stay organised) have had an unloving way of erasing Mr Heseltine from television by arranging for him to clash with "Play School" and "Camberwick Green".

This time he spoke to the City and the World and did so with all the butter-cream passion of which he is master.

As he was doing over local government he could hardly lose. Creditably, the Tories are very down on municipal over-manning at the moment.

But it has to be said that Cato was upstaged in his little senate. The fierce little leader of Manchester Conservatives, Cecil Franks, with the bitterness of experience, described council officers who cut services rather than administration and kept all cuts out of their own offices.

"They train councillors to defend them like parrots (applause). They advance their careers by flattering the egos of chairmen (applause). The prudence of local government myth (applause).

"Did you get a good deal from local government? You got a rotten deal (loud and prolonged applause – as *Isvestia* puts it)."

In his own Manchester local government had created its own electorate from dependent employees. Clearly somebody was talking about something which the conference understood.

Now, in my notes, "A" stands for applause: Mr Franks got eight "As".

The asphalt was talking and Mr Heseltine, even though he broke into verse at one stage, never competed. There was a sort of perfunctory ecstasy at the end but that is only the due of all Conservative Ministers who can get through 20 minutes without actually falling down.

Earlier in the morning session, we had cold roast Norman. The Leader of the House/Chancellor of the Duchy/Minister of the Arts is, if not a one-man band, a rather compressed string trio.

He defended the House of Lords, and praised Lord Thorneycroft – "a public monument upon whom the Prime Minister has slapped a preservation order".

Lord Thorneycroft, who in this pallid and mannerly assembly, actually does command affection, spoke with relish from the grave of early resignation to which loving colleagues had confined him.

He had enjoyed his obituaries. We enjoyed his speech with its cavalier wisdom that "respect and affection between different parts of this party are a damned sight more important than

16

constitutional reform".

But he said one thing which in this numb and gentle dream of a conference rather startled one. "We give the Press such fun," he said. They do?

Some of us have had more fun at the General Synod.

Daily Telegraph, October 8, 1980

Over the new year 1980–81 Mrs Thatcher tentatively dabbled for the first time in the art of reshuffling her Cabinet, sketching in Tebbit and whitewashing St John Stevas. The Sunday painter went on to be an RA.

Looking around the newly-assembled House one is taken by all the new heads on the Government Front Bench and by all the old ones on the floor.

The late camper-up of the Duchy of Lancaster (in whose fall I had no part) entered the House about 90 seconds before Prime Minister's Question Time to the sort of Labour noises associated with football excursion trains and went to the remotest of remote back-benches.

Frivolous, irrelevant old Norman, despite hard things said, will be much missed by we frivolous and irrelevant people in similar danger.

But we are on to new Normans now: Norman Tebbit, a felicitous short-cosh merchant now charged with the nationalised industries, and especially Norman Fowler, whose Transport Bill occupied most of the day.

Persons more socially discriminating than your correspondent make biting and divisive remarks about the minister. But then in England a suburban accent and the use of Brilliantine are more important than the man's actual talent. For, by and large, what Fowler cuts stays cut.

His Bill concerns itself with the sale of hotels and ferry services and with the law on drunken driving. It is the legislative equivalent of ordering sphaghetti and chips.

The subjects involved attract the classier sort of bore. Sir Bernard Braine – "caring approach, carnage on the roads, largest single factor," and Mr David Ennals, the Gary Player of affable bumbling.

17

Sir Bernard thought that individual liberty in respect of the motoring laws was so important that it ought to be the object of new legislation.

Mr Ennals talked eloquently on compulsory seat belts, which are not dealt with in this Bill, but which for the former Health Ministers are, well, a sort of King Charles's seat belt.

"I don't like the expression 'random testing'", he said. He was simply in favour of the police testing drivers at random.

On the whole, the Minister was quite good; he is crisp and factual. He is *not* imposing random testing and he is selling off the British Rail hotels. Is there any chance, one wonders, that he might do as much for those refreshment rooms which draw so delicate a line between plasticity and raw squalor?

Prime Minister's Question Time was, as usual, an unconstructive dialogue between telephone vandals and an *Ansafone* mechanism. But something must be done about Mr Foot's habit of breaking the embargo on his own jokes and laughing at them in advance.

"Does the Hon. Lady, ha ha, think she has, ha, controlled the leaks in her Cabinet, or is she, wait for it, ha, ha, the chief leaker herself?"

A little effort was put into jumping onto the lads back from the Metropolitan Borough of Afghanistan, but unfortunately Mr Ron Brown (Leith) had withdrawn his toxic presence from a House always gladdened by his absence, and Mr Allan Roberts (Bootle) is such a sweet fool that no one felt up to being half adequately nasty.

Daily Telegraph, January 14, 1981

Before Mrs Thatcher defeated the miners in 1984 she surrendered to them in 1981. Oddly enough she was not on hand to do the surrendering herself. One has someone do that for one. Poor Mr Howell was indeed duly pushed off the sledge.

Always given to gentle civility, Mr Merlyn Rees remarked that yesterday's announcement about pit closures did not represent a U-turn so much as a car skidding out of control.

It was, he said, a jack-knifing of policy.

18

Alas, at least insofar as Mr David Howell is concerned, not only does he turn, but we can all hear the gallows creaking. Metaphors of death leap up at one to fit the Secretary for Energy, the commonest in circulation having to do with his being flung very shortly from the sledge to those in pursuit.

For an understanding of why the Government is doing what it is doing, and what pains will flow, one does not look either to Mr Howell in statement-and-question session, nor to the Prime Minister. Of necessity they make mechanical devotions and try to ward off the mud and eggs of the delegated masses.

For understanding, one goes to the harder-bitten Conservative backbencher. Mr Terence Higgins, for example, one of Mr Heath's few really good appointments and an oversight of Mrs Thatcher's, asked whether concessions to the miners would not be reflected in a permutation of higher interest rates, higher prices in industry and other things which the gleeful Opposition are broadly against.

Mr Eric Cockeram (Ludlow) suggested that Sir Derek Ezra had lit a fuse and blasted money out of the Government.

All converse with the Opposition Front Bench was of an essentially trifling kind. Mr 22 per cent (Lab., Ebbw Vale) did his mid-Victorian actor bit, all scented sarcasm and hand-kissing tushery.

His promise of future bouquets to Mrs Thatcher as she adopted his policies was too much like a very late revival of George Arliss's Disraeli.

Mrs Thatcher's refusal of his playful and tiresome invitation to dinner was: "It is the lady's privilege to say 'no'." This set up a derisive cry of "not to the NUM".

That is the problem. It is not the actual decision which matters. That is seen broadly as a retreat to an unprepared position which was a whole lot cleverer than being kicked to death by Arthur Scargill in cleated boots.

What has hit the Tories like a meteorite behind the ear is the completeness of the change. Normally in defeat one climbs down; Mr Howell seems to have jumped.

Humiliation, like Justice, must not only be done, it must manifestly be seen to be done and in the process, the NUM, a gathering of often rather likeable men, is coming to look like a mystic force – the Executive Which Must Be Obeyed.

Daily Telegraph, February 20, 1981

Much of yesterday was given over to a restful and civilised debate on contempt of court presided over by the Attorney-General, Sir Michael Havers.

A delightful and soothing personality, he is the political equivalent of malted milk. Mrs Thatcher by contrast, when roused, is less like Ovaltine than ignited meths.

There exists between her and the more crudely Left-Wing peace, bread and unconditional surrender MPs a need for one another. There is a relationship or creative mutual loathing. It is like Punch and Judy with Judy using the stick.

Mr Norman Atkinson, who always sounds like a sergeant in the workers' militia, accused Mrs Thatcher of "harpie-like" operations in the United States which had brought nothing but shame to Britain.

To an unidentified backbench murmur of "Quisling" he called on her to apologise.

The Prime Minister, in her best ground glass manner, said she would leave shame to Mr Atkinson.

Naturally a Thatcher visit to the US is a sort of emotional therapy for the Left, some of whom have already promoted General Haig to the rank of Field Marshal, bombed San Salvador, in the mind at least, with napalm, and sent a nuclear mission to take out Mecca and Damascus.

Mrs Thatcher, by contrast, is busy being "staunch". That is a word one would advise her against. It is used, patronisingly but kindly, about one's feeblest friends, like those Conservative trades unionists Mr Prior is always going on about. To describe yourself as staunch sounds like patting yourself on the head.

Altogether it was not a happy afternoon for the Prime Minister. Her wholly admirable distaste for the Soviet Union and inclination for us to arm against it is diminished if she turns on the Liberals and starts accusing them of having no guts.

They haven't. But it sounds wrong to say so, and the impression was created yesterday afternoon that Mrs Thatcher, having lost to the miners, was going to take on the Russians instead. She sounds just a little like a West European Sukarno.

A foreign policy is, after all, the last refuge of a politician in general retreat. Any fool can have a foreign policy. I could have one. Even Mr Foot can have one. Controlling the money supply or getting trains to run is serious politics.

Not that one would want even foreign policy (or anything) to be in the hands of Mr Foot, who does increasingly now look like President Reagan's father.

Mr Foot's advice was that Mrs Thatcher should "learn the lesson of Vietnam". The lesson of Vietnam is to win.

The Opposition leader proceeded to denounce the lady in that slightly Edwardian prose style which recalls editorials in the *Morecambe and Lonsdale Herald* around the time of the Fashoda incident. He deplored her "bellicose demagogy".

He also, to the unkind amusement of the Government benches, lamented that she could not speak for a united country.

To have the part author of *Guilty Men* denouncing strong military stands and the president of the Labour dissolution damning the Prime Minister for disunity suggests that under that woolly muffler Mr Foot must have a fair measure of brass neck.

Daily Telegraph, March 3, 1981

The Budget of 1981 was actually rather important.

Sir Geoffrey Howe, speaking in a House sufficiently full for Members to be spilling over into their private gallery, committed his third Budget to the continuation of monetarist anti-inflationary policies consistent with the aims of the last 22 months.

The Chancellor enjoyed hush, whether sepulchral, respectful or appalled, for most of his speech which he delivered sustained only by a colourless, faintly fizzy liquid, at a guess mineral water.

His proposal to put up the duty on petrol by 20p produced the sort of response all round which goes with a finger-nail dragged across a slate backboard.

Inside the backbench Conservative one suspected that the stern economist was outnumbered two to one by the motorist and the prospective candidate in the General Election of 1984.

They did not care for it and outvoted his desire to cheer rather heavily.

The odd thing about the Chancellor is that although almost perversely mild and soft spoken (he doesn't just wear suede shoes, he talks in them), his wilfully grey manner conceals a taste in concrete policies for the dramatic. There is something endearing about his conjuror's ability to produce from a grey and battered hat a man-eating rabbit.

Whatever judgment may be made, no one will accuse Geoffrey Howe of seeing light at the end of a tunnel and then taking a 'U' turn back down it.

What Randall Jarrell said about poets is evidently true of Chancellors. "They begin as hypotheses, continue as facts and emerge as values." The value here is honest money, resistance to inflation and a refusal to go Macmillanning after cheap popularity with cheap credit.

For the wake of Nigel Birch*, the Budget could hardly be bettered. If it is wrong, it is wrong with a ferocious singularity of purpose.

This is underlined in a way, surely conscious and intended, when to the heavy tax on drink and tobacco the Chancellor coolly added an increase in the tax on matches and lighters. If Gladstone at the Treasury could collect candle-ends why ...

The delivery as usual was fairly awful. And it didn't terribly matter. The steady sustained mezzo-forte delivery habitual to the Chancery bar is burdensome to lightweight souls in politics and the Press, who want entertainment as well as death in the afternoon.

But then if you listened to Sir Geoffrey for his oratory you would hang yourself. This man is absinthe masquerading as barley water, as we would all know by now.

Still the hard matter of the policy came through if the minutiae of the tax adjustments for small business left an impression of cloudy approval. They are evidently good things, perhaps very good things, but one could do with somebody explaining them again ... slowly.

* Lord Rhyll, formerly Nigel Birch, had died that week. As a premature believer in not spending too much money he had resigned with Peter Thorneycroft and Enoch Powell from the Macmillan government, the original "little local difficulty" of which that Prime Minister made light so deftly.

However, the refusal to adjust the tax allowances by so much as one-tenth of one per cent produced the only real theatre of the afternoon. This is where you hiss the villain. Or, if you are Mr David Ennals, wave both arms about in opposite directions in very fair imitation of a man drowning on dry land. "Monstrous, unspeakable, you unparliamentary row of asterisks. Civilisation as we know it, good God, he's serious."

The response from the Leader of the Opposition began well with a number of the dry little jokes for which Mr Foot was so noted before the domestic tragedy of having to lead his party befell him.

Chesterton, Samuel Brittan and God all got a reference in no particular order of preference. But Mr Foot can never quite disentangle the conflicting roles of light cabaret turn and wind-swept, hillside revivalist. At the perorating end there was no question: Robertson Hare lost on points to John Wesley.

Daily Telegraph, March 11, 1981

Soon after the Budget, but not because of it we had riots.

The cocktail hour has acquired a rather special meaning wherever community workers, Rastafarians, and other Brixtonians are gathered together for practical criticism of police procedures.

So we had a busy time yesterday picking up the bits of South London which had fallen off over the weekend.

A good many sincerely-held opinions went unvoiced, since this was a serious moment. Only Mr Alexander Lyon actually attacked the police. Only Mr Harvey Proctor actually called for repatriation of West Indians.

The Labour side confined itself to an earnest, high-principled attempt to win votes at the next election, while Mr Whitelaw said that what had happened was utterly deplorable and not to be countenanced.

Mr Whitelaw could not, however, give satisfaction to Mr Hattersley, deeply dissatisfied that the official inquiry would not be widened – in scope so that the outrageous and direct consequence of monetary policies, the Department of the Environment and the shocking absence of a Labour Government could be examined – and in membership so that a mere judge,

Lord Scarman, might benefit from respectable and reputable persons familiar with "the community" (Mr Rudy Narayan perhaps?).

Mr Hattersley has, however, more wisdom than to attack the police (universal pastime though that seems to have become).

Mr Shelton (C., Streatham) pointed out that the Lambeth Council report on the area, which had been so adoringly praised by the BBC's dispassionate "community affairs" reporter, had described the local rozzers as "an army of occupation".

There was a good deal of the sort of talk we used to hear about Northern Ireland (not least from Mr Whitelaw) about "tiny minorities" and their virtuous antitheses "vast majorities".

The day a vast majority or even a moderately vast majority starts throwing bottles of petrol and setting on fire policemen provocatively on duty it will be rather disturbing.

Mr Enoch Powell, of course, the great unmentionable, expects nothing else. With an air of high Hellenic despair, he remarked: "We have seen nothing yet," and was promptly denounced for the obscenity of his remarks. Others, however, find the recent change in the colour of the River Tiber disquieting.

Sir Nigel Fisher, for example – a nicer, sweeter, unjumping Brocklebank-Fowler – was talking without apology about the need to use tear gas.

Like a call by Mr Douglas Jay for closer involvement with the EEC, Sir Nigel's hard line was surprising. Which is more than one could say for the observation of Mr Anthony Grant (Harrow) that the Asian population of his constituency were aghast at recent events.

On balance, one would expect the East Indians of Harrow to take a less sentimental view of the rioting West Indians of Brixton than your average guilt-stricken Anglo-Saxon.

Anyone who has ever watched a Delhi policeman swing a lathi might feel that some people in Railton Road do not know what they are missing.

Not that anything could stop the tremendous urge to browbeat the police.

"They lack training in race relations," said one Labour Member. "What happened to the police community liaison group?" asked a second. Surely there was a sad lack of social contact with "the community", said another. (Odd, is it not, that these days the word "community" means either the Common Market or Jamaicans?)

It was left to Mr David Mellor to make a cool, uncanting point from which discussion should have developed. Throwing bombs was not an act of social protest but of simple criminality.

From the reaction, that view has a large majority of the House behind it. Somehow one feels that training in race relations does not have quite the pull that it did.

Daily Telegraph, April 14, 1981

It was a hard afternoon in the Commons yesterday for the sipper of lemon tea or Ashbourne water.

It was Boozers' Wednesday, that part of the Finance Bill's committee stage given over to complaints about the duties on drink.

Mr Jack Straw, who got all those headlines about 12 years ago as a sort of post-graduate Kropotkin, has developed nicely into a bourgeois reformist politician with a pretty wit and sauntering manner.

He was concerned that the new duties fall so much upon beer and so little upon wine. "Beer," he said without going on too excessively about it, "is the workers' drink."

Half-hearted attempts were made by Mr Kenneth Lewis, the Conservative Geordie, to argue the unpersuasive case that there were Tories who drank beer. Doubtless there are, but like Tories who are Geordies there are not enough to make a statistically relevant sample.

If you had wanted to get class prejudice going – "classism" as some idiot will be calling it soon – there is no sweeter territory than the badlands where the supper of Ben Truman or Waddington is seen off by the not-at-all-bad-if-you-care-for-Loire-wines-that-is class.

Social class stalks the kidneys. No sniffer of bouquets or rotator of wineglasses can be a sound Labour man. Socialist, yes, but that includes all sorts of middle- and upper-class riff-raff.

It is a deadly weakness in the Social Democrats that they put up their sharpest political intelligence, Mr John Horam,* to

* In 1987 he left to join the Tories. The praise was premature.

25

argue the case for restraint on wine tax. Château Jenkins will be the death of them.

There was not much wine drunk in the working men's clubs of Blackburn, said Mr Straw with satisfaction. Now there might be, if there were more local vintages to drink. A Didsbury Sylvaner or a Bamber Bridge Riesling might catch on.

The great strength of Mr Straw's point is that on this issue he has got the workers and the patriotic card in the same hand. The unbeatable message is that the rich drink wine and foreigners make it.

Beer is drunk by workers and made here. So why are we hitting beer with twice the impost as wine? It is a good Labour line and we shall hear more about it if they know what they are about.

Involving as it does class, tax, nationalism and the EEC it is a club sandwich of issues to be eaten at leisure.

Mr Robin Cook, who sounds like one of nature's abstainers, pressed the EEC element. The inscrutable aluminium-faced men in Brussels had decreed that wine and beer taxes should stand in a certain ratio, one quite fortuitously favourable to the producers of wine and to the custodians of its lake.

There was not much the Tories could do against these amendments, apart from voting them down. There was no question of winning the argument, at least not with Mr Bowen Wells about.

That gentleman has going for him the solitary virtue that he is not Mrs Shirley Williams (whom he defeated at Hertford in the General Election). But he has the dialectical style of a brown bear.

Mr Straw had argued that the Government was seeking heavy additional taxation when it had promised lower taxes. "Mr Chairman, sir, we aimed to reduce taxation but we have been forced to increase it. Doesn't that prove that we are not dogmatic?' Some seats are better off unwon.

As it was the Tories huddled on the ropes and took the punches. They, the party of the brewers, had turned beer into a connoisseur's drink. Their fiscal policy was apparently in thrall to a French surplus production lobby. They had attacked the workers. What few pleasures there were left, they had put a tax on.

One waited with interest for Mr Eric Heffer, but alas that

26

five-masted galleon of verbal inconsequence was launched upon a sea of reminiscence. "When I was a boy in Hertford it used to be pub, shop, pub, shop. Hertford was that sort of town." Why ...?

I made my excuses and left ... for tea!

Daily Telegraph, May 7, 1981

The debate on foreign affairs, arranged with some foresight to coincide with the council elections when most of the more obsessive sniffers of this dubious glue would be stuck on the doorsteps in Salford and Sheffield Brightside, was a languorous thing.

Tempo di minuetto most of the time, it moved into Edmundo Ros territory in the speech of Mr Denis Healey.

Grave offence was taken in the gallery when Mr Healey, in flagrant breach of closed shop agreements, began to make a series of humorous remarks. As the convenor of sketch writers muttered grimly: "We make the jokes here."

Considered merely on their merit outside their context as scab labour on the floor of the Commons, the comments were variable.

To describe the Prime Minister as "Rhoda the Rhinoceros on the Rampage" gets a heavy endorsement for alliteration, something one is trying to stamp out.

But parts of the extended zoological metaphor like "passing the flamingo pool where we find the Lord Privy Seal, Sir Ian Gilmour, elongated pink and wet" would get a beta treble plus at least in our annual entry examinations.

It is rather sad to watch Mr Healey, one of the two great minds of the Commons, having a run for office. The old Denis was an unrelenting warmonger and fascist hyena of the very best sort who, at Scarborough once, turned on the unilateralists with some nasty details from the then Soviet leader's youth and said: "Can I get it into your heads, comrades, that Mr Khrushchev is not the George Lansbury type?"

Denis in this degenerate age has to go on about the Third World and the need for more aid, the virtues of an unreformed SALT II and the dangerous tendencies of the Americans.

In what one hoped was a cheerful spirit of parody he trusted

27

that countries like Norway, Sweden and Australia could play a part in helping the American pragmatists to win in Washington in their struggle with the idealogues.

At one stage he insisted that we were being disgracefully lax in not flushing vast quantities of money into the Third World, which presumably includes Africa, where otherwise people would starve to death in great numbers.

Three paragraphs later, having condemned the Government for vetoing economic sanctions on South Africa but not quite wanting to approve them himself in so many words, he proclaimed that Black Africa was more important to us than South Africa as a trading partner. The role of South Africa in feeding Black Africa was not discussed.

He was, however, agreeably rough on the Common Agricultural Policy. Dear old Sir Anthony Meyer, something of an old believer who wants European flags hung everywhere, intervened to say "the CAP was the *sine qua non* of more than one of our EEC allies".

The old Denis leapt into bloodshot and vehement GBH. If Sir Anthony thought that soaking our consumers (and German consumers) to pay a gross bribe to little groups of producers in France, Germany and Denmark was co-operation, he did not, and he was sure the Germans agreed with him.

No sooner was the spring-heeled hard man in action than he relaxed back into the senior tutor's manner and, as he often does, switched accents from Headingley to Balliol. He would take another intervention "in a moment when I have finished this little exordium".

Like Deacon Brodie of Edinburgh, he is a quick change artist. And it must be said that, for all the statutory feebleness he had to endorse, he is a superior article.

There is nothing wrong with Sir Ian Gilmour at the Foreign Office except that where Mr Healey is in personality terms a florid bloom, a purple and menacing rhododendron, Sir Ian, cool, civil, unassertive, is the white pale oxlip of politics.

"Was it not absurd," asked Mr Jessel, "to expect the Israelis to withdraw from a strategically useful territory?" "There was no reason," thought Sir Ian, "why Israel should continue to occupy land which in no conceivable way has it a claim to."

Mr Healey, less delicately, called Mr Menahem Begin a racialist. The combined bouquet from the British political garden will not flourish in the Negev.

Daily Telegraph, May 8, 1981

At Llandudno during Liberal Conference the leading figures of that party staged a public meeting with the leadership of the SDP with interesting consequences.

Llandudno, the flower of watering places all, is unchanged in its Edwardian stucco and wrought iron from the way it must have looked when Mr Lloyd George was President of the Board of Trade. It is a sort of Bad Ischl in North Wales.

Brutally, this conference is concerned about getting Liberals back into the contemporary equivalent of the Board of Trade. But at all conferences there are fringe meetings which, on the analogy of skiing, I think of as *après conférence*.

But the little meeting for which we hastened to the Pier Pavilion stands in relation to the Liberal Assembly rather like Slough to Windsor.

It was addressed, not by evangelising young men in corduroy jackets, but by the Leader himself, sourly described in some quarters as "the Wee Yin", by Mr Grimond, by the Moral Victor of Warrington, and by Mrs Shirley Williams, who, as we all know, has a part-time consultancy with the angels.

It was good, highly professional stuff. There were jokes about the Member for Rochdale (Mr Cyril Smith being a noted spitter in the sacrament of the alliance), which turned out to be references to Richard Cobden in 1861!

We had the uncanny experience of hearing Mrs Shirley Williams being incisive — especially when she talked of no longer having to look over her shoulder at Thought Policemen in the Labour party, something which set the pavilion thundering.

Certain clichés did, alas, bloom. Shirley, Roy and David between them "wished to break the rigid mould"; were "people who believed in the European ideal", and they denounced "false and outdated notions of class and dogma". Well, they would, wouldn't they?

At one point Mr Jenkins spoke of "the stultifying monopoly which the two major parties had too long enjoyed". Well now —

29

Minister of Aviation, Home Secretary, Chancellor of the Exchequer (an excellent Thatcherish one) and President of the European Economic Commission, you could call that enjoyment all right!

There are Liberals about, a sullen, youngish element who seem not terribly to like the Social Democrats.

There was something of an altercation just in front of your correspondent when a bearded young man in a corduroy cap muttered something about Mr Jenkins, and a middle-aged man in a Fair Isle pullover turned round and snarled, "Shut up, will you."

Overwhelmingly the meeting was in favour of Fair Isle pullovers. When Mr Jenkins offered them, in effect, alliance or extinction they cheered furiously, presumably for alliance.

What really did the trick was not the "mould-breaking" or the "caring passionately" about something or other – the high purpose language of politics.

It was a taste of low motives when Mr Jenkins, with a touch of raw, blood-and-intestines politics, said: "We are formidable." There was a roar. Temptation had come to the Liberal Party, which has long affected to be above politics, to sink a little.

Daily Telegraph, September 16, 1981

At one time the single most important issue in British politics seemed to be Mr Benn's attempt to become Deputy Leader of the Labour Party. It all seems as remote as the Battle of Bosworth!

"Sufficient" you might call Mr Healey's victory. At 50·43 to 49·57 that is the strongest word it deserves.

When the vote came Mr Benn smiled wanly. Dennis Skinner cast an arm round him and peaceably. Only a squeak and a handful of defecting backbenchers stood between the Labour party and Wedgwoodbennistan. The conference dissolved.

Those defecting Left-wing MPs, we calculated, had like ants dragged their sub-percentage of a vote with them, each to vast effect.

By a sweet and sour irony the Parliamentary Labour Party, seen here in the same light as the aristocratic estate at the

30

Convention of 1789, had decided the result.

It was not quite enough for the Transport and General Workers to have worked at treble bluff – for Benn last week, for abstaining yesterday afternoon and for Benn again after tea.

The miserable, wine-sipping, decadent MPs had delivered survival to Denis. Whether survival on such a percentage is worth having is debatable.

But for the Left abstainers, those Jenkinses in Kinnock's clothing, Mr Healey could have called it a day and gone off to run NATO in agreeable company.

Earlier, during the ballot, virtuous topics were raised by the Chairman of the Labour party who described himself as a grassroot and Brighton as the queen of watering places. I have always thought of this smart but flash borough as a shady baronet!

There was also the mayor, evidently a Conservative, who possessed either a masterly grasp of irony or wooden ears.

He urged the Labour conference, which contains some of the world's more than ordinarily not nice people and which frequently resembles unlicensed wrestling, to "proceed to their deliberations!"

He took great pleasure in the selection (pause) of this venue. There was a lot more in the ironic vein, about knowledge, wisdom and integrity and the semi-somnambulating Labour party looked up from its back-of-envelope calculations to clap absent mindedly.

The Chairman, Mr Alex Kitson, sounded in his Scottish way like somebody dragging the Clyde for the dead. He used a river metaphor on the Social Democrats. Actually "mud bank" was easily the most delicate description he managed.

They are "parasites" and "bloodsuckers". They stood in relation to Socialism like a vampire to a crucifix.

Trust between Conference and the Parliamentary party had been sucked dry by that bunch of opportunists. Mr Steel was "baring his neck to Mr Jenkins". All very hot and torrid stuff.

By comparison Mrs Thatcher was let off with a warning. She was only a neutron bomb, a holocaust and the personification of economic and military insanity – mere grace notes on the keyboard of abuse.

That is the sort of thing Denis has just rededicated his days

31

to enduring ... by 0·86 per cent. No one wishing this party well one would rejoice at the prospect.

The Orme-Kinnock group facing constituency firing squads, the struggle resumed, another election, more canvassing of union delegate conferences at Buxton Spa, and Denis not so much elected as impaled! A well-wisher would not be happy. As it is. . . .

Daily Telegraph, September 28, 1981

Monthly in Encounter *I have the opportunity to write at length. Here I took the opportunity to comment on an enormously successful, very bad TV serial adapted from my least favourite book.*

Brideshead Resisted

Chronicles of a Social Alpinist

At the time this appears the American public will be settling into the eleven-part serialisation of Evelyn Waugh's *Brideshead Revisited* which, with uncommon sharpness, we have unloaded on to their networks. Will the Americans coo or squirm? It is an important question from which they may learn a lot about their own state of political health.

Brideshead follows *Upstairs Downstairs* and *The Dairy of an Edwardian Lady* as an addition to the list of commodities marked under the trade label "Nostalgia". It is also a hymnal to the true English vice – not flagellation, snobbery! The narrator is dining with Rex Mottram, a loud, successful Canadian (based upon the real-life Brendan Bracken to whom Evelyn Waugh owed great obligations).

> I rejoiced in the Burgundy. . . . [It] seemed ... a reminder that the world was an older and better place than Rex knew, that mankind in its long passion has learned another wisdom than his.

Burgundy! But then the narrator, Charles Ryder, is that sort of young man.

Lady Julia (and we are frequently reminded that she is *Lady* Julia, daughter of the Marquis of Marchmain), describes her marriage to Mottram:

> Oh, Charles, what a squalid wedding! The Savoy Chapel was
> the place where divorced couples got married in those days. . . .
> My own friends came, of course, and the curious accomplices
> Rex calls *his* friends. . . . Mummy said we couldn't use Mar-
> chers. . . . There was great awkwardness about the tenants. In
> the end Bridey [her brother Lord Brideshead] went down and
> gave them a dinner and bonfire there which wasn't at all what
> they expected in return for their silver soup tureen.

Brideshead Revisited, novel and TV screen treatment, is a
desolating experience. More than anything else it celebrates the
aristocracy as a kind of virtue. To be one of the long-enobled,
to live in a house with wings and a chapel, is a state of grace
from which no trifling human defects can detract. Accordingly
the Flytes – drunken Sebastian, bitchy Julia, religion-crazed
Cordelia – are all the objects of Ryder's unpleasant combination
of euphoric adulation and cold-eyed determination to join.
There is quite a thesis waiting to be written on the distinctive
determination of ambitious young men in different parts of the
world to get on or, alternatively, to get *in*.

Now, although the screen version has been rightly praised for
its fidelity, the script-writer John Mortimer, a mild man of the
Left, has quietly toned down and filtered some of the very
worst Waugh, notably the treatment of Hooper, a clumsy,
uncultivated, lower-middle-class officer. That passage is fairly
near to being the apotheosis of Waugh's hatred for the com-
monality.

> "I told you to inspect the lines."
> "'M I late? Sorry. Had a rush getting my gear together."
> "That's what you have a servant for."

Hooper, it seems,

> had not as a child ridden with Rupert's horse or sat among
> the campfires at Xanthus-side. . . . Hooper had wept often,
> but never for Henry's speech on St Crispin's day, nor for
> the epitaph at Thermopylae. The history they taught him
> had few battles in it but, instead, a profusion of detail
> about humane legislation and recent industrial change.

That is childish and nasty but speaks eloquently for the author himself, a malevolent and spluttering version of Miniver Cheevy:

> Miniver cursed the commonplace
> And eyed a khaki suit with loathing
> He missed the medieval grace
> Of iron clothing

Brideshead Revisited is the story of Waugh/Ryder's shrewdly judged attempt to buy himself a season ticket into the landed gentry. It is interwoven with a very forgettable tract for triumphalist Catholicism, culminating in a deathbed reconciliation by the unbelieving Lord Marchmain to the Church of Pacelli, Franco and some very good families, which it would require a stomach of zinc not to be turned by. But Lord Marchmain does not rejoin his Church before stressing rather more important points.

> Aunt Julia knew the tombs, cross-legged knight and doubleted earl, marquis like a Roman senator . . . tapped the escutcheons with her ebony cane, made the casque ring over old Sir Roger. We were knights then, barons since Agincourt, the larger honours came with the Georges.

Ryder attaches himself at Oxford to Lord Sebastian Flyte, an alcoholic futilitarian upon whom some 40% of the text is lavished. As a college servant remarks, "A most amusing gentleman. I'm sure it's quite a pleasure to clean up after him."

Then he seeks out Sebastian's sister, Julia. They conduct a shipboard romance which comes over on television as if it had been written for a parodistic Fiona and Nigel, all sterile, significant pauses (by this time Charles has grown a moustache with which to brush Julia's cheek – and the actor, Jeremy Irons, had taken on the look of a higher-toned version of the young Hitler). Waugh, a relatively chaste author, does stipulate sexual intercourse, so Mr Mortimer, literal-mindedly and with an eye to the ratings, has Mr Irons in his underpants doing the standard RADA press-ups. Julia happens to be married to Rex who is a colonial and doesn't understand Burgundy, so that's all right. Except, of course, that Julia throws a religious tantrum next to the fountain in the park at Brideshead. She gets over it and has another agreeable turn of dalliance with Ryder. But when Lord

Marchmain comes back from his atheistical exile in Venice to run through his ancestors, find God, and die in the Queen's bed in the Chinese drawing room, Charles and Julia part, moved by a deep wisdom which evaded them for the previous 80 pages. Ryder has the consolation prize of God, awarded to him at Lord Marchmain's bedside: "a phrase came back to me from my childhood of the veil of the temple being rent from top to bottom...."

This novel and its television treatment are, not to be nice, trash. The thing is a species of epic novelette. Never mind for a moment its puerile snobbery and social finessing, parts of it could have been written by somebody on a six-books-a-year contract to Mills and Boon:

> ... the dark horizon of tumbling water, flashing now with gold, stood still above us, then came sweeping down till I was staring through Julia's hair into the wide golden sky, and she was thrown forward on my heart, held up by my hands on the rail, her face still pressed to mine.
>
> In that minute, with her lips to my ear and her breath warm in the salt wind, Julia said, though I had not spoken, "Yes, now," and as the ship righted itself and for the moment ran into calmer waters, Julia led me below.

The Television version, though sparing us some of this treacly dialogue and thinning out a little the spirit of clerico-fascism in which the book was written, remains dreadful and adds inevitable little dreadfulnesses of its own. Because Ryder, artist, *arriviste* and supercreep, acts as a narrator, he is not blessed in the text with a great quantity of dialogue. In consequence the actor Jeremy Irons, who plays this projection of a grander good-looking Waugh, hangs around a great deal rather like an under-employed footman.

Again, the producers commissioned by Lord Bernstein of Manchester's Granada TV (only a life peer, alas) have tried to waltz this tosh past us by dressing it up. Estimates of the cost vary but the location photography alone must have kept NATTKE, our sumptuously over-manned cameramen's union, on double-ply overtime velvet for months. It was shot at Christ Church, Oxford, in Venice, and at Castle Howard in Yorkshire. Great actors like Olivier and famous ones like Gielgud have also been brought into small parts to intimidate the feeble critics. If visual splendour could redeem narrative tat, Lord Bernstein would have done it. But alas, this gambit only indulges Waugh's vulgar dream of the great folk and their environment still further. Vast tracts of the film create the impression of having been shot through a slick of golden syrup. Sebastian and Ryder drive off into a haze of light and pause to picnic upon champagne in countryside which looks like the old advertisement for Summer County Margarine. Indeed one way and another advertising images are important to *Brideshead* partly because acres of the film could so easily dissolve into top-of-the-market plugs. Charles, stalking on the upper sun-deck before he gets Julia, really should have done a cologne-for-men or panatella ad. And, as another reviewer remarked, the Venetian trip is pure Martini all the way. For that matter the ITV advertisements seemed to merge with the show. A woman of stupefyingly gormless chic, in the early stages of seduction to a stage Frenchman for the promotion of Cointreau; a hostess surveying her super-splendidly laid dinner table before snatching an illicit After Eight mint under the eye of a roguish husband – they could all have been subsumed into the greater commercial called *Brideshead* and nobody would have noticed.

For *Brideshead* is soft-selling a social class to the Americans after having sold it with tolerable success to the general British public, and with no trouble at all to some of the more gushing reviewers. "Watching it has been like floating down a river as powerful as the Mississippi and as beautiful as the Loire.... Unfortunately Diana Quick has not the assured upper-class glamour of Julia. She gives her a touch of the schoolmistress. Lady Diana Cooper still has this glamour even in old age." (*Daily Telegraph* – who else?)

Brideshead is an advertisement all right – for every false, wrong, sycophancy-inspiring quality which is doing better than it should in Britain. Waugh trembled with rage at the encroachment of "the lower orders", not least because his own encroaching had been done very recently and because there were indications that he had only reached the banquet in time for coffee. The novel Waugh wrote in some hysteria towards the end of the last War is, when screened, smoother, sleeker and more palatable for the uncritical. It was a very apt production for the year of the latest Royal Wedding. It says: "Here are beautiful people living in beautiful houses (big ones) surrounded by culture and sustained by a very classy sort of religion. We trust that you know your respectful place."

Martin Wiener in *English Culture and the Decline of the Industrial Spirit* (1981) has a splendid phrase for what he regards as an English decadence: "The Counter-Reformation of Gentry values." For Wiener, we have been set in our country over many years on a false turning, best seen as the victory of Oxford over Manchester, of Gentlemen over men. Oxford, city of aspiring dreams, was never a more loathsome arcady than in the early episodes of the *Brideshead* serial. But is this decadence narrowly English or will *Brideshead* ring the bell for the AB yearnings in Kansas and Minnesota? For me Lord Sebastian and his teddy bear, Charles and his Burgundy, Julia using theology as a short cosh, Lord Marchmain and his noble ancestors, Anthony Blanche and his camp act, and the whole tribe of toad-eaters and servers-up of toad might well in some nice crude pre-Marxian revolution have been swept away by angry tenants not all contented with donating silver soup tureens. They are futile, feckless, unmeritable people; and the men who watch the charts and the polls seem to think that we like and admire them. Now is America – which confected its own plastic aristocracy in the Kennedy era and whose left-wing journalists can turn into running footmen at the lengthening of a vowel – is America sound enough, *republican* enough, to silence gentry values with the flick of a switch and watch something comparatively grown-up like *Kojak*? For, even if the supplier is in St James's, *Brideshead* remains soap. It is a bad novel by a good novelist, rendered marginally less offensive by Mr Mortimer's social conscience but drawn out from its thin substance like a piece of chewing-gum in the hands of the Inquisition. If America salutes *Brideshead*, the battle of Yorktown will have been a wasted effort.

Encounter, March 1982, Vol. LVIII, No 3
London Commentary

In the spring and early summer of 1982 a small war was fought between Britain and Argentina.

The House yesterday went vigorously to war with itself.

The cautious, polite unity of three weeks was broken in several places as the Leader of the Opposition and the Prime Minister faced each other, the one melancholy and lamenting, the other coldly outraged.

Mr Foot looks for rescue to the United Nations, where full and frank exchanges of views, not to say valuable consultations seem, he believes, a small price for not actually shooting, parachuting and launching rockets.

Mrs Thatcher responded with magnificent chilling disdain.

The prospect of military action quite soon has knocked the Humpty Dumpty of by-partisanship off his wall and broken him into pieces which will not readily be reassembled.

Parliamentary debate which had had all the gentle soothing tone of a garden sprinkler turned abruptly into the blast of a fire hose turned on in mid-winter.

Mr Foot informed the Prime Minister that if she did not make a proper response to the Secretary-General of the United Nations – the Peruvian, Señor Perez de Cuellar – she would be "inflicting a grievous blow upon our country's cause".

The Queen of the Iceni was in no mood to waste time in parlance with the Incas. She informed Mr Foot, in turn, that he was "putting our soldiers and sailors in jeopardy".

The Pastoral Age of civility has been succeeded not so much by Ice as by the Age of Broken Glass.

Mr Benn intervened loftily to observe that it was "clear that the Government had never had the slightest intent of using the UN. It was always going to be a military operation," he added in that special Benn tone of supercivility which merges imperceptibly into high Castilian disdain.

Mr Benn is an old parliamentary hand which is, no doubt, why Mrs Thatcher stamped on him. "The Rt Hon. Gentleman is talking nonsense," she said like Mrs Proudie crushing an uppity curate, "and I suspect he knows it."

However the remark which really turned up the central heating and made mild men snarl came from Mr Jack Dormand, a largish, grey-haired foot soldier of the residual Labour Right,

38

a minor key Jim Callaghan as it were.

Mrs Thatcher's belligerence in the last two days, said Mr Dormand, had misjudged not only the military situation but the mood of the British *people*.

The expression "wow", indicating violent and incoherent outrage, appears in your correspondent's notes at that point. If there is one point the Tories are hot on over this conflict it is that they are breathing in and out in perfect tempo with the Broad Masses.

If Mrs Thatcher's supporters are clear on one topic in international relations it is that while power may corrupt its absence paralyses. If there was no military pressure there would be no withdrawal.

We accepted the Security Council's resolution, but the Security Council had no way of enforcing it. Mrs Thatcher did not quite describe the SAS as the secular army of the UN but for practical working purposes that is the burden of her argument.

Labour, by contrast, regarded military action in a somewhat Augustinian fashion. They were in favour of it, as the young Augustine favoured chastity, but not yet.

Appropriately, at this point, Mr Norman St John Stevas, like a slightly battered archangel, restored good humour by calling for mediation by the Pope.

It will take more than pontifical and apostolic authority, one fears, to bring Mr Foot and Mrs Thatcher and their parties back into the ecumenical fellowship of the last few weeks.

Daily Telegraph, April 28, 1982

It was, you might say, the day after we sent the gunboat.

Older and wiser councils had *not* prevailed and the Commons was celebrating a victory which some of its Members cannot bring themselves to believe in, and which others will never forgive.

Attempts were of course made to detract from the triumph but it was all Crufts to a ginger kitten that a triumph was what it would be.

Mrs Thatcher, at last out of black and into a blue suit of a fairly hefty voltage, was her own best categorical self. The usual filter of subordinate clauses of a diplomatic and ambiguous sort had disappeared.

The word "surrender" appeared in the first sentence of her statement. And in its last sentence she spoke of the "defence of our way of life and of our *sovereign territory*".

By contrast, Mr Foot had a dreadful time. One does not want to be unkind and he had been, after Monday's interim late announcement, all grace and good manners.

Alas, yesterday he went on to auto-flannel. He lurched with sober incoherence into a great prose poem about the United Nations. The United Nations does for Mr Foot what the liquefied blood of St Januarius does for the more superstitious Neapolitan.

It was clearly necessary to get rid of the false and misleading apprehension that soldiers had gone 8,000 miles, lost comrades, risked their lives, and fought battles with guns just for some vulgar golf club and four ale bar notion of "British territory".

"International agreements," he said, and "UN trusteeship territory", like one platonically stricken by an abstract notion. The question mithered blamelessly and irrelevantly on to a background of polite exasperation.

Conservative feeling for the UN is that it has all the excitement of a monochrome rainbow and all the immediate utility of the next galaxy but three.

"I cannot agree," said Mrs Thatcher, "that our soldiers risked their lives to obtain a UN trusteeship territory. They did it for this country."

Suddenly the old verities are back and Plastic Internationalism is keeping its head down. Or, if it is wise it is.

Mrs Thatcher got her antennae exactly right, replying with great care and civility to all the factual and detailed questions coming from Opposition Members – if anything, pulling her punches in the business of putting hostile people down. She is eight foot tall at the moment and does not need to bully.

But she did not waste genuflections on the UN. If anybody threw Resolution 502 at her, with its implied requirement of negotiation and accommodation, she tended to answer in heavy type.

"But 502 was **not honoured**. We **don't need** to negotiate with the UN or **anyone else**."

Mr Foot returned to the need for international approaches and generally went on long enough to sufficiently little purpose to lull a conurbation into a light nap.

But the criticisms were a parenthesis in the general relief and pride. We have an anti-Suez on our hands.

In our vulgar, anachronistic way we have won a victory (something long thought passé and quaint).

The language of the 1st/7th Gurkhas, the taking of Mount William, the 1,000 Harrier missions from *Hermes*, and General Moore accepting surrender had taken over from communiqués, aides-mémoires and the "role of the Secretary-General as honest broker." It is all very embarrassing!

Daily Telegraph, June 16, 1982

I can only imagine that we were in the middle of a railway strike.

Anyone reading this on a railway platform towards the end of the first hour of his wait for a train is begged not to throw himself on to the line. The prospects of a swift termination of his distress are much reduced due to non-availability of drivers.

But one has to say that the Commons spent much of yesterday discussing the plight of the commuter and, in the highly Platonic fashion of this House, in bopping ASLEF.

The debate, literally won in a raffle by Mr George Gardiner, was a miniaturised class war. Mr Gardiner himself is an unreconstructed petty bourgeois. He sits for Reigate where, it is supposed among Northern Labour members, the entire enemy class reside – amid golf courses constructed with the surplus value of handloom weavers.

Mr Frank Dobson, who opposed him, though a member of the relatively sweet-souled NUR, represents Holborn and St Pancras which, as Town Hallologists well know, is part of the peace-loving Workers Republic of Camden.

Mr Gardiner, No 4 iron in one hand, gin-and-tonic in the other, was quite good much of the time, suggesting a campaign medal for citizens in time of peace to reward the man in the traffic jam/on foot/sleeping under his desk.

But he grew a trifle Reigate in his denunciation of overtime

41

earnings spent drinking and then slept off in the railway cab.

If we had a Class Relations Board, Mr Gardiner would be up in front of it! Indeed his attitude towards members of ASLEF on class feeling was one which, in respect of race, would have passed without notice in the Orange Free State!

His view of ASLEF is the succinct and evidently popular one that we should "break its back".

Mr Dobson, by contrast, spoke with reciprocal fervour of the job done by railway workers "clearing up the filth and stink the general public leave behind in carriages" and all, so he argued, for £50 a week. Clearly there are two social classes touching at no known point, the pixilated railwaymen and the unclean passengers!

Mr Dobson, who is an intelligent and amusing speaker, suffered one attempt by his professional jargon to stage a coup d'état and take over his speech. "What they [the NUR] entered into, Mr Speaker, was to enter into meaningful talks."

Similar difficulties faced Mr Harry Cowans, the stenographer-defying Geordie, who represents Newcastle Central (the Grampound of the 1980s). Intervening in a speech by Mr Cockeram (Cons. Hard Man Ludlow) he proclaimed: "I have been listening very vividly to his remarks on investment."

Actually Mr Cockeram is not so much vivid as absolute. He is as categorical as Kant in a nasty mood.

To call the money spent on the railways "investment" was a distortion of the English language. There was nothing paid on that investment. Quite the contrary: what was put in was written off.

"If people invest," said Mr Cockeram, doing his Jacob Marley bit, "they expect a return. What do they get? Not a penny."

He then proceeded to mention the bus services. "What profit did they make?" asked someone unwisely.

"Ah," said Mr Cockeram gratefully, the National Bus Company's profits over the last year had gone up from £10 million to £26 million.

Actually the profit and loss approach is a great deal more effective than the "Why aren't the workers putting their backs into it?" stuff which from Reigate to the Lenin Hills is the recurring conversational motif of those whose backs will not actually be getting put in.

Simply by sticking to the figures he was able to do ASLEF a great deal of injury, linking moneys lost in strikes and marginal lines vulnerable to closure.

ASLEF will make BR review marginal lines, he said. "Who will have killed them? Mr Buckton and his executive."

It is much wiser politics to show the other side breaking somebody's back than to rant on about breaking his.

Daily Telegraph, July 6, 1982.

It is with the utmost hesitation that one intervenes on Finance Bills. They abound with such private communications as "No, no, the Rt. Hon. Gentleman is mistaken: such a move would increase the CGR and not the PSBR."

But, hanging desperately to the few strands of rope which one can grasp in the upper rigging (if that is quite a happy term) of public finance, it does rather look as if something rather drastic is about to happen.

Ministers, of course, rely on the built-in stupor which the report stage of the Finance Bill (New Clause 1) can be expected to induce – it had the effect of virtually emptying the Press Gallery.

However, in their boring old way the Government appear to have sought unlimited powers of borrowing.

Mr Jock Bruce-Gardyne who, in a gentlemanly way, has the essential characteristics of an absent-minded Fellow of one of the remoter and better-castelled Oxford colleges, diffidently suggested that he was concerned to "restrain the monetary aggregates" and achieve "sound monetary conditions" – set forms of prayer with which the congregation are familiar.

But there is something about borrowing without limit so as to promote sound monetary conditions which sounds a trifle odd.

As Mr Shore said with some feeling, he had wanted higher borrowing sometime before and had been seen off with the argument that it would "crowd out" private firms' borrowing.

But the difficult questions came from Mr Terence Higgins. Mr Higgins is by nature not a rocker of boats nor a maker of difficulties but he is that fearful thing, an elucidator.

He pointed out that though M3 had all sorts of cabbalistic

significance for members of the Government, when they were obliged to choose between it and interest rates they had on a previous occasion preferred to try holding down interest rates.

"It is quite simple," said Mr Higgins depressingly. "O-level stuff." (But not to the hapless onlooker.)

One could choose between controlling a commodity or controlling a price but Mr Bruce-Gardyne despite his long lineage and his golden tongue could not do both. The price it was to be, and for price read interest rates!

Mr Higgins spoke sadly about how Sir Denis Robertson the Cambridge economist had sought to illustrate the subject by reference to *Alice in Wonderland*, but doubted if that could be followed. Let us try.

In these highly technical matters, the Dormouse (or Chancellor) has been preoccupied with the level of tea actually in the circulating pot, T3, but unbeknown to him the Mad Hatter (or bankers) has arranged at a price (interest rates) for private supplies of tea bought in vacuum flasks which the assembled tea party are delighted to consume.

Anxious about the overall tea aggregates, the Dormouse relaxes control of the tea in the pot (or T3) in order to drive down the price charged for the Hatter's private tea.

Mr Bruce-Gardyne may faintly resemble a dormouse but it was the argument of the half-dozen people who seemed to understand the situation, that he had been very fast on his feet in creating unprecedented powers to borrow and to crowd out the over-active banks.

It is all very technical and expert and etiolated, but sounds very like the sort of reversal of policy which a shrewd Government, putting its most absent-minded Minister forward, would wish to keep that way.

Daily Telegraph, July 13, 1982

The intrusion into Buckingham Palace of a stray eccentric put on circulation for newspapers across several days.

The Queen's Police Officer is one of those characters, like the Official Solicitor, who were not known to exist by us of the brutish multitude until the sad moment when they briefly astonished us, the one by being called in to get a Government in difficulties off the hook, the other to be stoned to death.

Mr Whitelaw, who made yesterday's announcement about Mr Trestrail,* has a lugubrious expression even when announcing the afternoon off and free beer all round. Yesterday he sounded like a funeral mute pressed into saying a few words.

Mr Roy Hattersley, in no narrow party spirit, thanked him and appreciated the difficulty involved.

Though how are we to be shocked? At the rate things are going the arrival on the Royal lawns of an Unidentified Flying Object containing time travellers from the galaxy Alpha Hercules will be no more than "a further extension of the difficulties relating to security at Buckingham Palace".

But this was only an Overture played before the Symphonic Poem of Mr Patrick Jenkin's announcement that Buzby† was to be turned into a limited company and the equity sold off in the market – perhaps, muttered a Labour voice, to foreigners!

The Labour party is devoted to British Telecommunications, which it defends as it would have defended hand-loom weaving if there had been a Labour party in 1770. (Come to think of it they would probably have set up a nationalised corporation called "British Handloom Weaving".)

Labour seemed particularly depressed by the fact that Mr Jenkin does not actually plan to commence his fell and midnight legislation until after the next election.

A wonderful opportunity, one would have thought, to have convinced the electorate of the obvious absurdity of privatisation and the shimmering efficiency and cheapness of the present telephone system. Somehow they didn't seem to see it that way.

Mr Ian Wrigglesworth, an excessively clean-cut and respectable-looking Social Democrat, complained that this decision would turn British Telecommunications into a political football.

He seemed quite to miss the point that 12 to 18 months as the party committed to turning Buzby into a feather duster is as good a way of winning the next election as any other.

Somehow, things accomplished are never quite as exciting as

---

* The Queen's gay detective, later to resign.
† A bird used in Post Office commercials, later to be withdrawn.

45

things undertaken to be done.

There was a strenuous work-out on the Labour benches by the abomination-denouncing and horror-expressing formation team who have won any number of silver rose bowls by the depth of their feelings for shattered humanity and, a golden oldie, their rising sense of outrage.

They could also have picked up an award for obtuseness. Mr Jenkin, though rather too silken and barristerly, is perfectly articulate. If he explained once that pension funds were secure and not to be raffled off in Lombard Street he did so (unequivocally) five times.

Daily Telegraph, July 20, 1982

The SDP at this time favoured mobile conferences, moving in 1982 from Cardiff to Derby to Yarmouth.

"Something must be done." The Social Democrats at Derby sounded rather like the late Prince of Wales. Except that they have a deplorable habit of adding chapter, verse and amending footnote of coercive detail about what should be done to whom.

The Assembly Rooms in the city of Derby, in the beautiful Walter Johnson country, are less appealing than St David's Hall, Cardiff, being constructed, unwisely of firebricks, as a futurian fortress for the repulsions of Venusians.

It is not made more agreeable by the orthopaedic chairs which, like the SDP, are good for us but not very enjoyable.

Delegates show signs of being refractory.

"All right," said a trade unionist, pressed to conclude. "I've just got one more paragraph," he added magnificently.

Then there was the bottle blonde in powder-blue trousers, who attempted to extend the floor debate at the expense of either Mr Roy Jenkins or lunchtime, in so far as those two can be distinguished.

When Mrs Williams overruled her, the lady turned on a rant which would have been highly commended at Blackpool, accusing her of "putting her belly before the future of the party". Authentic, fully assayed vituperation of this kind is a collector's piece here.

One can vouch for Mrs Williams – she spent *her* lunchtime at a fringe meeting on a platform shared with cheese, biscuits and Dr Stephen Haseler, the insistent quintetist, who, from outside Parliament, stood so neatly on Mr Rodgers' hand in the presidential election.

The trouble with the SDP is that it is the natural party of civil servants, and fairly bossy ones at that; and it is getting virulently progressive at the edges.

Mrs Shirley Hewson, in a voice acquired either in the lacrosse field or the more demanding Verdi roles, boomed, "I am a white person. I am the host country. And I am *ashamed* to live in a country with an ethnic sub-culture."

Mr John Leopard, anxious to reduce the prison population in the approved caring manner of releasing criminals prematurely on to the neck of the poor, was so blown along by rhetoric that he involuntarily addressed the conference as "prisoners".

The debate, which was wound up by a lady rabbi, demanded more "powers and resources" for a stronger race board, and demanded "positive anti-discriminatory action". As Mrs Neuberger artlessly put it, "There may be minorities we have not yet discovered."

A low Conservative such as Mr Cecil Parkinson, with the tasteless aim of separating the electorate from the SDP, could spend a useful weekend with the transcript of yesterday afternoon's Human Rights debate.

They are, as they say, "a party of principle" (Mrs Ann Smith). But they do sound like a party whose time came round about 1967.

They desire only the best for us and, with the combined tolerance of Beatrice Webb and a one-way traffic system, will permit us no other.

Mr Charles Westerly put it best in the trade union debate. He wanted "to capture the hearts of people, white or blue". Only when he had corrected himself did we realise that the SDP embraces everyone, regardless of race, creed or collar.

Daily Telegraph, October 14, 1982

The process of privatisation, or the issue of equity in the
family plate, began to roll steadily with the accession of a
Mr Lawson.

Mr Nigel Lawson is a quite splendid chap and the Labour party
does so hate him.

When he arrived to make his statement about the tendering
for shares in Britoil he had, in the Labour Members' view, the
tone and manner of a dubious parson with a good graveside
manner burying grandma while keeping a deaf ear to her
unreasonable protestations of not being dead.

They would have felt fairly rough about any Tory Minister
carrying out this little job for, after all, the Britoil which has the
brokers swinging from jeroboam to jeroboam was once BNOC,
an upright patriotic luminary of the public sector.

Britoil – an unhappy name which suggests something out of
a simulated cut-glass bottle which Nigel might put on his hair –
is private, capitalistic and thus a spoliation of Britain.

The Labour party comes over all Falklandish when faced with
the public sector. A chorus of "Hearts of Oak", is in imminent
danger of being struck up when some low fellow tries to sell
anything. Or, as Mr Lawson, being a low fellow, would say,
"dispose of it".

But their displeasure at the operation is as the displeasure of
a thousand when Nigel is involved.

Most Conservatives cultivate a certain boring mildness by
way of protective cover against the hunting and predatory party
opposite. They seek not to give offence.

His worst enemy has never alleged anything of the sort against
Nigel Lawson. He has a civilian version of military self-assurance; a sedentary swagger as it were.

Without raising his voice or indulging in the unsubtle boasting
of, say, Peter Walker, he can affect the Labour party like a
hangnail. He is in Labour's eyes the ultimate wowser in a chalk
stripe suit selling unauthenticated Rumanian bonds dated 1938
at a premium.

What was particularly annoying yesterday was that the Minister gave every impression of being quite intolerably reasonable.

He was selling by tender and not by one or other of the more
unorthodox methods which would have entitled Labour to send

up cries of "slicker". And a lot of good it did him. "Slicker," they cried!

He had made elaborate precautions on behalf of the small shareholder. When Mr Merlyn Rees, working himself up to the periphery of animation, demanded to know whether a balance sheet was attached to the prospectus, Mr Lawson replied with the quiet scorn of a man who would not dream of selling Brooklyn Bridge in any but the most correct and ethical fashion: "Of course there is a balance sheet. It is a very full prospectus."

It is a sort of soft-sell insolence which Labour detests but cannot quite cope with.

Mr Dick Douglas lurched into the patriotic bit and complained about "flogging the nation's assets".

Mr Cryer did one of his snarl-and-whimper turns about how "none of the shares could be bought by people on supplementary benefit"; how it was "a bonanza for City slickers"; and how "millions were going straight off to the Minister's friends in commission".

Some Tory ministers would act affronted; some would be hurt and regretful. Nigel, the unapologetic face of the futures market, looked him coolly over as if he were three-months tea during a glut and regretted that time had been taken from someone who might have had a serious question.

Daily Telegraph, November 11, 1982

There is something about the prospect of cable television which brings out the chairman of a £100 company which lies lurking in most Conservative MPs.

Just as naturally, it brings out the regulating, censoring, co-ordinating and suppressing instinct which hangs like a pale golden light around the generality of Labour Members.

In America, as we were inevitably reminded, there is a gentleman by the name of Ugly George who makes cables to burn bright by persuading young women to take off their clothes in Central Park.

We had no Ugly George yesterday, only Handsome Roy, the Shadow Home Secretary and the Labour Party's answer to Peter Walker for 12-foot-high crafted brass *chutzpah*.

"I do not want low quality pictures of girls persuaded to

49

undress in Regents Park," said Mr Hattersley piously, but with a certain syntactical ambiguity which left free the option of high quality pictures of girls persuaded to undress in Regents Park.

He conjured up a vision of the small screen horror comic, the rainbow-coloured baby's dummy which capitalism has created.

But, for a man who gave the impression of deriving aesthetic pleasure from the contemplation of Aeschylus, he rather spoiled the classical unities by complaining that not only was cable TV likely to be sordid and nasty but that it would not be immediately available to everyone.

He was joined in his strictures by Mr Barry Sheerman, a good chap but liable, like that symphony by Nielsen, to become known as "the Inextinguishable".

Like Handsome Roy, Interminable Barry saw cable TV as something half-human, half-American. But he offered one point in favour of the custom-built wilderness into which we are about to go. "For actors and writers," said Mr Sheerman, "the future is gloomy indeed." The thought of anything being bad for the arts mafia sweetens the day a little.

So does the other Sheerman prospect, of "minority interests" suffering under the evil reign of cable.

Putting aside the low but irresistible thought that girls taking off their clothes is clearly a majority interest, did this mean rather less than more of the Pakistani chat shows and caring, concerned and compassionate Leeward Island logothons deep into the night which have so characterised Channel 4?

If so, chaps who care passionately about developing commercial television as the dynamic, throbbing, new revolution, in which their brothers-in-law have a nice piece of the equity, should recognise a good selling point when they see one.

Indeed, earlier in the day there had been a particularly happy note struck when the beaters-up of Channel 4, led by Mr John Gorst, had obtained from Mr Whitelaw expressions of unease at the state of the greatest television service in the world.

Within the limits of ministerial language, Mr Whitelaw seemed pretty miffed.

The martyrdom of Jeremy Isaacs is too high a prize to hope for, but we can dream.*

Daily Telegraph, December 3, 1982

* I was prophetic but in the wrong.

The joy of Mr George Cunningham is that he is to abstract nouns what disinfectant is to germs (or rather, since we were discussing penal policy, to the germ community).

Mr Cunningham had started a debate on the social consequences of crime, and he began as he meant to go on by an aggravated assault on a Chief Constable.

It was Mr John Alderson, lately of Devon and Cornwall, now a candidate in the Liberal interest, and a man nearer to God than a middle-rank Archangel, who coined the term "community policing".

"I'm tired of all this rubbish about 'community policing'," said Mr Cunningham with all the delicacy of an armoured column. "The word should be banned. It is a substitute for thought."

Now one knows that it is all futurity against a wholemeal bun that anything will ever actually be done about the crime rate, but at least with Mr Cunningham on the premises the verbal necrosis which surrounds the subject is scorched and cauterised away.

"I'm afraid I take an old-fashioned view, the correct one," said the George Patton of debate. "Forget this post-Scarman outlook. If somebody goes out with a petrol bomb that is not the fault of a parent, of society, of the victim, or of me, but of the person with the bomb."

How were we to deal with the question of control over the police – the Livingstonisation of Law and Order?

We all knew what really happened, didn't we? When the police in Northamptonshire had overstepped the mark in vetting juries, it was the Home Secretary "who with a bit of huffing and puffing, fixed the Chief Constable".

Mr Cunningham, who seems to know the streets of Islington and the 20-year transformation made on them by a shortage of prison space and the taking of tolerant views, made the sort of speech which if retailed nationally might even get the Social Democrats back on their feet.

But he is one of those free intelligences, staters of the forbidden obvious, jargon-free political irregulars whose presence in a party, at once limp, anaemic and well-intended, is fortuitous.

Mr Cunningham crackled like burnt bacon. "Vulnerable to delinquency! Does that mean that they do it?"

So if knocked down and rolled on for your wallet you should recall that the parting transitive boot in the ribs is given by a victim, one of life's unfortunates, someone "vulnerable to delinquency", and to very little else!

Daily Telegraph, February 8, 1983

The EEC imposed its own rules about awful long-life milk against which we ineffectually protested.

ULTRA HEATED MILK OF UNKINDNESS

And take my milk for gall, you murdering ministers,
Wherever in your sightless substances
You wait on nature's mischief!

Lady Macbeth was going on a bit and she wasn't even on to the Ultra Heat Treated stuff, whose importation on EEC orders had the lads on the shop floor quivering with Francophobia yesterday.

Mr Walker's tactic was a variant of "when you have a bad case abuse the other side's attorney" or, as the case may be, his milk.

"I have often boasted," said Mr Walker (with perfect truth) "that my dog eats Lymeswold cheese. But he won't drink UHT milk."

Nothing like dragging animals into the argument to get the British agitated, though any Frog to have turned up in the Commons yesterday would have suffered the fate of the monkey in West Hartlepool. They would have lynched him.

Many Members look upon Europe as a place of extravagant hedonistic luxury, with the members of the assembly reclining against spare bolsters, consuming champagne and subsidised oysters.

The brutal consequences of the co-responsibility levy and positive MCAs in terms of evil French milk being sold by the loss-leading *Mafiosi* of the supermarkets, while blameless British door-to-door milkmen were cast onto the scrap heap of society, had not dawned till yesterday. But, my, did we make up for lost time!

The House positively sang a Cantata on Milk (a response,

perhaps, to Bach's celebrated Coffee Cantata). Mr Walker took the melodic line. He damned the French for trying to sell us a concoction roughly as attractive as liquid peat.

He exalted the British milkman as an on-going frank and full dimension of civilisation as we know it with added moral fibre for roughage.

Mr Norman Buchan added a harmonic line, agreeing with Mr Walker and also thinking that our milkmen were wonderful. Mr John Morris, like the good Welsh lawyer he is, decorated the theme with the artful suggestion that legislation passed to comply with the EEC should be prepared "carefully rather than hurriedly".

Agreement was so universal, the French castigated in terms so liturgical, the roundsman so garlanded like a Hindu bride-groom, the Labour, Conservative and Social Democratic parties in such honey-kissed amity that the interruption of Mr Campbell-Savours was quite monstrous.

"Is French milk so unhygienic?" he asked halfway through one of the hosannas. "And aren't we trying to protect our farmers and plan European trade in a very Socialist way?"

The House was deeply shocked. It was like spitting in the sacrament. And, anyway, Campbell-Savours is a Labour MP; what was he doing making cracks about Socialism?

Decent-thinking men averted their eyes and Mr Walker did his Lady Bracknell act which wants for nothing but the lorgnette.

Yet more shamefully, up jumps Mr Lamond of Oldham, whom we had thought a friend of Kolkhozes and mobile tractor stations, to suggest that if our product was so good why did we need to beat up the French product's reputation?

"Why not let the customer decide?" he asked in tones which would have won him a small rosette from the Adam Smith Institute.

The love-in was over. It had, anyway, been too bad to last. We were back with *Macbeth* where someone threatens to "pour the sweet milk of concord into hell". There, alas, it will encounter an import levy.

Daily Telegraph, February 10, 1983

It had seemed as if the superfluous debate on the Boundary

53

Commission would be a secular cantata.

The Opposition would go through the pious motions about the general atrocity of it all, while Mr Whitelaw said that all was very broadly, taking everything into account and not wishing to overstate the case, much as it should be.

For some time we were not disappointed.

Dr Edmund Marshall, who has taken on the unenviable job of Second Sherpa to Roy Hattersley, a man well-known for hugging the exciting bits of the brief, did us all proud. Some people are sensationally boring, Dr Marshall is just boringly boring!

At one stage he proclaimed with a flourish, apropos some piece of delegated legislation, "I could quote some 12 statutory instruments" (the legislator's equivalent of Lear's "Now could I drink hot blood").

"Go on then," said Mr Jim Lester with unwise light humour from the Conservative benches. He did!

Later he launched a terrible warning. The Conservatives had changed the boundaries in the second great Reform Act in 1867, so had Mr Gladstone in 1884, and the Conservatives again with the flapper vote in 1928. And all had lost the subsequent General Election.

The ability of the Labour party to find common ground with the first Duke of Wellington and Lord Liverpool on the fundamental unsoundness of reform and the need to sustain the decent order of things never ceases to delight.

However those who had fled from boredom had taken no account of Merlyn Rees, speaking from the back benches. The former Home Secretary, described by a colleague as "demob happy", was superlative.

He did not give a fig for the party issue. Either party would have done its bit about gerrymandering had it been in opposition. He was not complaining that anything was unfair. It was "the daftness with which the fairness was carried out" that bothered him.

Did the Boundary Commissioners know anything about the places they carved up – his part of Leeds for example? He had asked and had been told, "No, but one of them has a sister in Horseforth and sometimes came to see her."

Did not they realise that the River Aire in Leeds was wider

than the Vistula and three or four others put together but, no, that had not stopped them from crossing the water on foot and sticking a ward on to the new constituency.

The Commission, said Mr Rees with feeling, was made up of lawyers. Some of his best friends were in the legal profession.

Struggling hard, he mentioned a couple of useful things once done by lawyers ... "I think there is a role for judges," he added rather magnificently. But what did they know about Hunslet?

"I once sacked a Boundary Commissioner," he added wistfully.

"Yes, by all means have some judges on the Commission, or anthropologists if you liked for respectability's sake", but what was wanted to run a Commission was a decent politician with fingertips who had represented a place and knew it had an identity.

Even though he then went on to be rather rude about the writers who made a living sending up politicians, it was the sort of speech one would pay to hear.

Ministerial rank casts a shadow of anxiety and fills out a flesh of self-regard on most men which usually gets worse on retirement.

They remain responsible long after responsibilities have gone into other men's red boxes. But every so often one of them escapes.

Daily Telegraph, March 3, 1983

Something will have to be done about ex-Prime Ministers in this place.

They come back at you like ancestral spectres, African thought forms, or possibly something debilitating in the woodwork. It is a case, if not for exorcism, then for some more elegant SW1 version of Rentokil.

"In the period when I was in office." "I recall a breakfast with Giscard and Schmidt at which I took the view..."

Their pasts, which alas are our past, float by us as they get watery-eyed and Proustian from chosen corners of the Chamber, and begin to hector Sir Geoffrey for not being the men they were.

Incorporeal status as a former Prime Minister or Chancellor gives one position without obliging one to keep it up. So Mr Heath, grey, dignified, dapper and snide, could mock poor Sir Geoffrey for not having joined the EMS.

The £ had moved between $2.40 and $1.50. Had it been too high or was it now perhaps too low?

The Chancellor so derided had just got back from Mr Heath's beloved Brussels where, as chairman of the International Monetary Fund, he had been patching the wretched EMS together.

Mr Heath, oddly enough, said nothing about the $6,000 million believed to have been spent by the French lately for the privilege of staying in the EMS and *not* devaluing.

The Government was also much moralised at by these self-regarding manifestations from the spirit world. They remembered when they were Chancellor ... they deplored this pre-occupation with the PSBR (which Mr Heath kept calling the PSRB).

In the good old days they had concentrated on the broad balance and on growth, said Mr Callaghan.

Had not such a concentration ended in devaluation on top of ferocious expenditure to stop devaluation? asked Mr Timothy Eggar.

But ghosts are impervious to sword play. The gibbering nightmare of the then Chancellor, a Mr James Callaghan, in 1967 was brushed aside in 1983 as one of those difficulties about which contrary views are held.

Two of the most panic-stricken Ministers of the post-war world held forth with the serenity of unreal people. Together with Mr Jenkins and Mr Rees they sat like four Edwardian gentlemen at the front end of a punt, praising the last four bends in the river and upbraiding the fellow sweating away with the actual pole. Their anxieties were yesterday's anxieties. Mr Heath spoke contemptuously about "people who believe that markets decide everything", but did not explain how the goodwill of oil producers could keep stable that price which the absurd market was unwilling to pay.

On similar lines, Mr Callaghan went on (and on) about the need for goodwill from the trades unions and how he had bequeathed it to Mrs Thatcher without saying how much trade union goodwill had cost.

He did not say whether a government which has the trade unions in the sort of spot where Tsar Alexander had Napoleon in 1813 has any great need of such expenditure.

There had been a great deal of harking back. Hadn't Bretton Woods been a great thing? And what about Marshall Aid? It was for the most part rubbish, but a better class of rubbish, of the sort which senior Privy Counsellors are by custom and precedent entitled to utter yearly.

Nostalgia tempered by powerlessness is the order of the day when old men do not alas forget, but remember without compunction.

Yesterday and yesterday and yesterday ... to the last syllable of recorded time.

What was it Mr Malcolm Fraser* said last week? "I don't think ex-Prime Ministers should spend long hanging around Parliament."

Daily Telegraph, March 22, 1983

Foreign affairs are rather like a dream. Given that they were answered for the first time by Sir Geoffrey Howe, that dream took place in a deep and contented sleep.

The link between foreign affairs questions and anything at all, leave alone this world, is tenuous enough. Member follows Member demanding that this Russian prisoner shall be freed, that that Chilean trades unionist shall be released, for all the world as if the amiable tax lawyer from East Surrey could shift a properly placed iron bar one millimetre by his best efforts.

For the record, the Chileans seem to have been let out anyway, while Mr Scharansky and Mr Orlov remain in the condition to which it has pleased somebody with more immediate authority than God to place them.

Members were on the whole in an eirenic frame of mind, having early yesterday morning added a useful supplement to their expenses. But, though they are now paid more, they are not discernibly more productive.

Indeed age cannot weary Mr Hugh Dykes nor custom stale

* The former Australian Prime Minister, defeated and resigning his party leadership.

57

his somewhat limited variety; he was back as the cheer-leader and bottle-holder to the Vision and the Ideal of Europe.

It was necessary, he said, to recreate enthusiasm for the EEC (he can say that again); so why didn't we join all our friends and partners within the Community in a non-inflationary expansion of the budget?

Sir Geoffrey, looking like a man who has sniffed hydrocyanic acid in the peach juice, regretted that he could not follow his Honourable Friend.

Mr David Couch, nicer but on occasions less clever than Mr Dykes, suggested that we should trouble ourselves less about the EEC budget (the money they get out of us) and set about developing Europe as a political force.

Sir Anthony Meyer said that we should seek "to catch the imagination of Europe" and work in closer co-operation in social and political fields with the EEC. For *this* they get a rise? The wonder is they are paid at all.

The far-flung bit of foreign questions was no more real. Labour got on to one of its United Nations kicks (and the UN is to Labour what glue is to the wayward teenager).

Even Mr George Robertson, one of the best Labour men around, proclaimed that the threat or use of force to settle a dispute was forbidden under the United Nations Charter.

One puts such sentiments down charitably to insincerity: Mr Robertson is much brighter than that.

What commands no charity at all is the sight of Mr James Lamond demanding that we, the British, should utter a caution to the Americans for trying to keep Cuban ships and rockets out of Central America.

Mr Lamond has always put a Comintern view in foreign affairs, indeed all other affairs, and it is a small pleasure that we should be powerless to oblige him.

Indeed, Sir Geoffrey made the point a little later that the ratio between Cuban and United States military aid to that part of the world was in the order of 10:1, Cuba clearly not having read the United Nations Charter with sufficient attention.

The usual groups did their usual things, half-informed armies skirmishing in the late afternoon. The Arabists wanted us to scrag the Israelis (well, morally, that is), the Friends of Peace wanted us to quarrel with America and the SDP managed to drag proportional reresentation into foreign affairs.

It was a pleasant enough afternoon in Plato's cave, watching the shadows lengthen on the wall – shadows of the world we do not influence. Most of the questions, from Left and Right, could have been put with more relevance 120 years ago ... to Lord Palmerston.

Daily Telegraph, July 21, 1983

The Union legislation of Mr Tebbit had for TUC Conference a fascination both professional and nightmarish.

"They're all Tories now," said a wiser and elder colleague when Clive Jenkins came to the tribune to advocate talks with Norman Tebbit. Mr Jenkins bared a ritual incisor, denounced the undemocratic procedures of the General Electric Company and did his usual radical bit before calling on Conference to support détente with the Prince of Darkness.

It was a case of the Lord High Executioner waving a rubber axe.

There was a diverting moment when, apropos of absolutely nothing at all, Mr Jenkins said that our friends in the black African unions would expect us to vote thus. They would?

Is the feeling strong along the Zamabesi that Composite Three, with its instructions to the General Council "to convey their reasoned opposition to the Employment Secretary's proposals and to dissuade the Government from taking further legislative steps", is the issue of the day? It seems that in the kraals of Lilongwe they speak of little else.

However, if it is the form with Right-wingers like Mr Jenkins to go through ritual calls to arms before surrendering, that is not the way of the Hard Left. Mr Ken Gill, the hardest of hard men, a CP member whose union is not called TASS for nothing, delicately described talks between Mr Tebbit and the TUC as "a dialogue between a vet and a tom cat" (this is not really a family show).

Mr Gill, one of those subtly frightening men who never raise their voices, moved softly from castration to capital punishment, suggesting that talks with the Minister would be "like testing the strength of the rope with the hangman".

What a martyrdom-fixated lot they are!

When did they first get interested in torture and execution? How do they feel about Joan of Arc? Have they always found violence so soothing?

There is a whole new branch of medicine – to be called psycho-syndicalism – with a glittering future in guineas-per-hour, holding the hands of the emperors in their Surrey palaces and talking them off the ledge of their own rhetoric.

Alas, Mr Arthur Scargill who had been expected to jump, delivered instead a speech as flat as over-exposed keg beer. He also dragged in executions (*and* Taff Vale, *and* "our fore-fathers" *and* "collaboration"); but the authentic banana milk-shake was missing. The long slide in Scargills continues, and brokers are recommending holders to conduct a damage limi-tation sale.

As a Mr McKenna put it for the Bakers' Union, "in countries like Uruguay trades unionists disappear and are never seen again". Not just in Uruguay, Mr McKenna; poor Arthur, like King George V, is slowly sinking.

Not so Len Murray. I have never heard Mr Murray so good – sharp, snappish, percussive and treating fools with none of his usual sedulous charity. "We recommend accepting the motion and rejecting the first two amendments; as for number ten, it's not to be taken seriously, I haven't time to talk about it. Dismiss it. A one-day strike as a first step? Where to? – Oblivion? There will be no blank cheques to break the law."

We are accustomed to Mr Murray as the TUC's civil servant loyally walking through hell and defending the indefensible with a melancholy digestion. A turn of the political cards and he is free to speak private thoughts publicly – and, suddenly, the civil servant turns out to be Sir Humphrey Appleby.

Daily Telegraph, September 7, 1983

"At the Metropole Hotel, comrades, there are blue ice cubes in the toilets and carpets on the ceilings. Can we tolerate this inequality? No, we must sweep it away. And, one last word, comrades, forward with Socialism!"

For such barley-sugar baroque, such Socialist surrealism, we are indebted to Mr Eric Segal, who is devoted to cheering us all up on an otherwise morose and resentful day.

He was speaking to a motion for the defence of British Telecom, which the Tories are selling to their brothers-in-law, while Labour are pledged to defend Buzby to the wishbone.

Mr Stan Orme, the nicest and most human personality on what might be called the mid-Left, adorned an otherwise sound and bouncing little speech with a resonant warning about life after privatisation.

"It will mean the end of the telephone box as we know it."

Mr Ken Cure, for the platform, denouncing the Victorian values of the privatisers, proclaimed that Victorian life "had a very seamy side underneath".

The seamy side for most dispassionate (all right, hostile) observers came yesterday morning. An internal memorandum in your correspondent's notes reads simply: "This party is not going to recover."

Mr Healey, to be sure, was gay in the manner of a fiddler hired for an Irish wake. He made the best of the policy he does not believe in and lethally compared Dr Owen to Mrs Thatcher in a trouser-suit.

But the operation to graft unilateralism on to a policy of residual defence is not working; the graft will not take.

Terry Duffy of the engineers was hissed before he started to speak and booed when he did. It is fascinating to see how much hatred can be carried by campaigners for peace; no American four-star general (indeed no Soviet marshal) can approach the stored, concentrated rage of these lovers of humanity.

Interestingly, although the mild Mr Duffy was snarled at for his multilateralism, nobody barked at Paul Gallagher.

Mr Gallagher, a hard-bitten follower of the school of Frank Chapple, bristling with facts and as truculent as any disarmer, has the emotional stamina to take on the Surrender Lobby.

Nobody dared boo him except of course when he referred to "the murder of the 269 passengers in the Korean airliner".

But this moment of storm came with the case of the People versus Callaghan. The calamitous Gavin Strang, one of those urgle-gurgle Scots who grind this party under their rolling 'r's, received thunderous applause for denouncing Mr Callaghan's "sabotage of Labour during the election".

Uncle Jim clearly doubts his ability to smash up a scrap-yard.

He remarked mildly that, if his remarks on defence had been made before any previous election, they would not have rated a paragraph.

"You," he said (ominously using the second person), "lost millions of votes by going unilateralist." No man has elevated genial unpopularity as far as the last Labour Prime Minister.

Which, come to think of it, he probably was!

Daily Telegraph, October 6, 1983

It is the special art of Mr Austin Mitchell to send clichés into orbit.

Denouncing the nexus between the boss class and the Conservative party, he said that what applied to the employee goose should apply to the employer gander and that the present state of affairs should be brought to its swansong.

Not since George Orwell quoted the jackboot which was to be thrown into the melting pot has an imperfect command of the English language reached such a level of elegance.

Not that Mr Mitchell did not have a case, if he had been able to make it. An impressive list was read out of company chairmen, their corporate contributions to the Tory party and details of their subsequent elevation to the *Donatage*.

Mr Mitchell and the massed ranks of the Labour Party fell into that condition of horror and outrage which stands perpetually waiting for it, like a cab at the door.

Mr Mitchell made another of the dreadful puns about which a man's best friends are sometimes afraid to tell him. "The Tories," he said, wanted "a quo pro quid". The House parted like the Red Sea.

"On a point of order, Mr Speaker," said a Labour voice, "Conservative members are leaving the Chamber." "They often do," replied Mr Weatherill succinctly.

Despite the awful jokes and the losing battle with the English language, Mr Mitchell was in the happy position of being able to put on the Zola. "I accuse" was the motif of the afternoon.

He indicated Lord Matthews, £40,000 before the peerage and £40,000 after, Sir William Cayzer, Sir Robert McAlpine, it was like one of those sing songs from the Labour party song book,

"Oh how the money rolls in" and "I am the man who waters the workers' beer".

The message seemed to be that the Conservatives had indicated to their friends, "Give until it feels nice."

The private Tory response is probably that there should be a free market in blue ribbon and gilt and enamel pendants, just as there should be a free market in everything else.

Knighthood futures eased slightly with a decline in seasonal demand but the new tap stock of $7\frac{1}{2}$ per cent hereditary Viscounts was well received, and penny stocks like OBEs all showed upside potential.

Useless for the Labour party to protest with Mr Norman Atkinson that Labour would not on principle take money from a limited company. To vary the metaphor a little, that sounded like a proclamation of chastity from the undesired.

Except, of course, that this stricken lady with the frugal figure and cast iron countenance has been known in earlier and happier days to hold hands in the summer house.

This was brought home to us by Mr Cranley Onslow, who lingered with tenderness upon the episode of the lavender notepaper and Lady Falkender's little list.

Labour is, of course, as blameless as Miss Prism, but she is touchy on that subject upon which a sensitive and compassionate fellow would not dwell. Which is why Mr Onslow went on about it. Both parties now got down to the simple scurrility which they do best.

Mr Mitchell had got his figures about businessmen's contributions from the Labour Research Department. That body, said Mr Onslow, used to be proscribed by the Labour party.

Eight out of the 11 members of its top committee had Communist affiliations, which had not stopped Mr Kinnock from belonging to its editorial board.

At this there were cries of "How many fascists have you got?" and we knew that a state of normal creative futility had been resumed.

The Swindlers' party and the caucus of Reds relaxed comfortably in their agreeable places, deeply content with the balanced picture of British political life which they combine to project.

Daily Telegraph, December 7, 1983

63

Mrs Thatcher, opposed on moral grounds to the Trade Union closed shop, endeavoured against the wishes of Cabinet Ministers to make membership of a Trade union illegal at GCHQ Cheltenham.

"And who is the Mephistopheles behind this shabby Faust?"

Connoisseurs of Parliamentary metaphor will recognise the educated bludgeon work of Denis Healey, the thinking man's ruffian, and in his Faust, the Conservative party's answer to the sprung interior, the shock-absorbent, go-and-get-the-kids-to-dance-up-and-down-on-him-lady-he-won't-mind political mattress, Sir Geoffrey Howe, custodian of GCHQ Cheltenham.

Dialogue between Mr Healey and Sir Geoffrey is that between a high-kicking boot and a punch ball, and actually the Foreign Secretary did not fall apart in public, make a gaffe, blunder or otherwise delight the Coliseum season ticket holders.

He delivered his defence of the indefensible in terms sufficiently lawyer-like and reasonable-seeming to numb the Opposition into offering no more than a low rhubarbing accompaniment.

But there is no getting out of the fact that the Government had one of its nastiest days on record. It was not just the inherent implausibility of the argument that the GCHQ had been a secret until the recent Prime spy case, hence the "anomaly" of 40 years of trade union membership now just being tidied up, nor was it just Mr Healey – a remaindered line, outselling the newest things into the shop.

The Government got real and sizzling-hot Hell from senior Conservative backbenchers, which is like being handbagged by matrons of honour.

Mr Charles Irving, who represents the Gloucestershire Spa and Spy town, spoke of "ineptitude and insensitivity beyond belief", and, wondering how the whole matter had ever come up in the first place, blamed it on "some bright berk in the department (or in the US) who had suggested introducing the lie-detector".

At this point the lamentable Colonel Mates, presumably fishing for Front Bench favour with some loyal intervention, rose.

64

"Oh, how terribly nice to see you, but I'm afraid I never take interventions. We don't want to start any more precedents," said Mr Irving, stopping the House for eight seconds and the Colonel, one fondly hopes, for longer.

At seven o'clock, as we reactionaries call it, Mr Gorst spoke. Now Mr Gorst is well-known in trade unions circles, much in the way that the seven-headed giant is known to fractious children; that, if provoked, he will treat them like shredded wheat.

But then, Mr Gorst built his reputation as the Enemy of the Closed Shop; supporting the right *not* to belong to a union, he is irksomely disposed to a narrow consistency on the right *to* belong.

The Government reminded him of the thinking behind the Test Acts: Roman Catholics and Non-Conformists then (as Trade Unionists now) were barred from certain offices as men who could not be trusted because of their "divided allegiance".

On he went to describe the £1,000 offer as the 30 pieces of silver, a metaphor lifted from everyday Labour parlance – not that they minded – and to quote Pitt on liberty into Tory teeth. He had evidence as well, but really one couldn't see the straw for the bricks.

Most of the afternoon, though periodically joined by Mr Tom King, Mrs Thatcher and Sir Geoffrey sat huddled and hunched up together, while living robbers like Mr Healey, Mr Callaghan and Dr Owen, and ghostly figures like Mr Irving and Mr Gorst, lurked and flitted behind the trees.

They looked uncommonly like Hansel and Gretel lost in the wood.

With Dr Owen threatening to divide the House one is glad for them that a friendly wood-cutter exists in the person of the Chief Whip to come to their rescue. Though if there is to be a happy ending to this horror story one would like to be shown it.

Daily Telegraph, February 28, 1984

Harold Macmillan, having virtually ended the hereditary peerage, suddenly, to the private displeasure of the resolute commoner, Edward Heath, agreed to become a real Lord.

It is not every day that we get ourselves a new Earl. Accordingly, the House of Lords, that Gothic lullaby by Barry and Pugin, was crowded for the occasion.

It had been remarked that since the '60s their lordships had nothing more glamorous to induct than a Life Baroness. Now, with a rush, here come the hereditary nobility.

It was not without dignity, either. Lord Stockton, in a voice strong and gravelly, swore his allegiance and listened attentively to the slightly pre-Raphaelite prose of the Letters Patent conferring upon him status, dignities, titles and honours of the Earldom of Stockton: and there was a warm, sincere little cheer when the ceremony was concluded.

Quite a ceremony it is. There were the sponsors, Lords St Aldwyn and De La Warr (earls only at this level), Black Rod plus a couple of additional senior lords and a chap in a splendid part-coloured doublet, the Garter King of Arms, whose job it was to marshal the group.

He first brought them up the Chamber to where Lord Hailsham, the Lord Chancellor, was waiting. Then he brought them back to the other end for a sort of mime which had echoes of the fourteenth century and the drill hall about it.

The posse of Lords doffed and put on long black bicorne hats, stood up, sat down, stood up again and generally did things by the book.

The former Mr Macmillan cut a good figure. He is a very old gentleman, but the dignity is undiminished, the manner slow but very competent. "I Harold Earl of Stockton" is a surprising exclamation to hear from the chap who seemed 20 years ago to be phasing out our hereditary tendency.

But, really, who begrudges him it? Whether the House of Lords will live up in its debates to the high ceremony or Chinese opera, according to your taste in these things, is another matter.

Lord Hailsham, who presided, looks the part with an astonishing resemblance to a Lord Chancellor in and about the time of Lord Hardwicke in the 1730s.

But what will Lord Stockton make of Lord Hatch, who

66

commenced business after the ceremony with a long tirade about development aid?

He is bidden by Her Majesty's Letters Patent to "enjoy the pre-eminences and advantages of this estate".

But is he really to *enjoy* Lord Avebury (Eric Lubbock to most of us) rattling on about support for Nicaragua, or Lady Gaitskell doing her Third World recital?

All of that is miserably available in another place, and some of us are tied to a wheel and obliged to listen to it.

Lord Stockton, always the man for style and the sly, pose-puncturing, accidental-on-purpose remark, may need all the irony he has in a House increasingly reminiscent of the retired House of Commons which it actually is.

However, there are always the bishops, however progressive. There were 10 of them in yesterday for the investiture, in proper clerical lawn and black among the sub-fuscous of those unfortunates, the working peers.

The day might be given over to Lord Cockfield, talking about productivity (11 per cent up under Mrs Thatcher) and Lord Barnet (Joel Barnet) deploring our balance of payments (in the red).

But into this quotidian world of deficit and production we had arranged a splash of the thing we do best – ceremony in primary colours – scarlet earls, black and white bishops.

We may or we may not know how to run the economy and Lord Cockfield's answers tended to the second theory. But we know how to run a ceremony.

Daily Telegraph, March 1, 1984

Mr Heseltine being reasonable induces a feeling of unease; rather like Goering playing the piano, it doesn't seem quite right.

When he announced conversationally to the House without swinging from the chandeliers or breaking the Mace over his knee, that he was concerned "about the central formulation of advice on defence policy", the words were the usual alphabet soup of obscurity until Mr Heseltine suddenly said: "I intend to create a combined defence staff."

Thus is the better sort of coup d'état carried out when the constitutional Head of Government supposes the High

Command to be playing golf. And there is about Mr Heseltine just that touch of the Junior Sudanese Colonel whom one watches rather edgily.

A certain casualness affected Mr Davies (Llanelli) for Labour – not known as Devious Denzil for nothing. The Heseltine move was of course a gross act of centralisation which should have been good for the statutory Labour rumble about "concentration of power, authoritarian tendencies, first crocus of the Fascist spring" and all the rest of it.

Unfortunately for Denzil, that rewarding line could not be pushed as hard as he would have liked, the Heseltine *anschluss* being only the logical conclusion of staff work done years ago by Major Healey who did to the Service Ministries what is now being done to the staffs.

Accordingly he wandered off, like Captain Oates, into an Antarctic of vaguely vituperative generality: "The Minister's Walter Mitty world of being a wizard at management – the symbiotic relationship between the Ministry of Defence and arms manufacturers."

Having Mr Davies as your opposite number is like having toast under your poached egg. Nobody else, apart from Mr Powell and Mr Merlyn Rees, remarkably succinct on the back benches these days, made much impression on Captain Splendid, apart that is from the never-to-be-under-estimated Mr Campbell-Savours.

The Minister had been having it entirely his own way as Officer Commanding an accomplished fact, driven at speed in the departmental jeep, until Mr Campbell-Savours cast an elegant handful of tin tacks into the road.

Might there not be manpower implications? he asked, and could the Minister say how many?

"Yes there were. No he couldn't," said Mr Heseltine, acknowledging the right question.

Now Labour being Labour it is not altogether clear whether the party line is to be indignant about jobs lost and people cast heartlessly on the scrap-heap after a lifetime of service to whatever, or delighted at a cut-back in the number of hired killers.

Meanwhile the Heseltine operation has been carried out, the radio stations have been seized and are playing martial music,

Nelson and Wellington stir in their tombs and a thousand years of comradely inter-Service backstabbing, part of our national heritage, have been swept away. Or not, as the case may be.

Daily Telegraph, March 13, 1984

If monetarism was to be phased out, what better person to do it than a supposed monetarist? Cometh the hour, cometh Nigel Lawson.

Once in a rare while a politician puts up a performance which not only transcends his broad reputation but which shifts him into a higher class altogether.

We have all had fun about Nigel Lawson's "cleverness" which has generally been taken as proof of his being, as Jeeves defined Nietzsche, "radically unsound".

Yesterday we learned that Mr Lawson is clever without inverted commas, for he gave a performance of sustained mastery which slew the Tories and left Labour drooping.

Not that he didn't terrify us all at the start with his run-through of the technicalities of monetarist terminology. M3 and M1, like the old classes of railway carriage, we had heard of: but M2 is dodgy and as for M nought – now the favoured measure – one rolls one's eyes and agrees hurriedly.

Likewise, "broad money" and "narrow money", which have the ring of ecclesiastical controversy about them; Trollope writing about intrigue in a bank might have spoken of "a new cashier who was notoriously broad".

Labour, who were to have a comprehensively awful after-noon, brightened a little, hoping to hiss the villain, only to be told, "Sit quietly. You've got a lot to learn."

The news came in ways which wrong-footed the Opposition. Abolition of the Investment Income Surcharge should have been good for a ten-second moan on the wealth and privilege circuit, but such was the spontaneity of the Tory roar that simulated indignation was swept out to sea and washed ashore days later.

The bits which are good for Labour's constituency, like the National Insurance Surcharge (abolished), were handled with Cyrano-like panache and a mocking echo of Left-wing rhetoric – this tax on jobs ... introduced by the Member for East Leeds,

I propose to abolish altogether.

The villain having provided annuities for orphans, radical man was left like Mr David Nellist sounding more like Gladstone than Trotsky: "How are you going to pay for it?" groaned this sound money man.

Again it was unfair of the Chancellor to indulge in a sport of import-bashing by his adjustment of the rules on VAT collection in a way which will infuriate the EEC and which delighted Mr Dennis Skinner.

This is precisely the sort of thing Labour would have done if they had thought of it, and very annoying it is to have your clothes stolen before you have actually bought them.

The one possible political error in an otherwise subtle and sharp-minded Budget was the affair of the Chinese chippy. Looking around for a touch of spare revenue to finance his tax reforms, Mr Lawson hit upon (a) cigarettes – which are immoral and bad for you and (b) the blameless take-away shop.

It is not good politics to put VAT on Chicken Chow Mein. For one thing, as Labour, armed with this frail spar, will reiter-ate, crispy noodles in tinfoil are the workers' delight; for another, citizens of Chinese extraction and into the catering trade tend to be solid Tories.

It is a pity to penalise them, but VAT confined to Vindaloo shops who usually put up Labour posters could mean all sorts of trouble with the race relations people at Ethnic House.

When Mr Lawson came to his conclusion and commended his radical Budget, the applause was long and vehement. In this place one learns to distinguish between the semi-automated waving of Order Papers out of team spirit and the real delighted thing; Lawson, as they would say in the pops, scores.

Mr Kinnock, by contrast, failed to come up to the standard expected even of back-of-the-envelope speeches.

No one expects technicalities, sight unseen. They do expect a crisp little speech grasping two or three weaknesses, deploring the Chancellor's extravagance/rapacity, over and out.

They got 26 minutes – not of detail but of macro-twaddle, the florid oratorical generalities of a peroration in search of a speech.

Daily Telegraph, March 14, 1984

The Church of England has the beatitudes. Sir Geoffrey Howe making a statement on Europe to the Commons is the nearest we shall know in this life to the dismalitudes.

Like the good lawyer he is, Sir Geoffrey uses tedium like cuttlefish ink to obscure bad news.

The temptation to hide one's head under the bedclothes until the Foreign Secretary has gone away should not hide the facts that we haven't had our rebate, that we are paying this year's contribution, and that "own resources" (VAT money for barley barons) will be going up. Not that Sir Geoffrey would be so crude: that was left to Tory backbenchers.

One is impressed with the growing exasperation at the fish soup of Euro-negotiations of so many Tories, not just the Teddy Taylor element, who have been warning us from the heather for years, but of middling men, even, most significantly, of young, ambitious men.

Mr Tim Yeo said flatly that we would be justified in withholding payment if the other side didn't come up with the rebate. Mr Alan Howarth coolly contrasted a régime of financial discipline at home and of paying up and up and up abroad.

'He'll not get a PPS," said a morose Labour voice. I wouldn't be so sure about that; the days when Rodney cared passionately about Europe with half an eye on becoming number four at the Environment are long past.

The days are also running out for Sir Geoffrey to make responsible lettuce-eating noises about these being extremely difficult matters.

"Yes we know that," snapped Mr Budgen. Old Foreign Office lags like Sir Anthony Kershaw are wheeled on like Opera House claques to praise "the Secretary of State's high degree of flexibility which deserves our support".

That is a move congruous with President Johnson, contemplating re-election in 1968 and employing, for want of volunteers, an organisation called "Manpower, Inc."

Mr Jenkins, that fragrant echo of passionate Europeanism, loyally advocated less use of the veto, one of the few defences left to us. "They'd sell their own grandmother that lot," observed the future Viscount Bolsover.

Mr Skinner also managed to produce the best mixed metaphor of the week. "We know all about Europe: it's a gravy train propping up the Mafia." He then launched into a wonderfully irrelevant speech about the rights of Scargill's First of Foot.

"Order," said Mr Weatherill in his kindly way. "There is no way the question of coal can be related to EEC negotiations."

"Helmut Kohl," someone called out. The House laughed immoderately, but men enfiladed between the murmuring tedium of Sir Geoffrey and the juddering demented tedium of Mr Skinner must find such solace as they can.

Earlier we had enjoyed one of those totally confected, synthetic and Formica-topped outbursts of Labour indignation which are among the glories of this place. Mr Gerald Malone, also on the topic of miners, had referred to those involved in riot as "common criminals".

This was in urgle-gurgle time when Scottish Questions are taken. Labour member after Labour member, Baillie, Writer to the Signet, wee Advocate, or Member of the Working Classes, leapt to his feet to expound the doctrine of *sub judice*.

"This tin-pot lawyer over there," gnashed Mr Canavan.

"One law for a miner, another for a layabout lord," said Screaming Ron Brown.

"One of the men charged," said Provost Clarke, "is a highly respectable councillor." Mr Malone was asked to clarify the matter but, not being born to soothe, sprinkled paraffin on the flames.

A shocking wrong had been done to men entitled to justice, and a pleasant afternoon excursion had been enjoyed by all.

Daily Telegraph, June 21, 1984

All statements about the EEC (or Community as some call it) follow a similar pattern. Down the line, burn-me-at-the-stake chaps who got it wrong to a power of five a decade ago leap up.

"What a wonderful achievement this is," they say and isn't it an honour to be paying out money to preserve democracy and stop the French and Germans going to war?

With such people, led by Sir Anthony Meyer and Mr Hugh Dykes, no one much concerns himself. They are the nearest thing to a headless torso this House has had to offer and their contributions are in line with that unhappy condition.

The Prime Minister tells us that, while she hasn't got every-thing, it was a jolly good deal (Conservative cheers) and far better than anything Labour ever achieved (further Conservative cheers).

Mr Kinnock says, at length, that it is really a terrible humili-ation and is it not the case that ...

In fact the deadly questions yesterday came from other tech-nicians on her own side, deeply unimpressed by this fiscal disco-dancing.

Mr Higgins, not a Europe-hater but pretty good at counting, broke up the fiesta time which Mr Kinnock's ineptitude had brought on.

"As it is not a permanent settlement, should we not refuse any increase in Own Resources [that's VAT money for sweet-ening the peasants of the Loire] until agricultural expendi-ture is reduced. If it is not reduced, what is the point of all this?"

It was pretty much like that yesterday. Mrs Thatcher had a good day in a rather meretricious way.

She is a technician and she is always at her happiest where large sums of money, preferably recalculated through abstract units like the ECU (European Currency Unit), are being shuffled about through several years of back and prospective payment.

Mrs Thatcher moved off into high-speed hypothesis and would not stay for an answer.

Similarly, Mr Peter Lilley, one of the two or three brightest among the new intake and not a Europe-hater, asked for prior enactment of control in Common Agricultural Policy expen-diture before we legislated to spend more VAT.

"Was it not," he asked, "like asking an alcoholic to give up drinking by promising him more whisky if he did?"

"All analogies break down," said Mrs Thatcher like late November, but she did not make it clear where.

Indeed, much of Mrs Thatcher's rhetoric, good, accomplished and proficient as it was, hung upon the need for Spain and Portugal to come in and how this all strengthened democracy.

She was not terribly helped by some of those seeking to support her. Congratulations from Mr Rippon went down like cocktails in Teheran.

It was Mr Rippon who blithely got us into this unimaginable

mess 13 years ago. Any more sensitive man would have been in penitential retreat.

Not much more could be claimed for Sir Anthony Kershaw, the portable loyalist. We had a Prime Minister "strong in commitment" (derision) – Labour at least knows where to laugh though not much more on the strength of yesterday. "A Prime Minister who fights and gets an agreement."

A nice man Sir Anthony, no government should be without one.

In fairness to Mrs Thatcher her command of the House despite so much high velocity answer-avoidance was impressive.

She does grasp figures, she was impressively calm and she played the card of Mr Kinnock's incredible prophecy that she wouldn't get this settlement with class and timing.

Lyndon Johnson used to talk about "poor-mouthing". "If you have low expectations, pronounce them terrible in advance. Everyone will be impressed by their being better than hoped and some fool opposite may have made a prophecy of under-achievement."

Poor-mouthing had a triumph on the neck of the poor, prophesying, talking-too-much Neil. It's one way of learning.

Daily Telegraph, June 28, 1984

An attempt by Mrs Thatcher to win popularity by abolishing the Greater London Council had the immediate effect of losing popularity and, through the vote of the Lords, failing to abolish that Council. Mr Patrick Jenkin took the blame.

It is murder writing about Patrick Jenkin. As self-evidently as any of the truths to be found in the Declaration of Independence, he has made the cumulative four-star hash (with whipped cream added) to end all hashes in respect of the GLC "Paving Bill" and yesterday, to howls of uncharity from Labour and snide civilities from the Tory wets, he climbed down.

And yet he is a nice man, however inept, and there is no pleasure in his discomfiture. Also, one couldn't help thinking, as the Opposition spat into the open grave, how very difficult it will be for Mrs Thatcher to sack him.

He announced the extension by a year of the GLC's life-span, since transitional rule by Quango has been slung out by their Lordships.

Would he say, asked Mr John Fraser, if his own term would be similarly extended? "He has a great career behind him," spat out Mr Anthony Banks (Newham) with the charm of a puff-adder.

Mr Peter Tapsell from the Gilts Market rejoiced unconvincingly on "the return to constitutional practices", and said that all true Tories would share his view.

With enemies like Mr Banks and Mr Tapsell, Mr Jenkin acquires charm. Anyone so damned will finish up Attorney-General.

Yet he is so slow-footed and literal-minded in argument that one winces. "The Hon. Gentleman is making altogether too much of this," he said to a Labour critic: Labour, not unreasonably, fell apart.

We have been round seven rows of mulberry bushes, Ken Livingstone has been turned into a sort of Bagehot, a pillar of the constitution, and the Government has ash on its forehead and egg-foo-yung on its face. It is not possible to make too much of it.

Asked by Sir Anthony Grant to do something about the GLC spending millions on free advertising, he agreed it was a grave matter, that he was looking urgently into it, but that he could give no assurance.

There is a leaden infelicity here, a want of the right words, the right tone of voice, the knack of pleasing one's own friends. Mr Jenkin is so little of a politician, so unattuned to nuance, that it probably reflects deep credit upon his character.

He even let slip in his micro-statement the lawyerly cliché "I am pleased to announce..."

Earlier, at Prime Minister's question time, the mid-morning reluctance of the Government to make a formal statement, something they changed their minds about after lunch, was played by Neil Kinnock with some skill and blessed brevity. "Whose frit now?" he asked, recalling Mrs Thatcher's agreeable lapse from elocution English into Kesteven dialect.

Mr John Heddle, who is marking himself down as stooge material, not to say part of the queue for PPS-ships, attacked "that wolf in sheep's clothing, Ken Livingstone" under his leader's watchful and, one hopes, discerning eyes.

Supporting the Government over the GLC is like buying stock in a depressed market – quite shrewd really.

A little earlier, Mr Greville Janner had raised the very important matter of fish and chips – up 15 per cent since uncaring Lawson duffed up the takeaway shops with his lead-weighted VAT.

"This was due," said Mr John MacGregor for agriculture, trying to send up political language for all time, "to thermatic conditions." He means the sea has got colder. Nothing to do with the Budget. Good heavens, no.

Daily Telegraph, July 6, 1984

Public hangings, once a popular feature of our heritage, much as UEFA Cup matches are today, have largely disappeared.

It was ironical then that the parliamentary equivalent of capital punishment should be staged.

Mr Dennis Skinner, that finished primitive, who has grown systematically less amusing, more odd and so burdened with chips on the shoulder as to have become the pearly king of resentment, blew it again.

We were into the Prime Minister's statement on the GCHQ judgment when Mr Skinner, subtle as a Wagner tuba, asked how we could be assured that the Prime Minister would not bribe the judges?

It might still have gone through, one more dreary piece of abuse ignored because of the inconsequence of its author.

However, a lot of people have lost money underrating Mrs Thatcher's strength of mind. She intervened, white, cold and as amenable as radioactivity.

She brushed aside any ideas there may have been for the sort of settlement some people keep urging on Mr MacGregor.

Her demand for a full and unreserved apology effectively determined what would happen next since full and unreserved apologies come from Mr Skinner the way passion fruit is found growing in Banffshire. Labour were appalled.

They had been working up a nice little line in constitutional rectitude, the wisdom of Mr Justice Glidewell,* the need for "consultation now as common sense" (Mr Merlyn Rees), "the possibility of the Prime Minister thinking she might be wrong" (Mr Ron Leighton).

"Was she planning to push her appeal even further to the House of Lords?" (Mr Bob Brown). All of which made Labour sound as wholesome as wholemeal bread, then along comes this fool...

Official Labour did not actually divide the House against suspension after the naming.

The tellers for the "noes" on this occasion were not Labour whips but the two spray-on proletarians from the last circle of the Hard Left, Mr Jeremy Corbyn and the old Bedfordian, Bob Clay, open-necked in their defiance.

The figure, which somebody should pick up as significant, is that from a party of 206, with the Front Bench abstaining, 84 were to be found supporting the "judges may be bribed" lobby.

So 41 per cent of the *Parliamentary party* is willing to string along with the Hard Left! It gets more like party conference every day.

Earlier the Interrogation of Margaret had looked like one of those historical canvasses which pleased lesser Victorian painters so much.

Mr Martin Flannery, himself a lesser canvas of some sort, had done his revolutionary alderman act, stringing out clichés like links upon a mayoral chain.

Did the Prime Minister know she was plunging the country into *total chaos*?. *Draconian legislation* against the trade union movement would not work and, *as he had said* when the Rt Hon Lady was at Fontainebleau, *the inexorable march* towards a general strike had begun.

Mr Flannery does not belong to this world, and indeed a sale-and-lease-back agreement with the Peter Simple Corporation is being contemplated – for essential rights in Mr Flannery belong in the world of creative fantasy.

Or are we being naive while the Flanneries, like Triffids, take over the world?

* A judge who ruled against the government, doomed.

Mr Martin Redmond Proustianly denounced "those fascist states where the military suppress trade unionism". Mr Loyden, or "Analphabetical Eddie" as we call him round here, deplored what had happened at "GHCQ" and Mr Kinnock described Sir Geoffrey Howe as "a punchbag covering up a trail of guilt".

The Tory backbenchers went on unimpressively about "national security". Mr Winterton grew a purplish shade of patriotic and Mr Michael Morris was so loyal you could have walked on him.

Through it all the Prime Minister performed with the grim circumspection one longs for in England's middle order batting. But then this opposition is not exactly Malcolm Marshall.

Daily Telegraph, July 18, 1984

It is very hard to get over to Mr Prior the message that we are all going to miss him and that he shouldn't have taken our rougher words too literally.

Mr Proctor tried to say how he admired the Minister's courage. "I'm quite embarrassed," said Jim, "at the things they say once they know you're going."

We have, in fact, reached the stage of "well then forever and forever farewell Cassius" ... words uttered by Brutus shortly before falling on his sword.

Jim was up for his last outing at Northern Ireland question time enduring the Irish Republican declamations of Mr Kevin McNamara, a man who qualifies, with his allegations that British troops were searching Republican babies outside Armagh Jail, as Leading Bore First Class.

Nobody who listened to Mr McNamara could fail to sympathise with Mr Prior, and it is a source of relief that he will not be falling upon anything more lethal than his tractor.

It is very late in the year, very hot, and nobody thinks very clearly in late July. That is the best alibi one can dream up for the latest disastrous attempt by Mr Kinnock to get out of his rhubarb and cream rhetoric and on to the evidence.

"Would the Prime Minister undertake to stop the takeover of ICL by the American company, Standard Telephone?"

Mrs Thatcher, who relishes the Inca-Conquistador relationship which the Leader of the Opposition has with her, sweetly replied that the company was British, adding chapter and grinding verse when he tried to argue.

It was a bad day for the Welsh generally, not only is their man for No. 10 giving a fair imitation of systematic incapacity but they have a water shortage.

Mr Donald Coleman unwisely denounced the Welsh Secretary, Nicholas Edwards, as "the man who will go down in history for leaving the Welsh thirsty and unwashed".

Labour has a small mania about statements. Why was the statement on English water not until next week? Why no statement yet on Scottish water?

"We are trying a measured experiment," Mr Biffen said earlier, "to see what effects are caused to the weather by a series of Ministerial statements."

You don't waste irony on Ron Davies (Caerphilly). He turned on Mr Edwards; "Does he accept that his statement is completely unacceptable?"

Mr Davies, like so many with problems about expressing themselves, is a former teacher of English.

However it is a serious matter and one wonders wistfully about Mr Denis Howell whose appointment as Minister for Floods stilled the waters and whose earlier incarnation as Minister for Drought caused the heavens to pour it out by the celestial jugful.

Might not one of those temporary loan arrangements favoured by football clubs keep Mr Howell from the horrors of the next Labour conference and permit the Welsh to dance with hearts at ease beneath their sprinklers?

One hopes it rains if only to avoid the grim visitation of Mr Leo Abse, a politician so pompous as actually to talk about "grim visitations" and who sounds like a simultaneous translation of proceedings in the Roman Senate.

Not that Labour had all the nonsense to themselves. Something really must be done about the remarkable Mr Douglas Hogg.

Quite what does one say about a full-dress whip sitting on the Front Bench listening to a senior Opposition spokesman (Peter Shore), who responds to criticism of the Government by putting his thumbs in his ears and wiggling his fingers?

As we keep saying in mitigation, it is July. But really where Mr Hogg is concerned one thinks in terms of March.*

Daily Telegraph, July 27, 1984

The combination of the warm weather outside the chamber and Patrick Jenkin on a clause-by-clause session of the Local Government Bill within its air-conditioned walls is altogether too much.

One does not want to be too smart at the expense of Mr Jenkin, who has had a terrible year (not that he hasn't given us one as well); and anyway epigrammed politicians, like monogrammed shirts, are in doubtful taste.

Yet he does wear the spectator down. The voice at the Despatch Box as he copes with the re-hash of his paving bill is as lone and level as the sands contemplated by Shelley's Ozymandias.

Indeed the inscription "My name is Ozymandias, Secretary of State for the Environment. Look on my works ye mighty and despair" fits the general mood.

What Mr Jenkin is saying, that some big councils can't be trusted not to take money out of the rates and parcel it off to little councils of like mind unless he has the power to stop them, has a very likely ring to it.

But as counsel for the defence Mr Jenkin could get the Pope sent down for heresy.

His English is very dubious as well: "The extent *to* which some councils are prone *to* . . ." suggests that prepositions have been lightly tossed into sentences like cloves of garlic.

Also his denunciations of some GLC manoeuvre as "flouting the ordinary decencies of public life" sounds like Lady Bracknell going on about handbags.

Not that the Opposition are any more interesting. Mr Jack Straw talking lightly and conversationally of the Thatcher Reich, however good-humoured, is the sort of metaphorical overkill of which we can hardly have too little.

Most of yesterday's proceedings were of the time-filling,

---

* He did too. A few days later Mr Hogg jumped, fell or was pushed from a high window in the Whips Office. Keen like most Tories on spiritual values he has managed a quite unnecessary resurrection as a junior minister.

noise-making, on-the-record-putting sort which any competent politician can do in his sleep, something which explains a good deal.

Such colour as there was came from Mr Roland Boyes who, bursting overweight out of his scarlet shirt, looked like nothing so much as a giant legislative raspberry. He also intervened in debate but less effectively.

However the one point of real drama had nothing to do with the powers of metropolitan authorities or the crushing of municipalities under foot.

It followed a statement by Mr Malcolm Rifkind on the conduct of the European Assembly at Strasbourg which seems to have acquired a sentimental attachment to our money.

The language was milder than the X-rated stuff Mr Rifkind uttered on Friday, not "despicable" and "contemptible" but something altogether in the "A" category – "petty", "churlish" and "inept" not to say "hasty" and "intemperate". A child (accompanied by its parents) could have listened to Mr Rifkind yesterday.

But it was all too hot for Mr Edward Heath. The Man of Principle was on his feet deploring our abuse of what he called "the European Parliament". He stressed the legal propriety of the blocking, proclaimed us to be "isolated" at Ministerial meetings and demanded "an acceptable solution".

As the man who landed us with the whole banjaxed, deficit-sustaining, peasant-bribing mechanism in the first place, he might have shown a little penitent humility (how much has Mr Heath cost this country?), but that is not quite his style.

Daily Telegraph, July 31, 1984

The broad objective of the Liberals this week has been to keep the party's dignified side upwards. Bournemouth, after all, is where you go for a clean weekend.

Alas, yesterday afternoon the beards and woolly pullovers savaged a keeper and briefly escaped, spreading terror through the Pavilion Theatre. Order was restored by a round of tranquilliser darts fired by the party president, Lord Tordoff, into the microphone.

Trouble began for the chairman, Mrs Janet Sale, when Young

Liberals sought to bring a striking miner to the rostrum. If I tell you that when Frank Chapple was mentioned later the Young Liberals hissed, some idea may be formed of what it is that chairmen try to cover up and what Dr Owen hesitates to join.

The coal motion was one of those rolling majesterial evasions condemning Mr MacGregor, Mrs Thatcher and Mr Scargill in even-handed terms.

However, Mr Pat O'Callaghan, in one of those snarling Ulster accents associated with so many calamities, denounced "a cheap exercise in NUM-bashing", and failure to condemn what he sweetly calls "police riots".

"What was all this rubbish about the NUM not holding a ballot?" he said to some ecstasy. There had been no ballot on union with the SDP.

Towards the end of a debate with all the neat close-fitting shape of a caftan, the Liberal Friends of Arthur Scargill discovered that they were under-represented.

Why with a week's free television they expect any steering committee in its proper mind to frighten off the housewife with extra O'Callaghans heaven only knows.

A fierce little man in a beige pullover, a beard and a towering rage seized the tribune and demanded additional speakers against the motion. Mr George Binney smiled thinly ... and attacked the motion for being too soft on Scargill.

Beige pullover was now dancing with rage: and another Young Liberal – 6ft 6in, 20 stone and with an evilly-exposed navel, who should be on all Conservative video files – lurched to his aid.

Beige pullover tried to commandeer the tribune. Mrs Sale, to cries of "Stalinist", switched him off. But clearly the pullover had moved no confidence in the Chair.

Lord Tordoff functioning as constitutional back-up, kindly uncle and family solicitor, suggested that this sort of thing wasn't doing us much good.

The silent majority, which watches this sort of episode much as the Treasury monitors the dollar exchange rate, burst out of its silence and, at a bound, the Liberals were free.

The words of the fraternal Roy Jenkins earlier in the day were now sadly mocked. Mr Jenkins had called for a grouping "radical, rational, humane and internationalist". With uncharacteristic colloquialism he had called for "a bit of love between the parties". "Let us maintain," he said "the spirit of Llandudno"!

It is not the sprightliest of slogans, but the spirit of Bournemouth yesterday afternoon had tasted excessively methylated.

Daily Telegraph, September 20, 1984

Whatever one holds against the Tories – the usual impression they give of immersion in liquid sickly pale blue Turkish delight – does not derogate from the fact that they do not scream, hiss or shout; nor do they address the Chairman, Dame Pamela Hunter, as "Comrade Chair".

The Tories have certain clichés of their own. The "fabric of society" was one, also the expression "Arthur Scargill" is becoming rather hackneyed down in Brighton.

Accounts of the little unpleasantnesses facing working miners at the hands of what Mr Scargill calls "these magnificent men" – bags of urine, the blind son of a working miner threatened with a beating-up and the killing of his guide dog – were recounted.

Ironically, the Government's chief response was an account from Mr Peter Walker about how much money he was spending on the mines.

"There are those," said Mr Walker airily, "who want us to import foreign coal, but that would make us dependent on cheap coal" – instead of being dependent, as now, on dear coal!

He took credit (and Mr Walker takes credit like complimentary wafer mints), not only for doubling investment but for having, 10 years ago, started the landscaping of slag-heaps.

"This government," trumpeted Mr Walker, "will never let you down." He was not like the Socialist President of France who had *cut* investment in coal. That, in the view of the uncharitable, is nothing to boast about.

But, for Mr Walker, boasting is a form of oxygen. It seemed rather superfluous to have a debate on public relations on the same afternoon as the landscaper of slag-heaps.

However, there were other speakers, a formidable young man from Staffordshire, Patrick McLoughlin,* who announced

* Formidable enough in 1986 to win a by-election, not something much done lately by Tories.

83

himself as a working miner and a Conservative ... (rapture). He had only to speak ill of the clergy to hold the Conference in the palm of his hand.

Actually, a distinction is worth making. Conservative trade unionists are usually totemistic nullities – Wooden Indians aspiring to be Uncle Toms. Mr McLoughlin, who has fought a Parliamentary seat, is nothing of the sort, but a crisp, lucid, highly credible working-class Conservative. Backyard Tories used gratefully to vote for broadacres Tories. Mrs Thatcher may be exploiting the Jim Callaghan seam of society which is far from uneconomic.

Another most effective speaker from the pits, Irene McGibbon, did everything necessary for success, from quoting Mr Scargill's salary to damning the Bishop of Durham, for whom she uncharitably promised to pray.

The really worrying fact yesterday was the absence of any sustained attack on Neil Kinnock. He appeared as an occasional grace-note in a series of heavy chords in the key of A-major ... (Mr Scargill).

It is no small humiliation for the leader of Party X when the orators of Party Y cannot find it in their hearts to denounce him. The Tories swept Neil aside in the rush to lay violent hands on the president of a medium-sized extractive union (in every sense of the word) and a five-week-old bishop (in every sense of the word).

Perhaps he should hire a PR man.

Daily Telegraph, October 10, 1984

Michael Heseltine, hoarse and as politically passion-rousing as cheap scent, is of course a conference regular – a cup one wishes would pass by.

It is a peculiar talent of Mr Heseltine to make us appreciate the essential humility and good taste of Peter Walker! He is like some character from Restoration Drama: Sir Superlative Bombast or Mr Spurious Fizzbang; yesterday he was liquid kitsch.

The *Belgrano*? No problems: "Any other decision would have been unforgivable!" Troops? "They are being redeployed from the tail to the teeth." Labour? "They ignore the threat abroad; they *are* the threat at home."

But it was in the passage on this year's commemoration of the Normandy invasion that the Minister, head bowed, hands reverently clutched, voice vibrant, and awash with advantageous sentiment, surpassed himself. Not only does the cup not pass by, it runneth over.

Mr Heseltine has the sensibility and refinement of a brass bedstead, but he is an incomparable organist of that 2,000-pipe instrument, Conservative party conference.

Did they want justification for sinking the *Belgrano* – he pulled the *bombard* stop. Did they want to be reverent about the fallen – he snatched at the *Vox Humana*; and, pedalling deftly away, brought them to their feet in recycled rapture.

Meretricious it may be (meretricious it *was*), but it is more than Mr Nigel Lawson can do. The economic debate which *he* concluded had been an astonishingly listless and complacent flip of the wrist at conference.

It is not that Mr Lawson can't make a good speech – just that he didn't. There was a sort of fatty lassitude about it. It requires real enterprise, lethargy of a very dynamic sort, for a Conservative Chancellor not to get a standing ovation at conference.

The conference had been in a complacent, self-congratulatory mood. It took the Chancellor on a flat battery and with all the conviction of a man reading the Yellow Pages to stimulate them to a condition of perceptive inertia, clapping politely and sitting absolutely put.

Mr Lawson has great gifts and a diversity of high talents, but he came over yesterday as Renaissance Man who couldn't paint.

Daily Telegraph, October 11, 1984

An attempt by the government in a moment of ill-considered equity to charge the children of the well-to-do for the tuition costs of university courses had been abandoned in response to the clamour of the starving rich.

The ability of Scottish members to bore the rest of us to the limits of tolerance is wonderful.

On a day when one sectional interest, the grumbling intestine of the middle class demanding its free beer, had been bowed to by Sir Keith Joseph, another yet more dreadful lobby – the

85

unstoppable talking Scots, began an hour-long whinge *because they hadn't been granted a separate statement.*

A delegation from Hong Kong, brought to the gallery to hear the debate on the future of that city, complained that, despite excellent English, they could not understand.

The full extent of their good fortune has not been appreciated.

Perhaps Dr Alfred Adler, inventor of the inferiority complex and the notion of personal insecurity, might have understood better what lay behind the long, gravel-churning, index finger-wagging, disgrace-mongering, slow-minded resentment.

This came from a roll call of the House's leading dullards: Mr Ewing, Mr Eadie, Mr Robert Hughes, Mr Gordon Wilson – there may have been others, one tries not to think.

It arose, did this katzenjammer, because the Scottish Secretary, Mr Younger, had not anticipated at Scottish Question Time (2.30–3.30) the statement on educational subsidies for the well-to-do due to be made around 4.15.

He may even have pulled their legs a little ("Dis-grracefu', Mrrr Speakerrr").

Mr Wilson, a Scottish Nationalist who wears the chips on his shoulder like the military insignia of some sub-Carpathian republic, danced up and down, sat down, stood up, and repeated the operation half a dozen times.

"If it 'ad been me I'd 'ave been out already," commented Mr Skinner who is going through a phase of good humour verging upon statesmanship which cannot be good for him.

Mr Wilson, a prancing little dominie from Dundee, was put down temporarily by the Speaker putting his point of order for him and saying why he wouldn't take it till later.

We came through Sir Keith's statement and questions, after which the Scots were let loose on us like a battery of dental drills.

A better case for a separate Scottish State has never been made, subject only to an electric fence and the mining of the Tweed. Yesterday's episode was like listening to the affairs of a parish with three pumps.

As for Sir Keith's statement, it satisfied that large part of Conservative thinking which agrees with Bertholt Brecht, "erst kommt das Fressen, dann die Morale" (belly first, morality afterwards).

But some of the most obtusely truffle-happy Tories, like Mr Nicholas Winterton, whimpered after the subsidy, the full subsidy and nothing but the subsidy.

The slate pencil voice of Mrs Elaine Kellett-Bowman announced that the middle class were "quite unable to bear the burdens put upon them".

The Conservative Party was not seen at its most attractive yesterday. But there was one sweet moment when Sir Bernard Braine (aptly) spoke of "investment in minds". Labour, good-humouredly, chose to mis-hear this as "mines". It does set one thinking.

Are there uneconomic minds, minds which have not shown a profit for years or, keeping Mrs Kellett-Bowman and Mr Winterton fully in view, minds which are geologically extinct?

Daily Telegraph, December 6, 1984

What a rich diet they do feed us. Yesterday's proceedings were like one of those splendid and bad-for-you Sicilian pastries packed full of raisins, candied peel, angelica and maraschino cherries.

In the course of a single afternoon we had Mr Heseltine in his best "Fairly Secret Army" style committing himself to Trident to the end of time.

There was Mr Patrick Jenkin losing his temper and making a formidably good performance (both precedents) about a document couched in language as miasmal as the London fog (not a precedent).

We also had the Attorney-General looking over his benign-look gold-rimmed spectacles and saying through clenched teeth, "Oh, do shut up."

Finally, we had for a golden hour my own joint politicians of the year, Robin Cook and Malcolm Rifkind, debating the latest fearful stuff from the Eurocrats to the accompaniment of sub-machine gun obbligato from the men of little faith (Messrs Budgen, Marlow and Taylor).

When Mr Cook remarked that he approved of the entry of Spain and Portugal to the EEC, which is apparently spending money it hasn't got in a way which makes Mr Derek Hatton look sixpence overdrawn, Mr Budgen laughed his deep, villainous, Vincent Price laugh.

No such good humour informed Mr Heseltine's masterful time with defence. Quite apart from making a commitment to Trident so ruggedly absolute as to make real difficulties for the next Minister of Defence in the expenditure crisis of 1986, Mr Heseltine also ran up against Dr Patrick Duffy.

A question about low-flying military helicopters in County Armagh raised by Mr Alf Dubs (Armagh being an outlying district of Battersea) had Duffy up screaming about infamy and the Black and Tans.

"Sit down, you silly man," said Robert Atkins.

"Say that outside," replied the doctor whose urges to behave like a minor character in Davy Byrne's Bar are excessive.

The curse of Cromwell had no sooner passed than we were on to local government (Cromwell being easily the man best fitted to sort it out).

Mr Jenkin had a certain advantage in his statement yesterday, total obscurity being the greatest. "I also include the slope of the block grant poundage schedule" brought the House to its knees.

Conscious that he was one of three people present who understood the Volapuk in which Town Council spending is expressed, the normally depressive Mr Jenkin put, if not a spring, then a mild flip into his stride, turning on his persecutors of the past and using violent language like "an almighty scandal". Strong white wine for a sarsaparilla-drinker! Pressed for clarification of the verbal sludge of municipal-speak he civilly promised backbenchers "a child's guide" to it.

"Could you make a guide for a *simple* child?" said Harry Greenway endearingly.

Various slightly creepish Tories then rubbed their hands together and thanked the Minister for capping rates, and Mr Cunningham, always a mine of useful information, drew our attention to a billion pounds wasted by the same Department of the Environment which has 18 delinquent authorities hanging by the thumbs in its well-appointed dungeons for overspending.

Daily Telegraph, December 12, 1984

It seemed worthwhile to raise in Encounter *the mediocrity of petty change. There is enough homogenised prose-feed available in politics and journalism to make this topic a species of shop well worth talking.*

The Exaltation of the Commonplace

The Range of Change

"It was a bright cold day in April and the clocks were striking thirteen." The first line of *Nineteen Eighty-Four* is eerie because it says something alien. It is part of Orwell's affinity with so many of us that he cherished the familiar, the habitual: heavy coins, red pillar-boxes, "old maids biking to Holy Communion on misty mornings". Every country has an identity, a hearth fire before which it is warmed. What is depressing is the extent to which over the last two decades parts of that identity have been altered, usually for no very productive or irresistible reason, and more often than not by governments calling themselves Conservative.

Some of the changes have a half-validity but manage nevertheless to seem symbolic of a more general decline. It was quite reasonable to get rid of the heavy copper small coinage which Orwell found reassuring. Three true pennies in mint condition weighed an ounce and they were 97 per cent pure copper. With the price of the British currency where it was going, no one could afford a coinage worth so much more melted down than in circulation. But my complaint is against trivial, frivolous change, entered into for grand and sententious reasons as part of the river of progress and inevitability, which was neither inevitable nor progressive.

So much of the change referred to has the look of a frantic scurrying back and forth to create the impression of energetic activity on the part of men morosely aware of their inability to do anything that actually mattered. By no accident this orgy of horse-vaulting and wall-bar-scaling began in a period of acknowledged decline, the mid-1960s (incidentally, for no good reason we now call *PT* by the affected name *PE* when physical education for most people means something very different). We have not only changed the copper coins into dreadful unwashable brown discs which look as if they had been given away

89

with a packet of not very wholesome cereal, we have come up with a decimal system whose effect was to mask and, I rather suspect, to accelerate the extent of the inflation. The copy of Orwell's *Selected Essays* from which I quoted is 203 pages long (Penguin, 1957), cost 2/6 (or, in the brute locution of reform, 12½ New Pence), the slightly shorter *Down and Out in Paris and London* in an edition of 1968 cost no more than 3/6 (18 New Pence). But *Italian Short Stories* (parallel text), identical in length and published with *Down and Out*, but brought out in 1981, cost £1.50 (30 old shillings), a seven-fold increase in 13 years, but one sweetly lost in the mists of our Napoleonic currency. With the causes of inflation I am not here concerned, except to point out that a quick glance through books bought from childhood until now will give you a nasty reminder of how ferocious inflation has been.

What truly fascinates me is the idle-minded futility of a decimal currency. Less even than metrication can it claim to have done us any good. It was an act of conformity. Continental Europe does it; how anomalous, how reactionary for us *not* to do it. But, as Anthony Burgess pointed out at the time, mathematically speaking, duodecimal systems are more flexible. Twelve divides by two, three, four and six. Ten will divide by only five and two. It was also vaguely implied that, since continental Europe had a good growth-rate and decimal currency, lack of dots and calculation in tens might in some arcane way have contributed to our lack of dynamism. The currency we had was part of our identity. It made us different, and that difference, once treasured, was now seen as an anti-social act towards what we amusingly call "our Community partners". Indeed, British difference and British identity seemed to be bitterly resented by the most fervent of the good Europeans, whose streak of spiritual quislingism competed with the worst instincts of those who had other fatherlands – in Soviet Russia or mainland China. Orwell, again I'm afraid, returns to this argument with his doctrine of "transferred nationalism".

But transferred to what? Russophilia, however daft, has a long provenance. China is a great nation, however barbarised. But the dynamic men of the late 1960s and '70s, who were so keen to heave us into the homogeniser, created the impression of trying to make Britain as far as possible resemble Belgium.

No disrespect is intended by me to the southern part of the Low Countries, but Belgium (created in 1830) is the very model, down to the fact that it doesn't work very well, of an administrator's paradise.

Yet the precise people who wished us snipped and squared into an offshore Belgium were the first to lose their nerve when the first kilted ghoul snarled at them from a Scottish Nationalist platform. The Belgians, who have been around long enough to keep their heads about the mutual dis-esteem of Flemings and Walloons, would not have gone running as the entire consensus of received political opinion did here when the "Scot Nats", a truly unendearing body of men, won a few seats in Westminster. Panic is Whitehall's secret weapon, on which it falls back when complacency has failed. A Scottish assembly with imprecise powers but without the right to levy taxes would have meant one of two things: a fraudulent, superfluous tier of government (or *ersatz* government) created to deceive and placate; or a step towards separatism, a separatism which would have gained momentum from concession and grievance from disappointment. Devolution was defeated by a congeries of non-consensual politicians from Teddy Taylor on the Tory Right by way of George Cunningham, now a Social Democrat, and Tam Dalyell, that flailing and abandoned Labour moderate, to Neil Kinnock in an hour of glory. The *Civitas Dei* of politics never doubted its wisdom, never hesitated in its urge to reduce Britain to the condition of chopped liver. That we have grown, functioned and had our victories as a unitary state did not receive notice. Devolution was another of those imitations, another political *ersatz*. Germany was federal, Italy had regional government. It was, as they say in the dreadful shame-making manifestos which political parties put out, "Time for a Change".

The depressing thing about all the rather childish changes of the last fifteen years is their meaninglessness. Politicians have operated like the staff of a fussy purser on board not so much the *Titanic* as the flagship of the Ancient Mariner. Here, however, no albatrosses need alight; we roll our own. Accordingly we have earnest, thrusting activity within a painted ship upon a painted ocean. For, despite the footling dynamism of such people, Britain continues her quiet, grinding course of measured, secular decline, but with this difference; that we keep losing small parts of our map.

There is nothing in which frustrated, impotent men dressed in a little brief authority will not meddle. Take names. What does one make for instance of Amber Valley, Broxbourne, Castle Point, Delyn, Elmet, Gravesham, Halton, Hyndburn, Monklands East and West, Ravensbourne, Teignbridge and Wyre Forest? They sound to me like characters and locations from a new soap opera. Young Ted Hyndburn is the salt of the earth but you can't rely on that fly operator Jason Delyn, a dodgy character with a past, who has his eye on young Sandra Broxbourne who has come to live at Castle Point, that rather fine house on the coast, not far from Wyre Forest. But her uncle Sir Charles Ravensbourne sees the solid worth of young Ted and has set a private detective, rock-jawed, resolute Jake Elmet, to make enquiries into Jason's past. These bring him to the Colorado mining camp Monklands, in the once beautiful but now lead-polluted Amber Valley.... (More next week.) Why, one asks, must the Boundary Commissioners identify the shuffled and repointed constituencies with names which are meaningless, except in the occasional antiquarian sense, to the citizen? Hyndburn, for heaven's sake, is a tarted-up word for greater Accrington! What good will it do to a slightly battered brick-making town in Lancashire to have some verbal interior decorator give it a lick of paint and an alias? Hidden within the ranks of the British Civil Service there are evidently avid readers of romantic novels of the pastel-Gothic sort – witness Ravensbourne – and also men with a nostalgia deeper than my own. I simply have this soft spot for 1965; the chaps who renamed the municipality of Halifax as "Kirklees", out of deference to the Robin Hood legend, have a passionate yearning to get back into the snug 15th century. Indeed, although it is customary to blame Mr Peter Walker for the massacre of local identity in his Local Government Act of 1973, this is less than fair. Dearly as I lament the obligation to be nice to Mr Walker (not my favourite politician), it has to be said that his version of municipal boundaries and names, bad as it was, was solidly conservatory compared with the Redcliffe-Maud Commission advising him. Mr Walker simply dispatched to oblivion Rutland, Huntingdon, and a county peculiarly dear to this writer, Westmorland, as well as meddlesomely chopping bits off the others

92

and taking it upon himself, a mere ex-partner in Slater Walker Securities, to liquidate the Ridings of Yorkshire which antedate the Conquest. But the Maud Commission, God bless it, was all ready for the creation of six or seven regional sub-states, name-less lumps of geographical Lego to most people, but not without some inspiration from the Anglo-Saxon heptarchy.

Incidentally, those who carry out pottering changes on the face of Britain are very happy to indulge in a vast verbal inflation of their own titles. The rot set in here with Harold Wilson, now suitably if inadequately translated as Lord Wilson of Rievaulx. Harold Wilson it was, in his kindly way, who, after Barbara Castle had been badly thrown over trade union reform, tried rather touchingly to make it up to her with a grander and more resonating title to go with her diminished status. The old Ministry of Labour which had been good enough for Ernest Bevin ruling it like a benevolent Stalin was now frothed up into the Department of Employment and Productivity, and poor done-in-the-eye Mrs Castle became a full three-star Secretary of State with epaulets. It set a pattern which has continued unbroken down to Mrs Thatcher who actually turned Trans-port, least esteemed and sought-after of jobs, the chipped-off corner of another Ministry, into a full-blown Department with a Secretary of State. Housing and Local Government, with Transport added, long ago became the Environment (Depart-ment of), a piece of '70s chic. But, once separate, even Transport, even the present Minister, that stylish disaster Nicholas Ridley, has to be a Secretary of State.

As for the Board of Trade and its President (a nice Victorian title), office, name and size change with the tides; while the Ministry of Power is now the Department of Energy. All have won and all shall have prizes. The ranking of Ministers is reminiscent of the tendency in schools (which soon surely must become Education Centres) not to distinguish *alpha* from *beta* and to award (until the day before yesterday) passes so coded that only the very discerning can recognise them for failures.

I think I shall believe in the true seriousness of a Government when it demotes its Ministers to their true rank, when the glorious train of subordinates is diminished and its grandeur clipped. A nice story is told by one of Mrs Thatcher's Ministers whose chauffeuse had talent-spotted him over the head of an elder statesman as a man likely soon to grade himself (and her) up by getting into the Cabinet and winning for her the mark of such elevation – a Daimler Sovereign. "Well," she demanded after the crucial Downing Street interview, "did you get it?" "Yes," he said, "I'm going to transfer to ...." "Never mind about the Department," said the lady, "it's the *Daimler* I'm interested in." Defeat seems to have sharpened our appetites for the small change of office-holding – large cars and china cups. Civil servants wisely tend always to say "Secretary of State" in the vocative person – so much more soothing than "Mr Harris", and so fatuously Habsburg in every other respect.

However, not every disaster which has hacked away at us as a country latterly can be directly attributed to politicians. Part of the fair fatherland which, like Heine, we once had, was its language. It is not the fault of politicians if the Bible, which made the blood of that language run red, has been translated and retranslated into a sort of prose muesli, all second person plural and tin-eared. Try reading *Ecclesiastes* in the "Good News" version if you want creative dissonance, or if, for that matter, you want the banality of a straight talk to young men. Nothing in the several British (but hardly English) versions has quite the splendid absurdity of the American text which amended "And Saul went into the cave and covered his feet" as "And Saul went into the cave and went to the bathroom". They lack that sort of atrocious grandeur. But nothing resonates, the poetry is gone and no birds sing.

The custodians of what is left of Christianity, a highly residual faith in Britain, have consigned the language of Tyndale, Coverdale, Lancelot Andrewes and his co-adjutors to demotic marginality. They cannot have too little of it. Their text is intended for (and comes from) drab minds with no sense of time past or cadence. 16th- and 17th-century English is too hard, too demanding. So they have produced a text which is as little demanding as strained carrot! The Babyfood Bible has now been followed with the realisation of a spectre which has been haunting some of us rather more than any conjuration of Marx (who would have been as appalled as anybody): I mean a simplified, toned-down and modernised Shakespeare. Poor, bare forkèd creatures as we are, we might have been spared this. Worse, it is seen by its progenitor, the inescapable Dr Rowse, as an act of pre-emption. Worse would have happened, he tells us, but for his own clarifying text. The present generation, especially in America, cannot understand Shakespeare, he says. I detect here a wholesome lusting after dollars which at the present rate of exchange is most politic. But, if the past and High English are beyond the present generation, what does that say for the mental energy and intellectual fidelity of the elder generation who raised them? You have texts, you work, you come to understand. It isn't actually very difficult, any more than it was difficult for someone with an atom of energy or sensibility to understand the King James Bible. And like all acts of pre-emption this miserable text *won't* pre-empt. A thoroughly modern, probably socially aware and relevant Shakespeare must be only a matter of months away.

Identity in a people is a good thing. Names, words, texts, titles, the places where we live are all part of it. They can only be changed out of a sort of crassness or an active malice. The designators of new boroughs are not malicious. Indeed, they often act out of a spirit of rather touching (if meddling) anti-quarianism – Kirklees and the medieval sub-principalities of Wales, Powys and Gwent, that sort of thing – but the Euro-faddists have always imported a hint of dislike for this country into their discourse. There is a trace of voluntary subjection, of happy tribute-paying, in their Belgianising tendencies. Panic begot the abortion of devolution; vanity and self-solace among unsuccessful men in office started the bubble-titles of Ministers. But the rending (and I mean rending, in its Old Testament sense) of the Bible and the dilution of Shakespeare with Dr Rowse's water are acts of hubris mixed with malice.

This age has exalted the commonplace. Let us find whatever is not commonplace and bring it into low and level conformity. We had a source of rich communication, and this age speaks in obscenities and grunts with a vocabulary derelict of elegance or substance. Let that source dry up and diminish. Cathedrals are out, industrial building methods are in. As the Old-Hat Bible hath it: "God maketh man upright but they have sought out many inventions. . . ."

Encounter December 1984, Vol. LXIII, No 5
London Commentary

"I have kept my mind ajar." The words belong to Mr Patrick Jenkin (who else has such reflex infelicity of expression?) as we move into capped rates.

They conjure up an image of the Minister's mind resting lightly on its hinges: of PJ, as we might call him, relaxing like Rod Steiger as the Alabama police chief in *The Heat of the Night*, with the fan on full capacity as he lazily interrogates an overspending borough of the wrong complexion.

"How does a boy like you come to run a deficit of half a million dollars, huh?"

In the view of the Opposition the mind functioned, of course, only as a cat-flap. Mr Straw worked at his indignation over the Minister's lack of response to the just and well-founded protest of municipal man.

But even Mr Jenkin had fun reading through a briefing document or Ponting-sheet which had been circulated by Mr David Blunkett, Sheffield's rather bright left-wing boss. Caddishness, of the sort which so distresses Mr John Stanley, having reached the boroughs, Mr Jenkin was able to read off a catalogue of admirable low motives hiding behind the cloak of meaningful dialogue.

"Try to put the Minister on the defensive; make him look negative and unbending; avoid being accused of refusing to meet him", and, best of all, "dislocate the Department's time-table'.

It was very hard not to warm to Mr Blunkett, a man whose idealism and passionate commitment to whatever it was now stands redeemed by a streak of pure and uncorrupted cynicism.

Mr Straw, who is in business as one of our more ostentatiously educated politicians, beat the Government lightly about the head with their own philosophers. Did not Popper and Hayek warn us that centralisation of government would be foolish since it could not be matched by an equivalent centralisation of information? This is a good point but Mr Straw rather spoiled it by defining knowledge as "all those hundreds of councillors with skill and expertise".

They may well be very, very wonderful people, but somehow the image of your average toiler at the rate-face – reciprocal tripper to twin town in West Germany, organiser of lesbian day centres, proclaimer of nuclear free zones, non-nukable by

96

barbarous American or well-meaning Russian alike – is less clear-cut.

Lots of people rather dislike councillors.

Indeed had Mr Jenkin been here for something less milk-soppish than rate-capping, he might have been met with more enthusiasm. As it was, like the best, he lacked all conviction (leaving passionate intensity to the backbenchers).

"What if there is rate-capping?" morosely asked Hugh Rossi, who sounds at times as if he had been called upon to bear the rates of the world. The deficits could all be run, and would then have to be made up out of central government funds (tell that to Popper).

"Ah," said the Minister, "if that happens the auditors will be seriously concerned." Not much of a unique deterrent, is it?

It did fall out that what Mr Jenkin meant by this dark and menacing feebleness was surcharge and disqualification. But Mr Rossi was not impressed. Somehow one feels that, however indignant the Opposition gets, "hundreds of councillors with skill and expertise", linked with a spiral of rate increases fit to stand beside Trident, are simply part of our manifest destiny.

Daily Telegraph, February 26, 1985

Budgets increasingly resemble the 1,500 metres with Chancellors poised, like the Miss Budds of this world, to shave seconds off them.

Running on what we understand to be a mixture of white wine and mineral water, one way of diluting the excise duty he was about to increase, Mr Lawson achieved a new record – one hour and 12 minutes.

The style of delivery, though a vast improvement on that best-not-talked-about conference speech delivered in Brighton like a lettuce salad fallen on evil days, was strictly non-alcoholic. There were no gaffes and nobody ruined, in fact nothing to laugh at at all.

However, an excitable school of thought was to be seen rushing around drawing drastic conclusions for newspapers from the new open-ended employer's contribution to National Insurance in respect of the highly paid (not a point to dwell upon!).

Especially not, when it is linked with VAT for newspaper advertising and relaxation of the rules affecting unfair dismissal from large companies.

If the former City editor of the *Sunday Telegraph* and editor of the *Spectator* wanted to scare the maximum number of ex-colleagues discreetly out of their minds in one three-point package, he went the right way about it.

But from real radicalism of the sort which brings the owners of company cars down Whitehall with their placards Mr Lawson refrained, regretfully one feels.

The role of a fiscal Scarpia maintaining a Reign of Terror over occupational pensions, and all those other benefits which delight the Sunday morning car-washing classes, appeals to Mr Lawson. But he is under constraints.

Yesterday we had "Lawson Bound." Perhaps one day we shall have "Lawson Unbound". But the Prime Minister tries to minimise the Promethean potential of her Chancellor.

He was allowed only a passing melancholy sneer of the "foiled again" sort, at "the anomalous but much loved tax-free lump sum". Anomalous it may be, tax-free it remains.

Mr Lawson at that moment reminded me of a small boy wistfully contemplating an economically inaccessible custard pie.

However, to assorted cries of "looking after your mates again", he did abolish the development land tax.

When we got down to headline writers' territory – 6P OFF CIGS – he indulged in the singularly Sir Jasperish posture of exempting cigars, the preferred puff of the exploiting classes, from any increase in excise duty.

There were a few passages which looked as if they had been put in to make Mrs Thatcher happy – about "inculcating the spirit of enterprise".

However the heart of the Budget, a scaling down of National Insurance contributions to encourage businesses to take on more people, coupled with some modest tax cuts at the threshold, clearly pleased his own party.

Order papers, the basic test of a Budget, were waved, if a little languidly.

For the Opposition Mr Kinnock did what he usually does – began splendidly and went on too long.

If Mr Lawson, weighted down with the medium-term financial strategy, a review of the performance of the economy and his tax charges, can get as near to the one-hour-Budget as 72 minutes, Mr Kinnock's back-to-the-envelope civilities, quick critique and general deploring bit really should not take 21 minutes.

Mr Kinnock started sharp, pointing out the parts of the Budget lifted from Labour's election manifesto, asking a very dangerous question about long-term intentions on unemployment benefit and making a cruelly effective *ad hominem* crack about Mr Lawson "turning his back on the issues and waddling away from them".

If he had sat down after 12 minutes it would have been a memorable response. After 21, it was piped oratory, Neil Cassette.

Daily Telegraph, March 20, 1985

Having had time to reflect on the topic of the Falklands War, I came to very bleak and sceptical conclusions about it.

The Far-Away Falklands

Occasionally one lets slip a remark which has behind it deeper convictions than are acknowledged. I did so with an observation in this column about the Falkland Islands War. I find myself civilly taxed for it but feel profoundly unrepentant.

I will be asked: "Why bring this issue up? Why not accept that a highly satisfactory victory has been won, or at least that the world perceives it as a triumph?" But the present continuous tense in which we live is history and it is necessarily subject to revision, not least as the heady emotional moods of wartime recede. I acknowledge on my part an initial hostility to the whole business. I recall saying, "Bodies will finish in the water before this week's rhetoric is done." But, like very many people who entertain sentiments of ordinary respect and regard for their own country, I reacted to the start of the *fighting* by unequivocally identifying with our side, and saying so.

Time has passed. We are nearly three years on from that fighting, though the cash payments continue. It is time to look

99

back and wonder if the expedition makes sense in retrospect. I believe that it does not, that it was a misconceived enterprise, that the Government was itself caught up in day-to-day expedients and subjected to pressures which do not seem reasonable today.

I subtract not a farthing from the great heroism of those who fought. I acknowledge that nations have within themselves a need for self-respect, and that it is the strange nature of "little wars" that they release perfectly honourable, long-sneered-at feelings which I more than nearly share than I absent myself from. But wars, though sometimes necessary, should not be fought because they make you feel good.

And what about Grenada? If the Falklands is mistaken, can Grenada be right? Frankly, in solid Machiavellian terms Grenada made sense as the pre-emptive act of a great power which saw the early traces of another great power's influence within neighbouring territory, and acted. In terms of rational self-interest the Grenada expedition, for all the froth and drum-beating which followed, did have utility. For a country as little involved in the South Atlantic as ourselves, we have to ask what utility the Falklands War had. Alas, I see none.

How did we come to fight this infinitely futile, infinitely sad campaign, this toy-town parody with real blood? At the time we almost all cheered or at least applauded – and some are cheering still though the bills roll in and the utility of those few thousand acres of waterlogged, grade-five agricultural land, where thirteen acres will support a single sheep, seems more mystifying than ever.

Let me start anecdotally. The Anglo-German Königswinter conference of 1982 took place that April in St Catharine's College, Cambridge. We split for study sessions into four groups. I attended the one on foreign policy, and had just listened with mounting exasperation to an elder statesman expounding on the proper Foreign Office conduct of foreign policy as not understood by the Americans. "The Americans," he drawled, "have got themselves into a frightful tizzy over some place or other called El Sal-ve-dor. The Foreign Office is wiser in these matters. We would have trouble finding it on a map, and we would have left the whole matter in the hands of a junior officer...." (None of this, as one keeps having to say, am I making up.) He had no sooner sat down, with Americans duly reprimanded for their jumpy seriousness, than a messenger entered who handed to the Chairman a note. "I feel," said the Chairman, one of our most distinguished historians,* "that I should interrupt to let you know that Argentine forces have landed in the Falklands." That episode says more about the FO view than I could hope to.

What followed the world well knows, though it forgets bits. On the very next day, a Saturday, Parliament was recalled. The hysteria, violence of language, and abandonment of reason which took place that day mark it off as one of the worst performances which the House has collectively given. "All power to little silly men" seemed to be the order of the day. Mr Patrick Cormack was listened to seriously, an experience unlikely to be repeated. The old Tory Right, the Suez group, the men in mourning for an impossibilist dream of military authority within the world, came from the withered margins of politics and were listened to fearfully and with respect. Julian Amery's view of the world briefly came true. It is not something which must ever happen again.

For myself I remained certain that war would be unthinkable, that the talk of an expedition had to subside. I was utterly wrong. We went for several months through a period of collective irrationality and I readily confess, having initially used my mind, to having joined the mob and closed it again. I wrote in defence of this war, for which I apologise. Once a war starts, however foolish, however morally wrong, the feeling that this is, after all, our country becomes formidable.

One of the stories out of the great Falklands trek, recorded by Charles Laurence, who filed some of the very finest copy of the war, concerned the reliance by the British Army for its "yomp" upon Mars Bars. Since they are high in glucose content, this is entirely sensible. They helped sustain a brave and admirable army whose achievement is not diminished by the vain and desolating folly of those who sent them. But the rest of Britain was also on Mars Bars – which can be sticky, glutinous, and bad for your teeth. Fleet Street was at its most patriotic and rabid. If there had been a well-known Argentinian dog we would

* Michael Howard

have been encouraged to kick it. But it is also true that the British needed emotionally to fight *somebody*.

For a quarter of a century since Suez, the opponents of military reflexes had dominated politics. Suez itself, the last emotional blow-out of the Julian Amery /brigadier element, had ended in a humiliation which unpleasingly delighted the left. And in the last analysis the unintelligent but very honest patriot is a more attractive man than the sneering left-wing lecturer who enjoys national humiliation. After Suez, the cartoon character George Weber, in anorak and with placard, had had things pretty much his own way. The assumption that we are as a nation not entitled to stand up for ourselves – that the United Nations is a better homeland, that when humiliations come they should be welcomed, that the only good war was the sort waged by Ho Chi Minh or Robert Mugabe – represented a sustained inversion of natural loyalties which the generality of us find quite dismaying. But this outlook ruled as the bottom line of foreign politics. So much so that if General Galtieri had taken the precaution of being a bearded man in self-consciously worn, frayed fatigues, quoting Sartre to delighted correspondents, war against him would have been unthinkable. Would we, would Mrs Thatcher, have dared send an expedition against General Torrijos, who gave so much delight to one of the sour spirits of the age, Graham Greene?

As it was, poor Galtieri was an honorary South African, a right-wing *caudillo* of the kind which Spanish colonialism throws up all the time. War was deemed to be bad, but war against a South American dictator had two things going for it. On the Left of the spectrum, it was half-way accredited by being directed at an authentic two-star bogey. On the thinking Right, away from the Cormacks and Amerys, it had the virtue of being (like Grenada, later) winnable. Argentina is not a small country but, notoriously, it is inefficient, unheroic, and liable to fall over if pushed. The purpose of the Exocet missile however, like the revolver in Damon Runyon, is of being "the old equaliser". Even an Argentinian can sink a capital ship with one of these. How far Admiral Lord Lewin had thought that out, who shall say? But perhaps the true point of the *Belgrano* episode may be that the British military command did not at any time share the smoky euphoria of Parliament and Public, and looked upon any enemy ship as something to be dispatched to the bottom pretty damn quick by way of a "teaching strike".

Into such moral messes, such requirements of compounding death with death, do you get if war is undertaken to satisfy a yearning rather than as something within one's full capacities. For the conventional means of death, unnoticed by the uni-lateralist nuclear disarmers, have gone up a hundred-fold. The winners of all small wars are those whose new conventional rockets or armour-plate have done best in their field-trials. Alan Clark was quoted as saying that, if you fight a war, "world opinion doesn't give a damn, world opinion is queueing up to buy the kit you won it with. . . ." I have no indignant rebuttal for Alan Clark's cheerful cynicism, which after the mood of piety, and damp-handkerchiefed legal self-justification is some-thing of a relief. But the kit most people were queueing up to buy after the Falklands War was the Exocet, manufactured in France, supplied to Argentina, and used with some notable effect to sink British ships and kill British sailors.

This is a crude and obvious point which out of the delicate feelings we have for our own pride tends not to be made. What precisely did we get out of the Falklands War except a warm glow, the experience of feeling good, and a Roll of Honour?

We now have back on our hands what *The Times*, perhaps after conversation with the Foreign Office, called "these paltry islands". We have 1,800 people for whom the British government spent an uncomputable sum running into billions, when in respect of similar communities on St Helena and elsewhere it will not invest a penny beyond its fixed pathetic allocation to raise them from the chronic unemployment and depression which characterises such small groupings. So we didn't spend the money we spent, or throw away the lives we caused to be ended, out of disinterested concern for the Falklanders. It would have been possible at a trivial proportion of the war outlay, never mind the money which we are now spending, to have resettled every Falkland family bloodlessly in New Zealand, Westmorland, or wherever it is that shepherds and sheep like to be. Instead we budgeted for the death of troops and for the expenditure of money systematically denied to a hundred peaceful uses in the preceding course of the Government's expen-diture cuts.

A greater contradiction than combining strict monetary control with fighting a war in the South Atlantic is not to be found in the wildest jungles of fantasy. But that fantasy has been compounded by the subsequent "Fortress Falklands" policy, which involves a major garrison for this mudbank, and the building of Heathrow's long-awaited Terminal 5 ... at Port Stanley, so that Tri-Stars and other sophisticated planes can supply the Army of the South Atlantic. We are standing in the rain tearing up banker's drafts.

Sooner or later when the last brass instrument is silenced and when the red-faced patriots are not looking, the Falkland Islands, under whatever form of words we hit upon, will have to be ceded to the Argentinians because those islands are there and we are *here*. Stuff legal titles and stuff certainly the comic-opera nationalism of Argentina's own red-faced patriots. If the citizens of that melancholy country really want those islands, they will do the Argentinians no very great good and us no discernible harm, and it will not be irrational to hand them over. The British will come to see in time that the grotesque episode of 1982 was pure therapy. We were a great power; we have ceased to be a great power; we shall, alas, never again be a great power. We are afflicted by an inferiority complex and needing to cut notches on a stick.

The war we undertook nearly three years ago was fought by the men concerned very bravely and efficiently. We learned in the field what we knew in principle: that the reduced British Army is very good indeed. But did we deter any enemies, did we do ourselves any tangible good? Surely not. This was in all senses of the word, including the narcotic, a trip.

The British, with Mrs Thatcher at their head, came out high. It was a collective act of retarded adolescence and we all cheered. The patriotic card was played and we all fell for it. That is just a trifle hard. I don't personally think that the Government was wicked, cynical or calculating; and I find the Raymond Briggs – E. P. Thompson approach so much standard Left-wing knee-jerking. The British Government never looked as if they knew what they were doing. The Foreign Office, leaving a junior official in charge and pushing insouciance to the point of hilarity, managed to leave the impression with the Argentinians, mistaken or otherwise, that a cathartic act of invasion would actually disembarrass them. At the same time cuts in the Navy and in the Falklands garrison, reducing it to 80 men, suggested perfectly reasonably that a conquest was capable of achievement which, give or take a measure of puff-and-blow indignation, would not be resisted.

This was professional incompetence of the very highest kind. Those Foreign Office Ministers who lost their jobs afterwards deserved to lose them (and Civil Servants should have too). The newspaper image of chivalrous high mindedness by the resigning ensemble of graceful incompetents who brought off this alpha-class bungle is just one more piece of fatuous British deferential self-deception. The Falklands, if you really wanted them, could have been kept at the expense of another 100 soldiers and a plain, unequivocal, private statement that Argentine involvement of any kind was not wanted. If speech had not been fork-tongued, guile would not have doubled back and done us an injury. But when the paper-and-lath structure of defence and foreign policy first encouraged and then made possible an invasion, the British Government was trapped. It was given a choice between humiliation and war. With the baying dogs behind, it chose war.

This involved a measure of military gambling which made victory uncertain (not what any aggressor intends) and the deaths of very many servicemen a racing certainty. For, as the Government well knew from Day One, we had nothing which could remotely be called air cover. The extent of that gamble is underlined not only in the graveyards and plastic-surgery wards where so many Welch Fusiliers finished up, but in the fact that, if the Argentines had wired their fuses better, two and perhaps three other capital ships would have gone down. If they had, not even the *Daily Mail*, the Government's little drummer-boy, could have sold this bizarre war as a triumph.

As it was, the Government – to a degree we shall not fully understand until all the papers are released long hence – played a game betwixt bluff and war. The Opposition went along partly because the public mood which fogged the rest of us got at them, partly in an unacknowledged hope that things would come bloodlessly unstuck, that at some point south of Ascension Island we would turn and sail for home, muttering darkly and proclaiming in the accents of Suez that we had put out a forest

105

fire and that our mission was accomplished. Mr Edward Heath in one of his celebrated interventions called essentially for this. A large part of the Opposition, brought up like everyone else on the inevitable humiliation of the British in all modern conflicts of will from UDI to UHT, waited for withdrawal and made supportive noises until that humiliation should come. By a piece of good soldiering and by uncovenanted good luck from non-exploding shells (and because Mrs Thatcher plunged deeper at the gaming table than ever expected), the war was won and a gamble became a triumph.

It remains, as I now think, the most discreditable, amoral, and improper episode in British post-War history, a gamble not worth the taking, a war fought for reasons of *amour propre* mingled with electoral considerations as the long expedition went on, a pathetic attempt to pretend to ourselves that we were other than we are, a pantomime war in which men had their faces burned off.

Neil Kinnock got into dreadful trouble with the Tory press for responding to a heckler who alluded to Mrs Thatcher's "guts", that it was "a pity some people had to leave theirs on the beach to prove hers". In my view, Mr Kinnock was categorically right, and morally he scored right between the eyes when he said that.

This war was of no more import than the one between the big-enders and the little-enders. The most you can say is that fortuitously it accelerated the already expected interlude of liberal democratic government in Argentina which will precede the next military regime (the British are no more interested in liberal democracy in the Argentine than in Ungo-Bungoland; and indeed it is none of our business). At the end of the day Mrs Thatcher gave herself something to rejoice at, extricated the islands, and held a Roman triumph. But the Falklands remain worthless; the cost of supporting and defending them has turned nightmarish; and 1,300 men, 258 of ours, and over 1,000 Argentinians, were drowned, blown up, or scorched to death.

The *corpus delicti* remains, sodden, emblematic, morosely pleasing to sheep, and the inducer of folly in two second-rate countries in decline. It is as much material use as that plot of land for which Fortinbras went to war.

We go to gain a little patch of ground
That hath in it no profit but the name –
To pay five ducats, five, I would not farm it . . .
Two thousand souls and twenty thousand ducats
Will not debate the question of this straw.

What *have* we done to be drawn into such folly and death and
still be proud of it?

Encounter, April 1985, Vol. LXIV, No 4

Business questions every Thursday have, since the
accession of the great John Biffen, become the most cher-
ished part of the parliamentary week. An ironist cast
among accountants, Mr Biffen collects little, gently dis-
obliging things to say on Thursdays which leave PM's
questions looking dreary.

"As for the Hon. Gentleman's good-natured words, let me
disabuse him. I am a shameless bosses' nark and always have
been. I wouldn't do the job on any other basis."

There is only one member of the Government capable of
such soothing and self-derisive levity: the member for North
Shropshire, the Agnostic of the Cabinet table and the man from
whose palm the hawks and kestrels of the Left come to eat
Trill – Mr Biffen.

We were into Business Questions, that micro-prairie of a
debate which follows the announcement of next week's business
and affords members opportunities to ask for consideration
to be given to issues as diverse and unrewarding as Turkish
democracy and the Okehampton by-pass.

Both those issues were bounced off the wall, squash-wise,
yesterday afternoon in the company of Matthew Brown's
Brewery (about to be taken over – disgraceful!), the limitless
hypocrisy of the SDP (Prop. Dennis Skinner) and the need for
Parliament to operate a three-day week!

This piece of ruthless demanning came from Mr Madel (Con.
Beds S.W.) who begged for a long period of tranquillity during
which Parliament ceased from its labours in the public interest.

Alternatively we could start laying them off in the manner

already familiar to workers in the steel, textile and flange-bevelling industries.

The thought of men who have given a lifetime to the legislative industry being thrown on the scrap-heap because of Mr Madel's heartless ideological commitment to tranquillity pleases, but it lacks verisimilitude.

Business Questions are at least better than those devoted to agriculture where the maligned person of Mr Michael Jopling could be heard moaning in low tones about "the dreaded additionality question".

The Common Agricultural Policy, like the Mafia, has developed a vocabulary all its own, only properly comprehended by Men of Honour in good standing with the Family.

Occasionally, like a reforming Italian policeman, someone like Mr Dennis Skinner, will intervene to observe that "there have been 17 questions so far, Mr Speaker, and every one put by a Tory has asked for more Government intervention or increased agricultural subsidy".

In Sicily you could have yourself dropped down a disused sulphur mine for such indiscretion. Here Mr Skinner was simply ruled out of order.

Otherwise we were assailed by earnest disputation about the effect upon soft fruit growers in the South of England by the accession of Portugal.

Nobody, you notice, asks whether Portuguese raspberries might be cheaper. Debate relates entirely to the anguish of the producer and his right to produce in the teeth of demand or price.

Mr Proctor, for the Essex soft fruit trade, seemed inclined to argue for greengages much as Mr Scargill argues for coal. The Portuguese greengage, like Polish nutty slack, is a blow struck against men with guild rights.

Mrs Thatcher, never herself the lady you would cast as Cordelia (voice soft and gentle, an excellent thing in woman), has taken to accusing her opponents of being "excited and hysterical".

Mr Hattersley, who operates a superiority complex to snub an archduchess, which, come to think of it, is roughly what you need against Mrs Thatcher, awarded her, "as always, high marks for shrill irrelevance".

For a man trying to make a point about the rate support grant he sounded excessively like a Habsburg putting minor Balkan gentry in their place.

When Mr Kinnock is at the Despatch Box, whatever his failings (or more precisely his excesses), we do have a light-and-dark contrast with the Prime Minister's hauteur-on-draught.

With Hattersley posing as Lady Catherine De Burgh the rest of us simply huddle to escape the blast.

Daily Telegraph, April 19, 1985

There will be readers to whom the proposals in relation to Financial Services are a topic of such personal interest that they stand a-tiptoe, St Crispin's Day-style, to hear about them.

On the other hand the sort of reader who has anything to gain or lose by such legislation has probably picked the information up late yesterday afternoon off his custom-built terminal.

As for the generality of us – those for whom 500 shares in ICI represent the summit of a lifetime's furtive aspiration – financial services are a pain.

And, for those in pursuit of light, flippant reading, one can only say that, even with Mr Tebbit piloting the Bill, the risibility factor is very nearly zero.

Only nearly, mind you, because Mr Tebbit, to whom Freudian slips come like Halley's Comet, did sweetly change "market regulation" for something which deserves a modest immortality – "Margaret regulation". The Prime Minister is making her decisive way into our subconscious!

Otherwise one's heart went out to the Labour backbench audience which, most of the time, consisted of Mr Douglas Hoyle.

The cultivated and civil exchanges between Mr Tebbit and Mr John Smith, who just does, every now and again, look like the brightest man in the Labour party, were of a Claud and Cecil sort.

The High Hispanic chivalry of commercial technician communing with commercial technician was obsessed, pausing only to put one or two mildly critical questions "to elicit response, not to be of an enunciatory character" (Mr Smith).

It was, as the elder commentators like to say, "the House of

Commons at its best" – living death!

Though, on an afternoon calculated to lower the blood pressure of a coelacanth, one should be grateful to Mr Anthony Beaumont-Dark who is neither Claud nor Cecil and who tried to pick a fight with Mr Tebbit over the proposed role of the Governor of the Bank of England.

"A veto and a constitutional outrage," said Mr Beaumont-Dark, trying to get some blood on the moon. "I think my honourable friend, though he has a point, exaggerates a little," said Mr Tebbit wiping it off with a Kleenex.

In the light of such asphyxiating moderation one is grateful for the good old-fashioned political ill-will which blew up at the end of Question Time. This had been devoted to foreign affairs and had been as nearly perfectly irrelevant as maybe.

Had Sir Geoffrey Howe had valuable conversations on his visit to Czechoslovakia with Cardinal Tomasek? Wasn't it disgraceful that the Americans were giving so much aid to Costa Rica? What was the precise view of the president of Colombia in respect of the Central American crisis?

Various countries get denounced on such occasions – and a lot of notice they take of it. At such times MPs sound like the Synod of the Church of England talking about monetarism.

It is all a very beautiful, insubstantial experience and it keeps them off the streets. But, as Mr Eric Deakins admirably put it, the EEC, which had hardly been touched upon, differed from South Africa, Israel and Czechoslovakia in that, unlike them, it taxed us.

The House of Commons is very far from being an ideal place but at times it looks increasingly like a Platonic one.

Daily Telegraph, April 25, 1985

The Uses of Atrocity would make a tolerable title for yesterday's performance by Mr Kinnock.

At various times he spoke of "ratting" and of the Prime Minister being "a twister". While Mr Alfred Dubs abandoned his customary caution, and, like a fire bucket boiling over, accused the Government of "murder" – insufficient provision of cervical smears!

The new Kinnock was watched with some pride from the

110

gallery, not for the vituperative part of his act but for its sudden achievement of brevity.

For years now we have been urging that Mr Kinnock bears a resemblance to the V1 and V2 rockets with which Dr Werner von Braun contributed to the variety of life in Southern England during 1944–45.

It was said of the V weapons that they constituted no danger as long as you could hear their buzz. It was when the motor cut off that you flung yourself under the table.

Mr Kinnock has buzzed harmlessly, and at length over the innocently sleeping population. Again and again the advice, mentally given, has been, "Stop now, you've got a point." But, like the idle wind, in more ways than one, he regarded us not.

Suddenly yesterday he had a rush of concision, asking so much and no more, leaving Mrs Thatcher to a sort of amplified goldfish act – opening and shutting her mouth and saying very much the same thing.

Incidentally, Mr Kinnock managed and Mrs Thatcher did not an elegant welcome to Mr Weatherill, returned after unpleasant illness.

The immediate issue was Serps (employment-related pensions, expensive but promised and a source of fissiparous ill-will between Mr Lawson and Mr Fowler).

Mrs Thatcher had said at the election that she had no plans to change them. After her chat on Monday night with those two Ministers, would she say if that was still her explicit view? Too blandly for her own good Mrs Thatcher announced that she was conducting a "fundamental review".

Flying low over the marshalling yards, the K2 rocket quoted Mr Fowler in refusing to call the pension structure in question: "Reviews are part of government," he added just before switching lethally off, "ratting should not be!"

Labour, long denied blood and percussion by their leader's flying preacher approach, burst into the sort of ugly roar associated with blood sports. Staggering from reiteration to reiteration, Mrs Thatcher spoke of a "most fundamental review".

A second, if crudely constructed, K2 buzzed briefly about revision of the Welfare State, nearly overflew by getting on to the death grant (which Labour takes personally), then snapped shut and asked her why she was such a twister?

Vulgar abuse it may have been but it worked. Given his large optimism and erratic steering, Mr Kinnock has often had the look of Mr Toad. But yesterday he was Toad in charge of a motorised division.

For the first time in months the ambulance service of Tory sycophants was called upon to give first aid to the Prime Minister.

Mr Robert Adley leapt out, bandages and iodine in hand, and, interposing his person between Mrs Thatcher and her critics, asked the Speaker (happily back with us) if it was in order to use bad words like "twister".

Like a leading article in a magisterial newspaper Mr Weatherill inclined to the view that on the one hand robust debate was in order but that, on the other, so was moderation and that he deprecated its absence.

Mr Kinnock, now *three-quarters* in excelsis, jumped up to say how strongly he "supported your view, Mr Speaker. When policies are moderated, language will be moderated."

Mr Dubs, by the judicious application of excess, managed to get the allegedly inadequate screening of cervical cancer smears (and Mr Dubs) more attention than either could have hoped for. With a thousand preventable deaths taking place, he said, there was only one word for it – murder!

Actually, as any first-year law student could have told him, the most it could be is manslaughter. As for what Mr Kinnock did to the Prime Minister yesterday, it was a legitimate act of war.

The question is, can he keep the K2 rocket short on verbal fuel and close to target, or was yesterday just an aberration from the customary benign humming – overhead and out of range – so long associated with the K1?

Daily Telegraph, May 1, 1985

The De Lorean motor car which was to have revivified the economy of Northern Ireland proved downwardly mobile as it sank slowly into the ground taking reputations and subsidies with it.

"A project such as De Lorean would not now be supported."

The words of Dr Boyson would have seemed to most members the barest grudging minimum of residual humility and 20–20 hindsight to be expected when Government had sent valuable exchange into the shredder to the tune of £75,850,000.

Not a bit of it. On a notably crazy day Mr Roy Mason, the Minister principally responsible for the launch of cash into outer space, remembered his Clausewitz or perhaps his Scargill.

Treating attack as the best form of defence, he said that, but for the hard-faced Tories, De Lorean would still be in business turning cars off the assembly line.

Mr Mason is to self-doubt and humble regret very much what Dr Paisley is to Romanising tendencies.

The sum lost was, after all, paltry, a mere £75,850,000.

Compare it, he said in the grand way of a Victorian mill-owner boasting about bigger steam-looms, with Concorde. That had cost £795 million. None of your cheap imported muck but real British losses with a nap you could run your hand over.

Almost, but not quite, apologising for the modest, undersized, unassuming little loss he had begun to run up, Mr Mason turned to abuse the Public Accounts Committee whose chairman, the civil and admirable Robert Sheldon, had just led us through a chronicle of commercial atrocity recounted with too much British reserve.

The Committee was not well attended, he raged, giving figures for attendance.

Mr Sheldon quietly intervened and corrected him with the real numbers; "I can't be bothered with my Rt Hon Friend nit-picking on the figures" came the reply with the old-world politeness of the South Yorkshire coalfield.

Candidly, a more astonishing speech has not been delivered by a past or present Minister in my recollection.

He had rushed about as a Minister taking every precaution about the suitability of the De Lorean project, everyone had backed him, and the Cabinet, which had authorised him to go ahead, had had 18 members present, not the miserable six or seven of the Public Accounts Committee which had revealed the scandal.

Mr Mason has a thing about attendance at meetings. War declared by a quorum has clear precedence over an under-manned armistice agreement.

113

Of course American business had favoured such a deal. Mr George Parks (Labour) informed Mr Mason that General Motors didn't want De Lorean around their works at any price.

Anyway it was none of his fault. He had made the agreement but why hadn't the Tories amended it? But for them De Lorean could have been saved.

As for everybody else (including Mr De Lorean and I just think Mr Mason) they had done a remarkably fine job – "by our deeds we may be remembered".

The whole point about Roy Mason is that he combines the reserve of a go-go dancer with the approach of a rugby league forward.

He sees himself as a bringer of jobs, De Lorean as the sort of enterprising chap who could teach these fastidious City of London types how capitalism really works, and the whole enterprise as "a better weapon against the IRA than the British Army".

Unfortunately for the opponents of De Lorean, Mr Nicholas Winterton is one of them.

For, if Mr Mason sounds like a brass band at his own funeral, Mr Winterton resembles one of those characters with private placards telling you they have been cheated by the Lord Chancellor, the Archbishop of Canterbury and the grandmaster of the Freemasons.

And it is not in the least incredible that Conservative response to his cries may have been cynical, indifferent and incompetent (what are governments for?).

But, when a man starts telling the House that for his meeting with the Prime Minister he attempted to take his solicitor along "only to be confronted by the Attorney-General" who answered questions "like a Dalek", judgment is growing just a touch wild.

Somehow one felt that, right or wrong, Mr Winterton could best protect himself by sitting down.

Daily Telegraph, May 2, 1985

Never underestimate the power of a private member to seize the white gloves of a procedural traffic policeman and re-direct convoys of container lorries into the outer suburbs of Erskine May.

Traffic policeman for the afternoon was Dale Campbell-Savours. One could slot Mr Campbell-Savours without difficulty into a chaplaincy in the New Model Army. He would have led the psalm-singing at Naseby with authority.

Now, being a Puritan, Mr Campbell-Savours has a down on corruption; being a Labour regular, he has a down on the Alliance, and given the donation of £186,000 by the British School of Motoring to the Liberals he has an open goal.

The technique for such a coup, involving as it does the stretching of a point of order beyond the dreams of Playtex requires a misleading and disingenuous fairmindedness in the early stages.

So he murmured sweetly and consensually about a Private Member's Bill of agonising propriety and right-mindedness sponsored by a Conservative, Elizabeth Peacock, on the standards of driving instruction.

He ground on in the approved manner about opposition which had been raised by members of the Alliance. It was customary for those who opposed legislation to declare an interest.

Only those with a boring interest in politics to equal Mr Campbell-Savours' own could see where this was leading.

But this category includes the Liberals who, in the mild manner of their sort, muttered quietly under their breath.

"Mr Speaker, I am being barracked by Liberals. I seek your protection," said the member for Workington. Alas, in this place one is barracked by Liberals much as one might be torn apart by wild curates.

He referred to Lord Tordoff, Liberal leader in the Lords and a man to bring out the apathy in all of us. He had moved an amendment in the Lords – shocked Labour cries of "ooh" and "aah" – not even Hitler did that.

However, by a process, less evolutionary than geological, we came to the point. The objections in the Commons and the amendment in the Lords had been designed to protect Mr Anthony Jacobs' British School of Motoring, benefactors to the tune of more money than is altogether tactful to the Liberal party.

At this Mr Weatherill finally intervened. "I get the Hon Gentleman's drift," he remarked.

115

But Campbell-Savours is not content with drifts. He wants collision at high speed. "Mr Jacobs," he said "has effectively bought the Alliance."

Wearily, and with perhaps too much sophistication, Mr Beith, for the Liberals, pointed out that there had been an attack on the personal integrity of Liberal members.

But it was in vain for Mr Beith to protest that the Tordoff amendment made the Bill more effective or that it had been praised by the Labour Front Bench in that House, or that Labour had voted for it. We are into Smearsville and the evidence is strictly decorative.

Mr Campbell-Savours had had a coup, but whether it concerned anything relevant, truthful or accurate, was another matter.

Daily Telegraph, May 9, 1985

George Younger, Secretary of State for Scotland, a nice man much loved by all who have to do with him, miscalculated in a fit of transcendental inadvertence the rateable values for Scottish burghs, prospectively upping rate burdens by up to twelvefold. This had to be put right.

As a broad working rule sketchwriters respond to rateable values and Scotland much as your run-of-the-mill vampire avoids garlic and crucifixes. The tedium quotient of both is unquantified.

Not yesterday. George Younger, had he been a major American criminal, would have shown an unexampled grasp of the Fifth Amendment.

Being only a British politician, he was confined to blaming the Opposition parties for an alpha grade blunder attributed by leading scholarly sources to George Younger.

It was like being back in the carefree days of Edward Heath when the 'U' turn was as common as the *pas de deux* at the Bolshoi; for Mr Younger, whatever his blunders, at least goes backwards on points.

Nobody listening to the Minister's bland account of his intention of looking after one or two little anomalies by being exceptionally generous would have supposed that the groaning Burghs had come within an inch of filleting the Scottish Office.

The burden, at the extreme point of thirteenfold revaluation, has produced vistas of a Conservative-free Scotland rolling without interruption from Melrose to Thurso.

The Secretary for Scotland was thus a man trying to freeze panic into glacial self-assurance.

He is on such a terrible wicket that Labour and the Alliance couldn't bring themselves to be seriously unpleasant.

Mr Dewar contented himself with the hope that too much of the free money would not be concentrated upon Eastwood, Pollockshields and (significant pause) indeed Ayr, thus accounting for the seats of the junior ministers and the Secretary of State, none of whom would ever stoop so low as to hire the next election out of the contingency fund.

However, as Mr Younger took a firm grasp of the silken ropes cast into the pit dug by Mr Younger, he found consolation in one thing.

If he had blundered into the absent-minded machine-gunning of small town retail trade by way of a revaluation which is the very latest thing in inadvertence, almost the entire Labour, Alliance and Scottish Nationalist leaderships had been no better informed.

Luckily for Mr Younger the Opposition parties had reacted to rateable value with the same insouciant indifference with which we all regard other people's rateable values.

Not being a draper in Galashiels, Mr Dewar had not gone screaming up the wall, nor had Mr Gordon Wilson nor any Liberal spokesman.

Happy, hapless George had managed to get it wrong in company. He hung on to the silence and acquiescence of the other side like a shipwrecked mariner to a spare hawser.

As for money, money was of no account. The Scottish Office has always been awash with the stuff.

Of course the fishmongers of Dunfermline and the shoe-shops of Inverary (to say nothing of the hoteliers of Ayr) could have money. How much would they like?

The Liberals had spoken tentatively in the way of men not used to redistributing the Revenue like rice at a wedding. He, the Cash Pasha of crisis, would spend £50 million. The Lord taketh away and the Lord, running scared, giveth back.

The Polish Government announcing food price increases in

stern terms in 1980, the Duke of Milan faced with bread riots in 1628, have, when confronted with strike or riot, behaved with much the same reverse alacrity. Conservatives, who in Scotland struggle like ospreys against a hostile environment, offered thanks with the sincerity of Lazarus.

The feeling in that company is that the rules of annihilation have been suspended and, rather like Tom in the Tom and Jerry cartoons, each of them has been flattened by a steam roller, fallen 1,000 feet over a precipice, or been fed into the shredder before emerging in a leisurely way more or less intact.

The lines of Arthur Hugh Clough: "Hey ho, how pleasant it is to have money," which always fitted Mr Younger's tenure of the Secretaryship, have never been more apt.

Daily Telegraph, May 15, 1985

The massacre of a civilian population in Dresden from the air by the British in 1945 has long seemed dreadful. On the fortieth anniversary of the main raid I said as much in a Telegraph *leader which provoked a vast controversy. This* Encounter *piece extends the argument.*

The Candle of Dresden

An interesting occurrence in what I might call my other life – at the *Daily Telegraph* – has been to watch the controversy flowing from the publication of a leader to mark the anniversary of that wicked night of February 13–14, 1945 when the city of Dresden was turned into a fire of the sort which must have burnt in the mythological Christian hell. The leader went some distance to embrace the Willy Brandt view of the wickedness committed by one's own countrymen – acknowledging the evil and making a full apology for it.

I doubt if we have ever received so many letters for a single editorial (I have been given the figure 360), and what a diversity they represented – from the mature sense of a great news-paperman in retirement (Wilfrid Sendall), to the spluttering rage of a retired Air Vice-Marshal (Donald Bennett). The concern of most was to rationalise backwards, to invent a military utility which never existed; not a few talked the language which I heard privately from one of our elder television personalities, who

118

rejoiced that we had killed so many Germans. Quite as unwise were the handful of unilateralists who wrote to agree about Dresden and argue for the abrogation of our present defences.

For my part I have never been more convinced of what an evil the childish instinct of patriotism becomes. The British people will not grasp what was done in their name. They become indignant, and quite rightly so, if an Irishman sets a sophisticated fuse and kills a dozen people in what after all he regards as a war. The figures for Dresden are estimated by Max Hastings at "something upwards of 30,000 dead". And is it supposed that, if a German military leader could have been identified, as Air Marshal Harris was, with those deaths, he would not have been indicted, tried and hanged at Nuremberg as a war criminal? But the British in 1945 were the winning side, or more precisely a modest strand in it. Bomber Command was something we were proud of, though Churchill and some of the wiser military had their own sense of a wrong, and Harris was duly punished, not by a War Crimes Tribunal but by denial of the peerage he longed for. It was the British Establishment's way of setting itself at a little distance from a useful brute with whom it would not care to be too closely identified. Querulous and resentful, Harris left for White Rhodesia, which must have been a congenial place. Field Marshal Keitel should have had such luck!

Part of the reason for the Dresden crime, and the ones which preceded it in such cities as Hamburg, is fortuitous. We developed the bomber on a heavy scale and with un-British efficiency; the Germans pursued first fighters, then rockets, and the little-afflicted cities of England owe a debt to the lethargic incompetence of Hermann Goering. Fear of bombers, a "bomb culture" even, had been strong in pre-War Britain. Remember the trenches in Hyde Park, Baldwin's remark about the "bomber always getting through" and that premonitory episode in Orwell's *Coming up for Air* when George Bowling witnesses an accidental aerial bombing and identifies it as the future? Coventry, of which the British made a tremendous moral issue at the time, involved 584 deaths – a 1:50 ratio for those killed in Dresden in a single night.

We had the weapon of the bomber and had it in a period when laser technology for accuracy was non-existent. Any bombing would have been a bloody and haphazard affair but it took

"Bomber" Harris, like Leopold Stokowski, to demand heavy orchestration – the carpet-bombing which accidentally or deliberately set up the fire-storms. These drew living innocent civilians by vacuum suction into the furnace which he and the Pathfinders had lit. That such acts can still be defended, that the withered old men who took part have so little sense of the burning of human flesh as still to be writing to the newspapers in incoherent fury at criticism of "our brave boys" should, but does not, surprise me.

There was another aspect to the Dresden tragedy which is not readily admitted to. The inherent weakness of Britain as a military power at that stage in the War was clear enough. If we were one of "the Big Three" it was a sham position not warranted by our current contribution to victory. We may have been the heroes of the Battle of Britain, but we were the humiliated incompetents of Singapore, Dieppe, Arnhem and Crete. Bombing capacity was the one thing sufficiently matured in the aircraft factories and RAF training to represent a truly substantial British strength. Never mind the doubtful utility of much of it, never mind the misapplication of resources, in thousand-bomber raids. Here was a chance to swagger, an opportunity to keep up the Great Power posture for just a little longer. A candle of burning Germans to light the Russians on their way to Berlin was a fine way to ingratiate ourselves with the real powers.

The British have never come to terms with the extent to which their military permitted themselves at certain times to behave roughly like the enemy they were supposed to hate for his barbarism. The destruction of German cities, of which Dresden – wiped out a few weeks before the conclusion of a war – was the grand finale, had less in common with an aerial attack on a legitimate target (bridges, factories, marshalling yards, Luftwaffe bases) than with those acts of village-killing which put the Germans in so vile a light. Oradour-sur-Glane, Lidice, and Marzabotto (whose hero, Major Reder, received such a sympathetic reception when he returned to Austria earlier this year), these were acts of punitive destruction occasioned by local resistance. In so far as Harris's doings had a rationale, they served to cause terror; they were acts of exemplary death in great numbers: morally indistinguishable from Lidice, only bigger.

Dresden, for heaven's sake, was a ceramics centre full of frightened refugees. We couldn't see their faces (as the German officers could in those village killings), but surely even in Whitehall some half-farthing's worth of imagination might have been exercised.

It was wartime, and in wartime men's sense of right deserts them. They think, as our patriotic TV personality still thinks forty years later, that they are "killing Germans" and a good thing too, or that they are killing Jews or Arabs or Gooks or Ndebele or whoever's turn it is next at the hands of the righteous. Most countries and certainly most politicians are so misty-eyed with patriotism, whether it is the flag-saluting American sort or that odd, oblivious indifference to other people which the British and Chinese have in common, that it is a dangerous business saying "we were wrong".

However, saying that you are wrong is not and never will be the same thing as that terrible self-hatred which gripped so many Americans during the Vietnam War. Waving flags is childish; burning them is, if possible, worse. The unamiable defeatism which takes a pleasure in the victory of enemies, a spirit which was strong in the West in the 1960s and early '70s, one which demonstrated against war and in favour of the Viet Cong, seems to me not worthy of consideration.

Total pacifism is rather more respectable intellectually, but it is unknowing kin to flag-burning, the preserve not only of humane people making larger demands of the world than the world has goodness for, but also of the unpleasantly smug, the unco-guide and those who dislike not merely drumroll patriotism, but their own roots.

"Sanity" is a recurring word in the Peace Movement. It is even the name of one of their journals. But surely sanity in military matters is a rational balance between the commonsense ethics which make gratuitous killing wrong and that technically alerted state of elaborate defence which is most compatible with not giving in and not going bang. One of the many lessons from Ben Pimlott's fascinating biography of Hugh Dalton, Labour's first post-War Chancellor, is that it reminds us of Dalton's tough-minded efforts to snap Clement Attlee and the rest of the pre-War Labour leadership out of non-resistance. The language of almost pure pacifism was being talked in the highest Labour

121

circles, until very late, by men who somehow also wanted so much to oppose Hitler.

Yet, when they came to power and accepted the very war they had not been able to contemplate, neither they nor their Conservative colleagues did anything to deter the actions of Sir Arthur Harris. The fact of a war breaking out moves people from the most etiolated contemplation of their own ethics to acquiescence in fire-storms without their noticing. That is not sanity; and, more to the point, it is not good government. In fact it is not government at all. My own impression, from the biographies and histories of recent wartime politicians, is of the comparative helplessness of government when faced with the technical patter and insistent demands of the military.

We know now that bombing Dresden was a useless and superfluous act as well as a very wicked one. But armed services and their programmes have a momentum of their own.

Patriotic blackmail plus number-crunching (however bogus), plus the need to cut some sort of figure, all served to entrap men of Churchill's subtlety and moral quality into approving things which were as alien to them as I believe those Dresden raids were alien to England. For which reason we have to hang on to rules even in wartime, especially in wartime. We do not say, now or ever, "Oh, well, that was wartime. People get killed in wars." Nobody gets killed, somebody kills him.

That rule applies to the creative negligence of the Sabra and Chatila camps and to the new tragic events occurring in the Lebanon as I write. It makes Mr Justice Kahane, with his report apportioning guilt and contributory fault, like a true judge, the best sign out of Israel at a time which has not done that country honour. It makes the British cover-up on the *Belgrano* and the prepared truths and untruths of Mr John Stanley something to curl up at. Nobody's military can be trusted to abstain from the excesses we all attribute to other people's military. But the acts committed by our troops or by friends and allies actually have the same historical weight as those of adversaries.

Governments, alas, find themselves in war the custodians of acts committed by a military nominally subordinate, but for practical purposes in charge. If Admirals want to destroy a ship which constitutes no conceivable threat, for whatever reasons of miscalculation or military reflex, it is a government which

122

ends up by mendaciously misleading the country and protecting men over whom it had no control. A "Great War Leader" is, much of the time, a pure sham, wringing his or her hands and telegraphing assent, very nearly a constitutional Prime Minister in the sense that the Queen is a constitutional monarch.

Governments are slow to talk about indefensible acts, less because they commanded them (though clearly the Nazis and Stalin fit their own pattern of central-command terror) than because every shaft of light, every Ponting, demonstrates a government not in control, but on ceremonial duty. Which is why governments, which are not quite co-terminous with scoundrels, take refuge so frequently in patriotism. "These are our brave boys. . . . How dare any civilian protected by us during the War insult the heroic men of Bomber Command?" Only the losers run out of patriotism and say "*Befehl ist befehl* (orders are orders). . . ."

Patriotism excused the great cull of the First World War, the setting of citizens in the name of national glory to each other's extermination. The words were splendid. Lloyd George, that ablest and worst of men, spoke movingly; men wept, and the graves stretch out of sight. Generals had a wonderful time – all criticism was blanketed either by "national security" or "our patriotic duty". To one military historian even now, we under-fulfilled our quota of the dead. Faced with what military men do when they get near power – obtuse men like Haig, crude warlords like Harris, to say nothing of the little-known commanders responsible for action in the Afghanistan war – the less scope they are given the better.

If sanity keeps military men in the columns of newspapers in a permanent state of outrage it also has to do with printing the truth about past wars without benefit of patriotism. A lucid contemplation of what has been done in our name and which we ignorantly cheered on at the time, from First Ypres to the latest shoot-out in the Middle East, is education enough. We need neither bullfrog patriots nor the Surrender Lobby to disturb the melancholy condition which constitutes all the peace we are going to get.

Encounter, May 1985, Vol LXIV, No 5

It is always nice to have the *Daily Telegraph* on everybody's lips in the funereal circumstances of the Conservatives running third in a Gallup poll.

In the light of so much opposition, said Mr Wrigglesworth in the pedestrian, fair-minded way which will be the death (or the making) of the Social Democrats, would the Prime Minister stop carrying on?

"No, Mr Speaker," said Mrs Thatcher, nothing if not concussive. "I will not stop carrying on."

The carrying-on or Kitty McShane side of Mrs Thatcher's personality does not, indeed, grow less, whatever voice-massage or quantities of Dr Reece's sweetening tincture are consumed.

Mr George Foulkes is a moderately tiresome man but one who is in the answerable position of having been misreported for an incident on the Falklands visit.

He has been roundly abused by the Prime Minister and then been in receipt of an apology from the news agency concerned.

From Mrs Thatcher you get apologies the way tin is mined in Cornwall: the commodity exists but not in quantities which make extraction economic.

She was sorry that he had felt deeply wounded and was glad that he was withdrawing his remarks.

At which, as they say down-market, "all hell let loose", not the less impressive for being a gentlemanly hell articulated by a Liberal.

Mr Stephen Ross (Isle of Wight), an affable Paddington Bear of a man who normally overfulfils his quota of goodwill, was up and shouting above the Labour indignation: "The Hon member is completely correct. I was there and the charge is wrong."

Mr Willie Hamilton then made an historic call for courtesy and grace and, amid calls for the Prime Minister to withdraw, the Prime Minister withdrew.

More precisely she said that she thought she had already done so and added, "I withdraw then."

It was one of those small but destructive incidents which a less restless and fiery spirit would have defused with a swift ungrovelling expression of regret.

Mrs Thatcher is armed and weakened by a single-minded partisanship which sees civility as artifice. On such occasions the graces work to rule.

Mr Kinnock's part in the afternoon, though not particularly successful, did show the New Shorter Kinnock, an edition which, like the [Concise] Oxford Dictionary, is more in demand than the full compendium.

"Crime has risen since she came to power. What is she going to do about it?" may, as an observation, be hung about with *non sequiturs*, fallacies and other aids to cross-examination, but it is wonderfully terse.

Those who have watched Mr Kinnock producing words like a pasta factory on triple time observe the elegant arch of his learning curve and wonder if it will last. To re-phrase a favourite aphorism about higher education – less is better.

But Labour outrage took sail on a private notice question to the essentially functional Mr David Mitchell, of the Transport Department, which revealed extensive closures of British Rail workshops.

The case for closure may be legitimate, but hiring Mr Mitchell to make it is unwise. His style is that of the eternal underling, word perfect and bound to his text. Chained Bibles one has heard of, but chained Junior Ministers seem excessive.

Asked why he didn't do something about the secondary jobs which would be lost to major suppliers when the workshops closed and orders went abroad, he replied: "It isn't for me to do anything about it."

Now we know what he means (that companies must run for their own orders) but, as a sub-contractor for useful quotations in the next Labour manifesto, the toiling Mr Mitchell will never lack business.

Daily Telegraph May 17, 1985

"I am speaking from the heart, brothers," said Mr Ron Todd, advocating the motion which will end in the suspension of the AUEW. "Dinosaurs have hearts as well," said Mr Eric Hammond succinctly.

It is Mr Hammond's role here to spell out the full depth of the hole in which Congress finds itself; but the instinct of a TUC conference in such circumstances is to keep digging!

If the AUEW are thrown out for accepting a ballot subsidy, they will take their money with them. They will also take the

125

Electricians. And, as Mr Hammond sweetly observed, if anyone wanted to complain about "cowboys, scabs and other rubbish", they should watch those likely to rally to an alternative TUC. "You ain't seen nothing yet."

The episode is more tragic than comic. The offence is technical. Most unions take Government money for educational purposes. Indeed, Les Wood of UCATT said that only a narrow reading of the rules kept his union from appearing on the same charge-sheet.

Mr Clive Jenkins, clearly a reader of this column, pleaded that two valuable regiments should not be lost by having one of them confined to barracks (Mr Jenkins has formed his own campaign group: Hedonists for Common Sense!).

It was overall a rather grim morning. Mr Scargill, the voice of Physical Force Trade Unionism, demanded in that strange interplanetary voice that fines exacted last year should be repaid.

With 13 photographers clustered round, Mr Scargill smirked, preened, chopped the air, chopped logic and struck that peevish peremptory drone, favoured by Messiahs cruising on four cylinders.

More sadly, Mr Norman Willis opposed the motion. There is no pleasure in throwing rocks at Mr Willis, but inadequacy shines out of that speech. He is doing for coherence what Stockhausen did for the melodic line. After five miles' meandering in a mazy motion, he reduced one dedicated reporter to the cry: "I haven't got a single completed sentence in my book."

Mr Willis, a sweet man, all goodwill, is on the side of the angels, but he isn't doing them any good. The general effect is to make Len Murray seem like a fifth-generation computer, while poor Norman embodies Heisenberg's uncertainty principle.

Otherwise Eric Clark ranted, somehow dragging in Eddie Shah and British Rail. Jimmy Knapp, the gargling Scottish Tannoy, rushed to defend "so-called football hooligans", also prospective victims of Thatcher's authoritarianism, and announced: "Now they're coming after us" (the function of Mrs Thatcher is to flesh out paranoia and lend unpleasing similitude to things going bump in the night).

But the sweetest moment in the day came when Mr Alan

Sapper, who represents Video Tape Editors on £60,000 p.a. minimum, spoke for the working-class.

Not only had the miners been attacked by the class enemy; it had "*attacked us, the working-class*".

Mr Sapper is unduly humble. I have never seen him or his members in the same light as rumbling Jimmy's superfluous rail guards, Mr Duffy's spanner-men or Mr Leif Mill's shabby-genteel bank clerks. Mr Sapper is the carriage trade. Any class war against him would start from underneath.

It would follow the old Victorian Rookery principle:

"'Ere, Fred, there goes a toff,"

"'Eave 'alf a brick at 'im."

There was a brief respite to the class war and the miners' right to break the law when we touched in a short debate upon what were charmingly described as "part-time women".

The full androgynous possibilities of this term (we were talking about dinner-ladies) in fact fascinated Tom Sawyer of NUPE, Rodney Bickerstaffe's deputy. "It is a Cinderella job," he observed and, grasping double-entendre with both hands, went on: "Unfortunately it's Cinderella without Prince Charming. Even Rodney couldn't get the slipper on."

Daily Telegraph September 4, 1985

"*And, furthermore, Ealing is proud to have sent as its delegation a black woman and a gay man*" (loud applause).

The words of Mrs Valerie Vaz were timely provided to save the media from the gross effort of parodying Labour party conference.

The media, incidentally, according to a speaker in the "Black Sections" debate, were "trying to divide the Asian and Afro-Caribbean communities in Birmingham" – an act amid those burning shops surely of supererogation!

Bournemouth has not improved Labour conference but its sea frets and new facilities are well received. Reversing Kublai Khan, Bournemouth Borough Council has built a Misery Dome, one large enough to take the big grim conferences of the big grim parties.

One reaches it from underground through a smiling file of

"Maggie's boot boys" made necessary as a result of the crisis of British capitalism.

The conference centre works on different physical principles from the Earth, being pleasingly cool at its centre, the auditorium, and oppressively over-heated at its crust, the tea room and bar.

Coolness is, however, largely wasted on Labour delegates. There was much talk in that Black Sections debate about "the racist community", but it was dialectically satisfying to hear the High Left, in the person of the evergreen Ray Apps, opposing Black Sections for impeccable Marxist reasons.

Readers of the *Daily Telegraph* will appreciate the sophisticated distinction between the romantic and classical Lefts.

The gays, lesbians, feminists and militant blacks are very much at the Richard Strauss–Puccini end of the spectrum – all rising thirds and sevenths and general over-orchestration!

The High and Hard Left, with their concentration upon "attempts to divide the working class", are back there with Haydn, Mozart and sonata form.

Incidentally, they detest each other, and it was a sweet and peculiar pleasure to watch Roy Hattersley of the Old Right (cynical, opportunistic, careerist betrayers of the working class) fervently sustained by boatloads of proletarian authenticity.

Hattersley induces support with a balance of poignancy and assertion. "It is an act of Socialist faith that all men and women should be treated equally."

A form of words with which no rational person can argue, it was naturally disputed irrationally – by a screaming female contingent from the floor, defined by a more knowledgeable colleague as "the South Norwood claque". Hattersley rolled majestically over the South Norwood claque in his best ocean-going manner.

Roy Hattersley's rather classy eloquence, now tending to sentiment, now abruptly slapping down a nonsense, met his own rhetorical question, "Does it enhance the Labour party?" It did.

Daily Telegraph October 1, 1985

At the Labour Party's 1985 Bournemouth conference Mr Kinnock made a notable stand against the Militant Tendency. No one expected it. Everyone, especially in the right-wing press, now discounts it. There is no future in gratitude.

"You rat, you bloody rat. You sold us yesterday, you sold us again today!"

It was Neil Kinnock's lot yesterday to trigger almost all the qualities which distinguish the Labour party: human sympathy, idealism, shuddering malevolence and certifiable derangement.

They will talk about Bournemouth '85 as they talk about Scarborough '60, the last time a Labour leader, baited and abused by his Left, turned round and baited them back.

The story is told of how the young Neil, a few years back, had a punch thrown at him in the gents at Conference (for voting against Mr Benn as deputy leader), and how, being less meek than he looks, he "beat the daylights out of him".

Bournemouth Conference Centre was converted yesterday into a vast political washroom with overtones of Agincourt. Whether he is credited with a Crispin's Day speech or merely with thumping people, Bournemouth and Boscombe will no more come round from this day to the ending of the world, but he in it will be remembered.

"It was all reasonably calm," as the British Naval officer remarked reminiscing about the South Atlantic, "when suddenly there was this little red dot zooming in on us." The Exocet qualities of the leader lie in the sheer, abrupt, brutal lucidity of his attack.

One moment we were cruising on the affable lake waters of slogans and resolutions not being enough for victory, the next a viciously spinning disc had hit the hard Left in a soft place.

"Such implausible resolutions," said Mr Kinnock, "were pickled into dogma, ending with the grotesque chaos of a Labour council hiring taxis to scuttle round a city handing out redundancy notices to its own workers."

The immediate standing applause, the departure of Mr Eric Heffer in the stately waddle of an affronted Mandarin Duck, the frantic clapping of the Left and the operatic boos of other people, created what the French call an *évènement*, a happening.

The rest of the speech fell betwixt loathing and loving. Mr Hatton, the flashily-tailored representative of the authentic Working Class, gibbered like a sedentary King Kong. A woman in red in front of your correspondent muttered and snarled for minutes into her metaphorical beer, and of course there was "you rat, you bloody rat".

It is owed to Mr Kinnock to acknowledge not only the courage of the speech but its general high literacy and distinction.

The early parts, aimed at the Tories, were better than the usual humorous fluency. The dismissal of Tory aspirations – "waiting until some great non-unionised, low-waged, tax-dodging, low-tech privatised day dawns" – had a sharp burnished ring to it.

And indeed Mr Kinnock, who rarely rings when he can tintinabulate, had restrained the instinct.

For half or more of the speech he was trying to plumb an underground river – of diffuse, humane, generous, unideological good feeling which used to be the great glory of the Labour party.

He would not have succeeded as well as he did in his second assault on the Left without this search. For, after the ducks and delegates had departed in a demented huff, he alluded to his debt to the Labour party.

"Oh yes, careerism, betrayal, Kinnock in Number 10, lucky for some" trembled on glistening enraged lips. And, at that, he brushed all such abuse aside with an account of his life chance from Labour (housing, school, work) which was actually very moving.

He had reached the river and was floating sweetly upon it. Quite simply he could now ask the question – Do you want to improve people's lives or sit enthroned in purity, blaming somebody else?

As the party has spent years in abject purity, terrified of the electric malevolence which that commonsense question involves, the man who finally asked it has heroic status.

There is a very long way to go indeed, but yesterday offered the worst speech Mrs Thatcher and the Alliance leaders could have hoped to hear.

Daily Telegraph October 2, 1985

"We are not obsessed with materialism, with wealth in itself or with physical possessions." Oh, I wouldn't say that.

But then Mr Nigel Lawson, who made the feint at the ascetic vote, had such a large, if faintly meretricious success yesterday that one hesitates to cavil.

More of Mr Lawson in a moment, but the economic debate to which he replied and a great part of the day's proceedings badly needed all the back-of-a-lorry oratory they could get.

But first, as they say on American TV, a word from our alternate sponsors. Mr David Mellor in the drugs debate was fairly dire. Mr Mellor could well be commercially viable to the oil companies. One sees Texaco and Tricentrol buying large blocks of him and drilling in the fields they had acquired.

Flattery in the Conservative party, like Grievous Verbal Harm in the Labour party, is endemic. Even so, to express a warm tribute to the Prime Minister, the police, the customs, the judges and the Princess of Wales in the course of one speech seemed excessive.

If David Mellor were a worm he would send a vote of thanks to the harrow. Quoting some past threat of Mrs Thatcher to the drug trade, he proclaimed like a demented drum majorette: "The lady wasn't kidding."

When it came to politics, he threatened, "laws with the teeth of a shark" to protect us from "the nightmare world of the zombie". Such language might be taken personally by delegates to the Conservative party conference.

As for Princess Di, she got on to the Mellor servility circuit not only for presiding over an addicts' reclamation society, "but as a mother herself!" Mr Mellor, a fastidious admirer of classical music, has gone into a Liberace phase.

However, the day's heavy business, apart from the statutory Heseltine ululation – "Things for which brave men fought", "This party has always spoken for Britain", "We shall not fail" – was, thank God, concerned with the economy.

And very bad-tempered it became before Nigel the Great Healer brought things to a modestly triumphant conclusion.

Richard Fuller from the Federation of Conservative students was given Labour party treatment. He was hissed before he got to the rostrum.

Mr Fuller, a man of Gilmourisant reflationary views, struck

in thin code at Mr Lawson's fondness for the service sector and take-away joints by observing that the country could not be saved "by McDonalds alone, Mr Chancellor".

He also had a fable about a lady grocer whose penny wisdom about borrowing had kept her business stagnant while her virtuously overdrawn sister set up a flourishing chain of shops (dodgy metaphor that).

Mr Heath's mortician's job of impassivity cracked slightly while Mrs Thatcher favoured the youth with her sucking-an-underripe-greengage expression.

Into Mr Fuller tore Mr McDonagh, a rising PR man of South Sudanese economic persuasion. "Morally confused Robin Hoods," he called the reflators with their disposition to take a few billion and spread them around. He even managed to quote Livy, something not done at party conference since the better days of F. E. Smith.

He warned the Tories: "You know how to gain victories but not how to use them." Those words were originally addressed to Hannibal, and we know what happened to him! Central Office *delenda est*?

The Chancellor, quite apart from the economy, put himself right with his public by praising the police and by abusing the BBC, or the Britain Bashing Corporation as he called it, with the minimum of sensibility.

In such a climate, to use his favourite economic metaphor, a speech of small business proportions can achieve rapid growth and take-off. His points about Britain's economic growth (the biggest, or least stunted, in Western Europe) sounded less aridly statistical.

Into the uplift he dropped a hard promise: inflation below 6 per cent at the end of the year, and below 4 per cent at the end of next year.

From this modest spoonful of Bovril was a nourishing political speech made, though there was a raffish passage about people putting their money on the blue square, which will keep Mr Hattersley in moral infamy for months to come.

The statistics and the bombast were nicely balanced, which, since some statistics actually are promising, was legitimate. It all ended on a drum roll with the Opposition denounced for gathering under a white flag. "We will never surrender," said the Chancellor, with a faint touch of Dr Paisley. No matter. At the end Mr Lawson, if not the economy, was intact and floating upwards.

Daily Telegraph, October 10, 1985

South Africa, not one of life's naturally jovial topics, occupied the first three hours of debate yesterday.

It provided the Labour foreign affairs spokesman, the blood-soaked, metaphor-waving Major Healey, with two elegant animadversions and one rather dreadful lapse.

Lightly he congratulated Sir Geoffrey on the outcome of "his often weary negotiations ... with the Prime Minister".

Speaking of an earlier statement – that Mrs Thatcher had given Mr Botha a piece of her mind – he observed mildly that he would be cautious in accepting such a gift.

However, the Major Bloodnock aspect of Mr Healey got horribly out of control as hair rapidly grew on the backs of hands and he spoke of "another outburst, ho, ho, of Rhoda the Rhino, or rather should he say, ho, ho, 'Rambona'?"

May we take the opportunity to advocate the application of punitive sanctions, including withdrawal of IMF facilities and access to the gallery bar, on any journalist or politician to make one more "Rambo" joke.

Rambo must be outlawed, brought before the bar of world opinion, and made the subject of a report by Sir Shridath Ramphal.

Much of the debate was spoiled by the cricket-like interventions of Mr David Winnick whose squeaking abuse ("National Front", "spokesman for the South African government") never quite achieves the level of immaturity at which he is aiming.

However, this should not discourage us from drawing the line fairly sharply at his main target, the not excessively endearing John Carlisle.

Most Tories work on the "we deplore apartheid but ..." principle. Mr Carlisle's heart doesn't seem to be in the deploring.

It is perfectly valid to remind people of the unpleasant, undemocratic things frequently done in uncensured countries of

133

Africa, members of the Commonwealth in good standing.

But one flinches at the reference to Mrs Winnie Mandela as "the self-appointed spokesman for the so-called black majority".

Also the observation that "the security forces took the measures any government would have to take" opens up visions of ambush trucks being driven into Brixton to, ah, take measures. There is room, I find, to be very anti-sanctions and even more anti-Mr Carlisle.

But for much of the time it was a dream debate preoccupied on the Labour side with such observations as "morally this country needs the Commonwealth more than they need us" (Mr David Young, Bolton), "the world community at large" (Mr Winnick), and for the Tories, "there should be sanctions against the black African countries" (Mr Terence Dicks).

Any fool can compare the South Africans to the Nazis, and any fool did (Mr Winnick again). Only occasionally did it seem to touch on the actual predicament caused by the sub-continental provincialism of the Afrikaners.

Apart from an outburst of genuine, unfaked anti-South African passion from Hugh Dykes, a Conservative, who had been and seen and loathed the place, it was a debate in which embattled certainties withstood the onslaught of programmed indignation.

To paraphrase F. E. Smith speaking to a slow-minded judge, one was left none the wiser and very little better informed.

Daily Telegraph, October 24, 1985

Rioting at Broadwater farm estate in Tottenham did nothing for any of us, least of all our legislators.

One feels a bit rotten attacking Winston Churchill. He is an area of acute deprivation and verbal blight deserving understanding in a multi-talented society where everyone is cherished.

But his intervention in the Queen's speech debate was a wilderness, a great *karst* of cliché, which could have been made to advantage by a stone alderman clutching his lapels in Bolton park.

"A stark revelation to the country at large," he proclaimed, "cesspits of lawlessness and deprivation", "it comes ill from the Hon Gentleman opposite ..." "Left-wing activists, day-in-day-out, are undermining the work of the police", "in our modern technological society" and as champion entry, best in show, *we will rue that day*.

If we ever do televise the Commons, Mr Churchill will be the programme equivalent of *Emmerdale Farm!*

However, in the great struggle to turn a dishonest advantage out of the riots, the Labour party now has half a furlong's lead.

The urge among some Tories to think South African, in a genteel way, about the inner cities, requires more brutal resolution than is on view.

Rhetoric may be flourished but *sjamboks* will not be issued to the police. Neither, according to Mr Gerald Kaufman, will much else, like money.

Mr Kaufman, who mingles disdain with detailed grasp to a degree that makes Conservatives long for the services of his own personal crocodile, lingered not on the Government's promises, but its record.

"During the 31 minutes of the Prime Minister's strident speech yesterday, 207 serious offences were committed," he remarked rather boringly.

Without provocation he told us that one burglary was committed every 35 seconds, and an act of criminal violence every $4\frac{1}{2}$ minutes.

As a child one can see the younger Kaufman set loose on encyclopaedias and letting the whole of Leeds know the acreage of land given over to millet in Mauritius or the names of all members of the Slovakian string orchestra.

But he won his debate; Mr Hurd, for the Government, was mild, conciliatory and anxious to deaden the Rhine Maidenish echoes of Mrs Thatcher. But, to invent a barbarous word before the Americans, he was not impactive.

The Government is failing to put its mouth into its pocket, according to Mr Kaufman.

Though whether it is really the case that Treasury cuts among Customs staff have left certain ports coping with the drug problem by putting out honesty boxes for traffickers lacks perfect credibility.

Various attempts were made by the Conservatives to prove their just case by cries of "Bernie Grant".

Indeed, in Conservative hands, "Denounce Bernie Grant" already has the look of those faint, whitewashed signs one sees under bridges, like "Free Tony Ambatielos Now".

Mr Callaghan moved in like the Gas Board to turn off Mr Grant.

Of course policemen should visit schools as much as possible and it was very silly of certain Labour authorities to exclude them. As for Mr Grant, well he'd had a roasting and he clearly had a lot to learn.

He personally represented the oldest coloured community in Britain – the Bute Town district of Cardiff, "used to be called Lascars," he murmured.

There had been a riot in Cardiff in the 1920s, there had been a decline in morality in the country, but Mr Kinnock was "growing in stature".

That's all right then.

Daily Telegraph, November 8, 1985

To listen *seriatim* to speeches by Mr Hattersley, Mr Lawson, Dr Owen and Mr Heath is a Tennysonian and knackering experience. All day long the sound of battle rolls, but really they beat you to your knees.

One is impressed by Dr Owen: 25 minutes exactly, delivered with folded arms and no notes!

But he is into the moral equity of the next election, in which he has a substantial minority holding; gracefully getting us off the low and statistical ground of the Chancellor (scribe and Pharisee rolled into one) and Mr Hattersley (wounded man by the wayside).

Dr Owen is putting his money on the moral square. Disdaining what the *Daily Telegraph* was recurringly quoted for calling "dodgy accounting and electoral cynicism", he suggested that people didn't want to be bribed, an extremist position which has never troubled the Conservative Party.

As for the "budget for jobs", Mr Lawson would find that his own people might well disdain it. Such are the Samaritan economics of the Alliance; moral obligation brought up like artillery to bombard the secure and slightly guilty shires between Uxbridge and Penzance.

They are not to be shrugged off, which, by and large, the remarks of Mr Heath are.

The elder statesman was back on the beat of his *tour d'horizon* anxious that we should subsidise exports on the vast scale of the competition.

How else could we have won the lost Turkish bridge contract? Except that, when he was through, one had this image of the Humber Bridge being built across the Bosphorus and the Polish merchant navy being constructed again (with penalty clauses) entirely from revenue.

He was also anxious that we should sell keenly in China. With what the Chinese will buy from us was not made clear. Funny money is all very well, but there is no need for it to be hilarious.

However, the great burden of the day fell to Mr Lawson. Lawson speeches are as erratic as porkbelly futures and, in their singular devotion to the brute materialism of the City, not unlike them.

For a start he rolled over Mr Hattersley who had been justly sniffish about that dodgy accounting and the exact state of the PSBR.

On rolled the figures like an armoured division in open country: inflation, real take home pay, taxes on employers, growth, costs; all of them satisfactorily up or down according to requirement, none of them contributing anything to the dry well of Mr Lawson's humility.

"It seems," he said to Mr Hattersley, "that the Rt Hon Gentleman has as much trouble listening as he has understanding."

The Lawson and Owen speeches dovetail in a fascinating way precisely because the SDP leader permitted the Chancellor most of his premises about what was going well.

It was also a pleasure to hear a member of an Opposition party being unimpressed by his lachrymose old lordship and suggesting without affection that the Chancellor stood in a great Tory tradition.

The notion of Mr Lawson in apostolic descent from Supermac is painfully credible.

"All this," said the Doctor in magisterial recollection of another sixties politician, "is simply candy floss." The mantle of Harold Wilson descended from heaven.

Daily Telegraph, November 14, 1985

The Anglo-Irish agreement, negotiated with Dr Fitzgerald, marginally involved the constitutional nationalist Catholic government of the Republic with the affairs of its kin in Northern Ireland. Ulstermen proceeded to eat the carpet.

We had *Crescendo* yesterday, but it wasn't exactly Rossini. A Northern Irish Accent and a grievance converge upon one another with all the finesse of the iceberg and the *Titanic*.

So, Mr King, slow of speech, reflexively good-tempered apart from a very understandable degree of huffiness, and in every last particular an Englishman, stood and endured the rage of a different tribe.

The high point was, however, reserved for the Prime Minister, whose Question Time followed immediately after Northern Irish questions.

The Protestants, having become convinced, very credibly one must say, that the Republic is about to be cut in on their affairs, had rumbled on with that incoherent menace which is their speciality.

Mr Enoch Powell is not incoherent, but he is fatally attracted to the actor-manager school of declamatory excess. Did the Prime Minister not know, he asked in his best essay at the manner of Henry Irving (and if she did not, she would very soon find out), that the penalty for treachery was to fall into public contempt?

The mere word "treachery", flat and passive on the printed page, cannot convey what it sounds like in the mouth of a man not so much tearing a passion to tatters as putting it through the shredder.

Hairs stood upon the backs of necks, the House paused silently to see if Mrs Thatcher would shout him down or strike him dead.

Instead, and very wisely, she put everything on dignity. She hoped that he understood that what he had said had been "deeply offensive to her". Ice formed in the air, the rafters creaked and the mace rocked slightly on its stand.

Women are good at putting you in the wrong, except that Enoch was there already, spoiling a good case with personal abuse and the sort of theatricality you can slice and wrap up by the quarter pound.

Not that his muttering colleagues had helped earlier. Some of the Ulster MPs sound disconcertingly like first drafts of Arthur Mullard. Mr Ken Maginnis, for example, bawled out, "Ireland is our enemy."

All of this is very hard upon Mr Molyneaux and Mr McCusker; serious, anxious men preoccupied with a tragedy and suspecting, not very extravagantly, that something shifty may be pulled on them.

As Viscount Cranborne, one of Ulster's English friends, put it: "Had any member of the United States administration been made aware of the terms of the Anglo-Irish treaty?"

Since the answer to that question was "I cannot comment further", Mr Powell, whose hatred of the Americans leaves your average Greenham Common lady looking like a daughter of the American Revolution, will be sticking pins into an image of George Shultz.

Mr Peter Robinson observed that Mr King had not consulted the Ulster Unionists though consultation had apparently been extended to the SDLP (remember them?), the Vatican, the President of the United States, the United Nations and the EEC.

The question he should have asked was whether Sir Robert Armstrong, who is running this show, had consulted Mr King.

But Mr Molyneaux and Mr McCusker are burdened with their shards of colleagues, the hopeless primitives, over-matched in a County Council, whose resentments, even when founded in a shrewd sense of Whitehall/Downing Street duplicity, make onlookers resent *them*.

Daily Telegraph, November 15, 1985

Parliament, fearing the intrusion of the watching elector-
ate, rejected television in the same spirit as it once resisted
newspaper reporting.

Members of Parliament fear that television may trivialise them.
Mr John Stokes, a devoted reactionary who glories in the name
and is probably against the bringing in of railways, thought that
introduction of the thing, as proposed by Janet Fookes, would
change the tone of the place.

Members might be chosen for their photogenic qualities (Mr
Stokes has spent years perfecting the style and address of a
brigadier general retired to Upper Slaughter). Indeed, in some
places the presence of TV had created riots.

Mr Joe Ashton (Lab Bassetlaw), who is very much John
Stokes in steel toe-caps, agreed with him. Television had ruined
everything – football, religion and Arthur Scargill (Mr Scargill
had been turned by television into a cult of the personality).

It had even ruined Mr Ashton's own character; he reminded
us of an earlier debate in which he, the upholder of solid
legislative worth, had clowned about holding large white cards
with rude comments on them.

"And who was asked to come on television that night?" said
Mr Ashton. "Me! And who interviewed me? – Austin Mitchell."

Having deplored the fact that the low fellows from the media
would "turn this place into the chorus from 'Samson and Cle-
opatra'" (a show I must see) he apologised for leaving, but he
had to go and give a television interview.

However no grave and responsible comment on these deliberations would be complete without Mr Edward Heath, who
appears to favour televising the Commons on the grounds that
the rest of the media, led by your correspondent, are unworthy
of the House.

"Look at the correspondent of the *Daily Telegraph* every
day," said Mr Heath lapsing into the Ming dynasty imper-
iousness which has made so many friends.

"His sole purpose is to ridicule what goes on in this House."
Usually I find Hon members to do it for me.

Then we had Enoch Powell (against of course) striking that
note of melodramatic theatricality – half verismo tenor, half
demon king – which is doing nothing for his credibility.

"Destruction of Parliamentary debate", "misrepresentation", "caricature", "falsehood". He also dragged in "the homogeneity of society". Presumably life would be better if it were all white and untelevised.

This is a gross and trivialising caricature, but Mr Powell just does that to you.

We were blessed, however, with excellent speeches – from time to time – though the listener is obliged to hack his way through an undergrowth of neurosis, vanity and plain paranoia which was also on display.

Miss Fookes, introducing the motion, was graceful, sensibly playing out rope to a good dozen interviewers.

"If I'm allowed to get on with it," she said at one stage. "Of course," said Mr Robert Banks, "but before my Hon friend leaves that point ..."

A similar if elder grace marked Mr Foot, who can be the most endearing man in the House. He was also in favour of the devouring lens but lost his way in the century mostly sweetly.

He should do the progressive, up-to-date thing: It was "for us to say in ... *whatever the year is*".... that we would go together, or something like that. Only Mr Foot could mislay the year, but he isn't missing anything.

There was Mr Sean Hughes, who sounds like the sort of young member Labour doesn't quite deserve, quoting from the debate on reporting from the House in 1834.

A Colonel Evans, who could fit into either party today, had stated that the exercise was "in the first place impossible and if it were possible, it was objectionable in the second place".

Reporting had been authorised, said Mr Hughes wryly. Then, by an act of God, in the next year the Commons had burned down.

Daily Telegraph, November 21, 1985

Much of yesterday was spent in picking up the bits of the day before yesterday.

Mr Biffen, that discerning man, was faced with a number of irate questions raised under the device of the House's business session, on the constitutional marmalade which a muddle over a procedural motion had made of last night's division about television.

One member voted and was not counted; another member had allegedly been counted on both sides and, as was repeatedly alleged by the lens freaks, certain timidly ambitious Conservatives of the scampering tendency found themselves in the "aye" lobby only to discover that the Prime Minister was not there to tuck them up. An alleged flight of these free and sturdy spirits from one lobby to the other is said darkly to have seen off the sound boom and the zoom lens.

Mr John Maxton, an amiable Glaswegian given to constructive and civil unreasonableness, pointed out that Scotland had on Wednesday night taken a firm, confident hold on the future, with Scottish MPs voting 47:17 in favour. Could we please have cameras in the Scottish Grand Committee (a definition of aversion therapy if ever there was one)?

Mr Biffen outraged the legions of broken glass, tartan patriotism (and half of Fleet Street) by murmuring, "How can I be sure that English money won't be spent on televising Scots politicians?"

Mr Maxwell-Hyslop, who has a gift for inadvertent unmalicious absurdity, proposed in his scrupulous, pedantic, agreeably loopy way, that the problems of successive divisions which had confused voters on Wednesday could be put right by a sort of traffic light system *inside* the lobby.

The meat of the afternoon was given over to asking Mr Biffen questions. He functioned yesterday both as acting Prime Minister for her questions and authentic Lord Privy Seal for his own.

It was instructive to hear his reply to the upbeat enthusiasm about Geneva of Mrs Virginia Bottomley, a nice lady with just a touch of the Angela Brazil heroine about her. Mrs Bottomley, though stopping short of the word, thought that what Mr Reagan and Mr Gorbachev had pulled off was super.

Mr Biffen, who has lifted humane agnosticism to a new plane, expressed "a sense of relief" that the two men had survived the hazards of "high profile activity" without harm, adding that Mrs Bottomley had put the matter in a way which would appeal to the whole House. In other words: "We are all delighted that

Virginia is showing so much healthy enthusiasm for the school operatic society."

Mr Kinnock, civil but unexcited by the fundamentally dubious reconciliation of Holmes and Moriarty so oddly close to the Reichenbach Falls, moved crisply back to Wednesday's vote to keep a firm hold on the nineteenth century. He congratulated Mr Biffen as a fellow supporter of the cameras.

Mr Biffen had described the decision as the most important in its way since Disraeli's 1867 Reform Act – that "leap in the dark". It was, said Mr Kinnock, in that evangelising way of his, "a leap into the light".

"There is nobody," said Mr Biffen obscurely, "with whom I would prefer to share a disappointment" but we would be waiting for the light for a long time yet.

Daily Telegraph, November 22, 1985

"It is too late to save your soul with bunting," said Mr John Hume of Foyle (SDLP), quoting from Louis MacNeice. It was a memorable speech, if a little buoyed by uplift.

It was perhaps a mistake by Mr Hume, overlooking the Speaker at the end of his fervant declamation, to turn to the Unionists and say, "I will sit down and talk with you people any time," and then when Mr Ivan Lawrence asked him a question to say no, he couldn't deal with that at the moment.

Mr Hume is much regarded on the Labour benches and has a steady following among the Alliance and the more relaxed Tories. He is a nice man and a political moderate but with a touch of Celtic vividness which either cheers us up or marks off the barbarism with a black-edged effectiveness.

"The IRA," said he, "condemn Diplock courts and run kangaroo courts, they condemn unemployment and blow up factories, they complain about investment reductions and have just blown up two millions worth of investment in my constituency."

It was admirably put, entirely for the angels and ever so slightly like Neil Kinnock.

Mr Kinnock, speaking earlier, had been very moving and impressive but like Mr Gow, the resignation boy, he had demonstrated that 15 minutes has all the angles over 20 minutes.

In Mr Kinnock's case he spoke with quiet, insistent seriousness, aiming most of his remarks, remarkably in a Labour leader, at the assuasion of the Unionists.

It was good by reason of being different but it was pretty good anyway ... and then out of pure locomotive apathy he went into a party political routine about the Government, unemployment and, for all I know, "deep underlying causes".

Attention wilted like chicken fat in a micro-wave and a speech which had been registering in a silent house was disconnected.

The case of Mr Gow inspires two schools of thought: radical colleagues caught in the corridors were inclined to make retching noises as if they had been sipping maple syrup laced with paraquat; they also made un-Christian allusions to Uriah Heep.

But for most of the time it was actually rather good, making the valid point that the representative of the Republic at the standing conference would be seen as the protector of the Catholics.

He also had a rather injurious quotation from Mrs Thatcher speaking to Unionists in Belfast about "our two parties" and "never doing anything which will result in weakening the Union".

But a good speech which did for the Ulstermen what most of them lack the bland facility to do for themselves came hideously to a sticky end when he switched to his own role as resigning minister (it is Hell, I tell you Witherspoon, Hell) and to his continuing devotion to Mrs Thatcher.

He spoke of her as moonstruck subalterns were wont to speak of General Wolsey but this was moderation's second self compared with the golden syrup of his account of Mr Ian Gow. They should know that his heart "and it's a pretty big heart" was behind, hoping for the best.

"Half a mile more," said Dr Johnson of Thomas Gray, "and all had been marsh." Mr Gow will not be the last Englishman concerned with Ireland to be lost in a bog, but a bog of his own construction!

Mrs Thatcher herself eschewed the *Ecole des Larmes* of her television performance for what desperate men in search of a story call "a low key performance". There was nothing wrong with it and, probably on purpose, nothing very exciting about it either.

Mr Hume's scarlets and ochres, Mr Kinnock's tempered

144

excess and the shades of black favoured by Mr James Molyneaux were all avoided by Mrs Thatcher for a Civil Service general issue landscape of dun-brown cliché.

"The tide of violence", "darkened by the shadow of the gunman", they had "paid the price with their own lives" – actual awfulness of the kind that is taken away by policemen in canvas bags was represented by the executive banalities of people in office.

Her robotic account met, interestingly, with the devout support of Mr James Prior, former Ulster Minister and former Cabinet antagonist. He was ardently for "doing something", the prerogative of the hamster down the ages.

"There is no other way," said Mr Prior, a phrase which sounds faintly familiar.

Daily Telegraph, November 27, 1985

The episode of Westland helicopters was to transform British politics, leaving Mrs Thatcher, despite a subsequent recovery, not only weakened but disbelieved.

Not often does one agree with Mr Dave Nellist, that pale-featured Ice Axeman.

But, when he suggested in the middle of Mrs Thatcher's drab and unconvincing narrative that it would have been a good idea to have adopted a true socialist solution for the workers of Westland by nationalising the company, he must have enjoyed the secret empathy of the entire government. For a few miserable millions and a couple of civil servants on the board, they must have thought, there would have been:—

No Euro-furore ... no letter from Sir Austin Pearce ... no assurances that Mr Brittan was telling the truth; while the soft-voiced, wild-eyed patriot newly below the gangway would still be under restraint in a half-lit room under the sedation of high office.

As it was, the Government of Margaret Thatcher had to listen to a man, once defined as a bundle of liberal opinions housed within a fascist personality, talking with the quiet conviction and soft menace of a mid-afternoon strangler.

Mr Heseltine had new cards to put down, and with each of

them he won a gasp, not wholly simulated, from the Opposition benches.

The minute of the meeting which has not been recorded but which he was convinced could be found in the civil servants' note book from which minutes are constructed ... the instruction by the Foreign Office, through its Rome Embassy, to discourage Italian participation in the European consortium ... The instructions sent out from the authorities to prevent him from taking part in a broadcast.... None of these charges was quite calculated to make Mrs Thatcher look like the Angel of the Constitution.

All this came with the gift-wrapped knowledge of Mr Brittan's quite bottomless trouble over his conversation with Sir Raymond Lygo and the improbability of his version of events being correct.

Poor Mr Brittan barely featured yesterday: even at his own question time, which fortuitously fell just before the debate, he hardly answered a question, ferrying the work out to deputies instead.

In Mrs Thatcher's defence of the record Mr Brittan hardly appeared; the prospect that she might float off the rocks on his blood is not discounted.*

Poor Mr Brittan, who has attracted so much irrational hatred, is deemed to have exercised a lawyer's understanding of the truth in over-zealous service of his client.

The House was full of the feeling that, while the defendant's future was problematic, her attorney would undoubtedly go to the chair; if Mr Brittan had been a girl, he would have been named "Infelicity".

Mr Kinnock alone stuck to the Brittan issue. At the risk of seeming to push shares in the company, yesterday's performance suggests that recently detected upside potential in Kinnock is beginning to be realised.

His definition of Mrs Thatcher's style – "rule by over-rule" – deserves to stick. But his strength lay in *Litotes,* as we gents call understatement.

He did not rant on about resignation but wondered gravely how Mr Brittan could now bring himself to stay; and then wondered again whether the Trade Minister was culprit or

* She did.

146

victim, acting for himself or as agent?

At which he requested the Prime Minister to answer please and to the horror of the Tories sat down.

Mrs Thatcher by contrast went with a peculiarly drab authoritativeness through a list of dates and meetings, relying throughout on a sort of phantom mastery, as if rattled-off figures and remarks such as "No meeting was agreed to, therefore really there was none to cancel" were really convincing.

Not for the first time, listeners felt that a much happier time would have been had by a Government which had readily acknowledged a modest if irregular preference for Sikorsky.

Daily Telegraph, January 16, 1986

As a senior Tory put it afterwards: "It's all right for a novice MP to make a mistake like that but it doesn't look good if you're standing there in an 800 guinea suit."

For once in recent days Mr Heseltine had blundered and quite badly. He has this habit of rising to his full 14 feet while Labour fall as silent as a County Mayo congregation at the elevation of the Host.

He then murmurs something in a voice, softened beyond Sir Gordon Reece's dreams for the Prime Minister, a member of the Government collapses and Labour go off like Millwall F.C. Supporters Club.

So it had been until yesterday when Mr Heseltine gave a passable imitation of a matinée idol falling over the footlights.

Mr Brittan had made an allusion last night to a document. It was mentioned in column 1167 of Hansard. Was it in order for him to add a few words?

Now, in this place, as any PPS knows, the term "Is it in order?" is addressed to the Speaker, relates to Parliamentary orders, and can only be answered by him. Gratefully, Mrs Thatcher explained as much.

Labour were naturally heartbroken.

At the end of Prime Minister's Question Time they fell upon the Speaker's head demanding an answer even though time was out.

So did Mr Heseltine, pleading with a humility worthy of Nigel Lawson – "My relative inexperience of the back-benches."

147

It was relevant. It was urgent. It related to events now taking place which would be influenced by the reply (there is a good deal of the MGM trailer from old-style Hollywood about Mr Heseltine's sense of theatre).

It could be all of these things but, as backbenchers could have told Mr Heseltine if he had ever spoken to one, it was out of time and order.

But there he stood with the soft insistence of people who ultimately become intolerable, that an exception should be made for *him*.

Meanwhile, of course, Labour kept up its Neapolitan riot, absolutely sensibly from their point of view.

Mrs Thatcher finally responded by observing that if the famous remark in column 1167 was a quotation from a document the *whole* document would have to be disclosed of course (that is the rule round here). But was it? Could somebody please check?

After a few more special effects, including a compassionate plea from Mr Kinnock about the Speaker's "invidious position" – a case of demanding favour with menaces – the stately figure of Mr Cranley Onslow, chairman of the 1922 Committee and trainee life peer, rose in his place at the back.

Though only, in his Army days, a lieutenant in the 7th Hussars, Mr Onslow is one of nature's colonels, the sort who in a few brisk, verb-only sentences would put uppish chappies in their place.

As indeed he did. "Had read the section of Hansard. Doesn't mention documents." Since the entire Heseltine enterprise for the afternoon – right for disclosure of the document, "sinister implications, national importance, Mr Speaker" – turned upon this fixed regular rule that a document *quoted from* must be revealed while one *alluded to* lies, then happily on the shelf it lies. Stout parties collapsed on all sides.

Daily Telegraph, January 17, 1986

"A genuine misunderstanding between officials." That is Mrs Thatcher's story and she is sticking to it. Even the massed ranks of the Tories, ready to be loyal along Busby Berkeley lines of choreography, coughed unhappily over that one.

In the fullest account so far (and on this one we move in progressions) Mrs Thatcher left her backbenchers waving order papers through clenched teeth.

At its heart lay the Crown Jewels twinkling meretriciously behind the electrified grille. Mr Brittan had not "sought my agreement. I was not asked to give my authority and did not do so."

It was Dr Owen who took this line of argument to Sketchley's (which was just as well for the critics, Mr Kinnock having stumbled into a shouting match with what sounded like a hunt ball breaking up).

He had not helped himself either by a Freudian allusion to "the bid for Heseltine" when he meant "Westland".

Dr Owen took on the Tory claque with the sort of glacial indifference which would have quelled a rising in the Punjab with a glance. He also came to the point.

There were two and a half days between knowing about the Solicitor-General contemplating sending a letter and the near-instant leaking of it.

Had we really had Saturday, Sunday and Monday morning down to 1.30 without some conversations between her Mr Ingham and her Mr Powell? What were they please and how much did *she* know?

Here Dr Owen drew upon his own ministerial experience to point out that the Principal Private Secretary, Mr Powell (in the know) and the Prime Minister (not in the know) sit as close to one another in the same large office, as Dr Owen just below the gangway and Mr Speaker!

As for the other conversation which didn't take place – the one between Leon Brittan (guilty as hell, done the honourable thing) and the Prime Minister (nobody told her, been a bit sloppy) – Dr Owen made as clear as refrigerated civility permits that its non-existence was much more doubtful than God's.

Much of the Government case rests upon promoting the Prime Minister, in terms of the well-known typing pool advertisement as "sloppy girl" rather than "Brook St girl". Nobody has ever done that before and neither Opposition has any intention of starting now.

The questions remained unanswered, as they did for John Smith summing up at the end. For Mrs Thatcher's own speech had been an odd mixture of party conference percussion – random gruesome rhetoric like "not diverted from our task", and "bring power back to the people" (the people already!) – and on the other hand the message that this was her story and she was sticking to it.

"She was not told by Leon Brittan about the letter-leaking and she didn't ask him." That is the party's correct line and everyone, led by Mr Heseltine and Mr Brittan, whose intervention sounded as sad and loyal as anything said by Kamenev or Bukharin at their trials, is rallying to it.

Mr Heseltine made in capsule form one of those conference speeches which cause people to throw up behind the pillars at Bournemouth or Blackpool.

Mr Biffen, summing up, unwisely attempted a military metaphor. This was not Dunkirk, it was El Alamein. Actually it was more like Chalgrove Field in the English Civil War, a drawn skirmish.

Daily Telegraph, January 28, 1986

An attempt was made shortly after the Westland affair to sell two British motor firms to American companies. They were not well received and, close to panic, the Government retreated.

Reeling, you might call it as the hapless Paul Channon tried to defend the knocking-down of the motor industry to the Americans.

Now any contest involving Mr John Smith is liable to be unequal unless Mr Tebbit can be brought along in his dressing gown; and any contest involving Mr Channon, who has the style of a 50-year-old prep school boy, is, in a very different way, unequal.

The impression of this column is that the Government is in a fix and that the blues of retreat may be sounding before long. It is a very wide Tory goalmouth which Edward Heath manages to shoot into, but he did.

He burbled on, admittedly about European consortia and when he was minister of something or other. He also had effect; Ford sent their profits home, GM were notorious low users of local components, but wasn't it interesting that Leyland happened to have advanced robotics and truck technology. So why sell that?

The limp Mr Channon was unsupported by a single Cabinet colleague and subjected to cracks from the Tory benches about assurances not being worth a bag of chips. But no one wanted to be too unkind; it is like cruelty to a sandbag.

Interestingly, Mr Brittan, who presumably started this affair, was conspicuously absent from the Chamber, hanging on another gallows somewhere else no doubt.

Mr Smith is not cruel. He simply had in this debate the manifest destiny of a circular saw facing up to an upholstered toy. It was the sort of speech which Neil Kinnock should have made in the Westland debate – low-key, courteous, factual and murderous.

The thought occurs after Mr Smith's general performance in both crises, using his talents as financial expert and unpuffed, rational Scots Advocate, that he has effectively made himself the No 2 man in the Labour party. He was superb.

Desperate attempts had been made by the Tory Whips to push this debate down-column. Water was privatised by Mr Baker at twenty-to-four, and in the interest of ethnic balance and time-wasting Mr Edwards did as much for the Welsh for another three-quarters of an hour.

By such devices, observed Mr Smith, does one keep off the five o'clock news. But as Louis MacNeice once pungently observed:

> *You can break the bloody glass*
> *But you won't hold up the weather.*

Assisted from time to time by Mr Beaumont-Dark, who is taking on rather a Whip-resigning style, Mr Smith coolly examined General Motors' and Ford's rational self-interest.

Unlike Mr Heath, who judders at the name of Yank, he made credible protests of not being anti-American. "I am not denigrating General Motors. I am denigrating this Government."

GM had been known to be cruising, he observed, without success in West Germany or Spain and without giving a thought to castellated France. But they had finally come to light upon "the soft touch of Western Europe".

151

It made very good sense for them, eliminating useful competition, acquiring its capacity and markets and getting access to splendid plant.

He had a good deal to say about the effect on unemployment but said it quietly for effect, quoting from a component manufacturer who had written to him about the certain zero future which that firm would face. It was an unshoutdownable speech even if Mr Wakeham's militia had been in the mood to try shouting.

He got on to electronics and steel and the way they were inter-related with the motor industry. He stressed the 7:1 ratio of component to direct employment. To the approval of Mr Ken Cure of the AEUW in an upstairs gallery, he ran through the extent of recovery and change in working practice.

Also he had a horrible quotation from Sir Michael Edwardes, chief puller-round and re-assembler of BL in the days when Sir Keith Joseph and Mr Tebbit were spending all that taxpayers' money.

If the firm were sold, Sir Michael had written, it would become an off-shore assembly plant *and not even an extreme Right-wing Tory Government would stand for that*. Sir Michael has graduated in Labour circles from child-swallowing, South African Monster to wise old bird.

It was one of those debates in which one sees a Government lose its way, perhaps for ever.

Daily Telegraph, February 6, 1986

Collapse of stout policy. The Lady, it seems, is for turning after all.

Mr Channon, upon whom we must not be too hard – he is after all only a modality, a means of doing something – announced that "it was essential to end uncertainty and speculative interest in the matter of Austin-Rover and Ford".

This is Latin for saying that they were getting the hell out of the deal before the West Midlands collapsed underneath them.

It is a very odd state of affairs when, on successive days, first Mr Edward Heath and then Mr Dave Nellist makes a pertinent point.

It is not necessary to be a Trot, an ice-picker or to tend in

152

any particular direction to take Mr Nellist's point that "this Government is behaving like a headless chicken rushing around in its death throes".

Mr Roger King also had a nice point when, to general amusement including his own, he offered the heartfelt thanks of the workers of Birmingham.

Since Mr King represents Northfield which is preponderantly populated by the enfranchised workers of BL, their friends, relations, and shop-keepers to the point where it is lucky not to be called a *community*, the thanks of Mr King, sustained by a modest majority, were pretty heartfelt as well.

Not that everyone was falling about in delight. John Mark Taylor, who has Land-Rover to worry about in Solihull, was hotly interrogative and, as for Mr Heath, it was back to the basilisk (to the extent that he ever moved).

Nothing had been done to alleviate fears about the General Motors deal and the prospect of control going to Detroit.

Sir Kenneth Lewis, whose steady sniping despite a knighthood goes to prove everything that Machiavelli said about the advantage of expectation over gratitude, also intervened.

Might he congratulate his Rt Hon friend ... on his speedy footwork.

Mr John Smith, who works hard on being a progressive version of one of those Scottish judges who would tell the prisoner that he would be "none the worse for a hanging", not unnaturally took the credit for Labour.

Since this episode has turned out less like El Alamein (see Mr Biffen *passim* last week) than an uneasy combination of Dunkirk and Singapore with Hastings pending, Opposition pleasure was in order.

Mr Channon tried, ingeniously, to blame the Labour party which as the original rescuer/nationaliser of BL in the mid-seventies took this rather badly. The ever-better Mr Rooker showing signs of spontaneous combustion.

It was one of those days when a minister gets rid of 60 per cent of his trouble by simply giving in.

Daily Telegraph, February 7, 1986

Only Mr Barry Sheerman could have lit up a Monday afternoon

for Labour with a reference to 1985 being International Youth Year and drawing our attention to the importance of the Wolverhampton youth model.

But then Mr Sheerman was no more than a Gola League performer by comparison with Mr Alan Haselhurst, who was on a balloted motion and addressed the house on youth-training and education.

Mr Haselhurst is waiting for the natural captaincy of the team we send to Mexico for the World Boring Championships: he can do things with youth training which make comparative traffic jams, greens-I-have-three-putted and Whither Portugal? seem rather crude.

For a start he can speak in acronyms, hopping lightly to and from the CPV, the CVLP, and the TVLP with as much facility as the original bog-trotter moving from tuft to tuft within an Irish marsh.

His intentions are, of course, of the highest, but the language is a sort of coagulating miasma, marked but not lit by metaphors of a heavy and improving sort.

"He may run," he said with more optimism than effect, "along separate channels. But we must take care that they do not become tunnels." Yes indeed, what man of goodwill could be against that?

Indeed, all of Mr Haselhurst's exertions seem to be a test of character for the gallery, urging us not to shoot this tethered game fowl and, as it were, to become a better person.

No such luck. A man who launches on to "modular systems" or "vocationally-oriented" is running out of charity, and round here we run a quota on that as it is.

He gave a wonderful illustration of the euphemism which Orwell in a celebrated essay ("liquidation of undesirable elements" was his favourite) could not have bettered.

Proposing some scheme or other, Mr Haselhurst announced that it had "resource implications".

Consider that phrase, run it over the palate like a single malt, try it on the more discerning neighbours. What the man meant was that it would cost money.

There is nothing wrong with that – advocates of liberal causes should be able to say "it costs money and it's right" – but not Mr Haselhurst, he behaves like a Minister without being one.

Under the fast patter about modular systems and what my fallible notebook has as youth services being "an uncoordinated Cinderella" (poor girl), there ran a through bass of aldermanic heaviness, prose Brahms like "I am emboldened to make this remark" and "there must be parity of esteem", an expression which I thought had gone out with Attlee's first administration.

It was quite apparent that Radio Haselhurst had been seized by guerillas from the Jargon Liberation Front, the *Jargonistas*.

We must get him a knighthood.

Daily Telegraph, February 11, 1986

Gibberish from the governing (and opposing) classes is always welcome on a Tuesday afternoon.

Mrs Thatcher in her best duchess-opening-sale-of-work-manner might have carried all before her yesterday but for the little slip of the tongue which proclaimed to Mr Rees, in a slightly Irishman-in-the-pub-way, that she had seen off two Labour Governments and she was ready to see off the next one.

Not that she had incoherence to herself. Lovers of bipartisanship in the field of creative infelicity would have enjoyed Mr Kinnock's remark that the Prime Minister was "too old to stay, too old to go".

This was a contribution to advanced research in the field of meaninglessness which may be worth its own Nobel prize if Graham Greene, the Barbara Cartland of the devotional detective story, is to win the Order of Merit.

For what it was worth, Mrs Thatcher had the best of the 15-minute session, though in the hot house atmosphere of planted questions and slogan-shouting the garland is made up of half-hour orchids.

Half sale of work, half pep talk in the last bunker, her remarks were greeted with Mr Wakeman's chorus line of instant approval and, interestingly, by its mock opposite, Labour members encouraged, by Mr Derek Foster perhaps, not to boo the lady but, distressingly, to cheer her.

The last of my illusions has been exploded. The Labour party has taken up irony!

Inadvertence rather than irony governs Mr John Prescott, a much underrated politician, with a great command of detail but a tendency to drive through traffic lights pursued by hopeful ambulances.

Particularly liked was his allusion to Cambridge University and its "Department of Implied Economics".

Equally it would have been flattering to have coined his reference to "chief executives and their golden handcuffs" but I don't have that sort of flair.

None of which suggests we should take Mr Prescott lightly. Matched with scrapper Ken Clarke, he kept up a stream of technically informed vituperative scorn on the topic of the Wages Bill.

If he could be dissuaded from saying "They gainfully gain by that act" and lingering over "the decency threshold", which I had supposed to be about three inches above the knee, he would have been exceptionally formidable.

For Mr Clarke was doing down the workers in his sly way, not least by the abolition of the Truck Acts.

It had better be explained, before observers of what British Leyland workers are inclined to call the Midland Clearances have visions of contemporary Tommy shops like the Newport Pagnell Service Station providing 50 per cent of wages in kind, that Mr Clarke was only trying to arrange for payment by cheque.

He sounded rather shrewd when he suggested that wages councils were being slashed back largely to allow modestly paid women to be replaced in protected jobs by "YTS kids earning even less".

Since the women weren't on the unemployment register and the youngsters were, Mr Prescott, who has a nice line in low motives, had a notion of what was going on.

It was a good deal more credible than Mr Clarke's patter that all was for the progressive cost-effective best and that the unions only hung on to wages councils for comfort like Linus's blanket.

But how do we persuade Mr Prescott to say it all quietly?

Daily Telegraph, February 12, 1986

There is something very soothing about the absence of the Ulster Unionist members. The sullen and unbountiful countenances of resentful men from Lurgan and Larne were not to be seen in

156

their usual places and contortions.

This, in the circumstances of a well-advertised private notice question from Mr Archer about the loyal and patriotic practice of burning policemen out of their homes, seemed odd.

However, there were Englishmen enough (of the old and peculiar Lord Randolph Churchill/F.E. Smith persuasion), willing to be disagreeable on their behalf.

Mr Ivor Stanbrook, a lean, peremptory, umbrella-shaped man with the personality of citric acid, informed us that every responsible person condemned violence, "So let us not waste any more time on that".

Mr Stanbrook, like Sir John Biggs-Davison and Mr Ian Gow, was anxious not to be detained with the trifling inconvenience of arson and riot.

If decent Ulstermen feel the need to try to kill their policemen, clearly they have been grossly provoked by those trafficking in civilities with the black midnight forces represented by Dr Fitzgerald.

Enoch Powell, a man hideously shrivelled in recent years by the petty province which confines him, turned snarling upon the Prime Minister and Mr King.

They should remember that they were told in advance of the disastrous consequences of the Anglo-Irish agreement. "What shall be done to the evil counsellors to whom they listened?"

Now who is into evil according to Enoch's astigmatic soul – Mr Hurd? The Foreign Office? George Shultz? The Chief Rabbi?

The barking lunatic quality of the Tory Unionists is not to be distinguished in the Chamber from the barking lunatic quality of the Six Counties Unionists who were missing from it.

But missing to what end? Were they sulking? or were sensible men like Mr Molyneaux simply depriving themselves of the obligation to say anything at all for fear that the mob back home would be affronted by the least deviation into good manners?

According to Mr John Hume for the constitutional Catholics there could be less creditable reasons. "Some honourable members (I call them that because I am supposed to) may be engaged in *organising* the violence."

Cries of "Name them" were succinctly met by other cries (not from Mr Hume) of "Robinson", an illusion to Peter Robinson

(W. Belfast), a man often seen as making Ian Paisley look like Terry Waite.

The beauty of Ulster politics is that it keeps the British from getting too complacent about civilisation. Charges that, say, Mr Anthony Beaumont-Dark is organising riots in Bournville or that Critchley is planning to raise the Hampshire mob would lack conviction.

The opinions of moderate men were not helped by the obviousness of what they had to say – that stoning and burning people is not a nice thing to do.

A lame decency is the most that can be summoned up on behalf of the self-evident unless you have Abraham Lincoln around; and Tom King's kindest regarders do not quite see him in that light. The feeling is rather that, since we are always going to fail in the Six Counties, Mr King can be counted on to fail inconspicuously.

Mr Dykes, trying to come to his aid with an attack on Mr Powell, made a point which even this column found a touch arcane and allusive. Looking around for something rude to say to Mr Powell, Mr Dykes stopped the House dead in its tracks by condemning "the Jacques Soustelle of County Down".

To your average dyslexic politician for whom history began in 1974 and abroad is a long way off, the perverse intellectual who took the French Colonialists on to the streets of Algiers in 1958 could have been a skirt designer. Mr Dykes, who is a bit more *communautaire* than the rest of us, was pushing his luck with all this foreign muck.

That however was the only sweet moment of the afternoon. Otherwise one was taken only with the sour meanmindedness of the Tory Unionists, either refusing to speak against the violence, shrugging it off like Mr Stanbrook, or, like the oil-fired Mr Gow, with such unction as to turn the stomach and to send Mrs Thatcher out of the chamber.

Daily Telegraph, April 9, 1986

158

In a heroic moment, US bombers, based in Britain, bombed the palace of Colonel Gaddafi and missed.

With Mr Callaghan being elder and wiser, Mr Heath heavily reminiscent, Mrs Thatcher hard at her "what-Winston-would-have-done" act and Mr Kinnock being quite sensible, yesterday was a bruising and emotionally overdrawn day. Human kind can only take so much tremendousness.

When Mrs Thatcher gets into terrorism "sapping the will of civilisation" or Mr Heath tells us "that what Churchill said to me at dinner" or Mr Benn recalls that "when I was a little boy I was taken to see Gandhi", life grew as nostalgic as it was histrionic.

The real burden of the afternoon turned upon the utility of the Tripoli raid and Mr Kinnock, who is confined to this generation, rather creditably set about arguing, not that it was immoral or would have been denounced by Nye Bevan, but that it probably wouldn't work and might make things worse.

Incidentally, the Tory backbenchers, who have at times a distinct whiff of Leeds United, will have to find subtler ways of dealing with the Leader of the Opposition than trying to shout him down.

The tactics of the Westland debate – pettyfogging interruptions and massed choirs of derisive public school laughter at every third inflection – almost threw Mr Kinnock at an early stage.

But he battled through, saving his own laser-guided nasty cracks for the end.

These terms, "replacing solidarity with subservience", and "forsaking the role of candid ally for that of compliant accomplice", were nicely calculated to curdle the marmalade on patriotic toast all over residential desirable England.

The New Neil is pre-empting elder statesmanship. Though naturally the rougher sort of Tory interprets this as the old Labour belief that God would not have given us two hands if he hadn't intended us to wring them.

Mrs Thatcher, while being her solid competent self, rested rather heavily on her reputation for striving. It was a question of "terrorism thrives on appeasement" and, thrillingly, "the time had come for action".

She made the very fair point that much moderate Arab indignation was indeed moderate indignation – made with one eye shut and the other one winking.

Equally, few would contest her evident view of the Security Council as having the force and resilience of a piece of knitting. However, the prospect of Britain receiving special attention from unexpunged and ubiquitous terrorists flawed her argument like a hang nail.

Mr Callaghan, despite a touch of ex-Prime Minister's complaint, got sharply to the point: "You can kill Gaddafi. You can't get rid of terrorism."

He took apart American foreign policy.

Ex-Prime Ministers have their uses then, though one hesitates to be so enthusiastic about Mr Heath.

He also warned us of the dangers of another Suez, which, coming from the Chief Whip who maintained discipline in the dear dead days of putting out forest fires, seemed a bit rich.

Still it set one thinking of the received standard form of prayer used after that little episode trickled into the sand – "our mission has been completed" – forty miles short of the canal.

Mrs Thatcher and Mr Reagan have their faults but one wished them a better curtain line than that:

Daily Telegraph, April 17, 1986

Lawrence Durrell's Turkish friend Sabri observes somewhere: "To argue with a woman is Calvary – Golgotha!"

Those who are professionally employed to argue with Mrs Thatcher, a form of employment calling for asbestos suits, danger money and double time, know the feeling.

The Thatcher style, since Libya, has been variable: at first exultant, then as cagey as a man asking for his solicitor and the Fifth Amendment.

Latterly, with the red roses from Congressmen on the mantelpiece and the Congressional Medal of Honour surely on its way, she has grown chipper again, looking about for people to knock down.

It was thus inconsiderate of Mr Tam Dalyell to ask, in the grave, courteous manner of one in happy receipt of unsolicited information, at what point "the Prime Minister had been told of the use of anti-personnel weapons like cluster bombs in the raid".

Mrs Thatcher, who has a way of coining phrases better left at the mint, proclaimed at her stoutest and staunchest that after criteria had been selected it was "for the Americans to choose the weapons ..."

Her speech dissolved into a row of printer's dots for the excellent reason that it also dissolved into an aureole of oohs, aahs, and general issue shock horror noises from the Labour benches.

The notion of permitting President Reagan or Three Star Air Force General Weisenheimer a benign discretion in his choice of hardware has the wrong ring to it.

Somehow one has the feeling that "it is for the Americans to choose the weapons" could be doing duty with "the pound in your pocket", "at a stroke", and "crisis, what crisis?".

We know what she means. It is both true and inevitable. But the words are a little too candid ever to do her good.

Not that the truculence and desire to nail up the Opposition was diminished. Asked by Mrs Margaret Beckett if she did not think that "an eye for an eye" was an unsound basis for foreign policy, she replied in that heroic tenor she uses for issues of National Importance that the "only basis for policy was British interest".

Once again the sentiments, if banal, are unexceptionable. But Labour, who have taken to attending Parliament again, fell noisily apart laughing.

Mrs Thatcher came close to a personal Golgotha later in the afternoon while Mr Hurd was dealing with the expulsion, few and late, of those Libyans now suddenly regarded with dubiety.

Into the dispassionate and refrigerated environment favoured by the Home Secretary burst Mr Nicholas Winterton, a man who is to the Parliamentary landscape what a multi-storey car park would be to Ludlow.

Mercilessly he imposed his insignia of approbation on Mrs Thatcher. The Opposition's points had been "pathethic utterances", needed to learn the lessons of the 1930s, didn't we?

The accumulated wisdom of the Road Hauliers Arms flowed on to and over Mrs Thatcher's prone and luckless person.

"She was," he added, "one of the most stalwart defenders of *civilisation*".

We have been mildly critical of Mrs Thatcher on occasions at this address, but she deserves better than that.

Actually there were worse contributions to come. Terry Dicks, a man who leaves Winterton sounding like Vico, lurched to his feet and demanded, "Why have we not deported all Libyans?"

The little matter of there being some Libyans here who detest the good colonel and have been promised the gallows on return was not allowed to spoil Mr Dicks's style.

Anyway, why should it? He has two interests in life – deporting people and hanging them!

Daily Telegraph, April 23, 1986

The King of Spain paid a State visit and spoke to Parliament with the embarrassing good manners and restraint which distinguishes foreign eminences from our own.

The Royal Gallery, which accommodated the address of the King of Spain to Parliament, is not a room you would ideally want the neighbours in.

Altogether a glitzy, late-Victorian affair dripping with gilt and hand-carved all over the place to no very good purpose, it is adorned with violently undistinguished paintings of monarchs and a half-acre battle picture of the death of Lord Nelson at Trafalgar.

The irony is that here was the King of Spain, heir to splendid Castilian excess – inquisitions, *caudillos*, Spanish protocol, bulls in epaulets, policemen in patent leather hats and political power, and all the rest of that dreamy far away grandeur.

And what did he turn out to be – a nice democratic politician in a dark suit expressing impeccably liberal sentiments for all the world as if he were the Danish Foreign Minister.

It was a rotten day for romantics. Indeed the King looked faintly embarrassed, as well he might, at having to perform downstage on a chorus line of five elderly warrant officers got up to look like something out of *The Yeomen of the Guard*.

The once democratic British, clutching their economy about

162

them like a see-through skirt, are now so hopelessly into antique showbiz that they don't know where to stop.

We had a fanfare of trumpets. We had old, old irremovable Hailsham processing down the aisle in his *Iolanthe* costume and Mr Weatherill, the Speaker, also introduced with ceremony but managing in his full-bottomed wig to look more like a swinging, than a hanging, judge.

After all this flummery, on comes this Danish social democrat in the dark suit and chats about reconciliation and the EEC.

The proceedings had been opened by Lord Hailsham in a voice menacingly firm. The King, however, had a surprise for us. He said various pleasant affable Euro-blandishments and, being a pleasant, unpompous man, said them with more effect than is usual.

"On Gibraltar," said the Danish Minister, "there has been a step forward there but we have a long way to go." He looked forward to "the disappearance of the only problem that separates us".

This came shortly after he had praised the British for "their noble, sincere, participation" in helping Spain into the EEC (I always thought we were trying to give the French a poke in the eye).

But this lad is subtle with it. He got from Ferdinand and Isabella to laser beam technology without showing effort *and* put in a plug for getting Gibraltar back.

He began and ended to spontaneous applause (35 seconds at the end by my watch), not the response they would be handing out to certain heads of state.

It was such a pleasant occasion, despite the British flapdoodle, laid on, one supposes, by the Tourist Board, that the King must have gone home with hopes and possibilities.

Having been nice to us, having got himself praised (rightly) as "the guarantor of Spanish democracy", the man who helped deliver a liberal Spanish constitution, and a monarchy which makes ours look like the Ming in an uppity mood, he just might get a piece of the Gibraltar equity to take back to Denmark.

Daily Telegraph, April 24, 1986

Humour is not a Conservative strength. Not that anything is

very much these days as the Tories withdrew the sale of British Leyland.

But humour of the voluntary kind was attempted by Mr Robert Atkins, a sort of deep-thinking Geoffrey Dickens. "Why aren't you wearing a grey jacket?" he bawled in his imitation minor public school voice at Mr Kinnock.

This is an allusion to the Labour Party's new brochure which has slipped out of the customary street corner scarlet into something dove grey and seductive for the evening.

Jokes from Mr Atkins suggest that quality control through the medium of a Board of Hilarity may become necessary. Too many of them sound like flowers laid on Mrs Thatcher's grave.

Speaking of which, the Trade Secretary, Paul Channon, spent a melancholy time informing the House of the Government's determination to place its own plans for the sale of Land-Rover on the mortuary shelf.

Now let us not be unkind about Mr Channon. He is merely the boy with the telegram from Suzie breaking off her engagement, who tends in heated moments to get thrown down three flights of stairs.

Similarly, it is an act of supererogation to praise John Smith on this issue. He has been issuing subdued and magisterial Scottish thunder for some time now, like Lord Braxfield confronted with a parking offence.

"Climb-down," said Mr Smith like a man rolling the death sentence round his tongue, "humiliating", "total reversal of government policy".

"Apologise," he added, and "millions lost" not to say "furtive negotiations" before concluding that "this whole sordid episode demonstrated the unfitness of a whole series of Secretaries of State for their responsibilities."

The art of the political debate is to get the intellectual and psychological upper hand. Such are Mr Smith's slow-grinding ways, and such his masterful dismissiveness, that he conveys the impression of a lion matched with a lamb chop.

It was not generally a happy day for the Tories. Burdened with Mr Atkins' jokes and the Department of Trade's policies, they could have done without the Prime Minister's turn of phrase.

We had reverted at Prime Minister's Questions to Libya and

164

Mr Kinnock understandably made himself difficult by demanding that future requests from Mr Reagan would be rejected.

Mrs Thatcher appeared to accuse Mr Kinnock of "seeking to help *terrorists*".

The full text, like all full texts, is less dramatic, as she appended the need for terrorists not to know what reply Britain would give. But who remembers full texts?

For the third time in a few days she had left a phrase behind which sounded candidly disastrous. Labour received the gift by registered post and duly signed for it as Mr Kinnock got up and with annoying courtesy requested a retraction.

Sir Eldon Griffiths, arguably the most self-important man on the face of the earth, prolonged matters by protesting at the protest.

Humour is not quite Mrs Thatcher's thing, except involuntarily. Asked a question about some rowdy councillors in Lambeth, she intoned after 15 minutes of defending the Libyan episode: "Of course the Government always condemns the use of force."

Daily Telegraph, April 25, 1986

Selwyn Gummer was sent to negotiate with the EEC about food prices!

No one who has watched Jeffrey Archer wishes any longer to speak ill of John Selwyn Gummer.

Mr Gummer, now translated to the second slot at Agriculture (and with Mr Jopling down with anthrax he is battling up front), does not tell people to get off their backsides and go to Wellingborough, nor does he tell us how he came back from bankruptcy and licked the world.

Accordingly any ironies at his expense are entirely affectionate. Archer victims know what they're missing.

However, it was Mr Gummer's misfortune to have to present the latest fix with the Agro-Signori as a wonderful improvement.

Despite heroic victories on the sunflower seed and rapeseed front (you think I'm making this up, I'm not) the splendidness looked rather marginal.

Mr Marlow, (Northampton N), who lacks charity and community spirit, caught Mr Gummer as he breasted the tape of his 220-yard effusion and asked, since things were so broadly wonderful, by how much would surpluses in food production actually be reduced?

Mr Gummer said many things, some of them highly ingenious but he didn't say that the surpluses would come down.

The Government was tackling the problem in the right way and could not be blamed for the speed with which surpluses grew – something, he observed with a high innocence, "which nobody could have foreseen".

Well, actually, if you abolish the vulgar concept of demand, you may find yourself with rather more supply than you originally had in mind.

This little glitch has been troubling the great souls of the EEC for some time and what they come up with, as on this occasion, is solutions like the Cereal Co-responsibility Levy.

Readers are respectfully asked not to inquire what that is, only to accept that we have had one for beef for the last six years and that doesn't work either.

Trying to keep down EEC agricultural spending is very reminiscent of Mr Heath trying to control inflation. There is a lot of virtuous language about like "restraint" (presumably we are appealing to the better side of the Suffolk character) and any number of Widgett-triggering mechanisms.

And, just as the price index kept going up for Mr Heath, so the over-population of food rolls serenely on.

In Gummerese: "Despite the very real steps taken by the European Community to reduce the milk surplus culminating in the introduction of quotas, the community is still a substantial over-producer of milk."

Accordingly, the Ministers have gone for the nuclear option. There is to be a 3 per cent reduction in quotas (phased over three years).

Comment was not sympathetic, though Mr Baldry, a sort of free-lance hanger-on who for a lump of sugar will love anybody, informed the Minister that his announcement was fair, reasonable, non-inflationary and would achieve the best results for both the farmer and the consumer.

Mr Baldry should not confine himself: it is time to go public and launch the flotation of Loyalty Inc., the coast-to-coast corporation which provides calibrated gratitude, appreciation and warm tributes straight out of the micro-wave.

Mr Heathcoat-Amory, a useful if melancholy acquisition from the last election, suggested that the Ministry were treating the devaluation of the dollar, which has some very nasty implications for the Agrifix, as an exceptional event. What if it wasn't?

None of this nasty questioning and doubting had much effect upon Mr Gummer who is into optimism much as the great Khans were into world conquest.

The text drips a high, bright (and much loved) Gummerian élan. "I am glad to say we resisted considerable pressure for a price increase" (meaning it won't be going down).

"This settlement will have a negligible effect on prices" (meaning they will actually go up).

"Overall this price fixing has produced a highly satisfactory outcome" (meaning we got back from Brussels alive). "It is therefore," concluded Mr Gummer, "good for Britain and good for Europe."

Oh well, it's better than Jeffrey Archer.

Daily Telegraph, April 29, 1986

"Oh ay, she likes travelling now. She's taken wi' travelling free on the taxpayer. They're all the same."

The prize for detecting the unforgiving grudge-excavating voice of Dennis Skinner, rick-firer, machine-breaker and authentic voice of the working class to the carriage trade, children's parties, barmitzvahs and the universe, is something less than one segment of Bounty bar.

Of course it was Dennis, nobody else resents ministerial freebies the way he does.

Of course, with Mrs Thatcher reporting on her visit to the land of the flower arrangement, subtle water colours and predatory competence, he had something to grind on about.

Not that Mrs Thatcher was unreasonable. Despite much sychophantic encouragement from some of the plastic penguins on her own back-benches, she was quite restrained, keeping the duchess factor in a suitable lead-lined container.

There was, however, a modest amount of fall-out when she

turned upon Mr Kinnock. "Whatever he *tries* to say, I thought his own statement excessively banal." (Fires are still burning at the Thatcher reactor despite the efforts of helicopters to drop dampening quantities of sand and lead.)

Mr Ian Lloyd, who divides his time between persuading us that radioactivity is therapeutic and telling the Prime Minister that she makes "wonderful" seem a very weak adjective, was placed to follow both his hobbies.

Had not her visit been an outstanding success and were not the Greenpeace funk lobby liable to make OPEC, in its great days, look like an aid to production?

There is something about Mr Lloyd sneering, grand and patronising as he is, that makes the disinterested spectator instinctively agree with his opponents. Accordingly, Greenpeace looked rather sensible yesterday.

Mr Aitken, who once seemed sycophantic but in whom a sense of humour has rather got the better of things, drew Mrs Thatcher's attention to an alleged observation of Mr Shultz in Tokyo.

"Margaret really wrestled old François to the mat on this one."

The image of the President of the French Republic being half-buttocked into submission by the Finchley Footpad reduced Mrs Thatcher, creditably, to a mild fit of the giggles. But the idea of beating up the French will always have a certain charm over here.

The question which *didn't* get answered yesterday was asked not of Mrs Thatcher, but of the Foreign Office in the pained form of Timothy Eggar, a pleasant lad who deserves something better.

Mr Teddy Taylor, in his sedulous way, had asked by private notice why, when food imports were being banned after Chernobyl from every country in Eastern Europe, an exception was being made for East Germany, through which all those countries can send their produce.

Not much point, he thought, in banning goods from remote Yugoslavia when plums and pears in which the isotopes danced and cheese enriched with uranium would lightly be passing into Leipzig for re-export from all corners of Comecon under the terms of the inter-German treaty.

Mr Eggar made light of the matter and said that it was for the West Germans to check such matters.

Daily Telegraph, May 9, 1986

There is nothing like ill-will among lawyers to cheer us all up.

A modest part of yesterday afternoon had been given over to questions to the law officers, the gravely melancholy Sir Patrick and the coolly raffish Sir Michael, both of whom, unlike most of this Government, look as if they belonged in the job.

Was it not the case, asked Mr Greenway, a former school-master for whom even an MP's salary represents a pinnacle, that the recent so-called Satanist trial, lasting 36 days, had cost half a million and that certain counsel had each emerged £35,000 better off? ("Not enough," said a cheerful legal voice behind him.)

"The figure," said the Attorney-General, clenching his tongue between his back teeth to stop it bulging in his cheek, was "a gross exaggeration", but he didn't have the exact scorings made by the lads ready to hand. Clearly they can have made no more than a trivial £400,000 *and* had to share it between them.

The cheerfulness continued as Mr Stokes, who is prevented only by a fundamental sweetness of nature from bringing off the all-time portable parody of bristling backbench reaction, asked whether terrorism might not be treated as treason and thus receive capital offence status.

Sir Michael parried this by saying that the relevant statute was rather heavily concerned with the status of rival claimants to the Throne and, as it were, addressed itself to the burning issues of the 14th century.

"But surely," murmured Mr Rees, savouring the trouble he was making, such an idea had been broached by the Lord Chancellor, the head of the judiciary and all-purpose legal gargoyle.

The Attorney-General, who is kept from the great Seal of England partly by Mrs Thatcher's inability to retain Wimbledon in a by-election, partly by Lord Hailsham's magic glue-like adhesion to office in the extremities of antiquity, replied with feeling.

"On that occasion," he observed, "the Lord Chancellor was

speaking in his personal capacity." This translates as "the old fool was sounding off without getting a competent lawyer to advise him".

Less agreeable was the mini-debate gathered around the raids launched from South Africa, land of the *sjambok* and the flaming necklace. The House was full of people wanting us, the British, to do something about them. There is, in this yearning for authority in people who delighted in our divesting of power, much of the quality of a phantom pregnancy.

David Young, one of those slow-speaking Scottish Labour MPs, announced that we were "on trial in the eyes of the world". Mr Flannery, getting rather above himself, spoke for the civilised world.

Sir Geoffrey, sensible man, was into gravely deploring excesses and not actually doing anything about them. But he was somewhat persecuted from Left and Right by people wanting to draw irresponsible and uncalled-for analogies between Mr Botha's indefensible raids on the territories to his north and the Reagan-Thatcher raid on Libya which was a model of everything that is really wonderful.

The two cases, said Sir Geoffrey, to whom clichés are as dear as teddy bears, "were as unalike as chalk and cheese". Given the limitations of EEC dairying, the distinction is not as drastic as it sounds.

Mr Dalyell made the point that the West German police did not now connect the Libyans with the Berlin bombing (an important part of the Reagan–Thatcher justification). In which event the two cases may be at least as alike as Emmenthaler and Bel Paese.

Various Arabists took the opportunity to draw invidious comparisons with Israel's invasion of the Lebanon, another cheese surely of an overripe nature, but Sir Geoffrey, not knowing of a better hole, stuck to the one he was in.

That is: South African incursions into Zambia and wherever wholly deplorable, British-assisted American incursions into Libya an example to us all; other comparisons most unhelpful.

Daily Telegraph, May 20, 1986

You may have supposed that the Channel Tunnel debate would be interesting, controversial, exciting. Forget it.

Mr John Moore, who is very much the Charles Augustus Fortescue of this outfit, the one who succeeds by being clean behind the ears, kind to the cat and bringing in an apple for teacher, spoke with a level, corroding wisdom about the broadly progressive and desirable nature of what some here regard as the Margaret Thatcher Memorial Hole in the Ground.

Mr Robert Hughes, a truly nice man, now handling transport for Labour, made a great gravel-sifting travail of a fair-minded speech, trying to reconcile the interests of the NUR with those of the ecologists. Nobody, alas, got down to discussing the real issues, the second, all-road, tunnel with attached delta fanning out on to East Sussex, to be added after the next election.

What Mr Hughes did do, however, was to quote from "the Scottish play" along the lines of "if it were done when 'tis done ..." At this a Green Room howl indicated the unsuspected presence of Mr Andrew Faulds. "I must warn the House that to quote from that play is particularly unlucky."

This sounds like a promising line. Knowing as we do about the Scottish play and of those who have quoted it falling into the orchestra pit, or being bitten by the assistant stage manager's fox terrier (rabid of course after two years of the Channel Tunnel), perhaps we might hope that sufficient incantation of the choicer bits and the whole forward-looking enterprise may cave in at the high tide.

However, such hypothetical maledictions apart, some may feel that Mr Moore's proud boast that the thing would be creating "eight to ten thousand jobs over seven years" was oddly jinxed to have a quarter of that figure wiped out in an afternoon by Sir Terence Conran's forward-looking dismissals at British Home Stores. The Channel Tunnel debate was in fact a sad affair with the spirit and consistency of seaweed.

Mr Moore continues to sound and look like a character invented by Jeffrey Archer. Peter Rees, for the injured parties of East Kent, continued that course of self-hugging, tittering amusement at his own slender performance which marked the long pain of his Ministerial career.

Clearly the main attraction of the Bill was the ability of various Thatcher trusties to talk through to tomorrow and thus

171

deprive Mr Dalyell of his private business on Westland. This was much aired at business questions: the official line is that the Whips know nothing of this suppression of debate. No one doubts that, like the Americans in Nicaragua, they perform an interesting role as "advisors".

The rumour is that, if frustrated, Mr Dalyell will call a Press conference this morning. Mr Gerald Howarth demanded to know if the protection of privilege would be afforded to someone "using a committee room, Mr Speaker, to cast slurs upon one of our most honourable Prime Ministers?"

As one writes it seems very likely that Mr Howarth and his friends will have spent last night trying to prevent the question of Westland being aired, not something you could do in the face of Prime Ministerial opposition or indifference, not something which a confident Prime Minister would let happen.

As for Mrs Thatcher herself, we had her yesterday, at Questions, in full triumphalist throat. She had been asked about the wisdom of referring to "heaven on earth, an everyday attainment in Britain".

This naturally produced the allusion to Mrs Bonner and the usual sermon on the evils of the Soviet Union and/or "Socialism".

It gave Mr Kinnock a perfect opportunity to get out his pained but reasonable kit again, and to observe that some people didn't care much for either four million unemployed *or* the Soviet system.

"There are decent alternatives to both," he said quietly. (Seriously, the Tories want to start doing some real worrying about Mr Kinnock. He is striking a good note, different from the old Labour moan, and the Prime Minister keeps cueing him into it.)

Daily Telegraph, June 6, 1986

There is a tendency to see Mr Michael Meacher, Labour's welfare specialist, as a semi-disembodied idealist given to trailing clouds of glory and walking into the bollards of brute political life as he goes.

You wouldn't have said that yesterday. Having made £5 billion worth of cash promises to the lower social percentiles, the hard-bitten young idealist paused and observed, "Because all of those who are subject to these benefits – pensioners, mothers, the unemployed and the low paid – have a vote, a Labour government will not be long in coming."

For a naked pitch at the Ministerial Daimler Sovereign (with driver) you have to go back to Charles Haughey's promise in the Irish Republic of an international airport to service the shrines of Connaught.

Not that Mr Meacher is necessarily wrong. Indeed one rather sees the Tories anxiously conferring on the best form of passionate commitment to the pensioner/mother/lower paid consonant with keeping a firm hold of those Daimler Sovereigns.

Nor did any of this add distinction to Mr Meacher's discourse. Never happy with the English language, he does it as many injuries by dropping breeze blocks of clichés into it as any politician except Edward Heath. The rich have been enjoying, it seems, "a huge cash bonanza". The Government "has an obsession with imposing one law for the rich and another for the poor". The man spreads verbal dereliction without effort.

Mr Newton for the Government was drily insouciant about his opponent. Speaking first, he predicted correctly that the Member for Oldham West would be grinding on about the actual size of the new up-rating without reference to the fall in inflation or the fact that it was being made early and in the interim. The Labour technicians of social benefit, Mr Frank Field and the Fulham Wonder, Nick Raynsford, nodded shrewdly and made polite technical points.

Indignation of an old-style, levelling sort with a brand to burn down every merchant bank and a lamp-post to support every specialist in the dollar exchange market is confined to Mr Meacher, in many ways a touchingly old-fashioned politician.

Even the offer of, dare one say it, "a huge cash bonanza for the poor" goes with an antique style of politics as does the conflict of loathly opposites in perpetual struggle. It is only equalled by Mr Nigel Lawson's amiable caricature of a banker with a hundred dollar bill in his hatband clean out of socialist realist posters from 50 years ago.

Mr Newton, the fair-minded Conservative specialist, discourses civilly with Mr Field, the equally fair-minded Labour specialist, about the tropicana of welfare economics, people in the gallery listen respectfully and the House gets one of those awards for fair play which seem to be England's highest hope in Mexico.

Meacher and Lawson by contrast are pure agitprop, suave banker and overwrought agitator, firing water pistols over the barricades.

Various Tories, notably Tony Marlow who is declining into utility, politely asked Mr Meacher about the inflation angle and its effect upon savers. "Surely," said Mr Marlow, sounding strenuously fair-minded, "people who saved in the past have had their accumulation wiped out, why risk doing that again?"

The Labour spokesman, who has interesting reserves of *realpolitik*, glinted through his rimless Robespierrian eye-glasses and observed metallically that "the point for pensioners was not savings but pensions!" So much for the petty bourgeoisie then.

The Tories for their part should be grateful for Mr Newton. He is lucid, humorous and pleasant, given to arguing pre-emptively, and his remarks about the hurt done to savers through inflation in the seventies by an uncaring Government was a piece of linguistic irredentism to be treasured.

Daily Telegraph, June 12, 1986

The reactions to our blunders are deeply instructive about other people's sustained inner view of us.

Well-liked and respected figure stands on banana skin, does all the inevitable things and there will be at most a suppressed titter combined with a whir of real anxiety that dear Fred may have hurt himself. For others it is different; and sweating and cursing at the head of the column marked "Others" stands the Right Honourable Roy Hattersley, MP.

If Roy was thrown into a crocodile pit there are large numbers here who would be able to see the funny side of it. When as yesterday he was delivered to Mrs Thatcher's table as cold roast pork, hard-hearted fellows on both sides fell helplessly about for a good 30 seconds.

We were on to South Africa, prime indignation territory – why no sanctions, bar of World Opinion, liability of Government to be cut at garden parties by Sonny Ramphal, risks to our valuable trade with Guyana and various other forward-looking calamities, when Hattersley tried a frontal assault.

He may still be wondering why the House fell into the aisles when he said: "We are used to a combination of prevarication and bluster...." Mr Hattersley, himself, has a reputation for hesitant understatement appropriate to an American evangelist who had switched to the Metal Exchange late in life. It was very hard to see why the House couldn't stop laughing.

As for Mrs Thatcher, slow though she is to see crude things like jokes, she was set up like Mr Lineker to score one of his short-hand typist goals from three yards of an empty goal. "The Rt. Hon Gentleman is talking nonsense in his usual blustering fashion," she observed.

She was lucky in Neil Kinnock's absence at the Memorial Conference of Iron and Steel Trades Confederation, for her other utterances on South Africa were wooden and repetitive in the manner of mechanical devotions. She is against violence from either side. *There* is a breakthrough in dangerous thinking for you! She was against it five times yesterday.

Also she enjoyed re-using Dr Owen's speech against sanctions as a small personalised *sjambok* for Mr Steel who is in favour of them.

But there was little comfort (for the friends of the Veldt) in Mrs Thatcher's dull, departmentally vetted answers. Michael Hirst set up a beautifully sculpted question along the lines of deeply deploring apartheid but not employing sanctions because they didn't actually do any good. It was a clever query designed to make an affirmative answer seem not illiberal. She is against violence from all sides!

Mr Gardiner, whom one does not associate with subtlety (a firing squad has more nuance), also propped up the ball for her. While deploring apartheid, would she do nothing at variance with the principle she had previously defended in the House (like not imposing sanctions)? She was against violence from all sides.

One got rather to seeing the point of St Paul pouring out all that Helleno-Hebraic eloquence on an undiscerning congregation in Asia Minor and getting back nothing but "Great is Diana of the Ephesians". The way in which politicians will hang on to a safe, pre-processed phrase as if it was a spar in the

175

South China Sea is one of the melancholy certainties of a verbally uncertain and unfelicitous age – they all have football managers inside them wanting to get out.

There was much grim forward defensive play, though with a good deal more style, from Mr Rifkind, who after Chernobyl is stuck with telling the farmers of Dumfries and Galloway, Arran and Easter Ross that the slaughter of lambs is for the time being off. This is excellent news for the lambs to whom the odd bequerel of caesium in the system is hugely more healthy than MacCorquedale's cleaver. But with the Scottish MPs, a cantankerous lot on both sides, it went down less well.

They were joined by Miss Short, an Irish lady representing an English constituency, who announced, "I'm typical of many people." Let us just hope not.

Mr Home Robertson (Labour), who owns a respectable part of Berwickshire, annoyed Mr Rifkind no end, not something lightly done, by discounting the Minister's assurances that all was really quite safe with the words of Corporal Jones in *Dad's Army*: "Don't panic. Don't panic."

Nobody was panicking. However, now we have been given official assurances that no danger of any kind exists, this sounds like a good time to start.

Daily Telegraph, June 25, 1986

With apologies to Joel Chandler-Harris
Brer Newton he comes along the road loppity-lop. En he seeze this Tar Baby a called "suspension of 50 per cent mortgage relief for persons on supplementary benefit". "Yo sho' yo' self respectful tar baby," sez Brer Newton. En the tar baby he sits and sits en shoes no respect.

Brer Meacher he lies low and sez all kinds of things, it not being Brer Meacher's way to say nuddin'. En he makes a great courthouse speech on behalf of the Tar Baby, sayin' as how mortgage relief is accounted a mighty fine thing by Brer Newton when it get paid to the great folks in the Big House.

But when it comes to the chick-feed, potato patch folks that don't have no scratch but has been persuaded by Big Mammy Wham Bang Big-Money ter buy their two-bit cabins in the interest of creating a property-owning democracy, en they finds

176

theirselves not wanted on the plantation, Brer Newton his only concern is to reduce their relief en make them pay en pay.

Brer Newton didn't pay no attention to this great courthouse speechifying, seeing as how it was bein' made by Brer Meacher who notoriously didn't want no folks, rich or poor, to hev no mortgage relief. En he gets to an almighty literary turn of phrase and sez Brer Meacher is like Dracula a settin' up as a blood donor; only thing is, Brer Meacher is such a drained-out, white gilled sort of feller you get to thinking Dracula been done his work there long time past.

So Brer Newton he eyes the Tar Baby en demands respect en what he calls "equity", which is a five-dollar word none of the animals knows the meaning of. But the Tar Baby sits and sits in the insolent way of tar babies en sez nuddin' to Brer Newton.

"Tar Baby," sez Brer Newton, "I'ze a goin' to give you a whack". En he whacks the Tar Baby, only his hand gets all sticky en the Tar Baby he don't let go. En Brer Beaumont-Dark he get himself all worked up for the Society for the Protection of Tar Babies.

"What you go beat that poor thing fo?" he ask Brer Newton. En Brer Newton who is not goin' loppity-lop now, but more clumpity-clump, he mutters somethin' about equity en revenue en how most of the unemployed will be back in work soon, which comes as news to some folks.

"In which case," sez Brer Beaumont-Dark (that don't sound altogether like a up-country Georgia name), "why yo' tribulatin' yo' self for a whole heap of misery en a few cents? It don't make rational sense en it ain't generous-spirited."

But Brer Newton he was all roused and fractious like a fightin' rabbit en he hit the Tar Baby with his free hand. Bless me if the Tar Baby didn't take ahold of that hand, so Brer Newton he kicks the Tar Baby en finishes up all stuck en fixed to the Tar Baby so he can't hardly move.

Now when the animals see this they all come out of hiding en they talks of roastin' Brer Newton en fryin' him. En some of the unkindest things is said by the Conservative animals like Brer Raffan. "Ain't you got no compassion for the unemployed?" says Brer Raffan. "This mortgage relief, he go help de poor folks in Flint and Hollywell what I is accountin' on reelectin' me" (only he don't say this so direct more circumflexious and respectful like). En Brer Gwilym Jones, one of the 1983 animals nobody ain't never heard of, he get all uppity and critical as well.

Fact, nobody said much to comfort poor Brer Newton 'cept fo' Sister Currie (Little Mammy Thump-Crump Some Money) en nobody don'd get much consolation in this dang world hevin' Sister Currie a hollerin' fo' him.

The hardest time of it come from Brer Raynsford who in spite of bein' a terrible rad is a Virginia gentleman (fact, records says his first name isn't Nick like he give out but "Wyvill" which is a real great folks name).

But Brer Wyvill Raynsford he has all the facts an' figures about animals dispossessed from their warrens en chicken-runs for non-payment of mortgage obligations since 1979 when Big Mammy Wham Bang Big-Money come to power. En they gone up something grand. "Brer Newton," sez Brer Raynsford all friendly like, "this heah Tar Baby ain't a goin' to do yo' en yo' folks no good what with abstentions en rebellions and all. Why done you take a smart header into the briar patch where rabbits was born and raised? En we won't say no more to it."

But Brer Newton he got jus' like the Tar Baby and sits and sits. En last thing I heerd of him he still sittin' there all stuck with tar en mutterin', "Equity, equity."

Daily Telegraph, June 26, 1986

The habit of inviting distinguished foreigners to show us up in the Queen's Gallery is catching. President von Weizsäcker followed the King of Spain and spoilt everything by being even better.

The Queen's Gallery, which must be quite the most over-decorated corridor in any public building in England, is a wonderful setting for fraternal greetings (as we call them in the workers' movement) from heads of state.

These characters can be relied upon to sound off about peace and love among nations (in the case of President von Weizsäcker, rather movingly).

But all the time he is going on about friendship in Europe

one's eye edges up to the huge murals depicting the British crushing the Frogs single-handed at sea and then crushing them again, with a helping hand from the Germans, on land.

The real embarrassment comes, however, from the contrast between our chap and theirs. The Lord Chancellor of England is giving the impression these days of a parrot who has had his claws welded on to the perch.

He delivered himself of a speech designed to show off Hailsham as Renaissance man.

"One thinks of all the great Germans and their contribution, the composers Beethoven and Mendelzone, the philosophers, Hegel and Can't," he said without making any concession to pronunciation. "Einfeste Burg Istunser Gott, a hymn sung in every English church", "as Goethe once said", "was fur ein schoenes maedchen ist das".

Then he showed off his Latin: "A Roman statesman and jurist once said" (look, mum, I'm a statesman and jurist too) "Per aliquid sunt tu quoque, de minimis non curat nil desperandum, hic haec hoc, pro bono publico et cum spiritu tuo."

"Healing words of wisdom," said the Lord Chancellor, "the moving example of Willy Brandt, all for the best really, would you like some Greek, what?"

The last of his birdseed learning scattered before us was the proposition, presumably gathered from a Roman jurist or maybe Heine, that "human beings have a propensity to love one another".

Not after a speech like that they don't.

The German contrast was numbing. President von Weizsäcker is a trim, grey-haired-and-suited man putting one in mind of a pocket battleship.

So far from showing off smatterings, he spoke heart-breakingly perfect English and depressingly good sense.

He bashed the Common Agricultural Policy very satisfactorily, and observed sadly that this was a system of dubious morality and bad policy which directly injured the Third World.

He moved deftly on to anti-Americanism without prejudicing his presidential restraint, just suggesting that the impression of a politically withdrawn Europe, if given to the Americans, would do us no good at all.

The German President is a genuine intellectual, a nice man,

179

a little serious and given to talking rather too thoughtfully for our style which is dilettante when it isn't artisan.

A moving experience yesterday morning but rather a depressing one. We don't have anybody that good.

Daily Telegraph, July 3, 1986

All of what follows, however improbable, actually happened.

It is not every day that a former Prime Minister and First Lord of the Treasury falls sweetly into the River Thames but when it does we should make the most of it.

The cup of summer was overflowing during yesterday's Parliamentary Regatta. Chaps got up for Henley, girls got up to look like the chorus line of *Merrie England*, the Solicitor-General windsurfing down the Thames (I kid you not though actually, come to think of it, this was the last Solicitor-General, the splendid Sir Ian Percival).

All was going to plan in the best of English ways like a waterborne donkey derby, all proceeds for the church steeple fund, indoors in Westminster Hall if wet, quantities of Pimms and spritzers; eights being started by the vicar (in this case the Archbishop of Canterbury).

All was going agreeably to plan when a light aluminium launch carrying a number of labour MPs to the boat in which they would row as "The Labour 8" proceeded in a spirit of gross partisanship to sink, depositing the former Prime Minister, Mr Callaghan, 74, into the dun-brown water-course which divides Westminster from Southwark.

The raft is known in the boating world (and I am not making this up) as a Waliflote or, as some are inclined to put it, a wally float. Nothing of course went seriously wrong.

The St John's Ambulance launch bore down on the Callaghan party and dragged them kicking and spitting on board. Mr Callaghan, great professional that he is, went downstream after his breath had been recovered, waving cheerfully to the brilliant idlers who filled the terrace, and being cheered in a way Prime Ministers of any persuasion are seldom cheered.

It was a wonderful afternoon. Your correspondent, armed

with the binoculars of Another Newspaper to look like a bookie, spent the time standing on a table with a succession of pretty girls while successive MPs brought him soft drinks.

Disaster was not confined to the Labour eight. Another crew which had tried to sneak into the *Guinness Book of Records* by fielding the heaviest cox ever (Geoffrey Dickens: Saddleworth, 21 stones) found out, as anyone could have told them, that you carry a light cox in order not to sink.

The image of water washing over and over the stern of the Dickens caravelle as it proved scientifically the difference between toads and frogs was memorable.

Almost as grave, the panama hat of the Hon. Nicholas Soames, stern oar for the Eton 1 boat, blew away, but an anxious valet service fetched it by tug. Rumours put about that the tug was skippered by Mr Selwyn Gummer are quite malicious.

Eton had the satisfaction of winning its heat (against girls – "Avon Ladies") but as their stroke Mrs Celia Baker, wife of the Education Minister, put it succinctly to me afterwards: "The Archbishop made an unholy mess of the start, otherwise we would have beaten them hollow." A Tory added, with the venom of the new classes: "If that lot didn't learn to row at Eton they probably learned on their fathers' private lakes" – quite a bit of social flak about in the four-button party these days!

Unlike the Archbishop, the Prime Minister, who was giving the men in lurking security launches nightmares, gave an excellent start from a launch but a crew deeply sympathetic to her, an eight called "No Turning Back" stroked by Edward Leigh, veered to the right and coolly rammed the opposition.

It was a glorious day for Mrs Thatcher. Not merely did her boys: Hamilton, Robert Jones, Maude, Forsyth and others – a gathering so dry that they could have walked on water – get into the semi-final, but the arrival of an oil tanker, like rain in Great Missenden, brought the village fête to a premature ending so that nobody won and everyone shall have prizes.

Everyone that is except Edward Heath orating steadily about the need to punish South Africa on a day chosen by the Leader of the House when every MP in his right mind was on the river.

Daily Telegraph, July 17, 1986

181

In 1986 sanctions against South Africa were demanded. Mrs Thatcher and I dissented.

The Gathering of the Warlords

South African Turmoil

The miserable episode of South Africa and what we are supposed to do about it continues, showing Mrs Thatcher in a bitterly controversial light. She is widely damned for resisting significant sanctions against the Republic and is as little admired by Mr Brian Mulroney, the interim Prime Minister of Canada, as by Mr Kinnock, Leader of the Opposition, and – according to the *Sunday Times* – the Queen of England.

It is all very tiring, and none of it worth the time and emotion expended. For all her faults and limitations, Mrs Thatcher, despite slow footwork, seems to me to have been more reasonable than her opponents. She has taken a longer view of the consequences, and may just conceivably have come closer to the assumptions of the actual, fallible, unelevated British electorate than all the pieties of Sir Shridath Ramphal (Secretary-General of the Commonwealth) bound together and printed on vellum for presentation.

It is fashionable to say, and Mr Kinnock has said it, that itsily and bitsily, behind the curtains and with all due discretion, she doesn't like black people and sees apartheid as a much-maligned system of administration. Gathering up every caveat which that authoritarian and peremptory (not to say corner-cutting) lady inspires in me, I don't believe it. What distinguishes Mrs Thatcher from most politicians, apart from her heels-in-the-ground stubbornness, is an ability to read a balance sheet. She will understand better than most people that any sanctions against South Africa run the risk of escalation from the wrist-flipping gesture which makes people feel good into the real trade-denying, naval-blockading McCoy. In which case we the British, heavily involved for excellent reasons with investments of some billions put together over the years, are potentially the huge losers while various easily indignant parties have very little to lose.

Rationally she knows – and so does anyone who has given thought to this issue – that France as a trader and Israel as an

182

intermediary, almost certainly sustained by Italy, parts of the Arab world, and such West African countries as the Ivory Coast, would make possible for South Africa the buying-and-selling of whatever it wished to buy or sell. That will be so because trade is trade, and nobody but a fool passes it up. Indeed, there is a whole school of thought (which is hard to resist) arguing that this is actually a benign process. Trade and business are ultimately liberal agents. The black South African miner is not a rich man but by the standards of black South Africa he is very comfortable, and by the standards of the continent of Africa he has what the heart desires. He eats, dresses and is housed, and his children are educated beyond the dreams of Ghana, Nigeria, Angola, Zaire, Tanzania, or whatever African country you choose to name.

In the absence of trade this would not be so. Ironically in the absence of trade nothing would have shifted in the flat-earth mental standards of Afrikanerdom. Paul Kruger, for heaven's sake, wasn't a free-trader. The men of 1948, who created out of the conventions and half-laws of hung-over 19th-century racial assumptions their own Vatican of stratification and racial mastery, took a very ambiguous view of the windfall wealth of the Rand and of the English and Jewish entrepreneurs who set it rolling.

The South Africa of Malan and Strijdom has been undermined not by cricket bans or walk-outs from the Commonwealth Games, but by a growth rate which abolished the old, submissive, grateful black. The perception of Alexis de Tocqueville is the neon-lit cliché of the self-evident; poor, oppressed, hopeless men do not threaten revolutions, and the beneficiaries of rising life-standards do. Parenthetically it will be very instructive in ten or fifteen years' time to watch developments in countries like Brazil, where race is a relatively subordinate issue but where at present the gap between rich and poor is so vast as to make the people at the bottom extra-terrestrial beings to suburban householders. Perhaps Portuguese melancholy and good nature will find a way out, but equally – as hopes grow at the bottom – perhaps not; maybe that country will surprise us with a revolution which runs blood.

South Africa, of course, runs a little blood already. The Black Sash women, mostly white, who wanted to do right on principle have been superseded by the necklace crowds which by filling rubber tyres with petrol, putting them round the necks of casually accused submitters to the régime, striking a light, and setting fire have given the term "witch hunt" a new immediacy. To be completely candid, when Mrs Winnie Mandela says, "With our matches and our necklaces we will liberate South Africa," I am not drawn much to Mrs Mandela, the Mary Tudor of the townships, and I ponder what sort of liberation it will be that is achieved on heaps of charred bones and burnt flesh after the screaming stops. It won't be a liberal democracy; it won't even be a nice Czechoslovakian people's democracy. It could be a new kind of nastiness we haven't given much thought to yet.

How to obtain for other people in another country, over which we have no sovereignty, both the cessation of the *sjamboks* and the prevention of the necklaces is a problem beyond our devising or Mr Mulroney's or Mr Gandhi's. South Africa is not a wonky drain to be fixed with a couple of social-democratic plumbers, it is Purgatory with a running chance of turning into Hell. If Mrs Thatcher responds to so complex and nightmarish a proposition with a measure of considered political agnosticism, who on earth can blame her?

Mrs Thatcher is under fire from fellow Conservatives not on any great point of principle but because they favour the application of a measure of cold cream to the Commonwealth by way of specific sanctions, or the threat of them. It would have been much less dispiriting for Sir Geoffrey Howe on his forlorn errand to have had something to wave, but it would be better not to have undertaken the trip at all. It is not even illogical of the Prime Minister to say both that sanctions will be a futile gesture and that they may do real harm if they work. Probably they *will* be a futile gesture (certainly France will enjoy every particle of dropped trade she gathers into her unchaste apron); but, if the whole caravanserai moves onwards, if we get Sir Shridath Ramphal's dreams coming true (blockade, financial sanctions, the works), then repression and murder look like getting even bigger parts in the next revival of the show. Sanctions could fail badly and succeed disastrously!

There is at present a liberal buzz, a facile desire to do something to sign up with the angels and against the Pass Laws and the pre-amnestied South African police. But do what, and to what worked-out useful end? South Africa is built upon the journeys of the Voortrekkers and the assumptions of a closed remote community. A sort of South Africa well to the Right of the two Bothas, Mr Viljoen, or Mr Kornhoof could readily emerge. Without overstating the strength of Eugene ter Blanche, he is speaking the authentic Kaffir-blasting language of the historic Boer, a farmer incidentally, self-sufficient and indifferent to the degenerate world he sees outside.

There is reason enough already – and Lebanon should have instructed us – to expect the emergence of warlords. The African National Congress is one (the Comrades of the Soweto streets are a warlord army with no visible leader – but Mrs Mandela would do); the Government is another; Chief Buthelezi a fourth; and Mr ter Blanche a fifth. Is this a situation we actually *want* to worsen?

The critics of the British Government seem desperately parochial in their preoccupation with their immediate personal consciences, with doing right and feeling good. Most of the demands put up at the bidding of the busy Sir Shridath Ramphal tend toward destabilisation when they rise above self-admiring futility. Mrs Thatcher could have made things easy for herself by a few concessions. Perhaps they will be painfully dragged out of her; perhaps the Royal cherry of our Constitutional ice cream will play a political part out of the empty ringing pride which the empty ringing Commonwealth gives Queen Elizabeth. But the actual statesmanship and foresight have been Mrs Thatcher's. Even if she is bullied over the line into contradicting her instincts, she will still have been right initially. This is too vast a problem for progressive ju-ju to rectify. The potential for good, such as it is, still resides with business, with all the trade we can possibly do, and even, despite his recent actions in high panic, with Mr P. W. Botha – "*Het Kaapster vremdling*" (the foreigner from the Cape), as the brutal Connie Mulder called him.

Mr Botha and the men immediately around him do not actually rejoice in the State of Emergency, or in the cruelties which flow from it. They are in trouble in large part because they were marginal Fabian reformers in a country bubbling with irrational rage. They should not be despised by us. To amend St Augustine, it is better to evolve than to burn. Ironically Denis

Healey, shot to pieces for it in the House of Commons by Mrs Thatcher, was willing (when he was in the Labour Government as Defence Minister) to sell arms to Balthazar Johannes Vorster, ex-Nazi, Verwoerd's Police Minister, and all-purpose political ugly mug. Mrs Thatcher, who would like still to trade office machinery and soft fruit with the damned foreigner from the Cape, is told very foolishly by Neil Kinnock that perhaps deep down she is a racist.

She is surely right in her assumption that the only people who can liberalise South Africa, by painful and hesitant steps when and as they can next find breath from the Emergency, are the *Verligte*, the half-way sympathetic Afrikaners. Perhaps with the Zulus, another dominant tribe which had just mastered the other Africans when white men came over the Drakensbergs in 1836, they will dominate a future South Africa, possibly letting some welcome parts of it pass into federal autonomy and effective self-government, while holding what they need. If there is a Western line to the Afrikaner leaders, something may be mitigated; in good conditions something may be improved.

If we declare a holy but vicarious war, the mitigating voice will be alienised comprehensively. Having no friends – not even critical ones – South Africa, like Canada and Denis Healey, will do the easy thing. For those two it is a windy but expensive gesture; for the Afrikaners the easy thing will be to retreat into unblinking internal reconquest under a new leadership.

Do the people who gather for conferences, who demand action, who threaten grandly with their absence, ever contemplate the glass upon which we all walk?

Encounter, September–October 1986, Vol. LXVII, No. 3

The establishment, one weekend when the unions weren't looking, of Mr Murdoch's cost-effective press depended upon the co-operation of electricians and a fortiori of Mr Eric Hammond.

As a motion was passed late yesterday afternoon condemning the actions of the EEPTU at Wapping, a dummy with the mask of Hitler slipped over the balcony.

Thus, in the eyes of the committee, was Eric Hammond, class

traitor, fascist and superintendent of pieces of silver, hanged in effigy. As Mr Hammond knows better than most people, this was an inadequate substitute for the serious business of hanging him for real.

Some debates are more interesting for their psychology than their content. Yesterday's effusion was a matter of pathology.

Briefly, the EEPTU was arraigned for accepting jobs from Mr Rupert Murdoch's News International plant at Wapping. Crowds of extras from some documentary about the Thirty Years War assembled in zoological formation outside the conference centre.

Mr Hammond, who adores a fight, provoked deep feral roars and snarls simply by going to the rostrum. But then Mr Hammond provokes merely by existing.

Yet the terms of the debate were sublimely irrelevant. The Transport and General Workers Union has its chaps driving to and from Wapping. The National Union of Journalists of blessed memory has hundreds of desperate characters on its books (members in good standing) who politely decline to cease working for and being paid by Rupert Murdoch. Were they on a charge? asked Mr Hammond.

Good heavens no. They, the unions concerned, had issued directives to their members on behalf of union solidarity, their duty to the printers and printers' runners.

Tragically, and to the grief of angels weeping quietly in chorus, their members had, by and large, gone on driving heavy vehicles and writing nervous prose in the service of the Prince of Night, allegedly a good payer. But that wasn't the unions' fault, was it?

Mr Hammond spoke of a "ritual message" and "a washing of hands". With the actor's timing which is part of his appeal, he inquired with grief in his voice: "Why can't we be more like them?"

This, of course, is the essence of the quarrel.

Norman Willis, a nice man to whom one grows attached, is like the centurion in *Androcles and the Lion* who says to the stubborn Christian: "Drop a pinch of incense to the flame of Jupiter Minerva. Nobody believes in it but everybody does it. Damn it, regard it as a matter of good form."

What distinguishes the EEPTU in the form it has gradually

taken since Frank Chapple and Les Cannon drove out the old Czechoslovak leadership is a passionate, almost Protestant loathing of dropping pinches of incense to *any* shrine.

It goes against their magnificent and bloody-minded principles. But the afternoon was more about propaganda than principles; *adverse* propaganda, as the heavies who had filled a fair part of the gallery behaved in the way thoughtful men cutting film for Saatchi and Saatchi must long for them to behave.

After he had completed his speech, a deep chant was set up – "scab, scab, scab".

Masochistic, but light on his toes, Mr Hammond turned to his appreciative audience and gave a neat and grateful bow. They can't go on meeting like this.

The feelings of Mr Willis are exactly contrary. "Please don't clap me," he begged his audience. "I did have hopes of trying to get silence."

Like Bernard Shaw's centurion, Mr Willis is a sensible man, not a particularly coherent or razor-edged one (some of his speeches would need Talmudic glosses for better comprehension), but the broad drift of his oceanic style is eirenic. He would like this conference to go home without doing itself an injury.

It is one of those modest, unattainable ambitions which, for all his fumbling, make him such a creditable, decent person.

Daily Telegraph, September 2, 1986

With the Welsh, words have the function of drink, for which they have no great taste anyway. Mr Kinnock has no head for the stuff.

His entrance, as he falls over the cat and announces that he is Methuselah Jones come to redeem the wicked, makes it clear that he has been at the adjectives again.

Roy Jenkins, by contrast, carries it better and has more natural dignity. But, from his slow, measured walk supported by a couple of subordinate clauses, one realises that the great connoisseur has been sipping the old tawny abstract nouns all afternoon.

One is surprised when Mr Jenkins gets magisterial that anyone ever manages to disagree with him. He has the style of a lexicographer in a milk bar. Though one tentatively inquires if it is possible to form an adverb from "febrile", the construction "febrily", used by the member for Hillhead, strikes us as demotic.

But who can complain of a man who denounces "the political patois of hyperbole which repels people of sense and discernment from public life"?

Jane Austen, addressing the SDP conference, could hardly have put it with a nicer grasp of the proprieties, and one rejoices to hear the thunder roll over Labour's "fresh outbreak of ideological frenzy in that barren frontier, which divides the public from the private sector".

It suggests a landscape of East European barbed wire in the flat Silesian beetfields which mark the mined, machine-gun-implanted border between British Telecom and British Rail.

We had not come to this party to seek a seat at the top table of politics, but to overturn that table ... said the Rt Hon. Roy Jenkins, formerly Minister for Aviation, Home Secretary, Chancellor of the Exchequer, Home Secretary (again) and President of the European Economic Community.

Not only did Satan thus deplore sin, but Egon Ronay spoke slightingly of digestion.*

All of this was in aid of Robert Maclennan's plan to give us more local government than we thought there could be: "A parliament for Scotland, a senate for Wales, and regional assemblies with decisive power over the local economy for the rest of Britain," said Mr Maclennan.

Quite why the SDP think that the economy will come on flow, wheels turn, machine tools grind and the Taiwanese take terrified flight because Norwich city council has been given plenary powers is not clear.

And think of those Welsh senators. Whether they are toga-ed and scroll-bearing or julep-sipping filibusterers with iron-grey hair, they will be good at it. Ah, prejudice is a terrible thing.

Mr Gwynoro Jones in that debate, and Mr Tom Ellis in an

---

* I have made this point once before in the decade and the text but, contemplating Mr Jenkins denouncing ingested cake, the point is irresistible.

earlier one, are obvious senatorial material. Both speak in the plangent, catarrhal manner of North Wales: Mr Ellis to proclaim that "We are a revolutionary party", and to say of something or other: "This is single-issue politics multiplied a millionfold."

"I don't want to bore the man in the street," he had begun optimistically. Alas, the chair recognises (all too well) Senator Ellis-Hubert Humphrey in spades.

As for Mr Jenkins, he demonstrated the grandiloquent potential of one of those elder senators from Georgia or Virginia as he lamented: "The growing carapace of exclusivity, factionalism and self-righteousness."

But, like a man raised on mint juleps, Mr Jenkins can handle the long words and walk at the same time.

Daily Telegraph, September 16, 1986

"Thoughtful, rational, reasoned, fair-minded," said Mrs Shirley Williams only half satirically describing the Social Democrats. The trouble for sketchwriters is that by and large, and with occasional pauses for rest and recreation, they are.

One is correspondingly grateful for Mrs Pamela Holman and Mr Colin Smith who yesterday brought a blazon of magenta to the field-grey rationality of the SDP.

Mrs Holman, a jolly mum who looked as if she could have stepped out of an early draft of an advertisement for malted milk, lurched forward and struck the Chief Constable of Greater Manchester sharply on the jaw with a rolled-up brolly. (Looking back on that sentence, let us just hope to avoid prosecution by the Anti-Sexist Enforcement Authority.)

Happily and admirably Mrs Holman, speaking on the Stalker affair, was thoroughly sexist herself in the way that only a woman can be.

"I'm not a great admirer of the look of Mr Anderton," she said, adding inconsequentially "but then I'm only a woman. I don't care for large hairy men."

With the conference in oceanic delight around her, Mrs Holman went on to compare the body language of nice Mr Stalker and not nice Mr Anderton. Even Robert Maclennan, who rather looks upon a joke as a sacramental occasion, was moved to reminisce delightedly on "My brother Esau was a hairy man, but I am a smooth man".

Mr Smith gave equal pleasure by dragging sex into trade union ballots. It seems that some militant feminist in his union, one of those button mushroom Marats who plague modern life, had demanded the purging and suppression of all pin-ups and girlie calendars.

The rule of the barbed-wire bra appeared likely to prevail until the local union took up the Tebbit/Prior option, intended on the whole for higher things, and decided to ballot the members. They confined the vote to women members only and recorded a massive vote in favour of affront and exploitation.

One is grateful to Mrs Holman and Mr Smith because otherwise you would find light relief at this conference the way you would encounter Trotskyists at the Horse of the Year Show.

Meritorious they are – to the point of being good for us – funny they are not. Though we did have Mike Thomas conjuring up the image of "poor Norman Fowler – not just a prisoner at the Elephant and Castle but handcuffed to Edwina Currie, a fate worse than death".

I'm not sure about that. It depends with Mrs Currie whether you're looking or listening.

Mrs Williams made one of her Fidel Castro speeches, working her way like a methodical boll weevil through the economy, South Africa, the City of London, education, the health service, defence, and the Upper Zambezi Irrigation Board. It was a pious act, the telling of a political rosary, but it was well told. There is a disposition among the fancy to patronise Mrs Williams, but despite an aggravating itch to improve she is often traduced.

There was a mild scatter of clichés. Mrs Williams is not the Proust of the platform; fig leaves, yardsticks, twin tracks, yawning gaps, cold reality, disgust and disillusion took their appointed minatory places. But it was sound, persuasive stuff for all that, perfectly adjusted to the TV audience looking in.

Mrs Williams must come over to any casual listener as the least crass and abrasive of politicians.

Daily Telegraph, September 17, 1986

An otherwise inoffensive seaside resort in Sussex is perhaps best known for the quality of its low life.

At least the international-class murderers, Patrick Mahon and Dr John Bodkin Adams (acquitted but dead and in no position to sue for libel), all operated here, as currently does Mrs Thatcher's best PPS, Mr Ian Gow, while, at Bevindene, near the front, one finds, tastefully-fronted in white tile, the rest home and weekend spot of the Transport and General Workers.

However, it also attracts Liberals and, on a good day, David Owen. To set Dr Owen and Des Wilson, the Liberal president, in contradistinction on the same afternoon is like feeding junket through a grinder.

Mr Wilson, of the lopsided grin and the sobbing tenor, is capable of giving a content-free speech and winning a standing ovation. Give or take one or two very fair jokes, he did.

His parody of Mrs Thatcher's dreadful quotation from the blameless St Francis was rather nice: "Where she brought discord, let us bring harmony. Where she brought Bernard Ingham, let us bring truth."

Mr Ingham, that Trevi Fountain among directors of information, is widely seen as a one-man South Africa. Everybody is entitled to attack him – indeed Commonwealth Sanctions Against Bernard Ingham are only a matter of time.

But, if the Wilson jokes were acceptable, the Wilson performance was a sobbing tenor in spades, José Carreras going over the top: "I believe history will tell it differently ... will tell of your idealism and sacrifice and vision and, above all, your courage."

Then he was off on to Pericles speaking to the Athenians – in a translation worthy of Senator Gary Hart: "The secret of happiness is freedom and the secret of freedom is courage."

It had, did that oration, the intellectual consistency and nourishment of boiled plastic. He wants to create "the kind of global human organisations that produce alternatives to violence".

The other parties, said Des, in his best flip-witted idealistic way, "want power for themselves. We want it to redistribute and share with the people." We have it at last, banality on draught.

Dr Owen, by contrast, having come here as a devil figure with a Polaris substitute in his hip pocket, was oppressively exact. Flipping statistics of comparative warheads off the back of his wrist, concentrating minutely on the six-point type of dis-armament negotiations, he set out to elucidate the opposition into glazed-over cataleptic acquiescence.

Force-fed with expertise, the hungry sheep of Liberal CND looked up in hope of heartless outrage, and were offered rich handfuls of statistical budgie seed. There was a modest amount of uplift about disarmament but the moustachio-twirling Old Adam of "sound defence" remained at the core of his meaning.

Some people are born boring. Others have boringness thrust upon them. Yesterday Dr Owen, with malicious forethought, *achieved* boringness.

The place was alive with people longing to have a fight with him, but he was like a slimmed-down Japanese wrestler, so oiled over with detail and sweet reason that no one could get a purchase on him.

Having sprinkled iron filings over everybody's toast in his concern for gritty particulars, he was entitled to one woozy perorative sentence of a protein-enriched speech: "Let us go out from here to use the opportunity of coming together." Well, why not?

Daily Telegraph, September 23, 1986

On September 23, 1986 the Liberals, at the bidding of Simon Hughes, very nearly did for themselves. They did so by taking up a position almost indistinguishable from unilateralism. Arguably the long-term consequence was to make Dr Owen master of the Alliance.

On what must have been Norman Tebbit's most satisfactory day for years, the Liberals voted to split with the SDP on nuclear defence.

By a narrow margin out of 1,300 votes cast, they voted for a Canadian defence policy – membership of NATO but no nuclear weapons – with the disadvantage of not being Canada.

The Liberals have opted, in the words of Mr Brian May, for "a civilized defence policy to match our social policy", or, as Mr Viv Bingham, of Liberal CND, put it, they rejected "our current obsession with the security of Europe and the North Atlantic", preferring as Dr John Wesley, in a useful contribution, expressed it, "to make the whole world my parish".

The self-centric nature of the Liberals is fascinating. Perhaps only the Skibereen Eagle which warned the Tsar that it has its eye on him is quite equal to reporting their proceedings.

It was not until 5.15 pm, 105 minutes into the debate, that the US-Soviet accord received its first (and only) mention. Mr Chris Green, who believes that American bases, happily not the topic of debate, "merely lend the Americans street credibility", also demanded that "the Liberals should lead Britain and the world towards peace".

Mr Simon Hughes, the substitute Tatchell, in a speech which quite sweated piety, claimed that they would, if the motion carried, "start the catalyst which begins the process which removes the evil of nuclear weapons from the earth for ever".

He then added, to tumultuous rapture: "We are standing on the verge of responsibility."

No you're not, Simon – after this afternoon, responsibility is 15 miles down the road, a sharp turn right and up the drive.

When Mr Richard Holme suggested in his double-edged way that he would brief Simon Hughes if he was ever on a capital charge, a voice from the hall cried out: "You are."

In fairness, that sort of venomous righteousness, such a feature of tight Labour debates, was not general. But there was instead a tremendous amount of split Methodism: "In the Liberal Party we are accustomed to preaching the gospel of peace"; they were "fighting for the soul of the Liberal Party".

Quite why political parties – useful mechanisms for laying on smoked salmon, public attention, official limos and civil servants saying "certainly, Secretary of State" to one lot of mildly deleterious politicians rather than another – should *need* souls is not clear. They always strike one as superfluous to need.

As much can be said for democracy. It is a splendid rhetorical stress word, but when it extends to turning over the platform, arranging a split with the indispensable ally and delivering Premier Cru to Conservative Central Office, it is getting above itself.

The reason the platform failed to carry was that its speakers were sucked into a rhetoric of their own, which welded a bomb-sharing deal with the French on to a plea for wider disarmament and soused the whole with a vinaigrette of European uplift.

Jim Wallace, who believes in Europe the way County Galway believes in nodding Madonnas, gave it the half-horse power of his debating skill and sat down to the pale round of civil applause appropriate to a string quartet.

The unilateralists by contrast brought their own claque, a prayer meeting with overtones of the Stretford End. The unilateralists had their day and by the looks of it the Alliance, less split than chopped fine, may have had *its* day altogether more terminally.

Daily Telegraph, September 24, 1986

Councillor Cyril Smith, MP for Rochdale, a sour, unpleasant man who hates his colleagues, ended a long and pleasant boycott of his party.

Wholesome as a polystyrene drop-scone, Cyril Smith made his peace with the Liberals. The lugubrious Northern comedian gathered them tearfully into his arms like Albert Modley turned evangelist.

There has been nothing like it since substantial Cyril bowled a ruminative delegate off the rostrum some years back to announce sorrowfully to an audience which had never heard of her, that "our Gracie", Rochdale's other claimant upon civilisation, had passed on.

Gracie Fields, like a sensible lady, had spent the previous 25 years some little distance from south-east Lancashire in Capri, whose climate is better adopted to growing cotton than spinning it.

Any sensible party which had got Cyril Smith off its hands would have stumped up good money to confine that rumbling tumulus of cantankerous *faux bonhommie* in a similar if more frugal island retreat – Rockall perhaps.

Not the Liberals.

Disregarding Cyril's record of putting a size-22 boot into Mr Steel, and his long, soothing absences from Westminster, they swallowed hard and cheered to the echo one of the most touchingly insincere reconciliation scenes since Henry of Navarre's First Communion.

But, if Paris was worth a mass, Rochdale must rate a 20-minute sermon.

Speaking "here and now, on the record, in front of the British Press" (and through his teeth) he believed that David Steel was a great leader.

Mr Steel, putting Christian charity above his abhorrence of falsehood, smiled with the wanness of a five-watt bulb.

"I want to see him as Prime Minister," said Cyril, lengthening his nose by a foot and making the angels weep. He wanted to squash another myth and he is intended by nature for squashing things.

He had always been "totally in favour of the Alliance". (Actually he had said that the SDP should be strangled at birth, but let's not be tediously pedantic.)

Briefly deviating into good faith, he lingered resentfully on the salaries paid to Messrs Kinnock and Thatcher. They got respectively £42,000 and £45,000, he said.

While David Steel didn't get a penny piece above his salary – "the same as me", he added looking paternally at Mr Steel as if he were a chip off the old shoulder.

He then rolled his $3\frac{1}{2}$ hundredweight affably over the national Press – "controlled by the Tories, liable to be at your throats". No newspaper in its right mind would go for Mr Smith's throat, it is not at all appetising.

It is a measure of the depth of the Liberal mess that they responded to the return of this manic alderman from his three-year sulk the way Sebastopol greeted a detachment of cavalry.

He is to command, not troops, but something known with hob-nailed tact as the "Labour unit". Not a maternity ward, but a hit squad directing its efforts to winning Labour seats.

Incidentally, the national agent here is offering tuition in "rifle shots for beginners" which may be pushing the Liberal party's talent for dirty tricks rather dramatically over the top. Not that Mr Smith objects to dirty tricks, the speciality of the notorious Andy Ellis, Liberalism's answer to Titus Oates. He spoke lustily in praise of rough trade and the party of nice people roared delight.

Dr Owen had observed that, if the Alliance rejected sound nuclear defence, it would receive and deserve "a great belly laugh of derision". This was it and the casting was impeccable.

Daily Telegraph, September 25, 1986

Partnership for Progress sounds like a glossy brochure from the Eagle Star.

It is, in fact, the interim programme of the Alliance, but the debate upon it was like a parliamentary adjournment debate, a portmanteau occasion for all-purpose wittering, or, as the chairman, Roger Hayes, subtly assessed it, this was "a fairly major debate" but this is a fairly minor party.

However, to hear them is to be convinced that the Liberals are shortlisted as the most tedious grouping in Western Europe. There is quality opposition among the Flemish separatists, the German FDP, the Italian Republicans and those élite anaesthetists, the Swedish Social Democrats. But our boys have undoubted class. No emergent nation, no area of urban despair, no path to progress is safe from the juddering monotony of Liberal attention.

Neil Sherlock, a promising youngster, quoted Roosevelt, spoke of "despair, despondency and a crumbling environment" and claimed "tolerance, decency and justice" as the Liberal values.

It will come as very little surprise to experienced observers that young Neil offered to "heal the wounds of a divided nation".

Not that tedium is any obstacle to the bizarre. Miss Claire Brooks, whose itsiest whisper is anybody else's *Tannhaüser*, boomed out on her personal public address system her displeasure with the press.

Another of those sobbing types, she wept to think that we had tried to do the Liberals down (clearly nothing like hard enough).

Were they not a group of the most compassionate, caring people in the world? Had they not lavished upon us the most mature, caring (again) and profound debate on defence?

She was balanced by Richard Moore who had been in the party since 1951 and whose style was that of a master of foxhounds in perfunctory tweed mufti.

He spoke thoughtfully of "the fuchah of ah cantry". Like Nigel Davenport in melodrama, Mr Moore twirled a hypo-

197

thetical moustache and told us that "the fuchah of ah cantry" was "bound up with yerrup".

There were thus only two statesmen whom the Europeans "gave two straws about": Mr Heath – "wouldn't it be wonderful if he could join the Alliance and leave those banal little people", and Roy Jenkins – "an honour to be associated with him".

But, elder fogies apart, youth seized its dismal moment and lesbian rights were spoken up for by Helen Veasey, a nice-looking pleasant girl who talked like a badly programmed immigrant from Andromeda.

"The absence of mention of disability or sexual orientation is disgraceful and unacceptable. The document," said Miss Veasey, "was selling gay men down the river. That wasn't Liberalism." Indeed it wasn't.

One's heart bleeds a little for the grown-up Liberals, for Richard Holme, affectionately hissed, Eric Hammond-style before he opened his mouth.

Mr Holme, an apparatchik with the look of a respectable bandleader, gave a succinct and rather attractive account of the document he had helped assemble.

One delegate had spoken of having belonged to the Liberal Party all his adult life. Give or take the odd apparatchik, it is very questionable whether the Liberal Party has *had* an adult life.

As for the non-bizarre contributors, like the new MP, Mrs Elizabeth Shields, they incline to a lone and level mediocrity of sentiment which would turn champagne still.

"We are," said Mrs Shields, "the only party genuinely committed to the regeneration of the countryside."

Or, as another delegate put it, the Liberals "favour a fairer and more just society". They "are about social justice or they are about nothing".

Let me be even more unfair than Miss Claire Brooks supposes. After two and a half hours of this, they are about nothing.

Daily Telegraph, September 26, 1986

This is such a party as no peroration can mend. That said, Mr Steel did his best yesterday.

It was a pleasure to look at the surrounding faces – Alan Beith

198

anxious, looking up hopefully like a Bedlington terrier fondly worried about his master's prospects; Mrs Cooper, the Candidate for Knowsley, temporarily eminent and ready to cheer anything, and Simon Hughes, nervously clapping what he could and at other more essential times sucking hard on a mouthful of iron filings and shaking his head in earnest dissent.

And, of course, to introduce the leader in that lisping antipodean accent which can only be called "Thtrine" there was Des Wilson who has only to smile to lapse into the half-witted goodwill of a nice-natured rabbit.

Normally, when a conference has gone tolerably, a leader's speech is an exercise in cheering on and bucking up, a sort of cleaned-up baseball coach's half-time talk mingled with a little of that reflexive Methodism which, even in the mouth of a Presbyterian, makes the Liberal Party what it is.

But "normally" is not the adverb of the week in Eastbourne. We are in mid-evisceration. What was called for was less a pep-talk than a resurrection address. Did Lazarus run lightly from the Congress Theatre towards the sunlit uplands of the next Alliance government? Not really. Being a Liberal Lazarus, he squirmed slightly in his grave and began to heckle the preacher. Not nastily, you understand.

It is no accident that there actually is an Alliance candidate called Stephen Nice (SDP actually). But the Liberals heckled Mr Steel nicely, even lovingly, when he spoke of "victory having been temporarily put at risk".

They weren't madly keen when he said: "We shall update our capability until negotiations succeed." Had they fully comprehended that that means "we are keeping Polaris and will be buying a successor", they would have been even less keen.

That, of course, is the beauty of the Liberal Constitution. Anyone with a party card wandering in off the street can vote, and anyone wandering into the leadership can totally disregard that vote. It is like combining the purest form of New England town meeting in those parts of Maine and Vermont where Jeffersonian democracy subsists intact, with Hapsburg autocracy of the most absolute and peremptory kind.

Whether this disavowal will carry weight is doubtful. Mr Steel had his own Chernobyl to cope with and, rough little firearm that he is, people knowledgeable in the nuclear field fear that the effects of the fall-out may affect generations of Liberal candidates yet unborn.

Speaking from the heart, he observed that some of his friends in the hall had supposed that by rejecting the official policy they were strengthening his hand in negotiations with Dr Owen. They had indeed. The impression one forms here is that Dr Owen and the SDP are subconsciously regarded as sinister links with the late 20th century. They are without the apostolic authority which flows from Gladstone through Asquith, Lloyd George and Jeremy Thorpe. One speaker alluded to a "hundred years of Liberal thinking and five years of research by the SDP".

Apostolic Mr Steel may be, but he has schism on his hands. Any fool can get a round of cheers calling for "a new partnership in education", condemning the South Africans "as the negation of God erected into a system of Government" (Prop. W. Gladstone speaking of the Neapolitan Government), or saying that Cathy should come home. It's that bit about "updating our capability" which will have Lazarus out of his grave and tabling an emergency resolution.

Daily Telegraph, September 27, 1986

Labour latterly has been indulging in PR and roses, the motif which has replaced the spade as its emblem.

This is a maximum security conference, if not indeed an "E" Wing affair.

The press could have been identified at 3 pm yesterday afternoon as a gloomy queue of individuals strung out in a 40-minute queue far into the street while scanners and amiable heavies inspected them for the sub-machine guns, hand grenades and infernal machines which are everyday accessories in El Vino's.

Quite who, apart from Headmasters' Conference, displeased at the decision to nationalise private schools, and Mr Hatton, not overwhelmed by the abolition of Mr Hatton, seriously contemplates acts of mindless terrorism against the Dream Ticket, it is hard to say.

Mr Hatton had been the object of earlier anti-Press measures when his launch into eternity as they used to say in the Newgate Calendar went off without a hitch and *in camera*.

200

The same good taste which has led the Labour party to adorn itself with an elegant rose has encouraged it to smell even sweeter by discarding the hand-chopping designer atrocity from Merseyside.

That rose, which looks not unlike the one adorning the chocolate assortment brought to you by Lindt and Sprüngli under the brand name "Mountain Rose", was printed large on a background not of the usual screaming scarlet, but of faded biscuit pink several shades to the right of Dr Owen.

The people's flag is a pastel wash of refined taste.

Whether policy will be quite so elegant, with the platform overturned on education to the satisfaction of Mrs Frances Morrell, the ILEA's answer to Catherine the Great, remains doubtful.

With an eye to the Edwina Currie award for political finesse, she announced: "We must pass laws to enforce spending."

However, a high tone was achieved with the arrival of Master Matthew Leigh at the tribune. "Next week I shall be going up to Balliol," he piped, adding superfluously, "I am lucky." Others, he conceded, were rather less so.

Matthew, who talked of workers reading Robert Blatchford and being inspired by Shelley, would change all that.

He wanted all educational inequities ended and denounced "the weak-kneed ditherers on the platform". Details of his plans to study Shelley at Grimsby Polytechnic were not released.

Inequity has its charms as does Giles Radice (Winchester and Magdalen) who, in the manner of a rugby forward and retaliation, got his privilege in first, surviving to denounce its application for other people to Labour conference.

At the Winter Gardens, where Joe Loss performs nightly when one had supposed him to be at one with the Pharaohs, it was not surprising to encounter positively the last appearance of Ian Mikardo.

He took a last, lingering swipe at the People's Hedonist, Roy Hattersley, for speaking to bankers "in the lush surroundings of the Waldorf Astoria".

As for Hattersley, he proclaimed with a passionate ripple of jowl, that Labour was the party of investment, exports, production and jobs.

Disdainfully, but usefully, he observed that under the Tories imports of champagne had doubled. It is a good line, but some lantern-jawed Cassius might have been found to deliver it.

Daily Telegraph, September 30, 1986

As the Labour conference ambles on with all the controversy of an astutely researched wallpaper advertisement, we of the media, concerned to provide the "lies and distortions" which alone make it half-way interesting, are fascinated by Neville Hough.

The conference chairman, an amiable heavy from Brierley Hill, functions as the Big Louis of the platform. "You want me to lean on him, boss?" If possible he is more bored by what he has to listen to even than the somnambulating press.

Perorations are karate-chopped with brutal indifference to their social purpose. "And further I want to urge you to support the next Labour government ..." "All right, that's enough of that." "But I wanted to say our policy was wonderful." "You finish or I'll turn you off."

It would be quite nice in this age of miniaturisation if Neil Kinnock could be fitted with a pocket computerised Neville Hough. The idea would catch on, and a substantial domestic market, taking in the entire political spectrum, would ensure massive profits for the Alan Sugar enterprising enough to bring the Houghlet to the ordinary consumer.

Alas, even with the prototype Hough 86, a clumsy makeshift model, like all heavy machinery humming noisily, some good quality nonsense gets through.

There was a wonderful man from Brighton Pavilion, well-known centre of proletarian consciousness, a Robert Stamford who announced: "Every morning I wake up to face the reality of State power." Alas, under the iron court shoe of Thatcher, it's no better in Guildford or Winchester.

Mr Stamford, one of those Left-wing writhers suffering from intestinal *angst* whom the red rose and pink wallpaper operators have been trying to smooth into the wall, proceeded to tell us that Northern Ireland has been "crucified upon the twisted cross of British strategic interests". This is pretty close to the mainstream, middle of the road, half-demented opinion of the rank and file.

But with Neville on the board of censors it was as rare and

rewarding as a flash of knicker-edging in an Ealing movie.

Accordingly, during the Irish debate, that frantic daughter of Crossmaglen, Clare Short, was kept bouncing and squeaking, but off the record and in her seat.

Even on defence a fair measure of prophylactic quarantine was applied to the advocates of "getting out of NATO now", though we did have Mrs Little, the lady who mentioned our role as an accomplice in the crimes of the Americans. The smooth transition to respectable unilateralism, collar and tie disarmament, the policy of asking the Yanks politely to go home please, has been accomplished. The last thing the platform wanted was the representative loon voice of the movement getting to the microphone and scaring the horses or the electors.

Nor did they want trouble from old-style passé sceptics of Soviet good intentions. As Colin Gray put it with an eye on Mr Callaghan, they didn't want any ill-conceived or unfortunate differences getting aired in election year.

He may have to keep an administrative watch on Bill Jordan, whose views on the Soviets are concise: "Peace-loving they may be, but they have 9,000 nuclear warheads, many of them pointing at us."

Oddly, in the new, suave, Oil of Ulay Labour party, this is considered naive.

Daily Telegraph, October 3, 1986

Whether the Conservatives deserve Bournemouth, with its symphony concerts and floral undulations, is doubtful.

But hither they came, under escort with lonely multitudes of policemen drafted in from remote counties perfectly ignorant of Branksome Chine or Westover Cliff.

They do not know the way to the Winter Gardens. Like the helicopters and the marksmen on the Conference Centre roof, they are here in the same spirit as the Atlantic convoys – to stop something atrocious happening.

The delegates have the same feeling about a Labour government!

They are such loyal, uncritical people, the Tories, perfect cohort material, staunch as railway sleepers and as set in their ways as Chinese opera.

Speeches delivered from the floor at a party conference in Czechoslovakia could no more perfectly echo and sustain the opinions, held, authorised and distributed by the platform.

The contest was also on to find real life's answer to Leslie Titmuss.* It was readily done if "real life" adequately describes Norman Lamont.

Looking like a waxwork model himself, feebly touched by spasmodic animation, he spoke of the "spur to innovation", the "millstones around our necks" and other nickel-bright metaphors.

Laminated Lamont invoked Disraeli (and misquoted him) and spoke with pride of "the people's share club". My eye wandered to the paperback book beside me – *Heart of Darkness*.

However, Captain Kurtz in the form of Mr Tebbit had a very good morning. Talk of softening the Tebbit image is not, on the face of it, a more promising enterprise than casting Marvin Hagler as Wendy.

But the low-key Tebbit was impressive. We still get the Chingford Tiger, but he purrs.

Interestingly, he is practising a hands-off policy on Neil Kinnock, so well beloved as to make attacks counter-productive.

A velvet paw was drawn lovingly instead across the Great Belly of Sparkbrook – spending, investing, providing, caring, hardly taxing anyone and probably distributing red roses as well.

Particular pleasure was taken at the ingestor's plan to compensate the holders of private shares with the moral equivalent of War Loan.

On a day when wretched polls might have decreed that the Tory emblem should be a funeral chrysanthemum, Tebbit elegantly anatomised Labour policy, tinkling lightly on the harmonica of its jaw as he went.

Peter Clarke of Lothian, developing nicely as the Junior Enoch of Eastern Scotland, sweetly dissented from the platform optimism on education, reminding us that the centenary of Forster's Education Act was celebrated with a drive for adult literacy.

* The anti-villain of John Mortimer's *Paradise Postponed* showing on TV at that time. The serious view was that Peter Walker of Minchinhampton was the real model for castrol-smooth Titmuss.

I rather suspect that Mr Clarke, who is unrealistically intelligent for a Conservative, would put education out to competitive tender. But at least he broke the ice floe of competitive acquiescence.

Mr Baker was not amused. But then, as a hired Dubcek or acceptable face, he was concerned to get the Conservatives credit for common sense rather than intellectual cavalry charges.

Also as a good politician, seriously into votes, he lingered long and adoringly on Mrs Frances Morrell.

This lady, who does terrible, peremptory progressive things for ILEA, has Edwina Currie potential. Coupled with the latest blast of sex education, she makes good Tory reading – "Frances lives with Giles and Neil" was the unfair, effective message.

Daily Telegraph, October 8, 1986

A Leader's speech to conference operates rather like a highly sophisticated layer cake.

There are bits to please the faithful – an act of worship for conference, to adapt the BBC's title.

There is a statutory other side-bashing section: Labour here depicted as a conspiracy to destroy all that we hold most dear.

But after the prunes and moral fibre comes the bacon. Bacon in this case being the plain hint that we have an election coming up and that it will be fought, as nearly exclusively as may be, on defence.

Given the ability of the Alliance to tie knots in its own ears on this topic and the plans of Mr Kinnock to construct a barricade of moths' wings and thistledown in place of the unacceptable spiked railings of the nukes, Mrs Thatcher would be out of her mind doing anything else.

She has always enjoyed talking about patriotism in a style heavily influenced by the anti-tank speeches of Winston Churchill, and yearns for a Helden Contralto role for herself.

Things were said yesterday which lie heavily upon the stomach. Labour having got themselves a chocolate box rose, Mrs Thatcher felt compelled to announce that the flower in her corsage was the *rose of England*.

But then Mrs Thatcher always did speak in italics. The vein of opencast bad taste which has supplied the Prime Minister's domestic and industrial requirements for so long shows no sign of becoming uneconomic.

As much could be said for her useful patch of *chutzpah* or sheer brass neck. Running lightly through the list of accomplishments, rebutting the wicked Labour charge of "uncaringness", she referred to the Elizabeth Garret Anderson Hospital for women "which this Government saved".

Indeed they did save it. After a vigorous campaign of outraged protest from staff, public and patients, they saved it from their own plans for closing it! A political war must have broken out. They have just brought in the first casualty.

The first part of her speech was pretty dire, an undulation of unrelenting generality, marked here and there with the small wooden crosses of Mrs Thatcher's jokes – the Liberals described as "the Muddled Tendency".

The gist of her domestic case, wisely free of specific details, was that of the Hywel Bennett voice-over for British Rail – "We're getting there" but without his endearing note of self-doubt.

Still, Mrs Thatcher didn't get where she is today by endearing self-doubt.

Slipping into the mid-market tabloid prose which is instinctual to her, Mrs Thatcher promised us a *crusade* for People's Capitalism. This is no more and no less depressing than Mr Kinnock doing his thing about the Tories corrupting us with a quick buck.

Political speeches improve in inverse relationship to their moralising content. A "quick buck" and "a crusade for people's capitalism" are oxen yoked to a common banality.

However, despite a good deal of uncalled-for stuff about vision, dignity, rolling back the frontiers of the State and caring passionately, she got on to a winner and stayed with it.

Even a bad speech, and this was memorably a bad speech, can knock holes in Labour's defence policy.

Alluding to Hugh Gaitskell's promise at Scarborough in 1960 against the unilateralists – "to fight, fight and fight again", she observed crisply, "The fight is over".

It is just starting.

Daily Telegraph, October 11, 1986

*To the Parliamentary sketch we last year added the
Mansion House sketch. Disguised in Moss Bros tails I
watched Merchant Bankers dine and heard the Chancellor
purr.*

The Lord Mayor's banquet at Mansion House is capitalism's
answer to the Durham Miners' Gala.

Within a white-draped oblong of table (which could be claw-
foot Queen Anne or trestle for all I could tell), lie four inner
tables all housing grandees or littlees.

The Lord Mayor, Sir Allen Davis, sits with Mrs Lawson and
the Chancellor broodingly one place beyond.

There is muzak piped through the hall. No there isn't. This
minstrels' gallery actually has minstrels; there is Tafelmusik, a
consort of recorders with a cello continuo, discreet enough to
soothe the money markets.

Men in fawn breeches and plum-coloured livery walk decis-
ively about behind the diners, carrying to the Chancellor the
unmistakable tear-shaped bottle of Messrs Perrier: – import
penetration is carried up through the manufacturing deficit to
the very throat of the Treasury. Do they drink Malvern water
when the Bourse goes *en fête*? I doubt it.

"The Lord Mayor," says the toastmaster to the Lords, Sheriffs, recorders, aldermen, brokers, jobbers and runners, "will
drink to you in the loving cup." Or, as they used to say in West
Hartlepool, "His Worship will take wine with you." Another
French import goes the rounds.

Nigel Lawson is very eloquent and, being Nigel, very cutting
about other people, especially journalists. "They complain of
being confused; and, judging by what they write, some are
confused."

But everything is all right. It is just that as, bears of very small
sophistication, we miss the distinction between broad money
and narrow.

Broad money is on course (broadly); narrow money has been
quite bad and must come back every night next week. The
oil price has been worse and caused the fall in the exchange
rate.

The Chancellor, a man who pushes a sanguine manner to its
known limits, observes that there are also limits to the necessary

and desirable extent of that fall.

The phrase echoes sweetly in its masterful display of titanium nerve. But then Chancellors who twitch before lighting their Havanas have been known to start runs on the pound. And Mr Lawson is profoundly concerned to stop the present saunter on sterling from turning into so much as a jog.

As for interest rates, one per cent was wise, two per cent would have been excessive. Only the Press talk like that. Nigel, having got on the winning side suprême of a pheasant and the better sort of Riesling, is all resisting excess.

He is waiting for the pound "to return to the market" which lacks the natural felicity of the Chancellor.

All is for the best – "steady growth", "encouraging signs", "credible regulatory framework", "falling inflation". Only world trade, always something of a rotter, has disappointed by slow growth. The prospects are good; turbulent they may be but it will be offset by success.

The Lord Mayor, a man given to lapsing into agreeable low moments, had put it more directly: "Maybe we can make the odd bob or two," he said.

The Chancellor, standing amid the half-naked statuary and gleaming glass of the Mansion House, does not indulge in the fall-about stuff as he did at Bournemouth. The scriptwriter of *Yes Minister* has gone on sabbatical to make way for the J-curve, the big bang and the medium-term financial strategy.

Mammon which, like the discerning in the press, quite likes Mr Lawson, smiled and applauded. Aldermen, sheriffs, recorders, Lords, Ladies and Gentlemen all smiled, applauded ... and went away to make a few bob.

Daily Telegraph, October 17, 1986

There are newspapers which will be employing their sketch-writers to go on at length about the first ministerial appearance of Mrs Edwina Currie.

As there is far too much in the papers already about Mrs Currie, we (as Mrs Thatcher would put it) have decided to wait until parity of publicity has been given to some other appointee to junior office.

Until Archie Hamilton has received splash treatment, together with a write-up of the tasteful tweed ensemble he is wearing, the lady stays on stand-by.

Yesterday was basically the day of Gerald Kaufman, someone who may be relied upon to paint tomato sauce on atrocity and carry excess into overdrive.

The day is not usefully employed by Mr Kaufman upon which he has not planted a severed, papier-mâché head upon a spike; the noun is underdressed which he has not adorned with "infamous" or its adjectival equivalent.

He is a nice chap who enjoys making the Tories hate him, but he is distinctly given to statutory indignation. On the topic of visas, ruthlessly introduced by the racist Tories, according to Labour, he had rather the worse of things in his contest with Douglas Hurd.

Mr Hurd is in business as a new marque of Anthony Eden. He has a handsome, trance-like manner and is too far above the low side of politics ever to move to the caddish entrapment of emotion.

But the Shadow Minister was so patently over the top, through the fields and down the other side: "personal humiliation", "shaming to Britain", "degrading scenes", "human rights only for those with white skins", that any half-way competent minister (about a third of them), could have picked him off.

Labour, who do sometimes seem not to *want* to get elected, went on as if the imposition of visa requirements in Lagos rather than Heathrow was distinguishable only in degree from the world view of Krugersdorp.

It is never wise to call your opponent a scoundrel. Only on rare and delightful occasions is this actually true and the impression left is invariably one of operatic extravagance.

Whereas careful attention to the triumph of administrative mastery, which left Heathrow looking like Derby day in Karachi, would have had some impact.

As it was, Mr Nellist made comparisons with the Nazis and Sir William Clark claimed to be speaking for reasonable people everywhere; both statements about equally improbable.

Mr Kaufman asserted that the five black and brown countries given the local visa treatment accounted for only one third of the visitors from Canada, New Zealand and Australia. "*They*

209

go home," said an unidentified voice from the heart of the Tory soul.

Mr Hurd, who is actually quite good at the "mistaken and unwise" sort of thing – using understatement to make your opponent feel like the Duke of Edinburgh – dealt very beautifully with Mr Rajiv Gandhi who called us "racist".

With the kind of dignity which ought to be filmed for viewing by trainee Home Secretaries, Mr Hurd said that he had nothing but the highest regard for Mr Gandhi (who sounds like a pious pain), but that clearly he had said that when he was very deeply misinformed.

A better example of the British upper class put-down couldn't have been assembled in months.

Daily Telegraph, October 22, 1986

There was a moment late yesterday afternoon when Norman Fowler, grand superintendent of outdoor relief and workhouse master to the nation, lost his temper with Bob Brown, a rather ear-aching Labour member.

He quite lashed out. It was like watching somebody being mauled by a gerbil.

Communications between the parties on the topic of updated social payments is never promising. Labour had come to scoff and stayed to fall helpless in the aisle as increases in and around the 80p mark were announced.

The Tories, understandably snappy these days at all suggestions of hard-faced mill-ownersism, indifference to the halt and the lame, and a sneaking disposition towards infanticide, are liable to get very shirty, to quote the billions expended by them upon social solace and generally to wash their clean linen in public.

The days when Dr Rhodes Boyson was allowed out in public muttering about "less eligibility" and the bracing, therapeutic effect of hard times are over.

Even so, either Mr Fowler is living on his nerves or has reached the limits of constructive tedium as a debating mechanism.

Tormented by the Oldham drip torture of Mr Meacher – "scandalous", "miserly", "indictment of a civilised society" – and by the socially conscious chuckles which greeted such announcements as "child benefit will go up from £7.10 to £7.25 a week" and other suggestions of buttons being dropped into the poor box, he reached out and savaged Bob Brown, leaving tiny paw marks all over him.

"That was a pretty pathetic suggestion. He doesn't even understand the argument. The Government which had the misfortune to employ him as a member registereed 110 per cent inflation."

Good as that argument may be in principle, there is something so crashingly impolitic about an increase of 15p as to make no increase at all look like carnival.

The Transport Secretary is hardly more tactful.

Mr Moore (as in "Don't have any more, Mrs Moore"), announced a cut in the railway subsidy on classic pregnancy-mitigation lines. "It's only a little one!"

Also, according to Mr Moore, "subsequent fare increases should not be massive". Lord, there's a slogan to set the suburbs marching to the polls.

Mr Moore speaks almost entirely in clichés, spot-welded together, jogs, is ambitious, believes in efficiency and is really quite ready to be put back into a best-selling paperback book.

In a sales drive he might be given away free.

One of his Christmas cracker phrases is: "We shan't contribute to efficiency or solve a problem by throwing money at it."

At about the third reading of that litany, Peter Snape, a deliciously base fellow with strong ties to the human race, called out in the tone of voice that goes with throwing half a brick at a toff: "Tell that to the farmers."

Like all simplistic, jejune, crude slogans, it is unanswerable.

The notion of investors in the micro-prairies of Suffolk getting the branch line treatment is delightful but not for this world, until commuters outnumber landowners in the Cabinet.

Daily Telegraph, October 23, 1986

If Sir Geoffrey Howe were a Frenchman, he would be a member of the Académie Française, for he is one of *Les Immortels*.

Stuck with a pusillanimous performance by the EEC and by the clear evidence that a farmers' slush fund cannot be utilised as a warhead, Sir Geoffrey murmured that it was a matter for regret, most unfortunate, and generally observed his practice of tutting beatifically through calamity.

The Tories are very miffed. Mr Soames, who is in business as the plumped-out Skinner of the centre-right, went in for a little, casual Frog-squelching.

Had not our so-called allies been tawdry? And in particular had not the French been notably craven?

Politics' answer to Hanif Mohammed (arguably the most boring batsman of all time) "shared his Honourable Friend's disappointment".

Mr Faulds, who does a very fair Isaiah for the purpose of denouncing Israel, thundered about the invasion of Lebanon, the bombing of Palestinian camps and all the crimes of Ahab and Jezebel, which for him exceed the Syrian parking ticket.

Sir Geoffrey, a detergent sent by God, met this pillar of fire by applauding "the Honourable Gentleman's customary vigour".

He is a nice man, Geoffrey, impossible to dislike, impossible not to pull the leg of, and one who has raised boringness to the point where it is an adjunct of civilisation.

Civilisation, according to Labour, has nothing to do with the Government's plans for a work test to be set to the unemployed to see how serious they are about employment.

Clare Short, a lady permanently overwrought, shuddered about "the Tory wickedness of the means test".

David Winnick squeaked and twittered on his perch like a socially conscious mynah bird, and the Tennysonian roar of John Prescott rolled round the chamber.

The middle of the road impression is that the Department of Employment, though very far from rounding up the unemployed to send them to gruel farms – the broad import of Clare Short's observation – nevertheless hopes to get enough sick and invalid people into the sick benefit column to boil down the unemployment figures.

Give me an ounce of civet, good administrator, to sweeten my statistics.

Kenneth Clarke for the Tories – he masquerades as Paymaster General while acting as Lord Young's Vicar on Earth – tried to strike a genial balance between telling this obvious truth and endorsing the Labour view that it was Peterloo, Amritsar and Tonypandy rolled into a single questionnaire.

He struck a confident, jaunty note. The day he doesn't they will call in the doctors.

Mr Clarke is to bounce what Sir Geoffrey is to discretion, an embattled square-rigged barrister of proletarian origins. Less glossed than creosoted by higher education, he rides on the highest tides with a sort of inoffensive assurance. Just occasionally this confidence draws out remarks which could have been better phrased.

Anxious, on the analogy of the fox and hunting, to suggest that the bona fide unemployed would actually enjoy this questionnaire, he remarked: "People out of work are just as concerned at abuse of the system as members of the public."

And when they get jobs they will be allowed back into the public again!

Daily Telegraph, October 29, 1986

Westland remained interesting, involving as it did assumptions about Mrs Thatcher's conduct which in the US would have led to impeachment.

Readers of Richard Ollard's great life of Samuel Pepys will be familiar with the tactics employed by that great public citizen to get the Navy Office and the government of the day off the trifling charge of letting the Dutch burn the fleet at anchor.

Showing qualities which would have equipped him to head the Civil Service in another age, Pepys set about boring the Committee of inquiry to distraction with an interminable account of fluctuating prices of Riga hemp and Eastland timber, only adverting to the little matter of constructive treason by negligence when his hearers were lulled into a state of battered, if better informed, apathy.

For Pepys and the fleet read George Younger and Westland. Yesterday we debated the select committee report on helicopters and cheating. It was arranged that way, with great quantities of tedious rotor blade stuff intermixed with what might be called the Henry II question.

Who sent Sir Bernard and Dame Colette to the moral equi-

213

valent of Canterbury Cathedral?

Mr Younger lived up to the impression your correspondent has formed of him that here is a man who, despite, perhaps because of, impressing some as a career dowd, is uniquely gifted at using tedium to cleanse in circumstances where an enzyme detergent would cower in the corner of the washing machine.

In a 26-minute speech, he talked instructively for 23 about helicopters. Helicopters schmelicopters. What we wanted was the murder.

But Asbestos George lurched creditably on, filling his space with promising generalities.

Not having started the crisis, Mr Younger sees no reason to get mixed up in it now.

Sweetly reversing the order, Denzil Davies for Labour flicked helicopters off his cuff like ash and talked better than I have ever heard him talk about Mrs Thatcher.

The key thing when you have the goods on the other side (and indeed they have) is not to get excited and not to let your opponents pretend to get excited. Denzil Davies, a variable debater, came wonderfully good by mocking Mrs Thatcher courteously.

He lingered over her own phrase about "putting information into the public domain" and rolled it around his mouth like a 20-year-old claret.

She couldn't blame this one on the Labour Party, or the trade unions or the Russians or the BBC – long pause, Tories already pre-emptively wincing – it must have been a case of the enemy within!

Mr Davies's theory works like this: Forget about January 6, the day Dr Bowe was ordered amid expletives to ring up Mr Moncrief, "purveyor of news to the public domain".

That was the execution, what about the conspiracy – what about the 4th and 5th of January?

During all this time, Mrs Thatcher alternately tilted her nose in the martyred look she has been cultivating or examined the surface of her shoes very thoroughly.

A cottage hospital has been established for the truth, among which there have been heavy casualties. A majority was on hand to vote in its teeth in defence of her reputation. But though Mr Brittan spoke, damning Mr Heseltine and sticking to helicopters,

Mrs Thatcher did not speak.

That, as lawyers say, is her right.

Daily Telegraph, October 30, 1986

Mr Kinnock just seems to be getting things broadly right when his old Adam comes and catches up with him.

Words to the Leader of the Opposition are like alcohol to a wino. He has a talking problem.

A perfectly reasonable and quietly received question about Reykjavik suddenly took on the proportions of the brothers Grimm's magic porridge pot.

"Little pot, little pot, make me some porridge," said Mr Kinnock, who then totally forgot the words for stopping it.

Verbal porridge rolled in a slow deluge over the despatch boxes, the Government Front Bench and then the crouching PPSs in a sort of tepid eruption until the feet of far-backbenchers, like the disreputable bunch who sit around Nick Budgen, were awash in the pale grey, health-giving, oat-flavoured sludge.

One of the tricks the Tories have found out about Mr Kinnock is that, if on such occasions they shout at him, instead of cutting out his engine and bailing out he drones remorselessly on.

Group Captain Fanshawe-Kinnock of Bomber Command would have gone for Dresden and finished up in western Manchuria.

Apart from the Leader of the Opposition's skill in rolling up question and three supplementaries into a single club sandwich and ingesting the lot together with the toothpick, Prime Minister's Questions were not vastly rewarding.

Like Herculaneum most of it is still covered in lava and awaiting excavation.

The statement on teacher's pay from Mr Baker had its charms. Not often is a comprehensive climb-down presented with such purple-plumed panache.

Labour was put in the position of having to choose between gloating and whingeing, and, ill-advisedly, whinged!

Don Giulio Radice struck the table and shouted, trying to work some immoderation into his natural low temperature Fabian act.

A kindly and liberal figure, Giles is a night-light not a Roman candle, and attempts at eruptive atrocity *à la mode de Prescott* are misconceived.

Life was, of course, made even easier for Mr Baker by the presence of Martin Flannery, an ex-schoolmaster (with a little beard), so sour, so garlanded with withered rancour, and withal so patronising from a position four good inches above the ground, as to be cherished by the Tories as a walking argument for never voting Labour.

He attempted to snub Mr Baker, "new to the job – a lot to learn". This is a mistake. There is basalt under the blancmange.

"I gather he was once a headteacher," said the Minister, pausing to let the enormity of the implications for the trade sink in. "He may like to know that, on average, they earn more than MPs – an example, in his case, of water finding its own level."

The Tories were simply glad to be out of one hole, owner-occupied for the last two years, and not disposed to ask unhelpful questions about the new one into which a thumping increment of public payroll expenditure has landed them.

Only Nigel Forman, not exactly a Treasury whippet, dropped on the doormat something long-buried and better not contemplated. "We weren't getting ourselves into a re-run of the Clegg awards were we?" he asked.

That's negative thinking, Nigel. Of course the paying out of 25 per cent over two years to one lot of public payroll workers will have no effect on other public payroll workers.

The word "Clegg" (the name of an Oxford academic who let Mrs Thatcher in for £3 billion of uncovenanted money when she was new to the job and had a lot to learn) is not mentioned in polite circles.

Daily Telegraph, October 31, 1986

The BBC, in an unwise documentary, Maggie's Militant Tendency, *had libelled two Conservative MPs. This led to a paranoia at Central Office which led to many things.*

It was the day of the point of order. Mr Eastham had one as a result of a jackets-off session, Mr Dickens, in his quaint rambling fashion, had another.

The enemies of Norman Tebbit had a whole quiverful and

216

Mr Neil Hamilton and Mr Campbell-Savours endeavoured to prove a theological point by both dancing on the identical point of order.

Mr Hamilton, one is now at liberty to reveal without prejudice to the courts, is a thoroughly nice, funny and agreeable chap, doomed to upset the literal-minded by his mimic flair, but about as sinister as Father Christmas.

He had something of a complaint in respect of Dale Campbell-Savours, "the king of the bogus point of order".

Mr Campbell-Savours has been continuing the case of Hamilton and Howarth v Civilisation as we know it (aka the BBC) with allusions to Mr Tebbit's alleged wrist-twisting facilities in the basement of Central Office.

Mr Hamilton (and Mr Howarth), having won their case, are fairly fed up with all this and long to relapse into the blancmange-textured, pink oblivion of normality.

In fairness, Mr Campbell-Savours seems to see their point. He went to some length yesterday to distinguish the blameless nature of the defendants whom he knows, from the alleged black and midnight doings of Central Office.

But since Mr Hamilton's good name and democratic credentials are not in question, notably with his friends on the Labour side, the original programme looks even more bizarre.

However, Mr Tebbit, by bashing the BBC and not being available for comment in the Commons, has started more points of order than the Corporation has paid itself compliments.

Not just points of order. Mr Kinnock, commendably brief and on-target, wanted to know more about the Tebbit plan to subordinate the BBC. Since *he* was *her* creature, presumably *she* was behind it.

Whether it has been altogether wise is another matter. The BBC, which had been reeling, is now after assault by the chairman of the Tory party able to present itself as a sort of public service St Elmo – its intestines drawn out on a windlass turned by sinister Norman.

This is seen as part of the Countess of Kesteven's long-term plans to replace free-spirited Day and defiant Dimbleby with Radio Loyalty, a patriotic service with news bulletins checked for rectitude by Bernard Ingham.

Not surprisingly, Labour are rallying to the Corporation as

if it were a six-month baby in an incubator.

Wasn't it intolerable that the Chancellor of the Duchy of Lancaster only took five minutes of questions every two months, when in his other hat as Chairman of the Conservative party he was desecrating the Temple of Apollo?

Mrs Thatcher got very constitutional, always a bad sign with her, and proclaimed herself unable to comment either way.

Was "her creature" doing a Jekyll and Hyde, all bedside manner and cough linctus as Chancellor of the Duchy, and hairy wrists and butcher's cleaver as party chairman?

This was not a matter for Parliament to discuss (what is?). Only the governors could decide.

They don't answer questions in the Commons either, do they?

Daily Telegraph, November 5, 1986

It is always something of a treat to watch Nigel Lawson snubbing someone.

If he ever tires of the medium-term financial strategy and the contingency fund, he could always take it up full time, letting himself out professionally in the manner of the Duke of Plaza Toro, giving socially uncertain occasions a full sense of being part of the great world by the personalised refrigeration of undesirables provided under contract by this ducal personage.

As it is, he has to keep himself in trim by practising squash on the Great Wall of Birmingham, a Mr Hattersley, who wandered into Treasury matters a couple of years ago and has not yet found his way out.

The Chancellor was engaged in a major adjustment of policy wholly consistent with its long-standing commitments – a low and cynical hand-out carefully timed to suit the next general election.

It is claimed that we have been too narrowly rigorous at the Treasury latterly. By the rules of 1985 we don't seem, even on Mr Lawson's snake oil prospectus, to have been doing all that wonderfully.

Inflation is down, true, but so is growth. There is a wonderful deficit looming, mortgage rates are up (Sir Edward du Cann was to make a tragic intervention from the backbenches), and there is more money in circulation.

In another year Mr Lawson might well have done his Gladstone–Torquemada act, grieving as he turned the wrench, making a tourniquet of the national belt, so often exhorted by ministers of finance and so lightly worn personally on either side of the Treasury despatch box.

As it is, exhortation and hard times are out, blameless merriment and a little of what you fancy are in. Whether we fancy Mr Lawson and Mrs Thatcher, and if they will consequently be in, is an unworthy question. Why else would I have asked it?

In the circumstances Mr Hattersley could have done better. There is upside potential for biting irony in the conversion of this fiscal stalactite to works of charity. Nigel smelling the roses and talking about helping the needy is a deeply inspiring subject.

Not for the first time Hattersley lumbered uneasily through his homework like a man trying to dance a czardas in waders.

There was a lot of stuff about the sick, the poor and the homeless which, like a re-heated hamburger, is best left alone. And where there might have been irony there was that awful, Hattersley thing: "imputations". The Chancellor was fast losing whatever reputation he may have had for financial integrity.

Piety has its uses at the Home Office: a lot of tearful mileage can be got out of immigration officers standing, *sjambok* in hand, over trembling visitors to Sparkbrook from the subcontinent. But the Treasury reacts to this sort of sobbing-tenor-out-of-Leoncavallo with the numerate dispassion of people who long ago abandoned passion-tattering.

Of course, as Mrs Thatcher would say, Nigel is pulling a fast one. Actually it is less of a fast one than a leg break shown in slow motion. Indignation is the wrong response. So is the chapel scorn as Roydie does his bit about the money changers in the temple (Wedgie Benn on a glorious occasion had the money changers driving Jesus out of the Temple).

Not surprisingly, Lawson's lip curled and did his full sixteen quarterings act, remarking that the Opposition spokesman had missed Treasury questions in order to mug up the financial statement.

Otherwise he was concerned within the limits of incivility to oblige his honourable friends: Sir William Clark, who rises like a stick insect to ask assurance that everything is actually very wonderful; Mr Terence Higgins, who asks a question actually requiring an answer, and Mr Alec Fletcher, battling away with a liqueur-glass Scottish majority, wanting to get it on the record that the Tories have spent more money every year since 1979 keeping Hamish in English taxes.

Daily Telegraph, November 7, 1986

To witness the State Opening, with its splash of hats, colour and robes, is not just to attend a convention of Father Christmases and their molls, it is an open invitation to discuss *couture*.

The impression is that the ladies in the gallery, where straw hats of red and black were frequent, were rather smarter than the peeresses (who turned in 60 tiaras according to an attentive colleague) and who tended in their costumes towards the sort of unwise glitz which *looks* like rhinestones even when it is actually something more sought after.

The Bishops, who cover their lawn sleeves in what could well be polar bear capes, sat huddled together below the throne. Dr Runcie, sitting next to Dr Leonard, was actually talking to the man, which suggests that Christian charity has been pushed about as far as it should be asked to go.

The Judges, more reliable satraps of the establishment, sat back-to-back on what could well have been an inflatable life raft giving a little bizarre dignity to the annual dress rehearsal of *Iolanthe*.

It is very much "vesti la giubba" day, giving everybody a chance to dress up and make a splash in that terrible chamber, a dog's déjeuner of mid-Victorian architectural slap and tickle. The ambassadors come off best. Evening dress and a nice red and green sash (Order of St Bogomil) looks well among the folk supplied by Sears Roebuck to give away the presents.

The natural dignity of foreigners among the British got up for an indaba is usefully emphasised.

As for the contents, well it would sound better if one read between the polite words given to Her Majesty by the Government, the *real* burden of the message. It goes something like this:

My Government having found itself with a surprisingly good chance of winning the next election to its own very great surprise intends to go on about defence because that is a weak spot for the Opposition and don't they know it.

My Government will try out rating reform by way of a barely disguised poll tax in Scotland because the Scots aren't going to vote for them, and what is Scotland anyway if not to be used for the laboratory testing of dubious ideas?

They will go on about crime and drugs, not because they seriously expect to do anything about crime or drugs but because people expect that sort of thing.

As for the economy, while making noises about fiscal rectitude, they will shortly start distributing free money as they don't want you to start voting for anybody else.

They reckon that they can square the teachers, an ungodly bunch who have given my Government no end of trouble, but whether they deserve it or not we shall be glad of the quiet.

In case you are wondering about the TV cameras which have been used for the State opening for years but which they won't give a sight of in the Commons, my Government takes the view that anything scripted which they have control of is all right for you to see.

Daily Telegraph, November 13, 1986

Mention education and the chamber empties. The topic, never a promising one, brings to his feet the sturdier bore of our age.

And it functions as a numbing agent even on the talented. Time spent at the McAvoy* – face has done nothing for Mr Baker beyond cracking his benignity and bringing out a certain unsuspected snappishness.

Clearly he yearns to govern education after the style of France where the Minister of Education can tell you how far IV B have come in the Geography of the Balkans on a second Wednesday in February.

Labour is just naturally boring on education with the exception of Mr Fatchett. But the Tories are working on it.

One listens to a statesmanlike speech by Alan Haselhurst, a man who has put the lapel back into politics, fascinated by his impersonation of the dumb-language lady at party conference – and taking in hardly a word.

Sir Anthony Grant also has his charms, but jocose orotun-

* Douglas McAvoy is assistant general secretary of the NUT.

dities can grow oppressive, amusing as it is to hear – from a Conservative – that the NUT are obsessed with votes.

Most teachers, said Sir Anthony, were decent hard-working people, a fine body of men, then adding his real opinion, whose broad drift was that they were a bunch of pinko layabouts.

Mr Radice was not vastly better, sounding off unpromisingly and asking Mr Baker forlornly to "stand back from political advantage".

He then ran into an interesting case of cross-handed social enmity with Mr Hickmet. "More of the Tories should send their children to state schools." "Look who's talking," said Mr Hickmet.

"I went to a private school," Radice confessed ("Manners makyth Man," said Mr Hickmet, nastily identifying it), "but my children go to comprehensives." Nothing clever about that. Most people do it the other way round.

Thirty years ago you could have had a decent education in Chester-le-Street which he represents. You wouldn't risk it now. But then it is unlikely that the young Radices will be taking their chances far outside the Highgate zone of social desirability.

British class feeling can, on Lamarckian principles, become an acquired characteristic. Radice, translated Milanese intelligentsia, was swapping resentments with a man of solid Turkish Cypriot background (Millfield and the Sorbonne), like any pair of card-marking, azalea-snubbing native Brits.

However, enough of these petty differences, we had Derek Fatchett (Monks Lane Primary, Lincoln School and Birmingham University) who could give them both a social handicap of 24. What matters is that Mr Fatchett was so good.

Thought of as a Left-winger, he never raised his voice, repeated no slogans, and left fist and mind unclenched. It was the sort of speech the new rose-growing Labour party would like to get on to video. It inclined to regret the immoderation and precipitation of Mr Baker.

Memorably, he spoke of "Peace in Our Schools", a phrase with a charming echo, and civilly begged Mr Baker to resolve his dispute by a method widely favoured by Conservatives: a ballot. Nice to think of an anti-Currie, pleasant, useful, underpublicised.

If Labour could be half as good as this half the time, and on camera, they would win an election.

Daily Telegraph, November 14, 1986

Events in Australia began to preoccupy us.

Mr Ron Lewis (Lab Carlisle) is not a compulsive intervener in debates. An old-fashioned industrial worker in a party full of Lecturers Grade 2, he has better things to do than to be in a state of statutory agitation four days a week.

However, when Ron throws a spanner, he throws a spanner.

Since Mrs Thatcher was employing a former member of the Billy Graham Organisation (Harvey Thomas) would she observe that body's two guiding rules? One should always be telling the truth and never bearing a grudge against those who had disagreed with you.

Accordingly, would she expedite the overdue knighthoods of Mr Maxwell-Hyslop and Mr Critchley (collapse of entire House, Mrs Thatcher included).

She took it extremely well. One does hope she will also see its wisdom.

For the height of subtlety would be to humble Sir Julian and Sir Robin by thrusting upon them the code-brand of political inconsequence. A knighthood is the satin lining of politics. Only other people notice the wooden container.

Otherwise, life back at the ranch grew fairly rough with Mr Kinnock spotting a good thing and having the wit not to overload the circuit. Harassed by in-questions about Sir Robert Armstrong and his admission about "economy with the truth" Mrs Thatcher mistakenly fled to the *subjudice* rule.

That is never a very good idea with the disrespectful, since, as a reason for saying nothing, it draws excessive attention to the object of your discretion – much better to witter on meaninglessly about being full and frank.

However, it is especially ill-advised if the Speaker is going to rule that proceedings in an Australian Court are *not sub judice*.

Labour went happily to town. Mr Skinner, the frequent subject of postings outside the Chamber, pointed out that, when a member is in dispute with the Speaker, the correct procedure is for them to be asked to leave.

"This," said Sir Dennis a little sententiously, "is a classic example of where you should make full use of your authority."

The easy way out would have been an immediate bob at Mr Weatherill, an "Oh dear I seem to have got it wrong. I *am* sorry," to which there is no answer.

But why saunter along the South Col of a problem when you can crawl up the North Face? Mr Biffen was put up to suggest unhappily that since we were a party to the case might it not still be *sub judice*?

Mr Weatherill, who is not going to be made a Viscount unless he waits for Mr Baker or Mr Kinnock to see him right, replied, in the manner of a talking refrigerator, that he had prepared for this question *very* carefully indeed.

Dr Bodkin Adams wrung his hands and went on in his High Tory way about *Her Majesty's* Courts, only to bounce off Old Implacability who explained that Australia was an independent country (they do seem to be getting above themselves).

Neil Kinnock had an access of galloping statesmanship, regretted with word-perfect innocent malice the inadvertence with which the Prime Minister had misled the House and, grasping the beauty of the pudding, used egg very tentatively, suggesting time for reflection.

"Forty: Love," said the Speaker. Well actually he said: "The Leader of the Opposition is following a very wise course", but we knew what he meant.

After six interventions, according to my notes, lots of noise, Mr Kinnock's best short bout in months and a micro-crisis, Mrs Thatcher announced that she accepted the Speaker's judgment.

But he'll be lucky to get an OBE.

Daily Telegraph, November 19, 1986

The ghost of Sir Robert Armstrong, the noted truth economist, hovers about this place like the angel of death.

Sir Robert, very much the Ghost of Christmas Some Other Time, has been dragging a chain made up of defective injunctions, used stilettoes extracted from the Attorney-General, empty Australian lager tins and "blocks on questions", and making the most lamentable clanking noises.

Mrs Thatcher, having been told by the Speaker that the

proceedings in an Australian court do not benefit from the *sub-judice* rule, has thrown herself upon the national interest to stop people asking why the Head of the Civil Service is making a fool of himself among the marsupials, a wally among the wallabies.

The division of labour so far has been that Mr Jim Coe, Bernard Ingham's runner (there's glory for you), will abuse the Attorney-General while Mrs Thatcher herself will blame Mr Kinnock ... for partisan politics.

Partisan politics in the House of Commons, what horrors have we yet to see – bathing costumes at swimming pools?

Labour are less than chuffed at the subtle rule shift by which Mrs Thatcher, having first got her question block, then lifted it for the purpose of making points she found useful. Still less do they like off-the-record briefings by Mr Ingham's office on a subject forbidden to Parliament.

Like the experienced Parliamentarian he is, Mr Kinnock proceeded to make a point of order with the usual margin of elasticity, observing: "What the Prime Minister is not prepared to say in this House is said by a civil servant in private briefings."

For some reason the entire Tory party, led by a purple and swelling Mr Lawson (not a pretty sight), took off into one of those *ben pranzato* rages which show it to so little advantage.

Vermilion features above dark suits, bawling voices, stamping feet and other marks of loyalty disfigured the environment for some little time.

Mr Marlow, normally a cynical fellow, longer on derision than moral indigestion, said with a bitterness in his voice quite equal to his words, that Mr Kinnock was using "low, nasty party politics".

It was hard to understand the Tory mood unless Mr Kinnock is doing even better than he appears to be. Points of order get stretched in Parliament, much as apples get pinched in orchards.

This being an immoral, imperfect place, an Opposition finding Government up to its ears in ice-cold Fosters tries to push it under again.

This is politics. There is no percentage in wheeling on Shock and Horror.

Alan Williams, who is rapidly turning himself into a very

225

effective deputy floor leader for Labour, was able to make points to the Speaker about "the Prime Minister's arbitrariness and growing contempt for the House and her brazen refusal to make a statement", which hurt and got home.

Advice is not welcome, even from Tories. Nicholas Soames, who has a steady working relationship with common sense, suggested a select committee of Privy Councillors to sit on the Paranoia League in Curzon Street, and was told, "We must trust those in charge of security."

It is a memorable line, fit to stand beside "economical with the truth".

Daily Telegraph, November 26, 1986

Every day gets more like the one before it with the Prime Minister falling back behind the verbal ramparts of procedure and precedent – "It would be inappropriate to answer that question."

It is a depressing spectacle and despite the ready chorus line of spear-carriers, double-breasted young solicitors wanting a job, yeoman of the shire and people sent down from central casting, it isn't doing Mrs Thatcher any good.

The really serrated knives are pointing at the Attorney-General. To what extent, asked Mr Kinnock, had he personally taken decisions to prosecute in the Wright case?

"That," said Mrs Thatcher, "was totally unworthy:" Westminster pidgin for "Don't get rotten. It's more than my life is worth to answer that one."

It is very un-Thatcher, as we have most admired her, putting the safe line of solid chaps who knew one another at Harrow and don't see why the lower orders should be encumbered by information.

Part of the charm of Mrs Thatcher used to be that she wasn't at Harrow with the solid chaps.

As it is, she falls back on phrases like: "The Government is indivisible", which does for credibility what Oliver Hardy did for easy physical grace. The Government is about as divisible as a Camembert, section-wrapped in tinfoil.

There are one or two back-benchers, though, willing to face realities. Jonathan Aitken, not entirely uninstructed on the

226

subject, called for a moratorium on lawsuits in Australia.

Dully, like someone claiming Benefit of Clergy, Mrs Thatcher announced that she was following correct practice in the interests of preserving an effective secret service.

Benefit of Clergy was obtained, before some fellow reformed the law, by reciting three lines of psalm, known as "the neck verse" as proof of one's literacy and, by inference, clerical status and exclusion first-time-round from capital retribution.

Actually the neck at issue in this case belongs to the Attorney-General, whose propensity to chat instructively in the better sort of bar *and* prosecute chaps for breaking Section 2 of the Official Secrets Act is going to get him into terminal trouble before this row is out.

Much time was taken up by points of order by various hot and frothing Conservatives anxious to exact the wrath of God on the delighted head of Mr Campbell-Savours.

He is having the time of his life, listing every name in the Pincher and West books ever deemed to have conveyed information outside the rules of the Official Secrets Act and demanding a prosecution.

Sir Anthony Grant came on the club bore something terrible about Sir Arthur Franks, another of Mr Campbell-Savours' derisive "recommendations for prosecution" – "a very gallant gentleman, harrmph, a very splendid war record". Nobody talks like that unless he has taken lessons.

The inevitable Mr Nicholls and Mr Robert Atkins, who doesn't need to be inevitable with his majority, did their weary bit.

The Prime Minister is not talking because anything she said would get her, the Attorney-General and the Government even more deeply into the sea of tinned Australian beer into which the notion of discretionary secrecy, applicable for some, optional for others, has already got it.

Daily Telegraph, November 28, 1986

With the Irish and the Australian courts behaving in a thoroughly ungentlemanly fashion by declining to suppress what the mother country, her voice getting a trifle edgy, had bidden them to suppress, Mrs Thatcher has fallen back on the asbestos

227

overalls of a verbal formula.

Mr Hattersley did his heavily scornful bit – "taking nobody in … using the law as her private property".

Mrs Thatcher announced three times that *it was inappropriate to comment on security matters; that she was following precedent.*

She did this repeatedly in the sort of voice associated with Sung Eucharist, and evoked from the godless gathering opposite what might be described discreetly as enhanced derision.

Various Tories tried to get in on the "Neil did it" theory of history. But much of their effort was bludgeoned from behind by that well-intentioned Turk, Richard Saladin Hickmet: "None of these questions are planted."

Actually Mr Hickmet has produced a comeback to the two minutes' silence – the 30-second noise. Without reference to party, the House fell apart.

Much more depressing, Mr Cranley Onslow, the Headless Hussar who chairs the 1922 Committee, demanded that Mrs Thatcher should "have nothing more to do with a man who, *harrumph*, was no more than Mr Malcolm Turnbull's lackey."

Mr Onslow, we are told in the newspapers, is a former member of British Intelligence. On his performance here, he may have past connections with British Stupidity.

Mrs Thatcher declared herself astonished at Mr Kinnock. Not content with undermining the nation's defences he was now undermining Britain's security.

The style is roughly that of her reaction to the clergy at St Paul's who declined to turn the Falklands service into a Roman triumph. It was unengaging.

Happily, there are other things away from this sour topic – insider dealing, or Boeskenomics, among them. It is not a madly partisan issue since no official Friends of the Arbitrageur lobby exists.

But it gave an instructive outing to Mr Michael Howard and Mr Robin Cook, oil and cayenne seasonably mixed. Modifying Proudhon, Mr Cook announced: "Insider dealing is theft."

He followed it up with some rather interesting figures. Actual investment by the City has been about £6 billion – a mere 1.5 per cent of the value of transactions.

It was a good, lucid speech without that frostbitten arrogance which has spoiled Mr Cook for some of his colleagues. The virtues of the fact-ingesting Scotch dominie pleasingly re-asserted themselves.

Mr Howard himself was wonderfully bland, his customary high-IQ inoffensiveness doing its bit to keep the issue at room temperature.

Such civility could have gone on all night but for Mr Yeo who, as the City equivalent of a flogging lady in a flowered hat, demanded "a few prison sentences".

Has it occurred to nobody that poor Sid, when they tell him, may grow by penny points into a junior Boesky, creaming froth off Guinness with the best of them – Don't forget to tell Ivan.

Daily Telegraph, December 3, 1986

Yesterday's security debate produced some of my favourite things: Julian Amery and Sir Edward Gardner supporting the status quo like caryatids, one florid, the other the colour of institutional distemper.

Both were talking responsiblese – the gun wadding of sound men coming to the aid of the party when all its thinking members have slipped under the nearest bridge.

Not that Mr Hurd was better. The chemical reaction of that dust-flavoured prose which he favours and "an issue of national security" (which it isn't) combine to produce an esturial mud of non-communication.

There was, said Mr Hurd to a House too numbed to take notice, no political bias in the security service. Really the Home Secretary could induce hysteria in a litter of Melancholy Siamese.

I am glad to be paid to listen to Mr Hurd. One wouldn't do it for fun.

He and Dr Owen played a sort of limp-wristed ping-pong on the motion of a security commission. Dr Owen, excessively responsible and establishmentarian, spent half his time discussing status, and whether they might condescend to admit some wowser from the outside and then make him a Privy Councillor.

The doctor has had a pretty fair press from this column but he suffered yesterday from an onset of premature elder statesmanship which belied the neoteny of his features.

229

However, that may be the price of getting the Tories to listen, and to a worrying extent they nodded assent, gravely conceding the weighty meritoriousness of Dr Owen's contribution.

It is not clear who should be worrying, the Prime Minister or the leader of the SDP.

Mr Dalyell is not one for worrying about the Privy Council. Neither is Mr David Winnick who rather astounded us with a sensible speech.

"A line needs to be drawn," said Mr Dalyell between dissent and subversion. He wanted "a charter for dissenters – dissenters like me, Mr Speaker, who are not a whit less patriotic than the members of MI5".

Mr Winnick resented the Accredited Gents Only notion of a security commission, a row of buttered eggs unlikely to disturb the convenience of a Cabinet Secretary. After all, the traitors had not been recruited from Left-wingers in Parliament like himself.

It is a fair point. Evidence fit to be shown to Philby and Blunt is denied to backbench MPs of all parties a thousand times more loyal.

Dr Owen might have strengthened his case by suggesting that impeccable candidates for commission membership would be Mr Campbell-Savours and Mr Dalyell.

However, yesterday was above all else the day of Roy Jenkins and Gerald Kaufman. The Shadow Home Secretary never lets the terms of a motion come between him and the Government's throat.

He had a point about the 11-day lapse between the assertion that Sir Michael Havers had advised on a prosecution when he hadn't, which nobody else has dwelt on. It has a fascinating ring of Westland ethics to it.

The Prime Minister and the Attorney-General, instructively absent from the whole debate, were not able to register disdain and *Schadenfreude* respectively.

But above all there was Mr Jenkins. The Brussels *Eminenz* has touched ground and is holding hands with the human race again; all the old style and wit are back.

Civil Servants should not get too close to Mrs Thatcher, he said. Like a Upas tree, the branches were splendid but contact could be deadly.

230

Poor Sir Robert appears to be hanging from one.

Daily Telegraph, December 4, 1986

One of the joys of yesterday was Tony Marlow apologising to Helen Hayman, who has had nothing whatever to do with obtaining transcripts from Mr Turnbull, and for calling her a lickspittle.

"If only," said Mr Marlow to an admiring House, "other members would have the guts and grace to do the same."

For a supporter of the Arab cause, Mr Marlow has a line in *chutzpah* which would be celebrated in Jerusalem.

Our attention was drawn to this by the new, good-natured Tony Banks who observed: "He has called me 'a worm', Mr Speaker, but I don't complain. I called him 'a witless moron'."

Legislation can be fun.

There was a moment of pure unction when Mr Spencer Batiste demanded a code of conduct for Mr Kinnock.

But, as Mr Batiste is obviously a West Indian fast-bowler masquerading as a Tory MP, his contributions are taken with a casual good humour which rather overvalues them.

For real action Lord Rothschild stole the day. Mr Hattersley quoted the letter in this morning's *Daily Telegraph* and politely asked Mrs Thatcher to assure us that indeed he was clear of all suspicion.

She had seen the story. She was considering it. She had nothing to add. That is the sort of answer Mr Hattersley must have asked the Christmas fairy to bring him.

No one privately expects Mrs Thatcher to give instant clearance if only because of all the contingent, precedent-setting questions which she could be asked.

But there are forms of words which convey sympathy, urgency and personal regard.

Lord Rothschild received, vicariously, a fish slab of Dalek-speak, and every time the question was brought up again he got another one.

Robert Rhodes James, in whose constituency Lord Rothschild lives, begged for something better and received the same Ansafone message.

Unsurprisingly, Mr Hattersley fell about astounded. "An

extraordinary answer. The head of the research unit under Mr Heath, and the Prime Minister will not clear him of suspicion."

Labour voices called out: "He's suspect."

It was a dismal afternoon for Mrs Thatcher.

Not only was she left looking as graceful as a cherry-stone clam on the Rothschild issue where the right, generous words would have conveyed the message precedent-free, but she was reduced to the grimmest deadbat blocking of everything to do with the Wright case.

On top of which, she has surrendered the high horse, duchess and lorgnette act she has been running on the shameless Kinnock – in cahoots with the Australian enemy, not fit to receive security briefings, we don't talk to that sort of person.

Mr Willie Hamilton, not quite the picture of your lace-wristed courtier, pouring maple syrup over proceedings, observed: "She can suspend contacts with the Leader of the Opposition because none of us believes a word she says – about this or anything else."

With all the hauteur she commands, about 15 divisions, Mrs Thatcher remarked: "Normal courtesies will be maintained on this side of the House.'

Watching this miserable quarter of an hour, the Prime Minister exhausted, holding on to verbal formulas as if they were ropes, the Cabinet Secretary turning slowly in the breeze, Mr Wright's publishers multiplying the print run, and national elders publicly demanding exoneration, one wonders what on earth she thinks she has been doing.

Daily Telegraph, December 5, 1986

One of the beauties of this place is its ability to carry on exactly where it left off after a 25-day pause for rest, recuperation and deep thinking.

Mr Harry Greenway, with a question to the Attorney-General, was still hard at his entry for the Ian Gow Memorial Sycophancy Award, a bowl designed for use at floor level.

Would not the Attorney-General agree that if somebody behaved disgracefully in the manner of Peter Wright, seeking to reveal secrets for profit after he had sworn confidentiality, he should be duly punished?

Brown-suited Harry, to whom no one has explained the sartorial consequence of joining the chalk-striped, velvet-collared party, listed the things which could be done to Mr Wright: his pension stopped, the loss of all allowances, the end of all emoluments.

At this Tony Banks, who is working on the character of socialism's answer to Norman Tebbit without the subtle good taste, added that his balls might also be ripped off.

Decorum returned for the tributes to Lord Stockton. Mrs Thatcher, who does not excel at such occasions, may have been inhibited by the recollections of the concussive little briquettes of Keynesian mother wisdom which the late Earl used to pitch at her from the Lords.

She read her tribute from a piece of paper, and did so with the fervour, conviction and wristy vigour of a boiled cauliflower.

Mr Kinnock, being Welsh and good at adjectives, was more effective – recalling that as a publisher Macmillan had issued Keynes's *General Theory* in paperback for five shillings, and a treatise on monetary theory for thirty bob. No one was tasteless enough to point out that those were the prices you could charge in the days *before* inflation.

Mr Heath was not without his graces on the subject, but being Mr Heath could not keep "Yerrup" (the Continent lying south-east of England) out of it.

Mr Macmillan had tried to take us into Yerrup, which was the end of all argument for Ted Heath. Nobody was cruel enough to recall the words of General de Gaulle on terminating the bid: *"Ne pleurez pas, Monsieur."*

Mr Callaghan (Lord Ringmer in the autumn?) recalled Macmillan's devotion to India and the Trade Union movement: there is no moment like death for retrospective recruitment.

He also released to posterity one of those wicked little cracks, which were so endearing about the old chap. At a dinner party for ex-Prime Ministers he had murmured interrogatively: "What collective noun would we use for a group of former heads of government? Not perhaps a pride of Lions. What about a lack of principles?"

Life wasn't all posthumous testimonials. The arch mischief-maker himself would have enjoyed listening to Winston Churchill, whose middle name is "preposterous", harrumphing on about the dastardly attack on his honour made by Mr Campbell-Savours (charges of doing down Harold Wilson long ago).

"That," said silly Winston, "is a charge of treason against the Crown – something for which, uniquely, the gallows still exists in our laws."

String up Winston? Not us, but is there a monastery with strict vows of silence we could get him into?

Daily Telegraph, January 13, 1987

Yesterday was very much free bedsocks day. The sad condition of so many elderly people has brought out a free market in compassion between the contending parties.

Mr Major at Social Security promised an estimated £7,500,000 in emergency payments to old people, many of whom, in the leisured way of the retired, like to vote in elections. (Very good thing, Mr Major, watch him.)

Mr Kinnock was not content with this and used Prime Minister's question time to get even more excited in a rather counterproductive fashion. The Prime Minster by contrast did her nice Conservative child's refusal to share the same playground with rough, ignorant Labour children bit.

Keeping her pinafore nice and clean, but leaning out between the railings to stick out her tongue, she observed that she was glad Mr Kinnock expected higher standards of a Conservative Government than a Labour one.

The last exceptional winter had been in 1978–79 (nothing very exceptional if it turns up every eight years). Labour then spent £90 million on supplementaries, compared to £400 million spent by the Tories.

As this relates to built-in supplements which nobody understands anyway, and has nothing to do with emergency payments, Mr Kinnock worked himself closer and closer to cardiac arrest, less and less productively.

From the point of view of the millions not understanding the issue, he gave the impression of a man mourning a calamitous Tory policy which John Major, at a bound, had got them out of. One shared his grief; it wasn't doing him any good.

Rather as in the case of the Star of the Punjab Tandoori Restaurant and Takeaway, the urge to do the manly thing and take on any three of the unruly element in summary fashion may have been overdone.

The rest of us got no peace. Neil Kinnock was up and down, the Tories howling at him like acclimatised huskies gone rogue. Mrs Thatcher got progressively more pleased with herself, sounding like a butter commercial on overdrive.

The Opposition Leader got increasingly madder and in the middle of it all poor Jack Weatherill, our ever-more-appreciated Speaker, a *fino* to George Thomas's treacly *oloroso*, had lost his voice.

By lost I mean lost, not mislaid or put under a newspaper, or sounding no worse that a man talking through cornflakes. Mr Weatherill is required to keep order, shout down the shouters-down and do all the usual things with a larynx which must look like the entrance to Hell.

Faint deprecating noises came from him, like a rustle of wind in the wainscoting, as heartless members begged him for his guidance on this, his opinion on that.

Mr Kinnock, programmed for an indignant response to hard-hearted refusal to make emergency payments, had never come to terms with their low and crafty provision. He was still rushing around after PM's Questions in the manner of a headless robot, announcing that Labour would use its spare day tomorrow to debate poverty, cold, old people, and the economy.

The Tories grew almost equally overwrought. Poor Mr Wea-therill, who deserved butter, honey, cognac and the sympathy of the House, had to whisper calls for order and put up with cracks about Aled Jones. It shouldn't happen to an MP.

Daily Telegraph, January 14, 1987

Late, late in the week Labour discovered what it should have been talking about. Having stubbed a toe on the early rising shrewdness of Mr Major and (for the very observant) on the late night wit and detail of Tony Newton who took them apart on Wednesday evening, they needed something to go right.

In the person of Mr Ernest Saunders they found it. Swivel-eyed financial manipulators buying up their own stock through intermediaries less well regarded than Colonel Oliver North lighten the day for Labour.

235

For that matter they had a passably jolly time in the matter of Pilkingtons. One doesn't want to be unkind to Mr Paul Channon, but he does convey a measure of anguished ineffectuality which the Tories must be very happy to have kept off television.

Admittedly he was a whiz of on-the-ball mental agility compared with Sir Edward Gardner who woke from a hundred-year sleep during the earlier Private Notice discussion of Guinness ... to rumble ceremonially on about Pilkington.

"Fancy 'aving 'im defend yer," succinctly remarked Mr Skinner, never quite the fountain of public charity.

The general question of City of London naughtiness had already come up in Prime Minister's question time.

Mrs Thatcher, while in no way disconcerted, abandoned the flashing-eyed, two-gun cavalry style with which she had rounded on the congregation of the blessed over ice money.

Notably circumspect, she parried Mr Kinnock's call for a statutory supervisory body, but with hardly more conviction than panache. Per contra, Mr Kinnock, unnecessarily over the hwyl and far away on the snow fund, was calm, polite and difficult: "Are there then no circumstances in which she would not envisage such a body?" People on a winner often talk quietly.

Pilkington was even more fun because of the numbers of Tories displeased with the fruits of high octane competition. Only Mr Favel, anxious to buy stock on a falling market, spoke kindly of the Trade Department's non-referral of the BTR bid.

Far be it for your correspondent to voice – even hold – opinions on the merits of Smiggs plc or Spriggs International. But to hear some of the cross party rumbling one would have supposed that BTR is the Blood, Terror and Rape Corporation of Transylvania.

Equally, Pilkingtons have long enjoyed a place in the hearts of the centre Left as lovable paternalists, capitalism's answer to malted milk.

Labour MPs got out their newly polished Funeral-of-Lord-Stockton manner, kept back like founder's port exclusively for an approved, warm-hearted patrician or family firm.

The ambience was one of evil stepmothers slipping nightshade into the broth of virtuous infants, and paths of the wolf being perceived around Red Riding Hood's cottage. "Predator" was a favourite word, even among Tories.

Mr Channon, in part the prisoner of departmental discretion, managed to sound like a curate not really geared up to a stand on Sin: "It would not be right for me to express a view one way or another." We know what he means, but for high voltage infelicity he could hardly have done better.

Sir Anthony Meyer told him he would "rue the day when he washed his hands of an outstanding and caring firm". That is only Sir Anthony's baroque way, but the sentiment suffuced the chamber. One had the distinct impression of having been here before – of walking over Mr Channon's grave.

Was it not quite impossible for him to intervene over Land-Rover? And when 20 hundredweight of best bricks had been thrown at him, what did he do? Intervene.

Daily Telegraph, January 16, 1987

"The whole house," said Mrs Chalker not very convincingly, "will want to congratulate Sir Henry Plumb."

Well, nobody in any way dislikes the amiable arabalist lately made Mayor of the Palace of Strasbourg. Nor are they greatly worked up about it. Foreign Office questions subsume EEC questions and in the EEC, benchmark of civilisation, Mrs Chalker and a few huddled Old Believers keep faith.

Yerrup, as Mr Heath likes to call it, is after all the Con-solidated Fatherland of Charlemagne, Leonardo da Vinci, Beethoven and Stanley Clinton Davis. Yet its heroes, like Sir Henry, lack honour in Britain.

We are more disposed to follow George Robertson in his lowest, least Siegfried-like vein, calling attention to the rapidly accumulating cauliflower glut which is only disposed of in the classic Brazilian way with coffee, by burning it.

Mrs Chalker grew loftily, conducting herself on the higher plane, speaking of the "real and certain achievement" of the EEC – like rigging the price of cauliflowers.

Slightly more central to things was a statement on the man-agement contract for the Devonport Dockyard, coolly announced by Mr Archie Hamilton, which gives 30 per cent of the equity to Brown Root Incorporated of Delaware, USA.

At this Labour went into one of those patriotic orbits round

237

the golf links which is better veiled from the squeamish.

Mr Robert Atkins was also encouraged to reminisce about his ancestors. There was a great-great-grandfather who had helped build the thing. The notion of any family connection of the finely drawn and delicately tapering Mr Atkins, in muffler and cloth cap, humping a spade and actually moving something more tangible than amendments, is deeply shocking.

As for Labour's trip to the atrocity works, we had Mr Foot still in psychic touch with the 1930s through his vocabulary, going on about "profiteers" (a nice old word).

Mr Speed for the Navy lobby joined Labour in general denunciation, which suggests that the ministry must be thinking along the right lines.

Doubt was immediately cast on this assumption when Mr Patrick Nicholls of the Matterhorn School of Sycophancy came to the aid of Government policy. Mr Nicholls is, broadly speaking, the Ian Gow of real life, willing to please and not afraid to creep.

Mr Marlow, who is toying with crossing the floor to join the Monster Raving Loony party these days, accused the Labour party of "rampant paranoid spite" – and a couple of other adjectives which got lost in his slipstream.

However, Mr Hamilton's brand of cunning, sharp-edged perplexity – learned from watching the elder Whips – saw him through in spite of his supporters.

There followed a glorious interlude during a ten-minute Bill to abolish the Rent Acts, when Mr Michael Brown described himself: "I must be typical of hundreds and thousands of young people." Well, better such sweet-faced multitudes than that there should be thousands like David Winnick, the opposer.

Mr Winnick's agitative trill suggests a progressive budgerigar in a fighting mood. Much of that righteous squeaking and you could finish up voting Conservative, a fairly drastic step for some people.

The thought could be dispelled by watching the super-fine Nicholas Ridley observing his struggling critics when we came to the next stage of the Local Government Finance Bill. Jack Cunningham for Labour, mired in the treacle pudding of legal adviser's prose, did not have a happy time. But to watch Mr Ridley in conduct and expression is to observe a man with contempt in his finger ends.

Daily Telegraph, January 22, 1987

Mrs Thatcher started to send in the police to deal with her critics.

The displeasure of the Prime Minister, frustrated by treasonable types in defiance of an injunction, is memorable.

Mr Kinnock, forewarned of the Rugby XV liable to be set on him if he actually approved unlawful publication, confined himself to the sweet pleasures of governmental incompetence.

They had banned a film show about the Zircon satellite, only to have the *New Statesman* print the guts of it. What did Mrs Thatcher propose doing to mitigate the effects of the Government's incompetence?

The rage of the Government can only be guessed at. The full-dress uniform of the British establishment had been assembled: injunction from the Attorney-General, emergency ruling from the Speaker, the Sergeant at Arms* in his knee breeches, sword and funny rosette actually breaking up a film show and bidding the cinema-goers disperse.

Yet here were the *New Statesman* and ITN, not coupled on the injunction and blowing the lot. Tower Hill will be the soft option.

Mrs Thatcher fell back on her Britannia outfit and said that some people were "only interested in ferreting out information which would be of some use to our enemies". If by "enemies" she means Mr Gorbachev, what odds would the reader lay against his already knowing rather more than the *New Statesman*?

An intervention by Mr Heseltine, attempting pitifully to work his passage back, suggests the enemies may be nearer home.

"Was it not," he asked in his best sham major's style, "one more example of those who chose to abuse *the privilege of freedom?*"

"The privilege of freedom", there's a phrase to savour; issued only by teacher, like a gold star for exemplary homework and, in the manner of the pensions of ex-MI5 men, liable to be

---

* I am assured by the officer in question that he was wearing an unadorned grey suit.

withdrawn if we forget our obligations. For those who see freedom as a privilege, it is not hard to guess who is the enemy.

In the circumstances, Mr Kinnock was wonderfully smug. Confronted with the security lulu of the decade, he actually devised a way of gloating obliquely and keeping up his patriotic credentials.

He upheld the Government's purpose; his party had done everything to co-operate: "Not me, governor, he went that way."

However, would the Prime Minister please explain how they had let it all happen? Liturgically, Mrs Thatcher recited (three times) the terms of the injunction restraining, if that is quite the word we now want, "Mr Duncan Campbell, his servants or agents" from publishing.

The thought of Mr Campbell, a notorious progressive scruff, running a troop of lackeys in blue velvet coats with silver facings has its own antique charm. But the Government was stuck with Dame Partington's complaint. This was the lady immortalised by Sydney Smith for trying to keep a tidal wave out of Sidmouth with a broom end.

The Prime Ministerial temper held through questions on the satellite goof, only to erupt like Etna on piecework when Peter Snape enquired about Bernard Ingham.

Was it true that Mr Ingham had telephoned the proprietor of the *Daily Express* berating him over a critical article? Was it a proper use of her information officer to have him blackmail and bribe the part of the press not already kow-towing?

Incandescent describes inadequately Mrs Thatcher's Queen of the Night *coloratura* response. Life was extinguished within a five-yard radius as she challenged Mr Snape *to provide evidence*. Pistols at fifteen paces would have been more appropriate.

Daily Telegraph, January 23, 1987

A victory was won over the unpleasant long-term dem- onstrators at Wapping, but not entirely by pleasant means.

"Where ignorant armies clash by night," said Matthew Arnold, who hadn't looked in on the ball-bearing and drawn-truncheon party on Saturday night in Wapping.

240

Mr Hurd looked uncomfortable, and sounded less than perfectly briefed. But then it is an unenviable position to be caught between the brass knuckles of the proletarian vanguard and Thatcher's Mounted Militia. It is perhaps a sign of age that policemen look nastier?

Mr Hurd is a statutory liberal in an illiberal government. Most of his Tory listeners heartily approved of the cavalry charge, in the way of theoretical head-splitters everywhere.

Labour was even more embarrassed. They don't actually like the sort of people who throw ball-bearings, park-railings, darts and rocks, and are anxious to condemn them.

Equally, the most moderate of Labour politicians – Mr Shore and Mr Rees – gave every indication of not being overly happy with the tiny patter of police horse hooves.

This, of course, is treason. We know, if we are a backbench Conservative MP, that there are thugs and policemen – two categories incapable of overlap. We also know that if thugs throw rocks at policemen that is thuggery, and if policemen beat up thugs (or photographers) that is legitimate police-work. Only people with no pride in our great country think otherwise.

Not that the Tories have much to worry about with the idiot Left in attendance. There is something about Mr Jeremy Corbyn talking about "innocent and peaceful demonstrations" which lends colour to the otherwise wholly uncompelling case of the police.

All the same, an atmosphere faintly suggestive of Lord Liverpool and contemporary Czechoslovakia clung to the proceedings. Never more so than when Mr Chris Smith raised the raid on the *New Statesman* and Mr Duncan Campbell's house.

Nobody has been shot, nobody sent to prison camp. Verbal excess would be inappropriate, but we used not to have our papers raided, except of course by secret government agencies which do not actually exist.

We used not to have dragoon charges even of quite nasty crowds long after the actual incidents said to provoke them, or to have policemen who smash up TV and photographic equipment in the best Afrikaner style. Who can deny that we have made progress?

The business of nailing the Government was rather spoiled for Labour in the early stages by the persistent rugby club baying from the natural party of government. Also, Mr Kaufman is too much embroiled in the sheer pleasure of being hated by these people to make his point with the necessary low intensity concision.

Equally, Mr Hurd made an excessive virtue of his arms length position from the seminar conducted by Inspector Crunch. His account of the police action suggesting that Wapping High Street had been given over only to the sins of the crowd had the full, authentic ring of the Roman Colonial administrative mind taking a balanced view in Judaea at the turn of the millenium.

But questions were asked which even the most devoted interpreter of Mrs Thatcher's wishes will sooner or later have to answer. Mr Rees suggested, what all reports confirm, that at about 9.30 pm on Saturday something went badly wrong so that a charge was made when it shouldn't have been.

Mr Rees used to be Home Secretary. He is entirely well disposed towards the police. He has no rocks in his pocket. Perhaps he might hope for a response in calling for an inquiry. But Mr Hurd stood there, passive and inert – not a mounted charge, but not unlike the quieter sort of police horse.

Daily Telegraph, January 27, 1987

"There is no need to learn things which are being withheld from Parliament".

Thus did Cranley Onslow, scion of Whig grandees who talks with the prejudices of a man with a Toyota franchise, dismiss naive notions about freedom of speech and the press. A fit condition of loyal ignorance is all we can aspire to; we must model ourselves on Mr Onslow.

We were debating the Speaker's ruling preventing a showing of the Zircon film. As Mr Duncan Campbell has already published the contents one might suppose that the argument would have been theological – how many angels could dance on the head of the Attorney-General, that sort of thing.

Mr Biffen, briefed if not fee-ed to defend the indefensible, gave an honourable impression of not believing a word of it. At intervals he paused to transfer truly iniquitous points raised by questioners on to the ungrateful head of the Attorney-General.

As Mr Callaghan was to observe sweetly, one wouldn't on

this occasion compare him with Churchill, who was urged during the Norway debate not to convert himself into an air raid shelter. Rather (at which Mr Biffen was convulsed with hilarity), he was a building on which a dereliction order had been served.

The truth is that we are in the middle of one of Mrs Thatcher's fits of Metternichian authoritarianism.

Stendhal, describing a Metternichian state, has a chief of police humorously advising a young man suspected of liberal inclinations to see himself right with the authorities by taking a mistress of impeccably reactionary views. The Conservatives appear conclusively to have done that.

At Question Time when the same issues arose, her argument hardly rose above a droning mutter about "left-wing organs" which gave trouble. Listening to Mrs Thatcher in this sour repressive vein, it is hard not to feel that we are governed some of the time by a sort of toned-down Goneril, who wears most of her backbenchers as matching accessories.

Not that the official line of the Opposition is terribly heroic. They are wandering about arguing that the Government has botched its repression, surely the best thing about it. The point might have been put to Mr Kinnock: "Do we want botched authoritarianism or Rolls-Royce authoritarianism?"

Mr Shore, untrammelled by a security briefing and the sense of bright-eyed duty it imposes, was able to give us his best speech for a couple of years – not least effective when he quoted from such Left-wing organs as this newspaper and the *Sunday Telegraph*.

He delicately pressed the issue of Ministerial disagreement about suppression, citing the liberal instincts of the Defence Secretary, Mr Younger, who appears in military parlance to be a civil enclave within the armed camp of government.

Duty also obliges one to observe, despite having rolled tons of bricks on him, that Mr Tony Benn also made an admirable (and restrained) speech – the usual Benn passion for the 17th century, but in a very proper form.

He showed children and other visitors round this place and told them about Parliament asserting its rights against the Crown, and Mr Speaker Lenthall saying he had no ears to hear save as this House directed him.

243

Mrs Thatcher might perhaps worry a little about getting the worst of a libertarian argument with Mr Benn (and Mr Shore and Mr Callaghan). She used to go on about "the Nanny state". How long, one wonders, before Nanny takes over the radio stations and declares martial law?

Daily Telegraph, January 28, 1987

What one likes about issues of civil liberties is the way in which they bring out the real class among Tories.

"Did the Minister realise," piped one reedy, silly little voice, "that to put Duncan Campbell in charge of a series of programmes is akin to putting Myra Hindley in charge of a children's home?"

This is the authentic, fastidious voice of Twitney, MP, the sweatingly loyal backbench nullity applauding whatever petty iniquity the Government comes up with.

It was difficult for the rest of us, contemplating the BBC searches in Glasgow to know whether we were confronted with Captain Paul Waggett of *Whisky Galore* or with the first intimations of a serious Czechoslovakian strain in the Thatcher-Ingham Administration.

Mr Malcolm Rifkind, having been stuck with the consequence, took refuge in what Norman Buchan felicitously called "silly little legalities".

He, as Scottish Secretary, was not responsible for the Metropolitan Police and what they put in their warrants. He did not wish to comment on the merits of the case.

What merits?

The thought occurs to some that a lawyer like Mr Rifkind, responsible or not, must at least have been *interested* in a non-specific trawl through premises which went some little way towards setting aside the judgment of Lord Chief Justice Camden in Wilkes's case.

"General Warrants," declared Camden LCJ, "are illegal."

Mr Jenkins, discarding claret for hydrochloric, made himself heard above the idiot barracking of two Labour MPs to say something magisterial about a second-rate police state as illiberal as it was incompetent.

Thank God for the incompetence. The tigers of wrath are

usefully sabotaged by the warthogs of administration.

The Government's line is that it has no responsibility for, and thus by inference cannot have caused, the actions of the police. The Force is, it seems, an autonomous robotic instrument, self-directed towards office files, newspaper premises and private houses.

The Government meanwhile is suspended in a condition of holy ignorance, as much theological as constitutional. What they cannot answer for, they cannot, naturally, have caused.

"Not me, guv, them coppers done it." With such logic-shredding, the normally admirable Mr Rifkind seemed sadly happy.

He even preached us a little sermonette on democracy and freedom of speech, suggesting that it would be a sad day when any minister could *speak for the police*.

Even Montesquieu, who first identified (fallaciously) the separation of powers, confined himself to executive, judiciary and legislature and did not suppose the Bow Street Runners to be an estate of the realm.

It is a good working rule that what cannot be answered for is even less susceptible of rational defence.

All this we shall know more about today. For Mr Kaufman was successful in obtaining an emergency debate.

Interestingly, when the Speaker called for the House's approval and both Oppositions leapt to their feet while most Tories sat sullenly resenting this threat to national security, Sir John Biggs-Davison (God bless him) jumped up enthusiastically and was followed by half a dozen Tories.

On an afternoon when the House had rung to loyal cries of "treachery", "national security", "unfit to govern", to say nothing of Twitney's eruption, it was pleasant to find Conservatives in favour of debate.

Doubtless the Whips have their names and are talking to them. But then no minister is answerable for Whips.

Daily Telegraph, February 3, 1987

The Solicitor-General for Scotland, Mr Peter Lovat Fraser, has always seemed one of the most agreeable of Tory politicians. It is rather likely that this is now the view of the Labour party.

It is an intervention by Mr Fraser in a speech by Jonathan

Aitken – endeavouring to be helpful and spelling out the consultative, recurring, fully-informed role of the Lord Advocate – which blew sky high the version of the immaculate conception to which Malcolm Rifkind, Scottish Secretary, had successfully attached his party.

There is an old piece of French ribaldry which has Mary saying: "C'était le pigeon, Josèphe." For pigeon read "the Lord Advocate".

For according to Mr Rifkind a police raid in central Scotland is a rather wonderful and magical thing which happens through instrumentalities too mystical for human comprehension, fully independent and free of the gross carnality of politics.

The Government, like St Joseph, is surprised by the arrival of a little blue visitor waving a warrant and proclaiming search powers. So are those upon whose doorstep he appears!

According to Mr Fraser the Lord Advocate does not merely initiate proceedings, *he is consulted and kept informed*. He breaks the chain of governmental innocence.

Naturally the Opposition, who apart from Mr Kaufman's witty and resented speech had rather processed round the mulberry tree in search for someone to nail, took this up with Mr Rifkind, when he came, soon after, to wind up.

Now Mr Rifkind is arguably the best brain in the Cabinet. You hang him up by his thumbs the way you get Dean Jones lbw.

Yet by his thumbs he hung, asked a question by John Morris and manifestly failing to answer it – offered another by Donald Dewar and incredibly, for him, refusing to take on his shadow.

The pleasure of Mr Rifkind's mind is that it rejoices in rational argument, is perfunctory with party sloganising and, when hard pressed, escapes trouble by narrowing the terms of argument to what can be said with propriety.

As long as he stuck to his own departmental responsibility he was in a position of not knowing what he wouldn't want to know and being able to say with perfect rectitude that he didn't.

Once the question was switched to Le Pigeon, as we must now call the Lord Cameron of Lochbroom, the best thing for Mr Rifkind was to call up a good lawyer (which he did – Malcolm Rifkind is a good lawyer) and take his advice, which was to say nothing.

First Mr Millan hit him, then Dr Owen. He reeled back on his heels and then John Morris repeated the charge: did the Lord Advocate desire the seizure of the full six tapes, not just the Zircon film?

A non-answer was followed by the intervention of the official spokesman, Donald Dewar, and the champion failed to come out for the last round, indeed ended the debate a full six minutes early.

As Jonathan Aitken, not perhaps Mrs Thatcher's favourite backbencher, had put it in the wise, deft little speech which roused the Solicitor-General from the cave where he might wisely have slept another century – "There is a place in society for awkward questions."

Mr Rifkind, inherently a liberal-minded man, probably agrees but following St Augustine on chastity might murmur: "Not now."

The early part of the debate had been characterised by Gerald Kaufman being delicious if inconclusive – "the raid supposedly brought about by spontaneous combustion, had it been in Manchester no doubt we could have claimed divine intervention" – and Dr Owen, statesmanlike before his time, making a reasonable point thinly and often.

As for Mr Aitken, I hope he lives.

Daily Telegraph, February 4, 1987

We must not expect always to feed upon angel food. Treason, spies, the national interest, even Ray Whitney cannot last for ever.

Nor can the image of Neil and Momma swinging from chandeliers while taking pot shots at one another like 1914–18 War pilots.

Legislative tedium was always going to get its own back. But the Rate Support Grants Bill *and* Rhodes Boyson was revenge in spades.

Dr Boyson is not the man he was. The old Rhodes, when at education, was a cross between Dr Arnold and one of the more butchly predictable ironmasters – rolling his Rs and dive-bombing his vowels in the interesting, authentic 15th-century way of rural Lancashire, ready to hang, flog or teach Greek at the flip of a sixpence (old currency).

Whether by mellowing or perplexity, he traverses the Department of environment, a labyrinth lit by defective and flickering strip tubes, in a state of endearing incoherence.

The charm of his performance while introducing the second reading of the Rate Support Grants Bill (forsooth) was enhanced by the distinct impression that he understood it very little more than we did.

At times he simply read bits of the Bill in the way of a trainee newscaster confronting a news flash about Mongolia. Not that one mocks – "It had been so with us", as King Claudius put it in another context.

What is the lay civilian mind to make of recycled block grants, of supplements to grant-related poundages and of settlement assumptions at 5·75 per cent?

Dr Boyson established his credentials as a Minister by quoting the most reactionary line in Plato – the one about democracy being a charming disorder distributing to equal and unequal alike. Thus he said in a high-toned way what Mrs Thatcher would say if she wasted time on that sort of non-useful book.

Mr Heddle rather sympathetically announced himself as having failed O Level maths three times. The general view of Labour, whose councils will be suitably crunched, is that Mrs Thatcher, its true author, may have had problems with O Level magnanimity.

John Fraser, whose rough charm has not perhaps been fully rewarded, showed dangerous propensities for actually understanding the Bill.

He lingered with some amusement on the splendid catholicity of the financial memorandum attached to the Bill. It announces with all the gravity of a *Times* leader of the older sort: "The legislation may cause more or less money to be spent."

What would appear to be up amid the complexities, according to Mr Fraser, is that the money previously distributed from overspending councils to underspending councils is now the subject of a wise, unappealable discretion and will probably be redistributed to the Treasury.

All credit belongs to the drafters of the Bill who have treated clarity as a mortal sin.

Mr Fraser, perhaps because he *did* understand the Bill –

248

broadly, was down-market from the Minister, neglecting Plato for bookmaking to make his points.

However life wasn't all municipal finance. Tony Banks, who does grow on one as the most amusing heavy Leftist in sight, introduced a Ten Minute Bill for fixed Parliaments.

This would remove much of the terror and patronage, currently the prerogative of Downing Street. It was impeccably democratic.

But the prospect of victory and the enjoyment of unjust fruits has not faded from Labour. Mr Banks was asked who would help him bring in the Bill. Normally a dozen or so names are given.

"Not many takers for this one," he said cheerfully – quality rather than quantity, "Mr Austin Mitchell and myself."

Daily Telegraph, February 5, 1987

With that sketch concluded, I went away on a short foreign working trip and came back to find myself dismissed from sketchwriting for criticising Mrs Thatcher and the two police raids. That is an editor's privilege but it is something less than a triumph for a newspaper's independence.

INDEX